Zinsky the Obscure

A novel

Ilan Mochari

Fomite
Burlington, Vermont

ISBN-13: 978-1-937677-11-4

Library of Congress Control Number: 2011944247

Fomite
58 Peru Street
Burlington, VT 05401
www.fomitepress.com

Cover Design - Christina Regon
Author Photo -Kelly MacDonald

Dedication

To Heidi and Dov (my twin sister and younger brother), my best friends forever.

Thanks, too, to Stephen Lines, Diane Bernard, and Robert Peskin for their feedback, and to Jill Fraser for her guidance and inspiration.

THE PERSONAL HISTORY
EXPERIENCE AND OBSERVATION

OF

ARIEL ZINSKY

AN ONLY CHILD
FROM NEW HYDE PARK,
LONG ISLAND

Zinsky the Obscure

Contents

Book the First: Twenty Years of Solitude

"He beat me then, as if he would have beaten me to death....Then he was gone; and the door was locked outside; and I was lying, fevered and hot, and torn, and sore, and raging in my puny way, upon the floor."
— Charles Dickens, from *David Copperfield* (Chapter IV, "I Fall Into Disgrace")

"You have here, Reader, a book whose faith can be trusted, a book which warns you from the start that I have set myself no other end but a private family one. I have not been concerned to serve you nor my reputation: My powers are inadequate for such a design....

"And therefore, Reader, I myself am the subject of my book: [It is not reasonable that you should employ your leisure on a topic so frivolous and so vain."]
— Michel de Montaigne, *To the Reader*

Chapter 1 – Exordium

Here, for your mental-health inspection, is one day in the life of Ariel Zinsky:

6:00 – Breakfast. Then a forty-minute jog in Central Park.

8:30-6:00 – Work. I'm an editor at *Pigksin Prattle*, the football monthly.

7:00 – Home. Marijuana. Dinner.

8:00 – Masturbation. I obtain my nightly porn with three clicks of the remote.

8:10 – Televised sports. Football is my favorite, but I watch everything.

10:00 – Reading. Usually a 19th-century novel.

10:30 – Lights out.

So there it is: I seem like a common enough 30-year-old bachelor, do I not?

Ah, precious façade.

*　　*　　*

If your childhood is brutal, your adulthood will become a daily attempt to recover: a quest for ecstasy and stability in recompense for their early absence. In your mind there's a teapot shrieking, and your lifestyle aims existentially at its quietude.

Parents, if they do their job, produce a child who's not shocked or saddened by the world's indifference to his biography. My mother and father, may they rest in peace, failed in this respect. To this day I'm frustrated by the world's inattention to my circumstances. I recognize the lack of perspective in this position. But it's my position nonetheless. And it's the reason I took about 400 pieces of paper from the *Pigskin* offices not long ago: so I could tell the story of how I became who I am, and achieve – through the catharsis of setting it all down – a long-sought neutrality to the world's icy reception.

My only living family – also here in New York – are my stepfather and stepsister, Neil and Nicole. One day they will discover these pages and gain a greater understanding of their non-blood relative. My stepfather naively believes I'm going to "grow up" and become a family man. He says "grow up," as if his position as a parent is more elevated than mine as a bachelor. Not three months go by without his saying something like: "I also felt I'd never have children, when I was your age. Then I met Nicole's mother, and everything changed."

Nicole also thinks everything will change once I *meet* somebody. Whenever she says this, I smile and keep quiet. My goal is to avoid the jeers that would accompany my candid reply: that I've given up on romance and reproduction.

I don't want to go on dates. I don't want to be a father. I just want to stay home and smoke pot, whack off and watch sports. That way, there's no heartache on the line. That way, there's no breath to be held with each outcome or interaction.

When I was younger – when I was the naïve, 20-year-old Zinsky – I thought it possible for an ugly duckling like myself to succeed with a lover. But the older Zinsky can't be duped. He sees that the strongest relationships possess what his cannot: enduring carnality. For I know – I now have years of empirical proof – that women never burn for me. It hasn't happened yet and I'm only getting uglier.

Furthermore, I don't see what's so enjoyable about the state of affairs known as a relationship. My biological father did not teach me much, but he was right to emphasize that what women call a "relationship" is in fact a male subjugation.

Besides, if the Fates did send a hypothetical Helen to invade my solitude, Helen would likely desert me upon learning my aversion to reproduction. Some adults decide they don't want children because it is pricey, uncontrollable, and time-consuming. I, however, first foreswore fatherhood at age nine, when a series of events convinced me that my most selfless legacy would be the termination of my lineage.

You wonder: did you really feel this way at age nine? Yes, future mothers and fathers who would hang me for blaspheming newborns – I did. And to give that vital period of my life its proper due, I shall begin another chapter.

Chapter 2 – If You Ponder Suicide at Age Nine, You're Not Like All the Rest

My biological father left my mother and me in 1980, when I was five. He moved to Albuquerque with his slender paramour, Cam Clark, who'd been his accountant at OpenChain, his third software company. He sold OpenChain for a few million, financing his New Mexico retirement. He unretired seven months later, when the idea for his fourth startup came to him.

After he fled, my father visited New York two or three times a year, always on business. In 1981, when my mother was in her 36th year and I in my sixth, my father took me to the first baseball game of my life: a doubleheader between the New York Mets and Philadelphia Phillies. It was a frigid day in mid-April. Winds swirled throughout the skull of Shea Stadium. I recall sticking my gloveless fingers in icy Coke and *warming* them. Thanks to my mother's admonitions I've worn sweatshirt, jacket, and hat; but Robert Zinsky wears only jeans and a long-sleeve shirt, his muscular arms folded against himself for heat, his thick brown hair rustling, his mind doubtlessly drifting behind its dark brown eyes toward arcane computer code.

Between games we remain in our bright red upper deck seats, intending to play "War" with the cards Robert carries in his rear jeans pocket. I move over and he lays out the cards on the chair between us. He stacks his rusty keychain atop the deck, lest the breeze scatter our precious pile.

My father asks whether my mother has "any new boyfriends." I tell him about Barry Drinkwater and Tom Bryce, the two men I've met, two men who know absolutely nothing about sports but try selling their ignorance as wisdom to me, the precocious sports-expert. Robert Zinsky listens raptly as I answer his questions about their appearances and professions. Then he cuffs my frigid left cheek with an open right hand; just as quickly he blasts my face in the other direction with a hard left. I stare down at the soda-soaked concrete beneath the seat. My teary gaze falls on a trampled hot dog bun, smeared with ketchup and bright yellow mustard.

I know there are sports fans in the seats all around us; I can hear them chatting about the weather and the scoreboard. I imagine a few of them have witnessed Robert's behavior; I imagine they've observed me with pity but lack the nerve to interfere with family business. Robert leaves for the bathroom; he need not warn me to remain in my seat, for he knows I will. I watch his keychain atop the card pile. I readjust it whenever the breeze knocks it from its petty perch and it clinks onto the plastic seat.

Soon Robert returns and we watch the second ballgame as if nothing has happened.

On the ride home there are more punches. There are threats of further assault should I "breathe so much as one word" of the whacking to my mother. Robert double-parks his rented Nissan Sentra out on Townsend Avenue, in front of the Watching the Wheels bicycle shop, the store beneath the apartment where I was raised. He walks ahead of me up the sticky maroon stairs, his long legs taking two steps at a time. My mother, wearing one of her white headbands, seems surprised to see him at the door. She's been sitting at the oval table with her yellow legal pads, preparing a lesson on *Night* by Elie Wiesel, a hardcover copy of which rests on the table.

Sensing adult concerns at hand, I sneak to my room, peeking out to espy their interaction. Robert attempts to kiss Barbara. She lets him, briefly, before backing away. "I can't anymore," she says. His face is inches from hers. They are the exact same height: 6-2, to be precise. Robert seizes the copy of *Night* and whacks Barbara's face with it, first with a backhand slash, then a forehand thrust. And though *Night*, it must be noted, is a thin volume, the force of my father's blows gashes Barbara's upper lip and sends her stumbling to the floor. From her knees she screams, "Get out of my house!"

Robert Zinsky towers over her. "You fucking whore," he says. "*Your* house? Why, because you're banging two guys in the bed I bought? In the bedroom that's next to our son's, no less? You fucking whore."

"Get out of my house!"

He raises *Night* in his hands like it's a stone and my mother cowers: she's the unshielded Magdalene. Then Robert dashes the book to the floor. It bounces awkwardly, as hardcovers will, settling by Barbara's knee. He departs, slamming the door behind him.

I approach Barbara, who's stunned and floor-bound and staunching her inner lip with the headband. "I saw what happened," I say.

"And why didn't you stick up for me?" she screams. "Why didn't you stick up for your mother, Ariel?" She glares at me, and there's a scintilla of hatred in her indigo eyes.

"Because I was afraid," I mumble, hoping the scintilla will vanish. It doesn't. Barbara thumbs through one of her yellow legal pads until she finds: *Cowardice is no excuse for witnessing an injustice you have the power to reduce or prevent.* The six-year-old Zinsky is held accountable for his fears, is made to regret not using his body, Jesus-like, as a shield to block Barbara Magdalene's pelting.

The next day Robert calls to apologize to me and Barbara.

In later years I'll ask them both about the events of this day. And according to both of them, it was the first and last time he ever hit her.

* * *

But it wasn't the last time he ever hit me. You might ask: why did your mother ever let you in his sight again? I can't provide an authoritative answer. It is not something Barbara and I ever discussed. And though I didn't defend her then, I'll defend her now: My mother had no idea Robert had slapped me. Consider, too, that four-to-six months often elapsed between my father's visits, during which time many alimony checks and cordial phone calls – I often eavesdropped – passed between them. Finally, I speculate that few mothers would deny two or three annual visits to a biological father and generous fiscal provider.

I was hesitant to condemn my father. Had he not simply lost his temper upon hearing about the men my mother was seeing? If Barbara could forgive the violence of a heated moment, then so could I. Indeed, my lingering remembrance from that raw April day is not his violation of American child-rearing mores. All I recall is the abrasive sting of his frigid palm on my naked cheek.

But then it happened again. And again.

Over the next three years, on each of the seven occasions my father visited, he beat me. Twice it was merely slaps. Twice it was a mixture of slaps and gut punches. And thrice it was a wrenching, unremitting struggle, after which I was unable to recline on my back for days.

I concealed everything from Barbara for fear the pummeling would only worsen.

I will only tell you about one beating. It took place in 1984, when I was nine. It was the second-to-last time I'd see my father before our 13-year separation (1984-97). On this occasion I also had the fortune to be attending another baseball game.

But before I get to that particular ballgame, I should give some background on the nine-year-old Ariel Zinsky: an extremely tall and wiry boy with straight black hair and a knack for the multiplication tables – especially the "sevens," for multiples of seven were often the scores of football contests.

My third-grade teacher, Mr. Bradley, was a corduroy-clad unmarried man with thick-framed glasses and uncombed black curls. Despite my execrable spelling scores, he had taken a liking to me for reasons that will soon become clear.

There once was a class sewing project, the theme of which was "jobs." Each third grader was expected to create – with felt, thread, and stuffing – a doll-sized human, performing mommy or daddy's particular vocation.

The nine-year-old Ariel was the only child in the class requiring Negro-colored felt to create the skin of his stuffed human. For the young Ariel – instead of sewing a tall, bedenimed Barbara, standing by the chalkboard, or a goateed Robert, gazing intently into his personal computer – the young Ariel took it upon himself to sew a football player named Freeman McNeil who (at the time) was a star running back for the New York Jets.

Mr. Bradley asked if my father really was a football player; and he laughed aloud at my insistence that I'd been adopted at age two by Freeman McNeil himself.

I completed Freeman McNeil and brought him home. He currently resides in my bedroom. During football season I watch games with him.

But getting back to Mr. Bradley, baseball, and my beating: there was also, in my third-grade classroom, a banquet table, shoved against the far wall, covered with dark green tissue paper, on which sat the geometric puzzle known as the Rubik's Cube. Mr. Bradley had posed a challenge to the class: if anyone could solve the Rubik's Cube – so each three-by-three surface of the cube was all one color – that student would go to a baseball game on a sunny Saturday, courtesy of Mr. Bradley.

In addition to the Rubik's Cube, there were other puzzles on the table: a pyramid, a diamond, and a sphere. The solvers of these puzzles, we were told, would not attend a game, but would receive extra-curricular remuneration of a lesser ilk.

Not a single member of the class solved the Cube, though one of my peers attempted to cheat by peeling off the decals and replacing them to give the surfaces a uniform color. However, I and a boy named Archie Kong mastered three of the Cube's six sides. In addition, Archie – unlike me – solved both the pyramid and the diamond.

Now technically, neither Archie nor I deserved to attend the ballgame; and if anyone deserved to go, it was Archie, for at least he'd completed a few puzzles. But Mr. Bradley, as I've mentioned, was partial to me. Perhaps, too, he was sympathetic to the boy with the divorced parents; perhaps, also, he had a thought or two about the comely Barbara; and perhaps he feared the unfounded suspicions to which unmarried male teachers will be subject if they take only one child, and not two, to a ballgame.

At the ballgame with Robert Zinsky I was limited to one hot dog and one soda. Mr. Bradley set no such consumptive restrictions. Not an inning went by without Archie or me or Mr. Bradley smelling some food and subsequently ordering it: cracker jacks, pretzels, peanuts, cotton candy, frankfurters, soft ice cream in a miniature plastic batting helmet. The three of us sat in the red seats of the upper deck and we did not stop eating. Nor could we stop laughing. On one occasion, the peanut vendor climbed the steps of our section, looked down our aisle, and called out: "Hot *nuts*! I got hot, fresh *nuts* right here!" It was a declaration which, when interpreted obscenely, was enough to bring the most stoical of third-graders to hysterics; the sight and sound of which, during a balmy day at the ballpark, is usually enough to bring any neighboring adults into hysterics as well.

My soft vanilla ice cream came in the dark navy blue helmet of the Detroit Tigers. Archie's came in the lighter blue of the Kansas City Royals. Archie wondered aloud why the ice cream always seemed to come in the helmets of "lame" teams like the Royals or Tigers. It was a peculiar comment, because both squads were on the verge of excellence. The Tigers would, in fact, win the World Series that season; and the Royals won it one season later. But Archie had wished for a Mets or a Yankees helmet; and if not the Mets or Yankees, then at least one of their noted rivals.

I kept score of the game that day, and I still have the sheet – dated 5/14/84 – along with my Tigers batting helmet – in a box in my apartment. But that's not the only reason I remember that date.

Robert Zinsky had flown from Albuquerque to New York for a CEOs conference. He was staying in an uptown Manhattan hotel. He wished to see me for dinner Saturday night. Pursuant to Robert's request, Barbara urged me to ask Mr. Bradley for a ride into Manhattan after the game. "Why do *I* have to ask?" I said. Barbara replied: "Because your father refuses to rent a car. And I refuse to accommodate his cheapness by chauffeuring you to Manhattan. So, it can't hurt to ask Mr. Bradley, can it? If he says no, he says no."

Mr. Bradley agreed to my request. He took me to a city address that Barbara had scribbled on a torn piece of yellow paper from her legal pad. My father was waiting, holding a newspaper, standing under the hotel's dark green awning. I pointed him out to Mr. Bradley, who pulled into the underground parking lot.

Through the rear window I saw Robert following by foot. Mr. Bradley found a vacant space and parked. He unbuckled his seatbelt and was about to get out. But Robert was too quickly at the front door, literally obstructing Mr. Bradley's escape. My father poked his head through the open window and stared at me, sitting alone in the back. "Get out of the car, Ari, and wait for me in the lobby," he said.

I was at a loss. Was I supposed to just *leave*, without a word of farewell to my peer or teacher? Where was the lobby anyway, and how did I find it from the parking lot? I was frozen in my seat. "The lobby, Ari!" scolded Robert.

I slid out of the car and left the parking lot. Soon I was standing by myself on the cracked and gum-stained Manhattan sidewalk, smelling salty pretzels, watching yellow cabs whiz by.

I don't know what, if anything, Robert said to Mr. Bradley; both Bradley and Archie seemed their typical selves the following Monday. But the next thing I remember: Robert found his addled nine-year-old on the sidewalk, seizing me by the forearm and screaming that I was "an idiot" for failing to find the lobby. He gripped my forearm like it was a snake that would otherwise wriggle away. He led me to a trio of elevators. With his free hand he poked the "up" button several times in rapid succession.

In the elevator he poked the "six" button several times in rapid succession.

On the sixth floor, he steered me to his room. Once inside he slammed the door and finally let me go. He said, "Stay on the bed and don't move," and entered the bathroom.

I broadly interpreted his command as "don't leave the hotel room." I turned on the television and found another baseball game. Robert bolted from the bathroom and shut the TV with his right hand; then in a spry reversal of motion he caught my face with a backhanded slap, crashing my eye socket with his bare knuckles. On the reflex I covered my eye and turtled on the bed, presenting him with only a rounded back to beat on. I was not like the prideful, beaten children you sometimes see in movies or on television. I did not fight or talk back. I assumed a defensive posture and waited for the electrical storm of punches to pass.

"Do you know why I did that?" he said as I cowered on the bed. Out of my non-battered eye I tried peeking. "No," I whimpered. My eye socket, I already guessed, was fine – there would be no visible evidence for Barbara to discern. "I hit you," Robert continued, "because it seems to me you had a lot of fun today with your teacher. Let me ask you something, Ari. Do you think you and that Oriental kid are his favorites?"

I hesitated to answer, pondering whether "yes" or "no" might elicit another blow. "We won a contest," I said.

My father raised his arm, as if winding up to throw a ball. Seizing my neck with his left hand, he hammered my back with five clenched rights. Each blow knocked more and more wind from me, until I lay flat on the bed, on my stomach – the first time in my life I'd lost my breath. When I finally opened my clammy eyes I saw a filthy corner of the room where the red carpet met the striped wallpaper. Robert said, "Don't you know he takes two kids to a game *every* year? Don't you know he probably just wants to fuck your mother? Do you really think he's just being nice?"

I looked back at Robert, having learned the hard way, on another occasion, the consequence of answering him without eye contact. "I don't know," I said.

More fists to my back, followed by repeated blows to the arms and shoulders, as Robert shouted, "Don't say 'I don't know!'"

Robert continued: "You don't understand how men function because you are not a man yet. If you were a man, you could see your teacher is a loser. He has no friends, and no girlfriends, so he hangs out with kids on Saturday. Did you have fun with him?"

I pondered the consequences of honesty. "Yes," I said.

A dozen more shots to my nine-year-old frame. My back felt pulverized; my ribs could've been the bars of a battered xylophone, struck by a sledgehammer rather than a mallet. My back skin felt like melted cheese, scalding and slick; I thought of bright orange lava, slow-flowing over a solid land mass.

At length, the moist sounds of my breath-catching gave way to the chirps of the television. I chanced to look up at Robert, hoping his rage had subsided, dreaming we'd soon be at McDonald's, mollifying each other with milkshakes and apple pies. Instead, it seemed as though my expression set him off anew. With the heel of his hand he cuffed the back of my head. He climbed onto the bed, straddled me, and proceeded to pound my spine, ribs, and lower back. Soon the blows felt like they were landing directly on my bones, as if my skin were nothing but a paper cloth over the table of my back, wetted and weakened from spills and scrapes.

He left me crying on the bed. He ordered me to stay there while he went to McDonald's to pick up our food. I lay on my stomach, my forehead against the bedspread, my sobs soaking the sheet as if my eyes were icicles. Had life *ever* been this bad, I wondered? Did any nine-year-old on the planet, even the ones with no food in Ethiopia, or no freedom in Russia, have it worse than I did? Would I rather be blind, deaf, or paralyzed, than the son of Robert Zinsky? I remember wiping my eyes and wondering about these things.

My back was a landscape of lumps: Some felt dry and others damp, with my t-shirt adhering. The baseball game had finished and a rerun of "Diff'rent Strokes" was on. I reached around to my back, with both hands, and tried to take the measure of my pounding.

I did, to be certain, have an urge to call Barbara. But I feared a repetition of back blows if Robert returned to find me on the phone – or if he somehow found my call on a portion of his room bill. So I watched "Diff'rent Strokes" and valued his temporary absence.

Half an hour later Robert came back. We sat on the bed and ate from brown paper bags. And he said: "I know I keep doing this to you, and I know I keep apologizing, and I know you're going to hate me one day because of it. But – well, how's your food?"

"Fine," I said, sucking flat sugary Coke through a thick striped straw.

After eating we rode the subway to Yankee Stadium to buy tickets for a game when he next visited, in September. We then took the subway to its Eastern-most stop in Jamaica, Queens. From there, Robert called a taxi via payphone, reciting "234-46 Townsend Avenue, New

Hyde Park" with authority. When the cab arrived Robert handed me a $50, in the driver's view, and did not shut the door of the taxi until the driver recited the directions to my mother's apartment. My father waved goodbye through the rear window and I waved back.

My spine swelled against the soft leather seat, so I leaned forward for the duration of the ride. At one point the driver asked if I was okay. "Why?" I replied. "Never mind," he said, and we rode on in silence.

When I got home, Barbara was cuddling on the couch with a man I had never seen. I later learned he was an assistant district attorney named Jerry Schwartz. After Barbara conducted a cursory entrance interview – "Where'd you eat?" "McDonald's." "Again?" "I like it." – I went directly to the shower.

The hot water soothed my raw skin, gave me the notion that my back was de-swelling, congealing, morphing from black-and-blue to a restorative pink. I toweled off, changed, and went to my bed (Barbara and Jerry still couch-bound) for a late night of reading *Sports Illustrated* while lying on my stomach.

On Monday, as I have reported, Archie and Mr. Bradley seemed their typical selves. And perhaps I was too, since this beating, though the lowest moment of my life, was merely one of many. Still, what I recall about this Monday was one of my classmates, a tall red-haired boy named Peter Mauro, approaching me with a question about our math assignment. Peter raised his hand to insert a piece of gum in his mouth and I instantly assumed a defensive posture, ducking down and raising my forearms. Peter eyed me curiously and actually said: "Are you scared I'm gonna hit you or something?" I lowered my guard but remained tucked. "A little," I confessed. He told me not to worry. And then we sat at a desk and rode the rail of long division.

* * *

A permanent change to my personality took place over the next few weeks. I can summarize the prevailing feeling with a phrase that has since been co-opted by vendors of anti-depressants, but which I assure you was mine alone in 1984: *No one should ever have to feel this way.*

My mood contrasted sharply with that of my classmates. Daily they spoke of cartoons such as "G.I. Joe" and movies such as *Superman III* with a fervor that – to me – bordered on lunacy. They resembled in miniature that species of adult who runs red lights or ignores phone calls lest they miss a moment of a particular television program. They were so impassioned in discussion about dramas that *were not real.* I envied their ability to go home after school and savor scripted entertainments. I envied, in other words, their facile ability to be happy.

My de facto anti-depressant – in the absence of televised dramas – was professional sports. I was already an avid fan, but now I began following teams and players as if my life depended on them. You may say: all boys follow sports. I will counter: not like me. My lunchtime habit of reading all the local newspapers began then. I stole Barbara's yellow legal pads and filled page after page with the memorized depth charts of every football, baseball, basketball, and hockey team – college *and* professional. (Your typical boy might do the same for only his local teams.) I hypothesized selections for every round of the NFL and NBA drafts. (Your typical boy might speculate only on round one.) Did these activities make me happy? It's more accurate to say they prevented me from being wretched. You see, I knew that I'd have to see my father again in September. I knew another beating was coming. And I did not know, then, that September would be the last time I saw him for 13 years. I believed my foreseeable future would inexorably include semi-annual beatings.

I daydreamed of how things would change if I died in a school bus crash. That way, Robert would never see me again. That way, I would achieve the result of suicide without the damning stigma of the attempt.

By the time I saw Robert again in September of 1984, the bus-crash daydream had gone through several iterations. Perhaps my death was caused by fatally poisonous cafeteria food. Perhaps I slipped off the fire escape of our Townsend Avenue apartment. Or maybe I didn't slip. Maybe I leapt. Maybe my splattered carcass would show Robert and Barbara what they wrought for birthing me in the first place.

I contrasted my daily musings on death with the rampant flippancy of my classmates. How were they enjoying life so much, just because of cartoons and movies about superheroes who couldn't possibly exist? Superman was as dead to me as Santa Claus was to adults. The realities of my existence prevented my imagination from suspending disbelief enough to render plausible a caped, flying human.

You wonder: is it possible for a nine-year-old to ponder and feel all of this? Yes, it was. I daresay that those doubting my premature sensitivities only do so because the traumatic incidents of *their* lives took place after the age of nine. But mine did not, and thus I was thrust untimely into the darkened universe of adulthood's ruminations.

In the bathroom of our apartment I found my mother's razorblades and began a weekly ritual of *pretend* suicide: instead of fatally slicing my wrists, I minced my forearms (winter) or biceps (summer) until the slightest specks of scarlet appeared. Within minutes I covered my wounds with band-aids and cloaked the band-aids with my shirt, so that Barbara would never discover them.

My fall from paradise into awareness wasn't all bad. I learned to see the humor in any situation – to use humor as a psychiatric balm. I even prepared a few one-liners in the event Robert's beatings were once again a prelude to McDonald's. "See if the Happy Meals include Band-Aids," was my favorite. But I never got around to using this line or others. I was just too frightened of my father. His final visit came and went with many a bruise and nary a wisecrack.

So I was beaten badly as a boy and nobody knew, noticed, or cared. And by the age of nine I became a child who pondered suicide and hated living in a world where football seasons had to end and fathers had to visit. And I wondered: what was so great about our world that parents *continued to bring kids into it?* Especially if there was a chance of suicidal thoughts seeping into a child's disposition.

Mind you: I had not yet foresworn having my own children. That would take one final incident. And this time, my mother was the perpetrator.

*   *   *

In 1984, a fifth-grader from Great Neck – the affluent town where Barbara taught high school – committed suicide. Rumors abounded about how her parents' had pressured her to study SAT words and improve her sprint speeds so that she could be the consummate scholar-athlete by ninth grade.

The girl's death made headlines throughout Long Island. Grief counselors and other psychologists visited school districts and explored the topic of suicide in general.

The woman who comes to my fourth-grade class asks: "Now, have any of *you* ever thought about killing yourself?"

A lone left arm is raised, slowly, shyly, by the tall boy in the Jets hat in the back of the room.

"What's your name?" asks the counselor.

"Ariel."

"And why have you thought about killing yourself?" she asks, in front of the entire class, and in front of my teacher, Mr. Friedman.

"I don't know," I say. "I just don't see what's so great about being alive."

That night Barbara receives a call from Mr. Friedman requesting an emergency conference to discuss how Ariel is "functioning." Friedman discloses nothing else. Barbara hangs up the phone – so do I, since I've been listening in – and she enters my room. "What could this possibly be about?" she asks. "I don't know," I reply.

The next afternoon, Mr. Friedman and Barbara chat at his front desk. He shows Barbara a ledger containing my perfect attendance and mediocre spelling grades. He tells my mother everything in hushed tones while I linger in back at a circular table normally reserved for reading groups. I feign absorption in wooden blocks and hollow plastic chess pieces. There's also a globe that spins on an axle and has countries in yellow, blue, or orange, depending on whether the country is "first-world," "second-world," or "third-world." I spend much of Barbara's conference with Mr. Friedman slapping at that globe, getting it to rotate fast, until yellow, blue, and orange blur into one spinning smudge. Then I stop the spin with my own fingers to see, just for kicks, what country I end up in: Czechoslovakia.

When Barbara and I leave the classroom, we walk through a hallway flanked by endless rows of beige lockers and wooden windowed classroom doors. Once we are several strides away from Mr. Friedman's class, Barbara sears my face with a crisp deft smack. My eyes water and I step away from her, shutting myself inside a dark locker with a clumsy clang. She squeaks opens the door and says, "How could you tell Mr.

Friedman you want to kill yourself?"

"Because I do, sometimes," I reply, sobbing, leaning forward, sinking my head into her soft stomach.

"Why?" she says. "Why, sweetie?"

"I don't know."

"Does your father have anything to do with it?"

"I don't know."

"Well, I'm sorry I hit you."

We don't speak as we drive home in her brown Datsun.

We have a quiet dinner together.

And in my bed that night, as I finger the band-aids on my bloody forearm, I swear to myself that I will never reproduce as long as I live.

Chapter 3 – The Boy Who Lost His Hair Prior to Puberty

My father stopped visiting. My contact with him dwindled to an annual Christmas phone call. Was he ashamed of his actions? Did his second wife or his fourth software company demand more of his time? I never asked. Neither did Barbara. His child support checks kept coming. Over dinners together – on nights when she wasn't with one boyfriend or another, abandoning me to my *Sports Illustrated* and cold cereal – Barbara and I speculated about when he'd return: perhaps when Cam Clark divorced him; perhaps when New Mexico increased its tax rates. Or perhaps – cue the *Ode to Joy* – he'd *never* return. During Christmas, 1985, I overhead the following telephonic exchange:

Barbara: So is this it? Are you through with us?

Robert: I'm calling, aren't I?

Barbara: Well I do think you need to declare one way or another. I'm not banning you from phoning. But you can understand how from my perspective I want some certainty about your visits.

Robert: I can't give that to you. You know how unpredictable my schedule is.

Barbara: Why am I even talking to you? Shall I fetch your son, so you can speak to someone who believes such nonsense?

I carefully hung up the receiver. I picked it up again after Barbara shouted for me.

Ariel: Dad?

Robert: Barb, hang up the phone.

Ariel: She did, dad. She's lighting a cigarette.

Robert: Out on the fire escape, I hope. She's gonna give you cancer.

Ariel: So – how's New Mexico?

Robert: Look, Ari, I can't talk long. I just need to tell you that I have no idea if, or when, I'll see you. Don't pretend you're disappointed. I know I've been a prick. Just remember: You *will* see me again if you tell your mom about anything. Understand?

Ariel: Yes.

Robert: Okay. Take it easy.

And that was the last I heard of my father until Christmas 1986, when our conversation essentially replicated our 1985 dialogue.

Barbara and I remained skeptical; we felt his disappearance was too fortunate to last. But by 1989 – when I was a 14-year-old ninth-grader, and she was 44, still teaching at the affluent Great Neck North High School one town over – we had adjusted to his withdrawal. "I guess he's gone for good, huh?" I asked Barbara, after one of his Christmas calls. "Sure seems that way," she replied. And then we discussed at which Chinese restaurant we'd be dining that evening, and which movie we'd see afterwards.

Despite Robert's absence, my suicidal ideation did not abate. Although the threat of paternal pain was no longer imminent, I remained manacled by its memory. Other fathers taught their sons how to ride bikes, knot neckties, play sports – or how to *fight*. I entered the jungle of public school knowing only how to whimper. The result, I eagerly concluded, was my friendless existence: boys didn't bond with me because I couldn't throw or catch or defend myself. I saw myself as a helpless victim and traced my social disadvantage to Robert's absence, which I in turn traced to his beatings. I don't suggest that I was correct in doing so; I only say that in doing so, I continued attributing my hatred of life to a father who was only partly blamable.

I wondered why life was worth living. In retrospect, these emotions seem ridiculous: the best adults recognize life is worth living so long as your health is intact. But I was a teenager. Real life had struck, and I was too young and egoistic to count my blessings – despite Barbara's repeated advice to do just that, whenever she observed my moping expressions. I became an isolated, insular student to whom almost no one spoke.

I continued cutting myself with Barbara's razors. Still smooth-faced, I as yet had no reason to buy my own. So expert did I become at producing blood that my left arm always sported a series of healing horizontal gashes. On the rare occasion when my mother's new supply of blades was too shining and silver to be tampered with, I searched our garbage pail for my latest discarded bottle of Yoo-hoo chocolate drink. I smashed the glass with my foot and selected the largest triangular piece, discarding the rest into a brown paper bag. After washing off the syrupy chocolate and wayward shards, I pierced my skin below the elbow, reopening one of my wounds with a slow, savory, left-right stroke. My intensifying mouth-breaths fogged the sink mirror. After five such repetitions, I washed and bandaged my arm, telepathically telling the bathroom: "Same time, next week."

*   *   *

My only school acquaintances arrived in eleventh grade, when at the urging of a pre-calculus teacher I joined the "mathletes," a Tuesday afternoon kaffeeklatsch of equation solvers. The whole magic of this group was that I didn't have to try socializing. The teacher passed out equations and we discussed them.

My true best friend was my mother. She and I spent countless Friday and Saturday nights together. Our favorite dinner was pizza. After the meal we adjourned to the couch with our respective books and yellow legal pads. At 11:15 she'd turn on the television so I could see the sports scores before going to sleep. We did not have cable television, so I relied on the local news broadcast for up-to-date information.

The absence of cable epitomized how the economics of my life differentiated me from my classmates. True, Barbara and I were far from ghetto material. True, New Hyde Park was an upper-middle-class suburb by any stretch of the wallet. But as I grew more cognizant of our fiscal circumstances, I gained a measure of bitterness about the financial ramifications of Robert's behavior. No cable TV was the least of it. From what I could tell, based on mathlete discussions and general hearsay, most of my classmates lived in houses, not apartments; their families took annual vacations; they owned multiple cars; they took preparation courses for standardized tests; they took lessons in piano or karate or dance; they learned skiing or ice skating or tennis or golfing; they had catered birthday parties euphemized as Confirmations or Bar/Bat Mitzvahs; and very few of them held weekday jobs – whereas I'd been bagging groceries since my 14th year.

It was at Barbara's urging that I applied for the supermarket job at Waldbaum's, which was further down Townsend Avenue. "Look at it this way," she said, sliding the application across the dinner table. "Our groceries will be half price through your employee discount. We'll be able to afford more restaurant meals. We might even be able to see a show in Manhattan, or take a vacation, or give you music lessons."

"Maybe if you stopped buying cigarettes, I wouldn't have to get a job," I countered.

She glared. "You're right about that," she said wearily. "But don't you want to earn some money? You could get a subscription to *Sports Illustrated* instead of buying it at the store."

"Do I really have to do this?"

"No," she said. "Not if you really don't want to. We'll manage. All I'm saying, Ari, is cheaper groceries would make life a lot easier for us. You're growing so fast, and you're going through three or four boxes of cereal a week. Then there's the milk and the OJ. And all of this will be half price, if you just take a few shifts a week. I also think it would be good for you to get out of the house more. All you do is come home and make sports lists in your room."

"Okay," I said. Thus began my career as a part-time cashier and stock boy.

The world is rife with rich windbags whose storytelling efforts consist, in the main, of mythologizing their first jobs into vocational bibles. Show me an affluent man, and I'll show you – in four of five cases – someone with a paper-route parable of how success is born of punctuality and persistence. As I sit here typing in my Manhattan apartment, it is tempting to count myself among the windbags. But if you must say something about my generation, then you must admit: we are more sociologically informed than our predecessors. We recognize the tenuous correlation between money and merit. We rarely take undue credit for being "entirely self-made." And why is that? For some, the answer may lie in our exposure to backgrounds of true blight, oft-told through life stories of rap stars and athletes. For me, the answer lies in my supermarket experience. Within one week on the job an analogy formed in my head: Barbara and I were to the rest of New Hyde Park what my supermarket coworkers were to me: *poorer.*

I formed this analogy years before college taught me to term it "socioeconomic." Its genesis was not anthropological analysis, but basic questions: "Am I the only white kid who works here? Am I the only one who knows algebra?" In time I wondered: "I'm going to college in a few years. But where are *they* going?" This last query first crossed my mind in 1990, at age 15. The stimulus was a frightening supermarket incident:

When I arrive one Tuesday afternoon the aisles are packed. "I don't know what's going on," says my manager, an obese American of Korean ancestry named Victor Oh. "Get on register seven and put Omar on nine when he gets in." Omar, my cashier colleague, is 26. He's a black guy who's built like a welder, with disproportionately thick biceps and shoulders. He's also three inches taller than I, which is saying something: At 15, though I have (to my immense annoyance) not yet hit puberty – my voice still cracks and my armpits lack hair – I am six feet tall. Gigantic Omar has been with Waldbaum's twice as long as I have. He speaks impeccable English, leaving aside his colloquial lapses into ethnic parlance. And yet: Victor entrusts *me* to delegate Omar's assignment. And he entrusts Omar to listen.

And listen he does. Soon the crowd is gone and boredom prevails for us at the registers: fluorescent lights shine, listless instrumentals chime over the public-address system. Having already survived what seems like a marathon school day, I feel drained. But the eyes of Victor Oh are watching. So I greet customers with grins that seem right out of a yearbook. Products roll towards me and I lift them high like a doctor with a newborn, birthed or baptized on my black rubbery conveyer belt. Down to the ground they come for a rapid price scan before getting bagged for safe travel.

Soon employees are taking their meal breaks. The two meat men – Eli and Pete, long-haired immigrants from Macedonia who are fraternal twins – dine together, at which time a cashier covers sales at the butcher counter. The job typically falls to Roslyn, a revered 20-year employee in her sixties. Roslyn has great skill with meat-cutting equipment and a knack for weight estimation: if a customer asks for a half pound of potato salad or a pound of chicken curry, Roslyn rarely gives too much or too little. Such proficiencies offset her one weakness behind the counter: she walks with a limp.

Upon seeing Roslyn's wilted strides, most customers take pity and don't begrudge her lack of speed. Most regulars, in fact, know she's merely subbing for Eli and Pete, whose thick accents and work ethic are labeled "charming" by our unwittingly ethnocentric and condescending clientele. But Victor Oh – taking no chances – sends Omar to the meat counter to help Roslyn, just in case the supermarket again becomes "a mob scene." For my part, I begin – of my own volition – circling the store with a sticker gun: for Victor has instructed us not to "stand around doing nothing" when the store isn't busy.

My first stop? The dairy section. I recall how Victor once explained a little-known secret of supermarkets: they make no profits whatsoever from milk sales. "The only reason we even sell milk," he lectures, "is because it gets the mothers in the store every three days. We *lose* $.03 on every sale. But we deal with it, because of all the other shit the mothers buy once they're here. Fruit drinks. Cereal. Granola bars. It's like the amusement park that lets you in for free, then charges $10 for each ride and $5 for each hot dog. In business school, they call a product like milk a *loss leader.*"

I ponder his words as I kneel by the refrigerated section. Spare stickers protrude from the pocket of my teal Waldbaum's apron as I gun orange price decals onto cold slick cartons. I'm tempted to open a gallon of bovine beverage and start chugging. But then I hear shouts from the meat counter.

Omar has a hand on a customer's throat. Three other customers stand watching, too aghast to do anything. Roslyn sits in a chair behind the counter. "Omar!" I shout. He relinquishes the customer, a skinny, gray-haired man in his fifties, who immediately turns to walk away. My instinct is to chase him down and do anything to gratify him. But first there is Omar, with three more customers waiting for meat. "Help them out," I tell Omar. "I'll take care of this."

I catch up to the customer. "Sir," I say, extending my hand. "I'm Ariel Zinsky. Do you want to see the manager?"

"I'm fine," he says. "More shocked than anything. Really, it's no big deal. It only lasted a few seconds."

He stands there, in no particular hurry. "With all due respect, sir," I say, "there's no need to be diplomatic. One of our employees assaulted you. If you like, we can go to the office, and I'll get my manager."

"That would be great," he says.

Victor is in the office when we get there. He at once ascertains I'm mollifying a customer. He says, "Ariel, you can stay and watch how this is done." The customer gives his testimonial and completes a complaint form. We learn his name is Joe Deacon and he's been a patron for eleven years. He admits to provoking Omar by exhorting him to "hurry it up" on slicing three pounds of corned beef. Omar responded to Deacon's words by slowing it down. So Deacon remarked on Omar's bleak career prospects as a meat cutter. Omar emerged from behind the counter and grabbed Deacon.

At length Deacon departs, paying for his groceries despite Victor's insistence that he shop gratis. Soon Omar is in the office with us. Victor says, "This is not something I can be tolerant about, Omar. You smoke outside the supermarket, you show up five minutes late, even if you curse at customers I can live with that. Now I'm not saying you'll never work here again. But I have to fire you, and I cannot rehire you for at least three months. Do you understand?"

Omar nods and stands up. Before leaving he glares at me.

That night, walking home along a deserted and lamppost-lit Townsend Avenue, I'm shoved from behind and fall, ripping my gray corduroys at the left knee. A boot crashes into my sternum, rendering me breathless. Spikes pierce the back of my neck as a negro-colored hand seizes my collar. "I'm sorry, Omar," I say, squeaking more than speaking, owing to pre-puberty and my oxygen shortage.

"Oh, you sorry?" he replies. "Well here's what it is. When you gets paid Friday, we gon walk to da bank and cash ya check. And then I'm a get paid. And if you tells Victa or ya fat-ass ma, you gon feel a lot worse than *this*." He exhibits the source of my piercing. By lamppost light I see not a pocketknife, as I suspected, but a Chinese throwing star with eight silver spikes, emblazoned with an I-Ching symbol.

He walks away.

"See you Friday," I mumble.

When I get home I find Barbara reading *A Separate Peace* on her bed. I wave and lock myself into my own room. After ensuring my neck has stopped bleeding – I hold my ruined corduroys against my skin – I change into sweats for sleeping. As soon as Barbara shouts goodnight and clicks shut her bedroom door I go to the kitchen. I shove my corduroys to the bottom of the trash bucket, where they won't get discovered, since it's my duty to periodically remove the garbage bag. Next stop: the bathroom. I wash my face with soap and water before bedtime. My final stop is Barbara's door: I feel an urge to talk to her, with all that's gone on. But I don't want her to see my scabbed neck. And she won't, now that the light's off in her room. Without worry I twist her doorknob and creep into her bed for a cuddle.

I find myself wiping tears on Barbara's black sweatshirt. Her fingertips press the back of my head. She asks if something has happened at work. A few minutes pass before I develop a plausible lie. I speak through my subsiding, lachrymal heaves. "Mom," I say, "Who's going to teach me to shave?"

She kisses my head – a combed thatch of black spaghetti. "I will," she says.

"Why haven't I needed to shave yet?" I ask.

"Some boys develop later than other boys," she says. "You're just a late bloomer. It could be worse. Imagine if you were short."

"Did dad hit puberty late? Did you?"

"I was average. Thirteen. Your dad – I don't know if we ever discussed it. Is this all that's bothering you?"

"I just feel so young sometimes at work," I say. "But sometimes I feel old too. It's hard to explain. God, this is embarrassing."

"What's embarrassing?"

"Crying like this in front of you," I say. "I'm 15. I shouldn't cry anymore."

"Says who?" she says.

"Says I. You don't need to be saddled with a crying boy."

"Ari, I don't mind when you cry. I don't care if you're 15 or 50. You can always, always, *always*" – she seizes my shoulders on the third repetition – "cry when you're around me. Is that clear?"

I nod and bury my head in her chest.

I never see Omar again and my mother never hears of him.

*   *   *

There are stories like *Superman*, which require suspension of disbelief for maximum enjoyment. Then there are stories like mine – *real* stories – where for the most part, disbelief need not be suspended. There are no flying humans, no unfamiliar planets, and no optical illusions.

So what can I tell you now, when I've reached the rare juncture in my narrative that strains credulity? As I sit here typing, I'm puzzled: What happened to my hair all those years ago remains enigmatic to me. Doctors had no medical explanations, and I still struggle explaining it to myself. And I wish there were an easy way out. Or an easy lie I could tell. I don't have much experience discussing it. For who among us openly discusses his baldness? The conversational protocol is to treat baldness like obesity or a fatal disease: you rarely broach it with the sufferer. I can safely report that no one, outside of my mother, ever broached it with me.

Our world is one of minor medical miracles: we have all heard of eleventh-hour cancer recoveries when medicine has failed, occasioned solely by the patient's imperishable optimism. Crash survivors, bound permanently to wheelchairs upon initial diagnosis, sometimes learn to walk. In this context, isn't the notion of losing one's hair in a single moment *slightly* believable? Is it not possible that at the age of 16, when most boys are relishing the growth of hair in certain private places, I lost every single hair on my head?

It was wintertime: February, 1991, to be exact. The 16-year-old Zinsky was a friendless tenth grader. My appearance could be likened to a barbell on its edge: I was a narrow stick (now six feet, two inches tall) with cumbrous ballooning at the head (diameter: 7 and 7/8) and feet (size 15). And one morning when I came out of the shower my head had transformed. Seizing a comb in the anticipation there would be a wet mop attached to my scalp, I slouched before the de-fogging mirror and saw no follicles whatsoever – just an interminable Caucasian forehead. I was stunned. I had no recollection of hair coming off in the shower. I closed my eyes, hoping I'd awaken in my bed to find my baldness was only a vivid, palpable nightmare. But no: I was bald and that was that.

I checked the shower drain for traces of my long black hair but there was no sign of it. Again I palmed my head for confirmation: nothing but wet scalp. Again the mirror: my pate remained a bare mountain from the Caucasus.

My mother had already left for work and there was no one around I could talk to. And the shock of the morning's events wasn't enough to overcome the internal wiring – already there at age 16 – telling me I needed to catch the school bus at 7:30. So I threw on my Jets winter hat and went to school. I kept the hat on all day. I was quietly grateful that few teachers of my generation required hats to be doffed.

That night I showed my shocked-but-supportive mother what had happened. In the coming weeks she and I saw several dermatologists and hair-growth specialists, none of whom found anything beyond a sudden hair loss remediable only through transplant surgeries. They asked whether I'd been going through a difficult time.

No, I said. I'm fine.

I became embarrassed to walk hatless around school, though not a single classmate derided me. The hair loss was so sudden, so noticeable, that everyone seemed to assume there was a medical problem. I was thankful I'd attended schools in New Hyde Park my entire life. Though my peers rarely spoke to me, they were at least accustomed to me. If I had to italicize the meaning of their stares, the meaning would be *look what happened to poor Ariel*, as opposed to *look at that tall bald freak*. Trusty longtime peers such as Archie Kong still waved in the hallways. Others like Peter Mauro were not malicious but just ignored me. All told, I eagerly awaited my chance to escape to college. I still believed that in a new setting, I would finally meet the girl who would love me despite my baldness and boniness.

The hair loss triggered a deeper reaction in my mother than it did in me. It was as though Barbara became bent on becoming the girl of my dreams once my appearance made it apparent I wouldn't find that girl in high school. Granted: Barbara was now 46 years old, and her parade of boyfriends had slowed to a crawl. So she was more available on Friday and Saturday nights. Sometimes she'd stop at The Gap after school and come home with a new sweater or button-down shirt for me to wear on our dates. She could afford the clothes: she'd reached certain milestones in her tenure with the Great Neck School District, bumping her salary to the $40K range. For my part, my supermarket checks were roughly $90 per week after taxes. That was a fortune to a teenager like me, who spent not on smoking or sneakers but Yoo-hoo and magazines and library late fees.

Our typical Saturday date began at four in the afternoon. After spending my morning at the supermarket – where the reaction to my baldness was a similar mix of superficial concern and mannered indifference – I'd shower and don one of Barbara's purchases: a black button shirt, new jeans, and some hiking boots. Barbara generally wore black jeans and a white blouse, topped by a cardigan sweater. Her blond hair fell past her shoulders to the middle of her back.

Our first stop was the colossal Great Neck Public Library. Both of us usually had books to return and new ones to borrow. Barbara also enjoyed browsing the selection of VHS movies. Then there was the music section, replete with listening booths where library members could sample vinyl or cassettes.

The resources of the Great Neck Public Library – have I mentioned its microfilm archive, its collection of magazines and newspapers, its performance theater, or its private reading stalls? – dwarfed those of our local New Hyde Park library. Through her status as a teacher in the affluent town, Barbara garnered passes for us both. We treated the plastic orange cards like tickets to a luxury mansion on the hill. We especially savored the library during cold months, since the place was always warm. By contrast, our apartment became frigid three or four times each winter, through piping or pilot light problems.

Barbara and I referred to the Great Neck Public Library as the West Egg Public Library. We got the title from *The Great Gatsby*, in which the town of Great Neck is named West Egg. Sometimes Barbara drove to West Egg and sometimes I did. It depended on our relative levels of fatigue. On warm days we'd drive past the library, into the West Egg village known as Kings Point. There we sat and chatted at one of two outdoor locations. The first was an abandoned three-story manse off the Long Island Sound known as "Gatsby's House," which Fitzgerald had used as a basis for his protagonist's residence. Barbara and I parked the Datsun on the long gravel driveway and relaxed on a nearby bench. She smoked while I drank a bottle of Gatorade or chocolate milk. After two cigarettes, we'd climb back in the car and drive to the library or our dinner or movie destination.

Given the significance of Gatsby's house as a literary monument, we often expected to be discovered by curious strangers. But we were never intruded upon. At various points we wondered aloud whether we had the wrong place. But we were certain we didn't: for it was the only piece of property on a small side street called Gatsby Lane; the seaside view to the East showcased a harbor light flashing green; and beside the manse's withering yellow immensity was an empty swimming pool and a box-shaped ranch home, which Barbara and I guessed was the abode Gatsby rented to his neighbor, the 30-year-old narrator Nick Carraway.

Our second outdoor spot was a park to the North of Gatsby's reified residence: Steppingstone Park, an expansive green on the northwest tip of West Egg. Brown water met filthy sand at the fabled peninsula's beachy rim; seashells, broken glass, seaweed, and stones black and orange covered the coast, which stretched back to a ten-foot barrier marking the tide. The barrier wall extended for nearly 200 yards, covering the length of Steppingstone's northwest perimeter, separating that sandy stretch from the vast verdancy defining the park proper. Toward the entrance of the park, the wall diminished in height, sloping diagonally downward until it met the grass itself. Here there was a dock constructed of wooden panels painted gray and railings painted white. By day the townies of West Egg fished over the railings and sunbathed on the panels. Recreational sailors anchored their speedboats, stopping to eat or use the Steppingstone restrooms. The dock extended about one hundred feet into the brown Long Island Sound. At night, it was easy to see the hallowed green light of the East Egg peninsula.

When Barbara and I reached the park, it was usually still bright out. Foreign cars and luxury sedans filled the lot, as did the scratchy chirrups of crickets and cicadas. The West Egg Park District rarely skimped when it came to entertainment for its tax-paying residents; during summer there were always free cultural events: if not an orchestra, then a musical or a jazz jamboree.

The sound stage stood about 40 feet from the barrier wall, so that the beach and water were behind it and in front of it was the park's preponderance of grassy space. Lawn chairs, lounges, and blankets covered the grass, reaching from the very front of the stage to the rear of the park, where another sandy area delineated a playground for children: sandbox, slide, see-saw, and swing set. It was here that I learned to "pull" and "pump" as a child, so that my swing could soar without the assistance of a parental push.

One bright evening, as Barbara and I shared the swing set during an orchestral performance – she with her cigarette, I with my Gatorade – we were approached by a six-foot man with thick gray hair wearing jeans and a polo shirt. I didn't recognize him but Barbara stomped her butt in the sand and stood. "Holy shit," said the man. "Is that Barbara Pratt?" By his use of my mother's maiden name – and her reaction of embracing him – I took him to be one of her childhood pals. Barbara had grown up in Brooklyn and attended college at the state school in Buffalo, so through the years I had witnessed many encounters with people who knew her as Pratt.

The man stared at me. I wondered if he was shocked about my baldness. "Is that your son?" he asked.

"Ariel," I said, stepping forward, asserting my height advantage.

Barbara continued the introduction. In a matter of thirty seconds she explained away her marriage, my birth, her employment, and how we came to arrive at Steppingstone that evening. The man – Todd Winnick was his name – was not a high school or college pal but an old chum from a Pennsylvania summer camp. Winnick was alone and invited us join him on his picnic blanket, which was much closer to the stage.

"I'd love to, Todd," said Barbara, "But Ariel and I have plans to catch a movie. We were going to stop at the library too."

I felt like a hindrance. "Mom, why don't you catch up with Todd?" I said. "I'll walk to the library, return the books, and just hang out there. You can pick me up later."

Barbara wasn't biting. "Nice seeing you, Todd," she smiled. Winnick went back to the crowd.

On our way to the parking lot Barbara asked, "Did you *want* to go to the library by yourself?"

"I just didn't want to be a hindrance."

"*You're* my date for the evening," she said, curling her arm around my waist.

At the library we shared a mahogany table. With our book choices piled high, we read and made notes on our yellow legal pads. I happily recall how one of my books that night was a biography of Walter Camp, the "father" of American football.

Soon my teen appetite was rabid. Waiting thirty more minutes for our pre-movie meal seemed torturous. "Mom, want anything from the snack bar?" I asked.

After deflecting Barbara's predictable sallies about eating too much before dinner, I went downstairs, past the movie room and music stations, to the snack bar/cafeteria area. Posted rules forbade eating elsewhere, so I lingered on a bench and crunched on my Sun Chips.

A revolving door in the cafeteria led to a carpeted hallway, which in turn led to the library's performance theater. West Egg students could schedule rehearsals and shows on this stage; and during my trips to the snack bar, I often heard the distant dissonance of electric guitars or the operatic timbres of musical theater groups. It was this stage that introduced me to many of Shakespeare's works, and also to rock operas by Pink Floyd and The Who. But on this day, the 16-year-old Zinsky heard a lone female voice. She ranged high, then low, then high again. But her high voice seemed on the low side. I had read somewhere that contralto was the lowest type of female voice and quite rare. I racked my brain for the term that was not contralto but one higher: mezzo-soprano. Leaving my food behind, I passed through the revolving door and into the hallway, practicing the question – "So, would you call yourself a mezzo-soprano?" – I'd ask upon encountering her.

When I reached the stage I was too stunned to speak. A slender red-haired girl about my age lay flat-backed atop a wooden ramp near stage left. She was completely clothed, as was the teenage boy whose head was beneath her black skirt and between her tanned shaven legs. Her bare knees were back by her chest where she could hug them. My unnoticed visitation lasted for perhaps ten seconds, during which time my cock turned into a steel rod. I went back to the cafeteria to finish my chips.

There are, as I see it, two developmental stages to male horniness. The first occurs at a young age, when you notice the link between visual enticements and your organ's stiffness. The second occurs during puberty, when you discover ejaculatory release. Though I was 16, I was not yet accustomed to release. Through cultural osmosis the act of oral sex was familiar to me, but I never fantasized about performing or receiving it. Even sexual intercourse seemed strange: I had learned in health class that sex entailed a penis inside a vagina. But I remained uninitiated in the abiding forces compelling men and women to seek this thrusting, unified condition. So while what I'd witnessed on the stage aroused me, there was no correlative mounting of my own desires. Had I witnessed the selfsame scene three months later, my urge would've been to find a bathroom and beat off. But as a high-voiced, smooth-faced, late-blooming 16-year-old, the effect of my voyeurism was more contemplative than responsive.

Let me stress again: I was a "young" 16: I had yet to shave my face or require deodorant. Leaving aside my baldness, the only bodily manifestations of aging were my height and appetite. I devoured two entrees that night as Barbara and I dined at a Korean restaurant. We then saw a French/Polish movie called *The Double Life of Veronique*. My ability to suspend disbelief had not improved since my elementary school days. This film – where the same actress depicts two women, Veronique and

Veronika, who live in different European cities – was a severe challenge to my earthbound cogitation. Assisted by my caloric consumption, I fell asleep within minutes, slouched down in my seat so my head could rest on the seatback. It was the first time my bare scalp felt the velvety surface of a movie theater chair.

In future years, watching R-rated films would engender rampant masturbation. On this evening, my dry dream was only figuratively drippy: I discover anew the red-haired girl on the wooden ramp. She's fully clothed, sitting upright in her black skirt, holding a script. Her male companion stands twenty feet away at stage right. He reads the part of Cassius – and she Brutus – from *Julius Caesar*, Act IV Scene 3:

He: You love me not.

She: I do not like your faults.

He: A friendly eye could never see such faults.

She: A flatterer's would not, though they do appear / As huge as high Olympus.

Brutus hears me approaching and looks up. "Good evening," she says, jumping down from the stage to shake my hand. "I'm Katy." Cassius leaps down and introduces himself as Gregory, or Greg, whichever I prefer. Before long the three of us have switched to Act IV Scene 1. We read the parts of Antony, Octavius, and Lepidus. After which the questions begin: "Do you go to North or South?" asks Katy. She's referring to West Egg's two high schools. "My mom teaches at North. I live in New Hyde Park," I say, knowing only in West Egg do New Hyde Park roots yield street cred. Greg asks if I'd like to join them for dinner on Middle Neck Road, West Egg's main drag. "Sure," I reply.

Walking to a pizza parlor called Ellio's, Katy takes my hand. Greg doesn't mind. In fact, he smiles, and it's then I notice his braced teeth, verging on perfect alignment. I become conscientious about my own crooked choppers. Midway through our meal Katy, still holding my hand, asks why I'm not smiling. When I tell her she kisses the bare crown of my head. I notice now: her teeth are crooked too. "I thought all girls from West Egg had perfect teeth," I mutter.

And then I awaken. In future years, I will emerge from such fantasies with besotted boxers or sticky palms. At this point I find only a yellow legal pad on my chest, my left hand loosely gripping a pen.

Chapter 4 – The Spring Break Not Seen On Television

There's an old wives' tale linking hair loss to chronic masturbation. However, my days of jacking off only began *after* my hair loss. The girls filling my fantasy life were a mélange of slender assed or big breasted teens from the New Hyde Park High School hallways or the West Egg Library corridors. Most prominent was a mathlete two years younger than I named Charlene Chiu. She was the worst of the mathletes, the type who never solved any equations but showed up weekly to earn extra-curricular stripes. I never spoke to her, mainly because I only spoke about whatever problems were on the blackboard. But her specimen tantalized me: half-Chinese and half-Irish, she had the slanted eyes of the former ethnicity but the blond hair of the latter. Her body also reflected an ethnic dichotomy: Her legs and torso were lithe and Asian but her breasts floated outward and up like buoyant apples.

By the time I was a senior in high school I was thrilled Charlene waved to me in the hallways; sometimes she even called: "Hi, Ariel." I craned my neck to examine her bedenimed rear after she passed. If my next class was gym, or lunch, or something where tardiness was tolerable, I ran to a bathroom and beat off in a stall.

Charlene was the only girl I possibly could have asked to my senior prom. But when spring rolled around she began dating the lone Asian on our varsity basketball team. Once I learned this – I saw them necking in the hallway one afternoon as he "dropped her off" for a mathletes session – I scuttled weeks of rumination about how I'd phrase my prom invitation. I hopped a train to Shea Stadium and bought two baseball tickets for prom night. They would be Barbara's ostensible mother's day gift, and my instantly feasible excuse for bypassing a bally-hooed teen rite.

It was around this time that Barbara and I received a surprising postcard from Albuquerque announcing the birth of Sandra Clark, daughter to Cam Clark and Robert Zinsky. The card was followed by my father's first non-Christmastime phone call in eight years. Barbara spoke to him briefly and passed me the cordless receiver.

Ariel: How come she has Cam's last name?

Robert: In marriage you have to pick your battles.

Ariel: How come it took you so long to have a kid?

Robert: What is this, "60 Minutes"?

Ariel: We don't have to talk about it if –

Robert: Let me see if I can put it in terms you'll understand. Have you studied the praying mantis in school?

Ariel: What?

Robert: You know, the praying mantis.

His voice was moist: he sounded like he was chewing candy or to-bacco, like the saliva was tidal in his mouth.

Robert: You're aware that the female praying mantis, after mating with the male, bites his head off because, having captured his sperm, she no longer has a need for him.

Ariel: It sounds like an old wives' –

Robert: Ari, listen to your father. Because no one else will tell you this. Not your teachers, not your friends, no one. Women – are you listening? – women do not like *men*. Women do not fall in love with *men*. Women fall in love with *sperm*. And after they get the sperm, they become impassive to the sperm *supplier*. It's happened to me twice now, so I know of what I speak. I thought, after eleven years, that Cam might be different. But she's not. She's just like your mother, just like *all* of them.

Ariel: Okay.

Robert: You know that universal symbol of the female? That circle with the plus sign below it? It's bullshit. The female symbol is actually a praying mantis: a head with two antennae, the thorax, the abdomen. Think about it. Anyway, I gotta run. Talk to you in December.

More than a decade has passed since that phone call. I'm still uncertain whether his philippic was madman's contumely or prophetic wisdom.

* * *

My final high school grade point average was 89. My math grades were in the mid-90s; my English and Latin and Spanish and history scores were in the low 90s; but my science grades were in the 70s, thanks to my lazy effort and unskilled hands. (It once took me 15 minutes of class time to light a Bunsen burner.)

I had no clue what my job would be when I grew up. All I knew was that sports – and especially football – were important to me. I wanted to attend a reputable college that revered athletics. I wanted to study everything from lofty literature to sports broadcasting. And I wanted to leave Long Island. An escape to California wasn't necessary, but I sought *some* geographical distance between me and my past. I also didn't want to be too close to Albuquerque.

My choice? The University of Michigan. I got accepted in December of my senior year and applied nowhere else.

You can become isolated at Michigan if you choose not to align yourself with a fraternity, an ethnicity, or an extra-curricular activity. That's what happened to me. I spent entire weekends in my Washington Street apartment watching college and pro football (excluding the Michigan game, which I attended in person).

Following puberty's growth spurt I stood 6-8. Yet I was built like a broomstick and my weight remained a flimsy 180. If anyone had visited my college apartment during my first two years there, they'd have observed my toothpick frame and noted its resemblance to the halogen lamp standing next to my television.

My first instinct was to major in math. But calculus proved too challenging. Within one semester I was relying on accounting courses to fulfill university requirements. In my free time I made lists speculating on which college football players would best adjust and thrive at the professional level. There was, I won't deny it, an autobiographical impulse behind this research, since my own dominance in the sphere of math had vanished when confronted with tougher material.

So there I was in Ann Arbor: no hair on my head and, from the neck down, a flagpole physique with bony bulges at the knees and elbows. My uncomely appearance and reclusiveness led to the following circumstance: by my 19th year I had not yet mouth-kissed a single female. Nor had I come close. On the day I turned 20, in 1995, my mother phoned me in Ann Arbor. After extending birthday wishes and confirming my receipt of a $25 gift certificate to The Gap, she flat-out asked me: "Do you ever see any girls?"

"Nope," I replied.

She told me it didn't matter and apologized for not having more money to send me.

*   *   *

Almost every dime I earned went toward my tuition. I spent 10 hours a week washing dishes in the Betsey Barbour Dining Hall and another 10 hours performing clerical chores at Michigan Business School.

I used these financial circumstances as a specious pretense for flying back to Long Island – as opposed to Cancun or Hawaii – during Spring Break. The real reasons I returned home were my friendless existence at Michigan and the company of my mother. But I used the fiscal pretext with my mother too, since "I just want to hang out with you," is a corny and difficult thing to tell a parent.

Plus I knew any trips to Cancun would result only in my abject failure to kiss a woman.

One weekday afternoon, my mother opened the door to my bedroom without knocking. She observed her sophomore son face down on his bed, half-napping, jeans and boxers pushed down to his knobby knees, buttocks exposed. Indeed, I was in that pleasant, dreamy, postmasturbatory reverie. My eyes were closed, my mind was blank; my radio was tuned to the sports talk station.

The topic of the radio program was the upcoming National Football League draft. On my bed was a yellow legal pad on which I'd ranked the top 20 college quarterbacks. Beside the pad I'd arranged several football magazines, all of which contained glossy photographs of muscular players in colorful uniforms. And it was with my mouth drooling onto these gleaming pages that my mother found me bare-assed on that early spring day.

She said: "Ari, is there anything we need to talk about?"

Rather than pulling up my jeans I reached for my blanket and draped it over myself. I pretended to be groggy, not only to avoid conversation but also to keep the room silent, so I could hear radio commentary on which college players my beloved Jets might draft. "We'll talk later, I guess," said Barbara, shutting the door.

At dinner that night Barbara and I acted as though the incident hadn't happened. We ate quietly, our plates resting on the cream-colored oval table, which occupied half the open space in the apartment. Nearby were the lone couch, an ottoman (which Barbara and I had nicknamed "The Empire"), and a twenty-inch manual-channel television with a VCR stacked on top.

We sat angled towards each other, sharing one edge of the oval. Her back was to what we called "the TV area" (it was hardly a living room), while my back was to the window facing our fire escape. On the table's opposite curve rested Barbara's pocketbook, her yellow cigarette pack (American Spirit Full Flavor Menthols), and two of her yellow legal pads.

From the kitchen, where we kept the box radio that served as the apartment stereo, came the sounds of *Tupelo Honey*, her favorite Van Morrison album. When we weren't humming the tunes, Barbara and I discussed how her job was going. Currently she was teaching *A Separate Peace* to her three ninth-grade classes: regular, honors, and remedial. Students in all three were absorbed with Gene and Phineas, the protagonists; that the novel had World War II as a backdrop simply did not register. "A generation that only knows peacetime," she said, tonging salad onto her plate and sliding the bowl in my direction.

I mused on bringing up what my mother had walked in upon. I wanted Barbara to know that I had not been jerking off to football players, but to Charlene Chiu. Charlene had emailed me from out of nowhere – after two years – to announce she'd received a full scholarship to Michigan and would be visiting the campus in April.

I asked Barbara: "What were you thinking when you came into my room before?"

"I figured you were napping, and I just wanted to look at you I guess," she said. "I realize I barged in." She left the table to search the refrigerator. "I could've sworn I put out the Thousand Island," she said, her body half-hidden by the magnet-covered fridge door. She crouched, with some difficulty, inspecting the lower shelves.

"Right here," I said, holding up the squeezable bottle.

Barbara kissed me on the forehead before sitting. Her hair, true blond with scattered grays, went down to her breasts, which were safeguarded by a white blouse and black cardigan. "I don't know why I worry so much about you, Ari," she said. "I always love having you back here. But I guess – in my school, all the kids are talking about MTV's Spring Break, and – well, I know the big party has never been your scene. I guess I worry why you're not going a little crazier. College only happens once."

"I'm not gay," I said, "If that's what you're driving at."

"It wasn't."

"Whatever," I said.

"And what if it was?" she asked. "You'd be mad?"

"No," I said. "I know what motivates your question. And you should know that you can talk to me if, after all these years, you're feeling some latent lesbian tendencies."

"To the contrary," she said, chuckling. She proceeded to inform me about Neil Segal, a Manhattan attorney who was tennis-friends with one of her English department colleagues. This colleague had wanted to set up Segal and my mother for years. But Barbara refused to see Segal until his divorce was finalized.

"You've been holding out on me," I said.

"Sorry," she replied. "But as you know, I've seen way too many men go running back to their wives. Especially if they have kids. Neil has one daughter."

"You'd never date someone new before getting divorced," I said, alluding to a certain paternal personage.

"Well, he's stayed with her, I'll give him that," she said.

"And she's stayed with him," I added.

* * *

Later that night my mother and I were relaxing in our adjacent bedrooms with our doors open. I read football magazines while she read *Ordinary People*, which she generally taught after *A Separate Peace*. When the phone rang – a rare and cherished event in our household, except at Christmas – I somehow knew it was Neil Segal, calling to chat with Barbara. The way my mother said "Hi" – with that lifting inflection implying sexual interest – confirmed my presumption.

I stood in her doorway, eager to catch her glance and distract her. She was in her bed clothes, black sweatpants and a gray PROPERTY OF GREAT NECK NORTH sweatshirt. Around her forehead was a white headband. She sat up on her purple sheets and cradled the cordless between her ear and shoulder. Her paperback was folded open on its pages beside her yellow legal pad.

Through the years I'd watched my mom field many of these first-date phone calls. I knew what her next series of movements would be: she'd switch the phone to the other side of her neck, grab her pad, and then doodle (if not interested) or take notes (if interested). She'd test Segal's knowledge of world cultures and American letters, run him through a conversational gauntlet.

Within seconds she let loose a burst of raucous laughter, her chin doubling over as the phone fell to the bed. Her teeth, crooked like mine, were visible, their hue similar to that of Chai tea.

It amazed me that a suitor's call could still fill Barbara with laughter. Her risibility was a bodily sign of open hope, an audible denial of prospective disappointment. I was in my fourth lonely semester of college, and I still could not approach an attractive woman for fear of the emotional paralysis rejection might bring. But here was my mother, laughing like a hyena, as if the power of heartbreak had never lynched her.

One hour later I returned to her doorway and said, "There is something I want to talk to you about. How do you – life being what it is – how do you not get skeptical?"

"Cigarettes," she said. "Coffee. Daily vices."

"Masturbating?" I volunteered.

"I suppose," she said, staring at her pad.

"But isn't it such an effort for you? Not getting skeptical, I mean?"

"Sweetie, you have to give yourself something to look forward to," she said. "For all I know Neil may prove to be an asshole. But if I just relish the little fact that a decent man is calling me – that's more than enough sometimes."

"Yeah, but wouldn't it be nice for you – and for me – if just looking forward to a certain television show each week was enough? Those television lovers have it easy."

"Don't be a snob," she said. "Football is your television."

"Football is not television," I said. "Football does not have a script. Football isn't handsome actors with makeup and wardrobe consultants. Football is real drama. Real men. Real pain."

"Regardless," she said. "All I'm saying is it provides a regular dosage of events you can look forward to."

"Maybe I should try cigarettes," I said.

"No," she said, swinging her legs to the side of the bed. "But I'll be your best friend if you come outside with me."

We kept a beat-up wooden chair on the fire escape. A tin ashtray rested on it. With the ashtray on her lap, Barbara sat smoking in her slippers, still wearing her headband, having thrown a jacket atop her sweatshirt. I sat on the rusty metal surface of the fire escape itself. After finishing her cigarette Barbara went back inside to read a few more pages before sleeping; she had school tomorrow. But I was on Spring Break, so I stayed out. I absorbed the view of the Watching the Wheels parking lot and beyond it, the stretch of manicured lawns and midsized houses with darkened windows filling New Hyde Park's suburban streets. I wondered where my life was heading. The smell of Barbara's cigarette still wafted from the ashtray. I went back inside, retrieved my legal pad and a pen, and returned to the fire escape, sitting on Barbara's chair. I determined not to leave the chair until I'd devised a plan – an aim – giving me something to look forward to.

I still have this particular legal pad, in a desk drawer in my apartment. It reads:

3/21/95   LIFE PLAN: A LIST   ARIEL ZINSKY
1. Attend the National Football League draft each April at the Marriott Marquis Hotel in New York City

2. Prior to draft, forecast each team's needs and predict which player the team, given its sagacity or lack thereof, will select
3. Prior to draft, compile rankings of top 50 college players at each position. <u>Include statistics</u>
4. Print up all your writings and create an annual draft yearbook. Sell copies on campus and at the Marriott. See if you can figure out how to get them on the Internet. Maybe sell advertising?

Just then, our phone rang again. I scurried to get it lest it wake my mother. But Barbara had already answered. Charlene Chiu was saying: "I was in tenth grade when he was in twelfth."

"They gave you a full scholarship, did they?" said Barbara.

"Yes," said Charlene, her voice vaguely clammy, like my father's, but feminine, as though she were chewing a watery wad of Trident. "I'm choosing between a free ride at Michigan and a costly one at Cornell."

"Not that you asked," said Barbara, "but I'd go with the free ride. Ari's going to be paying off his loans for a long time."

"Hi, Mom," I said, finally alerting them to my phone presence.

Barbara hung up and Charlene said, "So what's up?"

"Not much. I just had a half-decent epiphany out on our fire escape."

"You're so funny, Ariel," she said. "I didn't know your mom called you 'Ari.' Does everyone at Michigan call you 'Ari' too?"

"No, actually, I'm not too popular there. Which you'll see soon enough."

"Right, well, I just wanted to call, while you were home and all, and confirm plans. I'll be staying with my cousin Loretta, she's a grad student, on Friday the 21st. Then with you on Saturday the 22nd, if that's still okay."

"Sure," I said, sitting at the oval table.

"Thanks for being so accommodating. So what was your epiphany?"

"Um – how closely do you follow football?" I asked.

"Not closely," she said. "I like tennis though."

"Well – my epiphany had to do with how I could, in a way, have a football career." I tried to determine how much of her chuckling was involuntary. She said, "Ariel, when did you get so funny?"

"I don't know," I said. "Did you know I'm not a math major anymore?"

"What happened?"

"I overrated my abilities," I said. "My new major is accounting. I prefer my literature classes but accounting is just so easy. It creates more time for football."

More laughs from Charlene. She said: "Well, maybe you're worse at math but you sure are funnier. I gotta go to sleep but I'll email you before I visit, okay?"

That night before going to sleep I reviewed my brand new life plan. Inadvertently, I'd agreed to host Charlene Chiu on the same day the NFL draft was taking place in New York City.

* * *

My mother's first date with Neil Segal was on the night before my return flight to Michigan.

On countless occasions I had met men who'd had enough of Barbara after one date. I had no desire to waste precious mind space meeting another. And I was repulsed by the prospect of fielding his benevolent social questions. Neil might ask what I'd been doing all day, and I'd say: "Watching college basketball." At which point I imagined his lawyerly, busybody expression would register a certain non-judgmental judgment, a certain, "Oh, isn't it nice that you, as a mere college student, get to sit around and watch sports all day." I didn't want to deal with it. I was 20 and I had already read *Catcher in the Rye* six times. Polite formalities seemed unbearably phony, especially coming from someone whose main interest was bedding my mother. Was I supposed to believe he really gave a shit about what *I'd* been up to all day?

I also fretted that Neil — based on what Barbara had told him — would perceive me as a geek. And so, in my undergraduate, don't-you-dare-pigeonhole-me way, I sought to impress upon him that I was, in fact, the *opposite* of a geek: a jock. A tough guy. To effect this impression, I would flee the apartment — ten minutes in advance of his arrival — and go for a jog. Then Neil would arrive, and Barbara would inform him that "Ari was out jogging." The spin-doctoring would be underway.

Barbara was attired like she might be for school — white blouse, black pants — but her blond-gray locks appeared firm and settled, as if commanded into place by the blow-dryer. She caught me checking her out and said, "I learned a long time ago not to dress up too well for a first date. Dressing up makes it seem like it's too much of an occasion."

"I'm going jogging," I announced.

"Since when do you jog?"

"Have fun tonight," I said, kissing her forehead.

Down the sticky stairs of our apartment corridor, past the Watching the Wheels storage area, and onto Townsend Avenue: it was a clear, balmy day in late March. The 20-year-old Ariel Zinsky began the first jog of his life.

I'm tempted to spare you the disgusting visual of myself, huffing and puffing through rhythm-less strides, beholding my perspiring pate in Townsend's glass-window storefronts. My hairless white head resembled a glistening scoop of vanilla ice cream; my gray Michigan t-shirt soaked into a charcoal color; my boney white arms shimmered with sweat drops, like fence posts after a storm; every thirty seconds the elastic waistband of my sweatpants slid down the slope of my buttocks. From my nose and mouth came not breaths but asthmatic acoustics: I snored like a blast furnace, a grinding, heat-generating tank overreaching its capacity. And my pace, if I could even call it that, evoked pedestrian wisecracks: one middle-aged man standing at a bus stop, holding a *Daily News*, beheld my slug-like approach and remarked: "The marathon's not till November."

I'd been running for only five minutes but gasped like I'd risen rapidly from the ocean's fathoms. Each exhalation seemed vital. I recalled stuffy-nosed sleepless nights as a boy, fearful a burglar might enter through our fire escape window and, in gagging my mouth, suffocate me.

Before long a sharp pinch in my gut slowed me to a walk. I trudged with wide, choppy strides; my face, reexamined in storefront windows, was taut from the exertions of bowel control.

I entered an Indian restaurant called Delhi Dining, aiming to squeeze past the front desk and zip toward the bathroom. In her accented English, the hostess asked if I was by myself. Flustered, I turned and exited.

I scrambled down a side street, finding myself in the Delhi Dining parking lot next to a dark green dumpster. I waddled into a tarred space between the dumpster and the restaurant's brick wall. By my feet was a long concrete slab, designed to prevent cars from overshooting their parking spaces. Assuring myself that no one was nearby, I hooked my thumbs between my waistband and hips and jerked down my sweats and navy Michigan boxers. Crouching, my naked ass about ten inches above the pavement, my left arm holding the concrete slab for balance, I released an enormous shit, closing my eyes and muffling an almost ecstatic moan. It was a clean break: I didn't need toilet paper in the slightest.

I pulled up my pants and boxers and stepped away from the mess, moving almost as quickly as I had during my so-called jog. Before leaving the lot, I spun around and inspected the cakey lump from several yards' distance. In the spring air I expected the brown mass to be steaming on the tar like a burger on the grill. And there it was, no more nauseating than a dog's output, only larger and perhaps more impressive in that it was not a few pellets but one solid oblong loaf.

The exercise was over. I felt relieved and a little exhilarated. Examining myself in the Delhi Dining storefront, I observed a reddish coloration in my normally pallid cheeks. My sweat-darkened Michigan shirt made it look like I'd just run a 5K. I almost looked vigorous.

I wanted Charlene Chiu to behold me *this way*.

*   *   *

There is a fine line between stalking and sincerity. I leave it you, my keen and unbiased readers, to determine my level of trespass:

I reentered Delhi Dining, calmly asked the overfriendly hostess for a phone book, and looked up Charlene's street address.

She lived on 77 Dominus Street, a northern part of town that was only blocks away from West Egg's southern school district. I walked there and when I neared her house I began jogging again.

House 77 was a two-story colonial. To my delight Charlene was out on the gravel driveway, her blond hair falling over an orange v-neck. I lingered by the front lawn. She squinted at first, as if she did not recognize me — as if 6-8 bald guys built like baseball bats routinely patrolled Dominus Street.

Her younger sister, Alison, emerged from the side door with a purple

Frisbee in her hand. Alison was three years younger than Charlene but already taller. She wore jeans and a white t-shirt. She stared at me the way most people do the first time they behold a giant whose elbows are wider than his biceps and whose knees, even in sweatpants, are wider than his thighs: Instant incredulity, followed by feigned nonchalance. The sisters Chiu crunched toward me on the gravel, their breasts jouncing ever slightly beneath those t-shirts. "So when are you going back to school?" asked Charlene, by way of greeting.

"Tomorrow morning."

"Can't wait, right?" she said.

I shrugged. "Same difference," I said. The sisters exchanged glances.

"Want to throw with us?" said Alison, wielding the purple disc.

"Okay," I said, though I'd never learned how to throw a Frisbee and catching was no guarantee.

Just then I was saved from athletic humiliation. The side door opened and onto the gravel stepped Maribeth Farley Chiu, mother to the sisters, in white sweater and khakis. She invited me inside for a glass of water.

The Chiu's kitchen had room enough for both a small table and a large one. We sat at the large one, wooden with green legs, filling our glasses from a jug of Poland Spring. Alison held the Frisbee in her lap, her slender legs bouncing. Charlene lifted her glass as if it were a graduated cylinder, inspecting the meniscus. Only Maribeth seemed sincerely interested in either chatting or avoiding a Frisbee toss. "So how do you like Michigan?" she asked. "I've heard it can seem too big."

"I like it," I said. "It allows me to drift around anonymously."

Charlene and Maribeth hiccupped with half-giggles. "See, mom, I told you he'd gotten funny," said Charlene.

"I really appreciate your hosting Charlene," said Maribeth.

More conversation ensued: the family feigned interest in my postgraduate plans, and I feigned interest in telling them. I played it low-key, mentioning only accounting ambitions and not revealing my blueprint to become an NFL Draft guru. When at last the time came for Frisbee, I begged leave, citing a need to spend the evening with my mother. Charlene walked me to the edge of the driveway. "I'd give you a hug, but your shirt's kind of gross," she said.

I reached out for her arm, yearning to say farewell with *some* physical contact. And there, resting plaintively on her tennis triceps, sitting boldly atop her mandarin shirt, was a three-inch insect, a shade lighter in greenness than an unripe banana. Two antennae poked upward from its oval head, like thin drones from a bagpipe. "Jesus," I gasped, stepping back.

"What?"

I pointed to her arm, expecting her to shriek when she saw it.

"What?" she said.

The insect was gone.

"Is it possible," I asked, "that I just saw a praying mantis on your arm?"

She sighed. "Anything's possible. Do you normally flip out over bugs?"

"No," I said.

"I'll pretend it never happened," she smiled. "Talk to you soon."

I walked home and tried myself to pretend.

*   *   *

I presumed Barbara would still be out with Neil Segal. But just when I inserted my key in the lock, she pulled open the door. Classical music piped from the kitchen stereo. On the oval table were two complete settings, four plastic containers of sushi, and a shining blue bottle of saki. Sitting, holding chopsticks, was a balding, bespectacled, and overweight man in a dress shirt, belted bulgingly into new blue jeans. He pushed out his chair from the table and rose to greet me. He was nearly a foot shorter than I was. I instantly liked him, mainly because he wasn't handsome. And based on his looks alone, I gathered he was auditioning to be far more than Barbara's temporary bedfellow.

Still, I was bent on playing the role of a jilted Hamlet, if only for my mother's edification. I glared at Neil like I wanted to pound him. He outweighed me but I was certain I could take him in a fight. My cumulative inner rage would carry the day.

"How was your jog?" said Barbara, disrupting my stare-down.

"Help yourself to some sushi," said Neil.

"No thanks, I better shower," I said. Their conversation resumed as soon as I stepped away.

After showering, I worked on my list of the top 50 quarterbacks in the 1995 NFL Draft. Amidst jottings on my yellow pad I fell to fantasizing about Charlene, goaded on by the breast size that her orange v-neck had accentuated. Before long my left hand was soiled and my head fell to my pillow.

When I awoke I heard some groans and giggles coming from my mother's room. With a mixture of curiosity and perversion, I approached her door, which for whatever reason – spontaneity? The presumption I was sleeping? – was open a crack. Naked Neil's balding head was between Barbara's sallow, drooping thighs. His gold-framed glasses rested on the purple sheet.

After a few seconds of spectatorship – and I won't pretend I was unduly shocked or disgusted – I searched the refrigerator for leftover saki. But there was none left. In terms of alcohol, there was only a single Budweiser bottle, hiding in the back corner.

I brought the bottle to the oval table and listened to the orgiastic orchestra emanating from Barbara's bedroom. I wondered whether I'd ever, in my life, get the opportunity to make a woman shout. And I wondered whether, if given the opportunity, I'd deliver.

Had a woman been sitting with me at the table that night, I might have sobbed to induce her pity. But even at age 20, I felt so numb to my solitude, so inured to a lack of companionship, I could not cry. Solitude was my childhood allergy; I'd learned to cope. Not through cigarettes and coffee, like mom, but through sports, books, and masturbation.

I strained to twist open the bottle before realizing I'd need an opener. I put my head down on the table and waited for my mother's noises, which sounded almost like cries, to subside.

Chapter 5 – Charlene Chiu and the *Fanshawe* Redemption

Behold: the Ann Arbor apartment of the 20-year-old Ariel Zinsky. VHS cassettes are everywhere: avalanching outward from the bedroom closet, blockading the path from the bathroom to the living room. Their content is not pornographic. Rather, the tapes – and there are more than 100 of them – are labeled by date and game score. For example: *10/1/94, Notre Dame 34, Stanford 15.* My methodology is straightforward: watch footage of every starting college football player, with a mind towards evaluating the best prospective professionals.

The first volume of *Ariel Zinsky's Quintessential Guide to the NFL Draft* is 100 pages long and contains no photos. I did the printing at a Kinko's on 54th Street in Manhattan. I handed my University of Michigan-emblem Visa card and a floppy 3.5 inch disc to an apron-clad employee and instructed him: please print 50 coil-bound copies.

When my *Guides* were ready, I stacked them into a shopping cart I'd hijacked from a nearby supermarket. Drawing glances from all passersby as I wheeled down Broadway on this mild and cloudless spring day, I focused on keeping the cart upright during bumpy, horn-honking transitions from sidewalk to street. Oh, what a picture I must have been, in my Michigan baseball hat and Jets t-shirt, my gangly frame curled over the cart, my pipette arms struggling to steer! Even the residents of Manhattan, for whom almost nothing seems to be a freak show, couldn't but stare at the long-limbed white guy hovering high over the clanging wagon. At length I completed the twelve-block, south-bound trek to the Marriott. The hotel doorman cast a suspicious eye but eased up once he saw my *Guides* pertained to the draft.

Barbara and Neil were expecting me for dinner at eight; that gave me three hours to peddle *Guides* in the lobby before catching a train out to Long Island.

I could have stayed on Long Island that night, but instead I splurged on a room at the Marriott. I wanted Barbara – and especially Neil – to take my budding business seriously. In my tenth-floor suite, I stowed 40 of the 50 *Guides*; the rest, I stuffed in my backpack. Then I headed to the lobby, and started selling. Seated on a burgundy leather couch with briefcases open on a glass table were two gentlemen dressed like executives. Beside them, well dressed but without a briefcase, was a young black man I recognized as Kordell Stewart, quarterback from the University of Colorado. I approached the trio and said, softly: "Hi. My name is Ariel Zinsky. I'm a sophomore at Michigan, and –"

"We're not interested," said the man sitting closest to the quarterback.

I turned away. After a few more failed efforts, I eliminated an introduction and hawked my books like a flea market vendor: "Draft guides – five dollars!" I shouted at every person who entered the lobby. I doffed my Michigan hat or pointed to my Jets shirt if I spied a fan wearing similar apparel. I sold only two copies but got several looks: many a draft devotee thumbed through a manual before returning it with a polite, "It's great, but no thank you." Several also told me that they'd already purchased their guides – glossy ones, with photos, produced by experts from ESPN or *The Sporting News*. What use did they have for my *Guide* the night before?

I trudged eight blocks south to Penn Station, trying to escape the rejection I felt. For an entire month I had toiled alone in my cassette-strewn apartment. I had revised my top 50 lists – and my prose – over and over again. And I was confident it was better, text-wise, than anything ESPN or *Pro Football Weekly* or *The Sporting News* had published. But now it was the night before the draft and the fact remained: only two people in the world, other than I, would ever read my masterpiece.

Nevertheless, I took the $10 I'd grossed from those two supportive patrons and purchased a roundtrip train ticket to New Hyde Park. I waited on the packed platform among workplace escapees bound for suburban Sabbaths. There were dozens of young, professionally dressed women, some wearing short skirts, others wearing tight tops. I entertained the idea that one of these women, staring East in hope of glimpsing the incoming train, was actually staring at *me*, her eyes captivated by my appearance, her emotions irrationally moored to mine. Then I laughed at myself. And I wondered, not for the first time, whether it was only the existence of Barbara that prevented me from throwing myself in front of an oncoming train. The whole intent of my *Guide* was to give myself an aim to sustain me. But now? I was a failure as a fledgling publisher. I was nothing but what I'd been *before* the *Guide*: a young man whom women never stared at. I doubted, though, whether all the ignored young men – surely I wasn't the only one – pondered suicide over their condition. Why was *I* doing this? How much of it had to do with my father and my childhood? And whom could I talk to about it? Not my mother. Not on this night, when what she needed was for me to suck it up and play nice with her new boyfriend.

At the New Hyde Park train stop I searched the lighted parking lot for Barbara's brown '82 Datsun. Instead I spotted her blond-gray head emerging from the passenger window of a shiny black '95 Audi, a two-door. On the phone she'd referred to this vehicle as "Neil's wheels." Squeezing my 6'8 frame behind Barbara's pushed up chair and into the Lilliputian back seat increased the shame of the moment. I felt physical torment, beyond the mental humiliation of cramping inside the foreign vehicle of my mother's affluent lover. From the offhand way he turned around in the driver's seat and shook my hand, I discerned Neil was so confident in my mother's affection he was passive about earning mine.

Not that jealousy robbed me of happiness for Barbara. Clearly, she was eager for me to observe her in twinkling, recently laid form. During our meal, at a trattoria in the town of Manhasset (East Egg, for you *Gatsby* fans), they held hands under the table, ate off each other's plates, and cracked in-jokes. I felt like more of a witness than a companion.

When Neil went to the bathroom Barbara asked about Charlene

Chiu's imminent campus visit. "You'll be back in time for her?"

"Flight's at two-thirty, I'm on campus by six, Charlene shows up at seven," I said.

After the meal we stopped briefly at home. Barbara beheld one of my *Guides* and said, "It's so thick. I can't even pin it to the fridge."

Neil went to Barbara's bedroom – had it become *their* bedroom? – returning with a Gap plastic bag. Inside was a ribbed brown v-neck. "Put it on," said Barbara. "I want to see you in this color."

Having donned the top I turned to my mother. "Yes," she said. "Neil, look at his *eyes* in this. Look at them!" Neil glanced up at my face, reluctantly. In his hesitance I sensed for the first time that he and I had an unstated understanding of our own.

Barbara seized my arm. "Come into my room," she said. "I want you to look at yourself." Neil remained in the kitchen while she steered me to the full-length mirror.

I could not bring myself to look in that mirror.

What was the point? To attempt to thwart my unassailable self-knowledge that not the finest Gap shirt, in the most flattering light, could render me handsome? I shut my eyes. When I opened them, I only gazed to the right or left of the mirror. I finally turned to my mother. "I'm so ugly, Mom," I said, and like a child I lowered my head to her body, wiping my eyes on her blouse.

"Nonsense," she whispered, stroking my bald head.

"Don't lie," I whispered, squeaking through half-formed sobs.

"Maybe if you looked in the mirror, you'd see I wasn't," she said.

I peeked at the glass. Barbara held me. "Look at those brown eyes," she said. "Believe me, sweetie. With those eyes, it's just a matter of time."

"Spare me the *eyes* bullshit," I said. Rather than being taken aback by my freshness, Barbara seemed relieved that I had returned from the brink of bawling. "You probably think," I said, "that Neil has great eyes, too."

"They *are* nice."

"Mom, you always think your boyfriend has nice eyes. Every woman thinks their boyfriend has terrific eyes. Who has ugly eyes? You know what eyes are? Eyes are subjective bullshit."

"If it's so subjective," she said, "then why do you take it so personally?"

"I don't know," I muttered.

*   *   *

Neil and Barbara chauffeured me to the New Hyde Park train station and I rode back to Manhattan. Before going to bed I sold three more *Guides* in the Marriott lobby.

In my hotel suite, I lubed my left hand with white body cream I'd found in the bathroom. Lying under my covers, I stroked myself while watching a pro basketball game. Once erect, I switched to HBO, hoping to find an R-rated sex scene that – when interspersed, in a mental montage, with selected images of Charlene Chiu – would produce a towering tumescence. I got my wish: a male actor seized a female actor from behind and used his hands to steamroll her breasts. I exploded, soaking a portion of the covers, moaning and wrenching with self-pleasure. Gradually my sounds mellowed into simpering wails. I curled up on my side and clung to the puffy pillow that had been sweet enough to sleep beside me.

*   *   *

I found Charlene sitting cross-legged on the stone steps out front of my Ann Arbor apartment. She wore an unzipped red ski jacket over a pink sweater and jeans. Black backpack straps squeezed the jacket's plump shoulders. With black gloves, she held open an *In Style* magazine. "I know I'm technically early," she greeted me. "But I figured there'd be other people around. Who else lives here? My cousin doesn't know anyone who lives on this part of Washington Street."

I stood in place, uncertain how to respond. Charlene rushed toward me on her toes with her head down and tried throwing her arms around my shoulders. She wound up embracing me around the forearms. My heart thudded against her cheek. I soon separated myself, lest she felt another organ throbbing against her. "It's good to see you," she said, stuffing *In Style* into her backpack, reverting to folded-arms posture. "I'm excited to see your apartment. I'm considering getting my own place as a freshman, just so I can study more."

Upon entering I was embarrassed at the dozens of VHS cassettes scattered all over the floor: In my bedroom and on my bed and beside my computer monitor, in the living room and on the couch and atop the television. "What are you watching so many movies for?" she asked.

"They're not movies," I said. "They're football games." From my large black gym bag I withdrew one of the many remaining *Guides*. She paged through it. "I don't understand," she said. "This is just lists and numbers."

"Lists and numbers of football players I'm evaluating," I said, holding up one of the VHS cassettes.

Laughing, she cleared away a pile and sat on my bed. "Seriously, Ariel. What movies do you have?"

"Seriously, Charlene. It's just football games. I'll show you." I handed her a tape marked *10/15/94, Oregon State 23, UCLA 14*. We moved to the living room. She reclined on my couch while I cued the action to a failed play-action pass. "See this UCLA quarterback? He lacks the mobility to avoid the rush," I said. "He gets sacked by the first defender who gets through. But next season they have a kid named McNown coming in. He's more of a scrambler."

"All these tapes on the couch and on the floor are *football?*" she asked. I nodded. "Ariel, that's so weird," she said. "How do you have time to watch them all? Don't you have to study? When do you go out?"

"I don't go out that much, I guess that's where the time comes from," I said.

"So what's our plan for tonight?"

"Well, I've heard people say it's easy to get into the bars on Liberty Street," I volunteered. "I mean, I doubt I'll get carded, since I look about sixty."

"I have my cousin's old driver license as a fake ID," she said.

We began preparing for a night out. From my closet, where yet more cassettes were buried, I handed her a green-and-white Jets towel. She fetched shampoo bottles from her backpack and marched to the bathroom. With my ear to the closed wooden door I heard the squeaking of knobs, then water-bullets slamming the shower mat. I fantasized for a moment.

We ate at the student union Taco Bell. Sitting at a turquoise table, surrounded by dozens of other students and prospective freshmen,

Charlene and I discussed the differences between life on Long Island and life in Michigan. Her hair was wet and redolent of raspberry conditioner. It was brushed straight back and it dangled over a tight black top. I wore jeans and the brown v-neck. "What do you miss about the East Coast?" she asked, toying with an unopened hot sauce packet.

"With the sports fans here, there's less sophistication-per-capita than you get in New York," I said. "The fans are so zeroed in on the Detroit teams – they act as though there aren't 30 other teams in the league. Whereas in New York, you never forget the national picture."

"*Besides* sports, Ariel," she said. "Do people here go to museums? Do they see movies besides the blockbusters? Do they buy music made by independent recording artists?"

"I don't know," I said. "Are those your tests for cultural sophistication?"

"Not as a rule," she said. "I know it's not a black-and-white situation. But, for example, my cousin Loretta said there was a clear divide between the in-state students and everyone else. Have you found that to be the case?"

"I don't know. I don't really know many people. I just go to classes, do my homework, watch sports, eat, sleep. I – I jerk off a lot too. I'll admit that to you," I said.

"*Okay*," she said, looking away, granting the word a facetious, upward intonation that made her pronouncement synonymous with the trendy phrase *too much information*. She stared down at her half-eaten bean burrito, resting on its unfurled paper wrapper.

"Oh, give me a break with that *okay*," I said, mimicking her. "Tell me it's news to you guys masturbate."

"We are *not* having this discussion."

"Yes we are," I said. "I'm just curious: did you, or did you not know, prior to this moment, that men jerk off?"

"I never really thought about it one way or the other."

"And your reaction – that *okay* – was that sincere shock, or just an expression of shock your manners compelled you to make?"

She mused on this. "The former," she said. "But it was less shock at the fact of masturbating than it was shock at your proclaiming it, out here, while we're eating."

"I'm sorry," I said.

"No big deal." She was quiet. Then she said, "I meant to say I like your sweater, by the way. It brings out your eyes. Is it banana?"

"Banana?" I replied, my face wrinkling in confusion. "I – I think it's brown."

She laughed, reaching across the table to squeeze my bicep. "I meant Banana Republic," she said. I nodded as if I knew all along and told her it was Gap.

Half an hour later we walked along Liberty Street, our jackets unzipped. We stopped at the back of a line about 30 persons long. We sought entry to Ambrosia's, which marketed itself a "New York style" club, with a bar upstairs and dancing downstairs. At the front of the line sat a bouncer on a wooden stool, admitting as many new customers as old ones departed. He collected $5 from each entrant and opened the door, treating the sidewalk queue to a brief, aural blast from the downstairs disc jockey.

It amazed me how so many students would pay $5 to subject themselves to such noise. What was the point of going out with a so-called group of friends, only to reach a destination where the music incapacitated your conversations?

(Today, mind you, I see the point of sonic immersion as a form of stress relief. Not that I ever seek it, preferring the control and tranquility of my apartment.)

Behind us in the line, punching each other's arms and practicing what appeared to be dance steps, was a group of six tall black men, half of whom were taller even than myself. I recognized them as members of the basketball team. I tried to see if I could identify each one. As I performed this mental exercise, Charlene began a conversation with a junior guard named Ahman Nesby, who stood about 6-3. She responded to his questions about her name and hometown. Then their conversation ran like this:

Nesby: That your boyfriend?

Charlene: Him? Oh, no – he's also from Long Island.

Nesby: So where else you applying?

Charlene: Michigan's my safety, actually, but I'm hoping to get a full ride.

At which point another member of the group, the only one whom I didn't recognize as a varsity player, approached me and put his arm around my shoulder. He was perhaps two inches taller than I and just as bald, though his shaven scalp plainly pointed to conscious choice. He steered me away from Charlene-Nesby and toward the parked cars on the street. He said, "Now don't worry about Ahman. He's got an Asian fetish but he wouldn't touch a high school girl. That boy goes to church every Sunday."

"But you're not on the team," I said to him.

Something about my non-sequitur jarred him. He removed his arm from me and said, "Hey, I'm just trying to help you out. I'm Jerod Wilkins. I quit the fucking team so I could focus on getting into med school."

The line began moving, as a pack of about 20 students exited in a burst. Charlene, Ahman, and the group of ballplayers walked toward the bouncer. I went back to where Charlene and Ahman stood talking. They were eyeing each other. I felt as I had when dining at the trattoria with Barbara and Neil: witness to a blissful rapport hovering stratospheres above my solitude.

Ahman addressed me: "You met Jerod?" he asked, gesturing with his chin in the direction behind me. I again felt Jerod's arm on my shoulder. "We've met," said Jerod, "and now we're going to take a walk." Once more he tried steering me away from the line. I didn't budge. Meanwhile, the bouncer nodded at the picture IDs of Charlene and Ahman and admitted them. Four basketball players filed in behind them.

I was stunned. I was incredulous. I rushed toward the bouncer. "There's a line, buddy," he said to me.

"I just spent 10 minutes on it," I replied, looking to Jerod, hoping his cocky, former-jock glance would validate my claim. But Jerod had abashedly turned toward the parked cars. He avoided my eye contact.

I seethed. I wanted to take a swing at Jerod. But his size intimidated me, as did his blackness. So I approached him, trying in vain to muster the menacing eyes I'd fixed on my future stepfather. Jerod sat on the sidewalk between two parked cars, his Timberlands resting in the gutter. Lamppost light shone off his bald head, which he encased in his enormous hands. He didn't wear a jacket, just a thick black roll-neck sweater that seemed large enough to drape a horse. He looked up at me; I held steady and glared at him. I had been hit before; what was he really going to do? He looked into my eyes and his expression seemed to change. "I can't believe what an asshole I just was to you," he said, staring through thick fingers at the gutter. "If you want to know the other reason I quit the team, it's because I wind up acting like such a jerk around those fellas. And I'm not trying to blame them for what just happened. It's my fault. I was the asshole." He peeked out from behind his hands which, like shutters, had hidden his moist eyes from view. "What's your name again, boss?" he asked.

"Ari. Ari Zinsky."

"Well, Zinsky, I want to apologize." He looked me over and seemed to be doing a double take, as if my standing length were newly impressive from his seated position. "You quit the team too?" he asked.

His flattering question cracked me up. "What's so funny?" he said.

"I suck at sports."

"You should come out for intramurals."

"I can't throw or catch or bully people," I snarled. "You might do better recruiting a sophomore who can stand up to Nesby's crew." Malice tinged my voice; in my heat I reverted to the Long Island accent I'd spent my freshman year trying to eliminate, if only so professors and classmates didn't deduce what Jerod was about to: that I was just another Yankee raiding a Midwestern state school, slinging condescension and fifty-cent words.

"Damn, Zinsky," he said. "You got some strange pronunciations. There's no W in *soph-o-more*. Where you from again?"

"Long Island."

"That explains *sawf-maw*. Good basketball out there. You'd have been varsity material anywhere else."

I laughed again. "That's the most flattery anyone's ever paid me," I said, enunciating the R sounds as if I'd been born in Saginaw. "But seriously, I suck," I continued. "My gym teachers ridiculed me. You haven't seen me play."

"You may just need some coaching," he said. "I got the best intramurals squad on campus."

"Jerod, I detest you right now. Where was all this friendliness before you helped Nesby seduce my friend?"

He rose from the pavement, his height surpassing mine. After exchanging nods with the bouncer he entered Ambrosia's. I zipped my jacket.

One minute later he emerged lugging Charlene on his shoulder, her legs dangling at his chest. Nesby followed them frantically. Rather than kicking or struggling, Charlene laughed and pounded playfully at Jerod's back. He deposited Charlene on the sidewalk next to me. "Hi, Ariel," she said. She waved at me, even though I was inches away. "I drank, like, two beers! I thought you were coming inside," she said. She smiled, her pinkish cheeks rising closer to her eyes, which were a worn brown, like dry leaves.

Nesby said to Jerod: "That's not right, what you just did."

"I don't intend to debate it with you, Ahman," said Jerod.

Nesby protested. "I really like this one."

"Go back in there, find another Asian, and pretend you never met this one," said Jerod.

Nesby hesitated. He waved at Charlene, who promptly waved back. "See you next year, I hope," he said. Jerod said, "I'll be in touch, Zinsky." The two big blacks reentered Ambrosia.

Charlene and I looked at each other. "Ariel, I'm so sorry about what happened," she said. The breeze toyed with her hair.

"Did it just *happen?*" I asked. "Or did you let it happen?"

"A little of both," she said. "I really like that guy, but I should've come out and found you. I don't know what got into me."

"I know what got into you," I sneered, racking my mind for what our next activity would be. "You want to check out the bars on Thompson?" I asked. "See if we can meet some more jocks?"

She smiled. "No, let's go back to your apartment and watch football."

"Are you serious?"

She paused. "I am kind of tired. Maybe we could just get a movie?"

I nodded, hiding my aversion to most things cinematic. There was a video store a few blocks down, on the corner of Liberty and Main. We picked up *The Shawshank Redemption*, based on Charlene's testimonial that her finicky sister Alison had raved about it.

Despite all the hints that Charlene wasn't interested, I could not quite lose hope that I'd get to kiss her on this cool spring night. Somehow, I blocked out her praise for Nesby and believed I had a chance. She was staying overnight in my apartment, was she not? She had repeatedly lauded my sense of humor, had she not? Her infinitesimal affirmations – the squeezed bicep, the sartorial compliment – filled me with belief.

I reached down for her hand and squeezed tight because I couldn't bear the thought of her gripping me loosely. And she said: "Oh, Ariel. That's so sweet."

When we got back to my apartment, Charlene prepared for bed. She pulled a tube of facial cleanser from her backpack and trotted to the bathroom. She returned wearing a red sweatshirt and Cornell boxers. I stared at her burnished, hairless legs as she sat beside me. "You never have to shave those legs, do you?" I said.

"Nope. It's a rare perk of being Asian."

"Rare?"

"Yes, rare. Did you see how red my cheeks got after two beers?"

She smiled and for a moment my eyes met hers. I leaned forward and attempted to kiss her – the first such attempt of my life. She turned her face and presented me with her cheek, no longer pink. She giggled. "Ariel, what are you doing?" Her chuckle sapped my strength. My head dropped, almost desperately, in the nook between her neck and shoulders; her arms came around me, and my head rose up. I kissed her cheek. I kissed her forehead. I kissed her eyelids. I kissed her nose. I kissed her hair. Then I dropped my head to her shoulders, and kissed her neck. She held my head but her grip was loose. I slid toward the edge of the couch, against the armrest. I was a good two feet away from her. "Where did all that come from?" she said.

"Where did it come from?" I repeated. "Jesus, Charlene. It came from everywhere. It came from my heart, my brain. It came from my soul."

"It did *not* come from your soul."

"Why split hairs, Charlene? Like you'd have kissed me if it came from my soul."

"I'm just in shock, that's all."

We were quiet for a minute. Then she began a speech, a variant of which I'd hear on countless occasions over the next ten years. "Ariel, you're a great guy," she commenced. "I've always admired you. You're smart — I think you're brilliant, actually — and you're nice, and I never realized how funny you are. But I don't know if I'm coming here next year. And I like our friendship. And I'm not sure I'd never hurt you."

"You can come right out and tell me I'm ugly," I said.

She paused. "What do you want me to say?" she said.

"I don't know," I said. "I would just ask that, in the future, you don't squeeze biceps or compliment clothing or let guys hold your hand. You gave me false hope."

"Don't be mad," she said, reaching out for me before catching herself.

"Do you still want to stay here tonight?" I asked, holding up the *Shawshank* cassette. On the cover was a luminous photo of the shirtless, rain-soaked actor, Tim Robbins, lightning flashing in the background.

"Ariel, I *love* hanging out with you. Aren't you psyched for the movie?"

I nodded. I ejected *10/15/94, Oregon State 23, UCLA 14* from the VCR and inserted *Shawshank*. I shut the room lights and sat on the rolling chair. "You can sit next to me, Ariel," said Charlene. I returned to the couch and tried focusing on the drama.

Within minutes Charlene's head was on my shoulder. I kept staring at the TV, wondering whether this was her attempt at reconciliation. Perhaps she was just tired, and my lean left shoulder, layered in brown Gap fabric, happened to be the nearest pillow.

I eased away and let her lapse onto her side. I retrieved my Jets blanket and covered her with it. I watched the rest of the film from the rolling chair.

The entire movie, a story about a falsely imprisoned accountant (Robbins) who escapes after over 20 years in jail, struck me as a metaphor for sexual triumph. In one of the climactic scenes, Robbins was literally ejaculated from a sewage pipe. And how had he entered the pipe? By chipping away at a wall and hiding his manufactured hole with a poster of the actress Rita Hayworth. This, I feared, was to be my life as a man: decades of work, all for the hope of one, and only one, meaningful ejaculation.

As my VCR hummed in rewind, I eyed the sleeping Charlene and thought: "I cannot blame her. Why would someone who could have her pick among basketball players opt for me?" I went to bed, wondering how I'd ever entertained an optimistic thought about her. I wondered how young men recovered from romantic rejections. Gatsby – at least he got to sleep with Daisy a few times.

*   *   *

When I woke Charlene was sitting at my desk, reading a copy of the *Guide*. Her stuffed backpack was next to her black shoes. My green Jets blanket had been folded squarely and placed at the foot of my bed. And now Charlene sat on my bed, the *Guide* on her lap. I placed my palm on her bedenimed knee. "Just let me keep it there for a minute," I whispered. "Touching your leg is the highlight of my year."

She smiled. "Good morning to you too," she said. "My cab's coming in a few minutes." She lightly tapped my hand with the *Guide*. "Since when did you become a sportswriter?" she asked. "You should write for the student newspaper. I've never heard of football players being described like this."

She pointed to page 74 of the *Guide*. Regarding Stephen Boyd, a linebacker for Boston College, I wrote: "*Boyd sprints toward ball-carriers with the self-importance of an ambulance. While most linebackers merely tackle ball-carriers, Boyd engulfs them, swallows them whole, absorbs them like an amoeba performing phagocytosis on a hapless organism. Some experts are down on Boyd because he lacks straight-line speed. They write things like "besides his slowness, Boyd is the total package." Well, besides my lack of eloquence, I'm Shakespeare. Far be it for me to ignore Boyd's tragic flaw. But I'll say this: speed is not as important in an interior linebacker as many make it out to be. In a 3-4 scheme, Boyd is as capable as any linebacker in this draft. It baffles me how he won't be chosen in the first three rounds.*"

The cab driver buzzed my apartment. Charlene gathered her belongings and embraced me. "Can I take a copy of your football book?" she said. "I think my dad might like it." I nodded. She stuffed a *Guide* in her backpack. "Email me," she said. She waved and departed.

I slept until about four in the afternoon, keeping my head ducked beneath the fibrous warmth of my blanket. When I awakened I could not get out of bed. My legs were capable, yes. But my heart, brain, and soul had no motivation. No NFL draft to focus on until next year. No woman to focus on until…probably until I myself was a grown-up accountant in a solitary, institutional struggle.

I knew I was not among the manic depressives. I knew I'd manage, in my own way, to rise from my mattress *eventually*. But I felt low. And it was different than the suicidal thoughts that had afflicted me from a very young age. It was romantic rejection – I wondered if it was the emotional equivalent of a beating.

And I had no friends or acquaintances to call about it.

So, indeed: I picked up the phone, dialed the familiar 516 area code, and reached out for the scratchy voice of Barbara Zinsky née Pratt.

I phoned home. I called my mom. I rang the apartment on Townsend Avenue in New Hyde Park where I was raised.

And a lawyer named Neil Segal picked up.

"How are you?" he said and before I could answer he said, "Let me find your mother."

My mom came on. "You don't have to worry about me," I said. "I'm going to get up soon. I am. I really am."

"What happened, sweetie?"

"Charlene dissed me. There's no football on. Classes are stupid. I'm not hungry and I'm not horny and I don't know just why I should leave my bed at this point."

"Do you have a good book to read?"

"I don't need a book because most books tell lies like the movies and make it seem like love is lurking around every corner."

"You need a book," she said. "Neil showed me a novel I think you might like."

"What the hell does Neil know about me?" I cried.

"Not much, but I read this too and I agree," she replied calmly. "It's called *Fanshawe*. It's the first book Hawthorne ever wrote, when he was only 24. He hated it. He wanted every copy to be destroyed."

Barbara and I spoke for a few minutes before I realized that it was a quarter-past-four – and Shapiro Library, the place where I could find *Fanshawe*, closed at five. I rose from bed, showered, and donned a navy blue baseball cap bearing a golden letter "M." I pulled on my jacket and left my apartment, strolling down Washington Street. A right on State, a left on University, and there I was: I climbed the stone stairs, two at a time, and when I reached the top I was huffing and puffing for breath. To feel myself respire, to feel my cheeks chill and redden on a windy April day – it was an improvement upon staying in bed, that was certain. I wondered whether Barbara had told me of *Fanshawe* to get me to read the book, or merely to get me out of my apartment, to put me in motion and color me purposeful.

In a small way she saved my life that morning. She was my best friend again, even if Neil was now hers.

End of Book the First

Book the Second: Wolverine

wolverine –

1. a carnivorous usually solitary mammal…
2. a native or resident of Michigan
— *Merriam-Webster's Collegiate Dictionary, Tenth Edition*

"It was unexpended youth, surging up anew after its temporary check, and bringing with it hope, and the invincible instinct towards self-delight."

— Thomas Hardy, from *Tess of the d'Urbervilles* (Phase the Second, "Maiden No More," Chapter XV)

"All one had to have was a pen and a pad of paper, a mic, a mixer, and a sampler. Thousands of kids labored over their raps in their dark bedrooms, then stepped onto the streets to learn firsthand the vagaries of hustling and distribution – all just so that people could hear their stories."

— Jeff Chang, *Can't Stop Won't Stop: A History of the Hip-Hop Generation*

Chapter 6 – Birth of a Family

When I think of how to tell the rest of Ariel Zinsky's story, I recall the nine-year-old Zinsky, spinning the colorful globe at the back of Mr. Friedman's classroom. The sphere of my biography whirls, twirls, and rotates, the yellow, blue, and orange worlds all blurring. Already, I have stopped the spinning by putting my fingers down on the state of Michigan. Later, we will touch down in New Mexico: home of my father, Robert Zinsky, his wife, Cam Clark, and their daughter, Sandra Clark. We will also, after spinning forward a few years in time, stop in Boston, Massachusetts. For now I intend to stop the globe on Long Island, for an occasion in January, 1997: the wedding of my mother and Neil Segal, ages 52 and 54. The ceremony took place inside a carpeted, white-walled room at a West Egg hotel called The Dutch House.

In the days before the wedding I spoke to Robert Zinsky for our annual Christmas call. "Still a virgin?" he asked.

"Still married?" I retorted.

He chuckled. "Yes, I'm still married. Now let me tell you about being a virgin: you're not missing much. Sex is overrated. Cam doesn't let me near her anymore and I don't even miss it, because she makes me work so hard I can't even enjoy myself. And then she gets pissed because I'm focused only on my own pleasure. You see, Ari, women, for all their supposed sexual liberation – still, about 90 percent of the time, the act of sex means too much to them. They sanctify it. You're what, 22 now?

Believe me, you don't need to be shackled with some woman who expects you to be in her service, just because she's willing to have sex with you. As your caring and responsible parent, who I remind you is footing half your tuition at that cow college, my preference would be that you find sex without shackles. Preferably with a woman who's so hooked on you, she feigns indifference to your performance. But to be honest I don't see that happening, with your looks."

"You haven't seen me in 13 years."

"Am I wrong?"

"No," I said.

"All right," he said. "Now, your mother tells me that this Neil is actually friends with his ex-wife. What gives with this guy?"

"He wants to befriend you too, actually."

"Shut up."

"He does. We were going to have you over for a game of pinochle, then we were going to read passages from *Night*."

He chuckled again. "You really are becoming a funny bastard."

"I became a bastard long ago."

"Well, I'm glad your mother has time to plan *this* wedding," he said.

*   *   *

Coincidentally – or maybe it was Barbara's taste in men – Robert Zinsky and Neil Segal shared two key traits: both were "only" children (just like Barbara and me), and both were born and raised in the Jewish tradition. Barbara, for her part, was a Protestant on paper.

I still have my copy of Barbara and Neil's four-page wedding program. On the first page, the ceremony is described as "Reform Jewish, with a single Orthodox flourish." Mozart's "Adagio for Glass Harmonica" breathed soft and precious through the clear passages of The Dutch House sound system. Rabbi Tahl Roth, sporting a chestnut mustache and jaw-line sideburns, presided. He addressed the betrothed on "the fundamentals of a fruitful marriage." He put one hand on Barbara's shoulder and another on Neil's. "Do one kind thing for each other every day," he said. "Even if it's just a smile. Do not raise your voices at each other. Err on the side of apologizing."

Soon we reached the lone Orthodox portion: the bride circled the groom seven times. I have since learned that this circling typically takes place as soon as the bride arrives beneath the marriage canopy, or *Chupah*. But Barbara and Neil weren't operating that way. They extracted and redacted as they saw fit. Barbara moved slowly through her revolutions, a sundial dressed in white. Her eyes locked onto Neil's. His yarmulke-crowned head swiveled as she traced a perimeter.

Barbara completed her second and third rotation with her gaze fixed on Neil. I wished for a moment she'd flash her pupils at me. I recall feeling guilty about that thought; I also recall wishing I could generate tears for my mother's big moment. But my mother's marriage to a random man named Neil Segal could not disrupt my solipsism. I stood rigid in my navy blazer and focused on supporting the *Chupah*.

At length Barbara completed her seventh circle.

* * *

Tuxedo-clad hotel workers threw open the doors to the reception area. Bartenders stood behind drink carts and a DJ's music ushered in the crowd. The hardwood dance floor was surrounded by gray carpet and dozens of white-cloth tables covered with wineglasses, champagne flutes, scarlet napkins, and silverware. White napkins were tied around the stems of the wineglasses.

Soon everyone was in the reception room except Neil and Barbara. The DJ told me they were due in ten minutes. That gave me time to mentally rehearse the toast I was expected to give.

I couldn't very well rehearse in the reception room, with the music and guests as distractions. Spotting a red EXIT sign above a door, I approached and pushed out, my shiny black shoes clacking onto parking lot pavement in the January cold. My breaths formed steam and I scented the marinade from a steak dish, which I presumed was being prepared in the hotel kitchen.

I paced back and forth within a single white-lined parking space. I was idly eyeing the foreign sedans and SUVs when whom did I see sitting on the closed trunk of a black '95 Audi but my mother, the newly named Barbara Segal. Wearing a winter jacket over her long white dress, sporting her scintillating diamond, arms folded and legs squeezed together for warmth, her breath billowed from her nose and mouth in perfect puffs. With her diamond hand she reached up to her braided hair and twirled an index finger within. She pried free a lengthy blond-gray tendril, which dangled jauntily from her forehead, rejoicing in its freedom from the braid. I went back inside, returning in moments with a cigarette obtained from a bartender. "What are you doing out here?" I asked, handing her the cigarette.

"You got a light?"

"Shit," I said. "No, I don't."

She smiled. "That's my boy," she said.

"Why are you out here?" I repeated.

"I just needed to give myself a minute," she said. "I told Neil I had to go to the bathroom. He's expecting me to take a long time, of course, because I told him I'd have to climb in and out of this gown, and find Nicole to help me tie and untie it."

I leaned against the Audi, put my hand on her shoulder, and kissed her cheek.

"God, Ari," she said, stowing the cigarette behind her ear. "I remember when your thumbnails were the size of gumdrops – and now, practically overnight, you're huge and I'm remarried. It seems so unreal I'm marrying this guy who showed up with sushi 21 months ago."

"It's so arbitrary," I said.

"But it's also tender, I think," she rejoined. "It's almost more tender because it's arbitrary."

"Is all this really hitting you *today*? I would think, after all the planning you guys did, it would have hit you months ago."

"It did, but now the day is here. I'm actually wearing the gown, wearing the ring, and going by a different name. Actual changes took place today." She clasped the cigarette, holding one edge of it near her nostrils. "Wanna run in and get me a lighter?" she asked.

I fetched a Zippo from the bartender and returned. "I got time for a few puffs before Neil gets suspicious, right?" she winked. She lit up and took a few drags, leaving a lipstick mark on the rolled paper. The air around her mouth and nose became a mixture of actual smoke and visible white breaths. "So what'd *you* come out here for?" she asked, her wayward tendril still flapping.

"To rehearse your toast, of course."

"Oh." Her eyes disappeared for an instant behind the mixed miasma, reemerging with a jocular gleam. "Nicole's becoming a pretty girl, don't you think?" she asked.

"It doesn't matter, does it?" I said. In the nearly two years since Charlene Chiu had dismissed me I'd reached the conclusion that my opinion on prettiness was irrelevant. If I were going to ponder my prospects with a woman, if I were going to open up the risky vault of romantic hope, then such hope could only be founded on a woman's inexplicable attraction *to me.*

Barbara shrugged. She tossed her cigarette, only one-third smoked, to the pavement. "I'm gonna sneak back in the front," she said.

Her heels clacking on the pavement, she left me in the parking lot.

* * *

Nicole Segal lived with her mother and stepfather in Scarsdale. She had wavy, syrup colored hair and blue-gray eyes like her father. Her hips were thick but you couldn't call her overweight. She was 16 at the time of the wedding and her breasts were fully developed. Every now and then, when I am over at her apartment examining the wedding-day photo album, I am repeatedly riveted by the black line of cleavage on her pale chest, squeezed tight by the top of her long shimmering purple dress.

Prior to the wedding I had only met Nicole once. We merely exchanged hellos: I was heading out for a jog the instant she and Neil arrived at our apartment.

Her father and I seldom spoke. Over summers, when I was home from college, he slept in Barbara's bed. I hid in my room or took late-night jogs. In the morning, when he drove his black Audi to the Manhattan law offices of Reynolds & Roberts (where he was a partner in the real estate division), he offered me rides to work, since I was interning nearby at the offices of an accounting firm. I refused his rides with a curt, "No thanks," opting for the train and my solitude with the sports section.

One morning, Neil spied me coming out of the bathroom and attempted to correct the slapdash knot on my necktie. I seized his hands and threw them off me. "Mind yourself," I seethed, reentering the bathroom and shutting him out.

It was the last time he and I conversed all summer. When Barbara was around, we were different: the teacher was back in the classroom and the two boys behaved, inquiring about each other's workdays. Otherwise, Neil and I avoided each other.

On those summer mornings I was despondent. I felt my individuality disappearing, compressed amidst thronging masses train-bound for vocational destinations, all of us bundled in suits despite the warm weather. How had humanity come to this? And how had *my life* come to this? Was I already resigned to becoming a nine-to-five working stiff, despite my *Guide* ambitions?

The highlight of my summer workdays was checking my az1@umich.edu email account. Not that my inbox was flooded with social invites and female flirtations. I had six correspondents. One was Charlene Chiu, soon to be a Cornell undergrad. The other five were the first cadre of loyal *Guide* readers, whose email addresses I'd solicited and with whom I bandied ideas for improving my fledgling publication.

One day amidst these correspondences I received an email from Jerod Wilkins. It was the second email I'd ever received from him. The first – which I still have saved – came one week after Charlene Chiu's campus visit. It read: *"Zinsky: join my intramural squad for a pickup game Thursday night. Nine pm at the CCRB. Our games for future reference are at the Intramural Sports building."*

His second email was more conciliatory: *"Zinsky: I can tolerate that you ignored my previous email. I deserve far worse. But I just want to tell you: I'm not giving up on my quest to make you a ballplayer. You can expect a visit from me once school resumes. Enjoy your summer. Jerod"*

He buzzed my apartment the first night I was back on campus for my junior year. He disrupted Monday Night Football. Despite my glum expression he smiled with teeth perfect as Chiclets and asked, "Do you know what's going to happen once I mold you into a player?" His big black hands cradled an orange basketball.

"I don't deal with farfetched hypotheticals," I replied. He followed me into my apartment. My football cassettes were strewn all over the hardwood floor.

"You're going to be *happy*," he said. "And then you're going to get laid, and you won't have all these pornos lying around your apartment."

"Focusing on my personal life is the wrong sales approach," I said. "Besides, these aren't pornos, they're football tapes." I handed him *11/5/94, Miami 27, Syracuse 6*. "This is one of my favorites. Ray Lewis is an animal on defense for Miami. Syracuse has a spunky little return guy named Kirby Dar Dar. He doesn't strike me as pro material, though. Whereas Lewis – "

"I don't follow the Big East," he said, sitting on my couch, helping himself to my open bag of Cool Ranch Doritos.

We sat and watched the television. Jerod crunched his chips loudly. I was quiet. After a few minutes he said: "I'm not going to use this football game as a superficial way to bond with you. You might not believe this, but I was once dejected and withdrawn like you are."

I sighed. "Jerod, I'm not playing basketball. And I don't understand why you keep after me."

"I just want to see you play once," he said. "If you suck, then fine – I'll leave you alone. But just do me a favor and try it. Don't tell me you'll hate playing for my team before you've played for my team. Just show up at the CCRB on Thursday."

I stared at the television. He departed.

And...three days later I showed up at the CCRB. There were three polished basketball courts, lined up beside each other. Full-court games occupied two of them. But Jerod was alone on the third holding his ball. "Time for the clinic," he smiled, patting the side of my arm. He taught me how to make a lay-up. He did not let me leave the gym until I made five in a row.

By the time I made my five several other undergrads had joined us on the court. They all seemed sincerely glad to meet me. (Of course, basketball players are always pleased to meet a tall teammate who is content not to shoot.)

We split into teams and we played three games up to 21. I was out of breath by the time the first game had a score of 4-2. Still, I kept running back and forth as best I could. I did not take a single shot.

I continued to practice and play with Jerod's squad for the remainder of my junior year. And by the time my senior year rolled around I remained the worst player in the history of Michigan intramurals.

* * *

The DJ handed me the microphone.

"It seems so strange," I began, pausing to take an amplified breath, "that a rabbi can utter a few magical words and *poof* – a stepfather and stepsister appear in your life. I look at Neil and Nicole, sitting over there, and a part of me wonders: *who are* these people?"

This candid remark had the seated crowd in hysterics.

"So, back in maybe 1985, my mom had just broken up with this guy named Dennis. I don't even remember his last name."

"Neither do I!" shouted Barbara from her table.

More laughs from the crowd.

"Well, when they broke up – I was just curious, so I asked my mom, 'Why'd you break up with Dennis?' And from our bookshelf she handed me *The Catcher in the Rye*, the purple paperback with the yellow stenciled letters. And she said, 'Read this. Then you'll understand why.'

"So I read it. But I still had no clue why. So I asked mom to explain. And she said, 'Do you remember the character Stradlater?'

"And I nodded. Stradlater was Holden's handsome and assured roommate. Then mom asked, 'What did Holden say about why he and Stradlater could never make great roommates?'

"And I remembered. Holden said that the best roommates are the ones who have the same caliber of luggage – and Stradlater's luggage was *way* fancier than Holden's. And mom said, 'Well, Dennis's luggage wasn't quite fancy enough for me.'"

This line occasioned more laughs. Barbara had locked hands with Neil, their bejeweled fists beside a breadbasket on the white tablecloth. Nicole, sitting next to them, stared back at me.

"So – let's face it, we all know Neil has more money than my mother does. But on some level, maybe not strictly economic, but nevertheless on some level – my mom and Neil carry a similar type of luggage. So I think they're going to get along. And Neil? If you're even half as deserving of my mother as she is of you, then you won't take her for granted. And you'll read all the books she asks you to read. Thank you."

There was applause; straightaway the dancing began. I went to my seat, relieved to just sit and munch bread.

During the meal, Nicole caught my eye and said, "You were great up there."

"Thanks," I said, looking down at my plate and knifing my steak, which bathed in a marsh of mashed potatoes.

We didn't mutter another word to each other until the end of the evening, when she kissed my cheek and said goodbye.

* * *

Neil kept an apartment in Manhattan. He and Barbara tended to sleep there on weekends and in New Hyde Park on weekdays. Nicole mostly stayed in Scarsdale with her mother. But she also spent weekends in Manhattan with Neil and Barbara. The three of them went to museums and movies, concerts and brunches. I continued to absent myself, creating whatever excuses I could muster. I suppose I wasn't thrilled about sharing my mother, or spending time with strangers who now passed for relatives.

Nevertheless, I had agreed to dine with them the Friday before I returned to Michigan for my final semester.

I had spent most of the Christmas break researching the 1997 *Guide* and practicing basketball on the concrete courts behind my old elementary school. My regimen of lay-ups and foul shots took about 45 minutes, by which time my frigid fingertips felt like thimbles. Then I trudged home, practicing my dribbling along the way.

Coming home from the courts on this particular Friday, I spotted Nicole, sitting and smiling on the fire escape, her teeth as white as milk. A wool orange cap covered her hair but not her ears. Those were encased by large black headphones. A portable CD-player rested in her gloved hands. She tapped her black boot lightly to the music; the fire escape responded with minute vibrations, perhaps discernible only to a veteran observer of the rusting edifice.

I can only hope that everything I've written so far provides some explanation for what I did next: I rifled the basketball at Nicole, taking dead aim at her teeth. The ball flew with shocking velocity and thwacked my stepsister in the nose, knocking the headphones from her ears. The Discman fell from the fire escape and crashed to the ground. The lid shattered on impact into three distinct plastic pieces. The disc inside was a rap album: *Ready to Die* by the Notorious B.I.G. I kneeled on the sidewalk, gathering the equipment. Nicole had covered her nose with her gloves. Then she spotted me. She looked as if she were about to cry. "I'll be right up," I shouted.

Once I came inside I ignored her. I went to my bedroom and jotted *Guide* thoughts on a yellow legal pad. When I put down my pen Nicole stood in my doorway, her bare left hand pinching her nose with a wad of moist, bloodstained paper towels. "You threw the basketball at me," she said flatly.

"I didn't mean to *hit you* with it," I lied.

"Well, whatever. You *did* hit me," she said. "What were you thinking?"

"I don't know," I said. "I'm sorry. You were just in a daze up there. I thought it would be amusing to snap you out of it. I was aiming for the ball to just land on the fire escape. But I misfired. Now you see why I'm out practicing all day."

"I think it's stopped bleeding," she said, examining the paper towels. Her black ski jacket was unzipped, revealing a white dress shirt with the first three buttons undone. I stole a look at her cleavage and jotted more meaningless notes. "I'm so sorry," I repeated, looking up from my pad.

"You should jump in the shower," she said, checking her watch. "Our folks are going to be here soon."

"Where are they now?" I asked.

"Looking at a house," she said. "It's in the town your mom calls West Egg."

"Oh – that's Great Neck, where she teaches," I explained. "Lots of rich kids, like in Scarsdale. There's a great library there though."

She nodded and excused herself. I went to the shower.

I lathered my left hand with Barbara's strawberry-scented conditioner and fantasized about Nicole sliding open the glass shower door, entering naked and embracing me. I imagined her wrestling me down to the shower mat, mounting me, arching her back, holding the edge of the tub for leverage, my bald head resting against the drain. In reality, I was standing alone on the mat, grasping the door handle for balance, interspersing my Nicole fantasy with flashes of Charlene Chiu's chest as I rapidly stroked myself. I ejaculated with an agonizing wail. Semen escaped in explosive bursts from my pumping tip, splashing my face and chest. I almost lost my footing. The ecstasy lingered in my cortex for minutes afterwards, reverberating against the shell of my skull like an ice-cream headache. It was the first time I had ever jerked off while standing up. I knew I'd never be the same.

*   *   *

I emerged from my primping in an outfit Barbara had bought me: brown crewneck sweater, black cargo khakis, and black belt with a brushed silver buckle. My shoes, black Doc Martens I'd had since high school, looked worn by comparison. Nicole immediately noticed. "When's your birthday?" she asked.

"Why?"

"I'm going to get you some new shoes."

Just then Barbara came into the apartment, keys a-clanging, greeting me with a smile and my stepsister with a kiss. She began describing the house in West Egg: vast backyard, finished basement, cul-de-sac driveway, and three bedrooms, for nights when both Nicole and I were staying over. Soon Neil came in through the open door, dropping groceries on the hardwood and embracing my mother from behind. "Anyone want some wine before we go the restaurant?" he said. "We picked up a few bottles of Syrah."

"Me!" said Nicole, raising her hand. "But Dad, Barbara, listen. I think Ari needs to rectify his shoe crisis before heading back to Michigan." My mother and Neil glanced downward at my feet, then up at each other, nodding. "We can go to Chester's," Barbara said. "They're open till nine."

There was something about being the topic of discussion – I daresay the object of it – that soured my mood. Who were these wine guzzlers and why did they care about my shoes *now*, after two years of silence on the subject? Today, I recognize the care underscoring their benevolent critique of my wardrobe. But back then, I couldn't fathom why they were so concerned over my *external* appearance.

I looked past them, toward the fire escape. Avoiding eye contact with my new troika of critics, I muttered stolidly, almost whispering: "Would you three mind if I just had a few minutes to myself?" Neil shuffled off to the kitchen. The two women exchanged conspiratorial glances. Their eyes contained a feigned shock, a shared sense of what made for reasonable adult behavior. I half expected a praying mantis to appear on Nicole's white blouse or Barbara's black jacket.

I backed into my room and shut the door. From behind it I heard Nicole say: "What do you think he's PMSing about? Was I being obnoxious about his shoes?"

"He just needs to be alone sometimes," said my mother. "He's like that. You know, no one understands him, et cetera. Come on, let's sit and have some wine."

I switched on the *Mike & the Mad Dog* sports radio program and lay on my bed. I was angry at my mother for ridiculing my retreat. But I recognized her need to bestow courtesies on her new family.

I skimmed an article in *Sports Illustrated*. Several college quarterbacks – Virginia Tech's Jim Druckenmiller, Arizona State's Jake Plummer, Florida's Danny Wuerffel, Colorado's Koy Detmer – were mentioned as "the cream of a decidedly non-bumper draft crop." The article did not sit well with me. I pondered the ages of the quarterbacks: 23, 22, and 21. All my life I'd been younger than the athletes I admired. I was a boy, and they were men. Yet now that I'd attained the seniority of these jocks, I realized: they were not men. Not yet. They were just...guys. Guys who practiced sports, guys who jacked off in the shower, guys who needed jobs after spending four years on campus. Like me, the jocks were in vocational limbo: none of them knew where they'd be in a year.

Decision time was drawing near. I had 13 weeks left as an undergrad. I thought about joining the nation's army of accountants. But hadn't I published both the 1995 and 1996 *Guides,* in accordance with my own life plan, to avoid that fate?

I shut my eyes and absorbed the sports-talk radio. I wondered: now that I was a published authority on football, why wasn't I hosting a sports show? Could I not try to get some airtime on the Michigan student station, WCNB, 88.8 FM? Could I not leverage Jerod's relationships with the basketball squad to score some sports interviews for

WCNB? Could I not try turning the *Guide* into my first career choice?

In my yellow-paged campus directory, I found the name of the WCNB program director: Shelagh Styne, a junior history major hailing from Berkeley, Calif. She resided on the campus's South Quad, was a member of the school's vaunted Honors Program, and also belonged to Phi Alpha Delta, which called itself "a pre-law, coed fraternity."

Hoping Shelagh would *be* in Berkeley, I dialed information, and asked for all the Stynes with a "Y." I phoned the first number I received. "Is this *she-lag*," I asked, when a highborn female voice (not "hello," but "hell-eau") picked up.

"It's pronounced Sheila. Who's this?"

"This is Ari Zinsky. I'm a senior."

"Oh, hi. Have we met?"

"No, but I saw that you were program director of CNB, and I was wondering if I could join."

"Well, definitely. What did you have in mind?"

"I want to host a sports show. I'm a published football expert."

"Well, we have a sports show, Tuesdays and Thursdays at midnight. I can give you the number of our sports director, Kris Holley. He's a good friend of mine. Also a senior."

I jotted Kris's number. "Ari, we're having an open house in Mason Hall on Monday the 13th. It's meant more for freshmen and sophomores who want to get involved, but you're welcome to come. I'll be there, and Kris will too."

I thanked Shelagh and marked the 13th on my calendar.

And I emerged from my bedroom, ready to rise to the social challenge of shopping and dining with my new family.

* * *

After buying my new size 17 Doc Martens at Chester's, we proceeded to Eddie's, a pizza place carrying a bit of personal history for me and Barbara. We went to Eddie's in 1987 to celebrate my first decent score (85) on a spelling test. The two of us also had had an early dinner there on the night of our non-prom date in 1993, before heading to Shea Stadium. We dined there to celebrate my admission to Michigan. And we had gone just one year earlier – only the two of us –

to celebrate her engagement to Neil.

This was the first time Barbara and I had brought guests.

The restaurant had two long rectangular rooms, each with its own heavy wooden door facing Townsend Avenue. One room, the dining area, was brightly lit, filled with oblong wooden tables and black wooden chairs. The other room was dimly lit, had a long bar counter, three booths, a corner with outdated arcade games, and a jukebox with timeworn tunes. A ramped entryway connected the two rooms.

The jukebox played "Cracklin' Rosie" by Neil Diamond; Barbara bobbed her gold-gray head and hummed affably. I stared down at the table. Nicole munched a breadstick. Neil asked what classes I was taking for my final semester. "I'm done with accounting requirements, is the good news," I said. I ticked off my classes: Modern American Lit, 20th Century American Art, and a history of Christianity survey.

Barbara said, "Ari used to love the video games here."

"What do they have?" asked Nicole, smiling at her father.

Neil arched back in his chair, tugging his wallet from his front pants pocket. He peeled off a few singles and handed them to her. "Have fun, kids," he said, as if our ages numbered 6 and 12, not 16 and 22.

We scurried into the other room. Nicole displayed her teeth to the bartender, who was pouring drinks at the far end. "So, college senior," she said to me. "You buying?"

I was amazed how easily she'd forgotten my attempt to deface her with a basketball. If she hadn't forgotten, she'd certainly believed my fib of harmless intentions. At any rate, she seemed inclined to amiable overtures.

When the bartender arrived he asked Nicole what she needed. "Two Coronas and some change," she said. I handed her cash to pay for two glistening lime-plugged bottles, which we placed down on the grimy red-tiled floor at the foot of a Ms. Pac Man video game. I clanked our quarters on the dusty plastic console beside the joystick. Nicole said, "Let's invent a drinking game: every time I eat a ghost or a fruit or finish a level, you have to drink. The same for me when you're playing." I nodded. She inserted two quarters and the machine burped an electro-musical *thank you*.

Nicole steered her Ms. Pac Man to the left and up toward the central box. Pursued by the red and the orange ghosts, she fled toward the maze's upper left power pellet. When she consumed the pellet, her two pursuers changed color to cold blue. Straightaway she ate the flashing ghosts, snaring one and reversing to chomp the other. "Drink twice!" she shouted.

By the time we completed two two-player games, I'd finished two beers, Nicole one-and-a-half. We gave our remaining quarters to a pair of middle school boys who'd been eagerly waiting. As we walked up the ramp to the restaurant's other room, Nicole's arm encircled my waist, her fingers pressing my hip. "I got your boy good and drunk, Barbara," she said. In our absence, a pitcher of Sangria – already half-empty – had arrived at the table.

"You don't look so sober yourself," said Barbara. "Not that I should talk. You do know, Nicole, that one of your father's best skills is designated driving."

Soon a waitress placed a steaming pepperoni pizza on a tray beside our table. Neil collected dishes and dispensed dripping slices. I played footsy with Barbara under the table. "Sorry I'm so drunk, Mom," I said.

"Oh, you deserve it," she said. "It wouldn't hurt you to drink more back at school."

"Sorry I'm not one of the cool kids."

"You know I didn't mean it like that."

"I know. You know I know."

And so we ate and drank as a quartet for the first time. We finished another Sangria pitcher before the night was through. On the way home, I semi-dozed in the back seat of the black Audi. Barbara napped in the front, her golden-gray locks against the headrest.

Back in the apartment, the Segals ministered to the ailing mother-son tandem. Neil steered Barbara toward their bedroom, while Nicole steered me to mine. I nodded off for perhaps an hour before a bathroom urge forced me awake. Exiting the bathroom, I heard Nicole giggling on the phone in the kitchen. She was in pajamas, a matching pair of red and yellow flannels. She sat on the kitchen counter cradling the cordless. Something in her expression seemed a bit too startled to see me; so I went back to my room and clandestinely lifted the phone to eavesdrop:

Nicole: He's a senior at Michigan but acts like he's never had a beer in his life.

Nicole's female friend: I think you have a little crush on your stepbrother.

Nicole: That's *gross*, Michelle.

Michelle: You're the one who said he's interesting. Which you also said the day after the wedding.

Nicole: He *is* interesting. But –

Michelle: But nothing. [Sings] 'Incest, incest is the best / Put your brother to the test.'

Nicole: We're switching subjects now.

Michelle: Your children aren't going to have any uncles.

Nicole: Michelle, shut *up*!

I gently hung up and waited until Nicole was off the phone. I found her at the oval table, reading the *Times* and spooning ice cream from a half gallon of Ben & Jerry's low-fat Cherry Garcia. Her breasts hung low and braless in her flannel top. "I'm sorry I hit you with the basketball," I said, sitting next to her.

"I know you didn't mean it."

We were silent for a while. She kept reading the Op/Ed page. "Well, I need to pack," I said. "Do you – do you have an email address?"

"Yup," she said. "It's NickySeegs@hotmail.com. You should write me."

"I will," I said. I left her at the table with her newspaper and ice cream.

I peeked in on Barbara and Neil. My stepfather had draped a dark blue blanket over her sleeping body and wedged a pillow beneath her head.

Chapter 7 – Otherwise Known as Shelagh the Great

I met Shelagh Styne at the WCNB open house. She was a trim brunette, six feet tall with straight shoulder-length locks. Her eyes were the color of wet soil; her thick lips, tinted like pomegranates, stood out against her caramel skin. Her breasts seemed like handfuls beneath her white sweater and her rear was firm and muscular in light blue jeans.

So I doubted anything would happen between us. My first thought, after the physical rush upon beholding her, was the conscious act of ridding myself of hope. I thought: why would this girl go for you, when she could have a quarterback?

I wore my preppy outfit – the same thing I wore to Eddie's – including my shiny new shoes. And on my head, bless my 22-year-old heart, I tied a University of Michigan bandana: navy blue with a golden 'M.' My backpack was filled with copies of the 1996 *Guide* and an early draft of the 1997 version.

Shelagh was one of seven students at the front of the classroom when I arrived. With a squeaking red marker she penned "WCNB Lineup: Spring 1997" atop a rectangular whiteboard. Nearby, a box radio rested on the diagonal slope of a lecture podium. Another of the seven students, a handsome red-haired young man with intense gray eyes and a pencil behind his ear, peeled off from the group and sat at a desk in the front row, pitter-pattering his fingers to the clarinet rhythm sounding from the speakers. He stared long and hard at a piece of pa-

per, which lay flat on his desk and appeared to be a carbon-copy regis-
tration form. Before I could introduce myself he looked up at me.
"Ever drop a class?" he asked. "What do you think I should put for
'reason to drop?'"

"What are you dropping?"

"Modern American Lit."

"That?" I said. "It sounds cool."

"That's what Shelagh says," he said, nodding at the tall woman by
the whiteboard. "But she's a junior. I'm going to law school next year,
and I just don't want to spend my last semester *reading*, you know?"

"I hear you," I said, though inside I was processing that Shelagh and
I were in a Lit class together. "So – do you know where I can find Kris
Holley?" I asked, recovering my purpose. "He's the Sports Director."

"Me," he said. "You want to join sports? You look like a basketball
player."

"I'm a football expert," I said, handing him a 1996 *Guide*.

"Wow," he said, skimming the pages. "You're that Zinsky guy, huh. I
never thought that you would be so…tall. Jerod Wilkins is your boy,
right?"

"Right," I said, unsure how he came to know this piece of info. But
I rolled along. "So – I can use Jerod's connections for you guys."

"Jerod pimps your *Guide* to everyone he knows," said Kris, continuing
to peruse. "Now tell me – what do you think of Rod Payne?"

"Best offensive lineman on our team, but nothing special," I replied.
"Of course it's seditious to diss him in Ann Arbor, because he's our
best prospect. But we all know this is a sorry excuse for a Michigan
squad, going 8-4 overall, 5-3 in the Big Ten, winning ugly over Ohio
State. Payne doesn't get enough leverage on his run blocks and he can't
overpower any legit nose tackles. His pass blocking is atrocious, and
God forbid you ask him to pull. Adam Treu, the Nebraska center, is
twice as talented."

"You'd be willing to say all that on the air?" said Kris, biting his pencil tip.

"Why wouldn't I?" I asked. "What's Payne going to do, come after
me? I should be so insulted, to be called an 'average' football player."

"It's not that simple," said Kris. "The athletic department won't let us interview coaches and athletes if we're critical. You have to express your opinions gingerly. Don't say Rod Payne will be an *average* pro. Say Rod Payne will be a *viable* pro."

"So can I get on the air?" I asked.

"Come to the station Tuesday at midnight – so technically I mean Wednesday morning," he said.

The room was filling with wide-eyed freshmen and weathered sophomores, all wearing jackets, hats, gloves, and scarves. They entered chattering and seized their seats, waiting for an official presentation to begin.

Shelagh finished writing on the whiteboard and moseyed to Kris's desk, trailed by a short young man with dyed-blond hair. Kris said, "Shelagh, Shane, this is Ari Zinsky, a football expert who picks fights with varsity athletes. He's joining the show."

We shook hands like good young pre-professionals. Shelagh said, "Oh, you're the one who called me." She touched my brown sweater on the left elbow. "I have to start this meeting, but I'll catch up with you later." She returned to the whiteboard.

After lowering the volume of the box radio on the podium, Shelagh introduced herself, Kris Holley, Shane Carson (the station's general manger), and four other members of WCNB management. For the ten minutes she spoke, I paid less attention to her words than I did to the bottom cuff of her white sweater, which floated at the level of her lower waist, rising a centimeter every few moments to reveal a flat stomach with a hoop-pierced navel.

Shelagh's speech was followed by ten minutes of sign-ups and schmoozing. Then the undergrads filed out, including Kris and most of CNB management. I remained at my desk, feigning absorption in my *Guide*, inconspicuously watching as Shelagh and Shane bantered. They shared a lengthy hug goodbye. As soon as Shane left, Shelagh, standing a few feet away and flipping through the signup sheets, said, "I love gay men."

"I love lesbians," I countered.

"But do you really? Are you actually friends with any?"

"No. Are you?"

"No. But Shane knows a few from the GLBT groups." She glanced at the *Guide* and asked, "What's that?"

"This? It's a football magazine."

"A football magazine. You buy it at the airport?"

"No," I said.

She picked it up and flipped through the first four pages. She sat on the desk next to mine, rather than in the seat. The flatness of the wood accentuated the muscular curve of her butt. "I have a confession to make," she said. "I looked you up on the Internet. All I found was this web site with a football magazine. I thought you were some crazy stalker, calling me at home like that. So I emailed Kris to warn him about you. And he replied he knew who you were. And now here you are, playing coy about this so-called football magazine which, from what I understand, is more than a hobby."

I was stunned she'd devoted an iota of thought to me. "It's just a magazine," I stammered.

She chortled politely and said, "I've always wanted to be as passionate about something as you are about football. Like – when did you know? Did you have to make your first magazine to realize football was your passion? Or did you always love football, so you started to make magazines?"

I told her about my life plan and my fire-escape epiphany.

"I once felt passionate about radio," she said. "When I was growing up, I knew all the stations in the Bay Area, their call letters and frequencies and formats. Then something changed. Now radio seems like it's just more work in a life where work is all there is. And I can't let on – not even to Shane or Kris, who are dear friends of mine – that my passion has slipped. I have to fake passion so people won't suspect my inner indifference."

"Sometimes you have to fake indifference, so people won't suspect your inner passion."

"Why would it ever be harmful to show your passion?" she asked.

"Because then, maybe, people think you're a stalker," I said. "Or they think that you've got too much time on your hands."

She placed the *Guide* on my desk and went back to the whiteboard, her black boots clicking on the tile floor. As she stretched up to erase the board, I noticed a bright green mark at the bottom of her spine, decorating the lowest rung of her backbone. "That a tattoo on your lower back?" I asked.

"It's the letter 'H' actually," she said.

"Like in your name?" I asked.

"I had the hugest crush on a guy named Harris in high school," she said, finishing her erasing. "We worked together on the yearbook. His parents went away one weekend, and I went over to his house to seduce him."

"That's preposterous," I replied. "No woman has the right to use 'seduce' in the active voice."

She threw on her orange winter jacket and red backpack. She tugged on hat, scarf, and gloves, all of which were black. With a grin she said, "Why does my use of that verb really bother you?"

Her sudden switch to frivolity unnerved me. She was pretending to ignore that we'd been plumbing deeper emotional levels, mining our Platonic landscapes for a nascent friendship's common ground. I stuffed my *Guide* into my bag and stood. "Are you going to betray the tone of our connection, just like that?" I screamed. "And are you now going to accuse me of being too serious, in accusing you of that betrayal, even though you know *damn well* what you just did?"

She stood frozen. Her lips pressed together, flat and horizontal like clamping calipers. "Don't look at it that way, Ari," she said. "I just have a lot of reading to do tonight. I wanted to find a polite way to excuse myself from a conversation that might've lasted a while. Plus, I heard you talking to Kris and I'm in your Lit class – so we'll catch up tomorrow. Where do you live anyway?"

I felt an overwhelming sense of relief.

* * *

A frigid breeze chilled our cheeks as Shelagh and I walked south on darkened State Street. We turned right on Madison and left on Thompson to reach South Quad, home to Shelagh and hundreds of others in the Honors Program. When we approached her doorway, she sped up and climbed the stone steps. She reached the glass door and faced me. "It was nice meeting you tonight," she said. "See you tomorrow." Before I knew it I had climbed the steps and leaned in to kiss her thick crimson lips, seizing her shoulders for balance after my hasty cinch. At first she did not move her mouth. But soon I felt her gloved hand on the back of my neck, its frosty fingertips inching beneath my hat, on the edge of my bandana. Her tongue darted between my lips. My own tongue lay flat, until I realized hers was prodding mine, goading reactionary movements. For the first time in my life I was kissing someone.

We broke from each other's warm mouths for a moment, which seemed like a frozen eternity. Then we resumed. "You're so beautiful," I whispered, stroking her cheek when she backed away.

"You're sweet," she said, reaching behind her and palming the doorknob. "I'll see you in class, okay?" she said. And she went inside.

*   *   *

In the aftermath of our kiss my emotions yo-yoed like never before.

The positives: I had kissed a great-looking girl. And she'd kissed back. The quivers and throbs of her tongue pressing mine, her hand on my head – I'd never felt anything like it.

I was dying to feel it again.

The negatives boiled down to my cold appraisal of how unlikely that was. For there was no mistaking her tone: "You're sweet," was a death sentence. If I had learned anything from Charlene Chiu, it was *that*. There was also the reality of my initial impression: she was *way* too attractive to have a legitimate interest in me.

By midnight, pessimism prevailed. So did fatalism: convinced I'd never kiss her again, I soon persuaded myself that she'd ruined my life. For how enjoyable could living ever be, if in future pursuits I was doomed to match the ecstasy of a kiss like this?

My feelings recalled Barbara's explanations for why I should never smoke: exhilarating as the stimulation of nicotine might be, the downside was an unhealthy craving – or addiction – for regular dosages.

Unable to sleep, unable to focus on *Guide* tasks, I phoned Jerod, who agreed to meet me at the gym even though he'd been sleeping. As a former varsity man, he had an electronic set of keys to the CCRB that the athletics department never repossessed. He used his access to our advantage as an intramurals squad. We practiced at midnight the night before our games and never left the gym until we'd rehearsed our first five plays. The mere fact that we *had* plays separated us from almost every other team. Owing to the plays, the practice, and our talent, we typically raced out to early 15-point leads and spent the rest of the game coasting.

Waiting in the piercing cold outside the locked glass doors of the CCRB, I pounded my ball on the concrete. Where the fuck was Jerod? I fumed. I presumed he'd gone back to sleep. I kicked the glass door as hard as I could. The glass remained rigid and the bolt rattled in its lock. "Take it easy," said Jerod, approaching from behind. He waved his keys in front of a black box by the door handle, from which flashed a pin-prick of red light. The red turned green, the doors clacked, and we pushed through, turning on hallway lights and then the lights of the actual gymnasium, which took minutes to reach full luminescence.

While I shot free throws Jerod casually mentioned that our towering teammate, Tim Nover, was on campus and would be joining us shortly. "I only told you he was gone so you'd practice harder," he admitted.

"It worked," I muttered brusquely. Indeed, one reason I'd practiced so diligently during Winter Break was because I believed our team finally needed me, with big man Nover taking a semester off.

Jerod stepped in front of me and stuffed my shot with his big black palm. "Tell me it's okay," he said. "You know because of how we met I need to hear it's okay."

"It's okay," I said, backing up a few feet, and then gunning the ball right at his head. I missed wildly and he came after me. He chased me to center court, caught me, playfully wrestled me to the painted floor, and began throwing pretend-jabs at my ribs.

Then Jerod's face got rocked by the flying force of a ball from the powerful arm of Tim Nover. Jerod appeared to be shaken up. He rolled off me and lay on the gym floor, those huge hands cupping his bald head around the eyes. Nover approached him apprehensively. There was no telling whether his injury was genuine or a trap to lure Nover into an ambush counterattack. Nover and I stood above him; finally Jerod opened his eyes and sat up. "You zinged me pretty good there," he said to Tim.

"You had it coming," said Nover.

"We'd never lose if you played as hard as you threw that ball."

"Eat me," said Tim.

Their insults, to which I was an amused bystander, continued until the three of us decided to have a three-point contest: each of us would take 25 shots, five from five separate spots, and see how many we could make. I went first, making only three, two of which fortuitously caromed off the backboard. Jerod made 17.

While Tim shot, Jerod asked me: "So what's going on that you needed to play right now?"

"I kissed Shelagh Styne tonight," I said.

"What?" said Jerod. He promptly picked up a ball and threw it at such a trajectory that it collided with Tim's, just as Tim's shot was arcing down toward the hoop.

"That was going in, asshole!" said Tim.

"Count it," said Jerod. "Whatever. Yo, you know that piece-of-ass junior who works with Holley and Calipari at the radio station?"

"She has a body on her," said Tim.

"Zinsky fucked her," said Jerod.

There was silence in the gym for the first time that night.

"I didn't," I said, my sneakers squeaking as I jogged to retrieve the balls. I tossed one back to Tim and pounded the other on the hardwood, seeking background noise for my confession. "We kissed, and I get the feeling she regrets it," I said. "And I'm all fucked up over it. Even though I just met her tonight."

"A big step up from high-school Asians," said Jerod.

"Why would she kiss me if she doesn't like me?" I asked.

Jerod and Tim eyed me quizzically and a little sympathetically. "You're too good for that bitch," said Tim.

"She's not a bitch," I said. "She's awesome. She's smart. And she's hot. She was grabbing the back of my neck, you guys."

"I need to inform Tim," said Jerod, "that you've never kissed someone before."

"Oh," said Tim.

"I'm only going to say this to you once, Ari," said Jerod. "You know how you feel about Shelagh? Well, one day some girl will feel that for you. She'll be irrationally, uncontrollably attracted, even though she's only had one conversation with you. Now I'm not saying you shouldn't try to fuck Shelagh, or at least get what you can. And I'm not saying chicks don't change their minds. But if it's a girlfriend you want, then don't waste your time with these indecisive foreplay sluts.

"Six hours ago, if I'd have said you could kiss Shelagh Styne, take it or leave it, you'd have taken it. Happily. So don't be sad. Just pretend she's got a boyfriend back in Napa or wherever she's from. Don't hope for more. Find another girl to target, or you're going to fuck up your final semester over this bitch. I can't have you acting that way. Neither can this team."

"But wait," said Tim. "Why are you so sure she's not interested?"

"Look at me," I said, staring down at the gym floor.

The boys were silent. Tim said, "Some girls don't care about looks."

"Thanks," I said.

"It doesn't matter," said Jerod, slapping the basketball from my hands. "Are you fags here to play ball or watch Oprah?"

Straightaway we played five games of 21. I came in last place each time. But I felt better. Shelagh still pounded at my mind but less fervently. When we finished playing at 3 a.m., my t-shirt and shorts were sopping. My feet throbbed. I thought I might need a chisel to remove my sneakers. "Well boys, I got class tomorrow morning," said Tim, sparing me and Jerod the embarrassment of being the first to cry fatigue or cite busyness.

When I got back to my apartment I pondered how elated I would be if Shelagh were there to greet my return home: a Penelope whose Zinsky-Odysseus had been gone for only two hours; a Zinsky-Odysseus who'd only been out playing basketball, not dallying with nymphs and other temptresses.

* * *

I was late to Am Lit the next morning. Not because I overslept. I spent 45 minutes deciding what to wear, having worn my primary "cool" outfit the previous evening. In the end I settled on jeans, a navy blue Michigan sweatshirt, and navy blue Michigan bandana.

The lecture was in West Hall in a traditional classroom: chalkboard up front and rows of right-handed desks bolted to a wooden floor. Professor Dalrymple, a pregnant, untenured lecturer in her mid-thirties, read notes on *Winesburg, Ohio* from a portable podium. She glanced at me wearily as the door creaked upon my entrance. I spotted Shelagh in the front row, her light brown hair wet and brushed; she glanced at me and then returned to her open spiral, resuming her assiduous note-taking. I unzipped my jacket and sat in the back row, beside a radiator with peeled silver paint that banged like a blacksmith. There were about 50 students in the class, and all of them except for me seemed to have tuned out the radiator.

Shelagh hunched her shoulders over her notebook as she wrote, as if fearing a neighboring student would copy or cheat. She scribbled intently, a stenographer without the stenograph. It surprised me she was not among the laptop-toting avant-garde.

When class disbanded Shelagh shoved her spiral into her red knapsack, zipped it shut, ripped her jacket from the chair-back, and sped toward the doors. I caught up to her on the West Hall stairwell, tapping her shoulder. We faced each other on the steps, two embedded rocks around which rivulets of students climbed and descended. "Ari, now's not the time for this talk," were her first words.

"Why is that up to you?"

"It's not, but I have a thing about being late for class, and this talk can't and shouldn't happen in thirty seconds. I'll call you tonight, okay?" she said. She touched my elbow before she dislodged, flowing upstairs to her next lecture.

I went back to my apartment. It was January and I had *Guide* work to do.

*   *   *

As part of my effort to promote the *Guide,* I sent monthly newsletters to my list of subscribers. I write "subscribers," but in truth the list consisted of any football fan who'd ever given me his email address. There were 61, in total. Hardly astronomical, but not bad, considering I'd only had five subscribers in the summer of '95.

I spent the next two hours writing the following message:

"Greetings, football zealots!

Welcome to the January 1997 Quintessential Draft newsletter, piped to you hot and bloody from the aorta of my apartment's molasses-speed Internet connection.

Before I get to the sex, let me warm you bitches up with some housecleaning foreplay. I'll enumerate, so as not to overtax the attention deficits of those knuckle-draggers among us, for whom the captions in Maxim *seem like the footnotes of Marx.*

1.Welcome to Kris Holley and the rest of the CNB sports department. I promise that starting tomorrow I'll improve your shows.

2.Please forward this email to all the sports fans you know. I have only 61 readers, while ESPN has millions. Where is the justice in that?

3.There might be a few among you who, upon reading foreplay item #2, are thinking: "Why should we put more money in your pocket, Zinsky?" To which my response is: What money? On each Guide I sell I make perhaps $2 in profit. That would be lucrative maybe if I sold more than 61. Besides, do you really think I'm doing this so I can buy a mansion with a pool in West Egg? No. I'm doing this because the only thing that bothers me more than getting kissed-and-dissed is an overpraised or underpraised athlete. Why that is, I don't know. Some can't sleep at night knowing there are famished families in Africa or Democrats running our Executive Branch. I can't sleep at night knowing ESPN's experts are foolish enough to believe Joey Kent, the stone-handed receiver from Tennessee, has a chance to even make a pro roster.

4.Having written all of that, I beg you: don't forget to send that $5 check to the address at the bottom of this email. You can also, if you like, pay by credit card at www.zinskyquintessential.com. The 1997 Guide will be released on March 31, meaning that — after this one — I will only send out two more newsletter-reminders.

To the sex: This month, we shall objectify the physical attributes of Derrick Mason, a receiver from nearby Michigan State, who's about seven times better than every receiver in this draft. Now, NFL scouts, like the ladies, prefer a player who is tall. But I have watched enough football — and y'all have played enough football — to know that height means shit if you can't catch!

And yet, the aforementioned Joey Kent; Kansas State's Kevin Lockett; and San Diego State's Will Blackwell — all of whom are over six feet tall, none of whom can catch — are all rated more highly by ESPN and The Sporting News *than is Derrick Mason, who (a) has the best hands of any receiver in this draft and (b) is as fast, in pads, as any of them, including the ballyhooed Ike Hilliard and the vaunted Yatil Green. Take it from me, folks: I've seen Mason play, in person. For four years. He's insane, both at the line of scrimmage and in the slot. He returns kicks. He goes over the middle.*

And if he turns out to be anything less than a viable, eight-year starter in the NFL, I will give you Guides, *for free, for as long as you live. Nay, if Mason does not make at least one Pro Bowl, then I am not —*

Ariel Zinsky

Founder and Editor-in-Chief, Zinsky's Quintessential Guide to the NFL Draft

U. Michigan Class of '97

I sent off my newsletter and lay down for a nap.

*   *   *

When I awoke I couldn't stop thinking about what I'd say to Shelagh when she phoned that evening. Having already spilt my guts to Jerod, I called the only other intimate who'd care about my situation: My mother. In retelling my story my rage returned and Barbara tried soothing me: "It's a good thing this happened," she said. "Next time you won't get your hopes up until you feel secure."

"Who *ever* feels secure?" I shouted. "Unless they're dating someone they don't like that much. Do you feel secure, even with a ring on your finger?"

She paused. "That was obnoxious of you, Ari, but I'm going to let it slide because you don't sound quite yourself," she said. "But for your information, the ring is a red herring. I wouldn't have liked Neil, nor would I have married him, if he made me feel insecure. And if you weren't so drunk on your own emotional self-absorption, you would realize that. Though I suppose your level of self-absorption is normal for men under 40."

"Sorry."

"It's okay."

We spent the rest of the conversation not exchanging feelings but clinically discussing the house in West Egg. She and Neil had formally closed on it. It was built of red-brick and had green shutters and a screen door in back. The backyard was bereft of foliage, but no matter — one call to a landscaper, problem solved. Barbara would now be a five-minute drive or 20-minute walk from her school. For the first time in her life, she owned a home.

*   *   *

After putting in my two hours of clerical labor at the Business School and another two washing dishes in the nearby dining hall, I spent the night at Shapiro Library, reading the gospels for my Christianity survey. To concentrate was difficult: Shelagh's forthcoming rejection played on my mind. Barbara's "self-absorption" remark lingered too. I tore a piece of paper from my spiral and penned a letter to Barbara, entitled: "*Reading myself in the* Gospel According to Matthew: *Zinsky as a Romantic Egoist.*" And I wrote:

"*The disciple Matthew believed he was recording a crucial bit of history, but he did not know with assurance what an immortal Jesus would become. Likewise, the 22-year-old Ariel Zinsky feels that the minutiae of his own biography are well worth recording, for the sake of some future fame that the world will eventually grant him. Upon which recognition the seemingly quotidian events of Zinsky-Jesus's life will assume a colossal, Gatsby-esque significance, the same way that the childhood toys and teenage scribbles of rap stars, news anchors, and mediocre actors all become deified by dint of the persona's prominence.*

"*The 22-year-old Zinsky is convinced that his prescient analysis of football players, and his rise from a suicide-pondering, single-parent childhood in middle-class circumstances, makes him worthy of (at least) national recognition, insofar that any connection between celebrity and merit can be proven to exist. If the connection does exist, then the rise of Zinsky will be the proof of it. Similarly, the contrapositive will be proven if the adult Zinsky turns out to be just another accountant, another set of Caucasian hands (invisible hands, according to Mr. Smith) turning the cranks in the white-collar sweatshop. Indeed: No fame for Zinsky will signal that any link between merit and celebrity is specious at best and, at worst, as spurious as most of capitalism's mythologies of ascendance.*"

I felt better. I knew my mom would glow upon seeing my letter in the mailbox and laugh like crazy upon reading it. She would laugh like she laughed on her first night on the phone with Neil.

*   *   *

When I returned home from Shapiro Library I waited in vain for Shelagh's call. I lay in my bed reading *Winesburg, Ohio* until I fell asleep.

*   *   *

Upon entering WCNB headquarters in the Student Activities Building, you heard whatever radio program was on the air through black ceiling speakers. A blue-carpeted hallway held entryways to two office spaces, one on each side. On the left was the sales office: a large rectangular table with a phone on top. On the right was the management space: a smaller room with a cherry wood desk, on which sat cordless phone, fax machine, and PC. Against the wall was a mailbox with slots devoted to Shelagh, Kris, Shane, and the other CNB staffers. The blue-carpeted hallway veered sharply to the left, leading to the actual radio studio. Through a wide rectangular glass you could spy each program's host, monitoring volume levels on a switchboard, taking phone calls, inserting or removing compact discs or audio carts. An ON THE AIR display, illuminated in fake-red like an exit sign, flashed high on the glass window.

Through the glass inside the control room I spied Kris Holley running a hand through his auburn curls. He unfolded his arms and cracked his knuckles. The hostess of the jazz show preceding Sports LateNight faded a Joshua Redman piece and cut to commercial. When the commercial began Kris raised his voice: "Where the *hell* is the cart with the Owens ad?" he demanded, frightening the bejesus out of her. I imagined that the short-haired hostess, who had a wide-eyed, smooth-faced freshman look, had hoped for a kinder reception from Kris, whom she likely regarded as some extracurricular deity. "Sorry, Kris, I haven't seen it," she muttered.

"Fuck," said Kris. "The sales guys have been nagging me all week: Play it *before* the show starts. Are you sure you haven't seen it? Shane said you'd have it right here."

"I don't know anything about it."

Kris saw me lingering in the hallway, eavesdropping on his form of flirtation. "Zinsky," he said, "you're early. Sit over there." He led me to a small room next to the studio from which you could observe the control room through another pane of rectangular glass. I sat at a long black table, at the center of which was a large microphone with a foam red covering. "I'll be back in a few minutes," he said. "First I have to remake this Owens commercial." And he left me alone.

When he returned, he slapped a white envelope down on the black table. "Found this in my mailbox," he said. "I didn't open it, as you can see, but I really wanted to." He smiled. A yellow post-it on the envelope read: *Kris. Please give to Ari Zinsky. Thanks. S.* Kris said, "What does she want with you? Over break, she emailed me asking all about you. Are you guys together?"

"I'm afraid not," I said.

"Well, you've got time to read it," he said. "Calipari won't be here for another ten minutes." He left me again and I opened the letter:

"Ari, I must apologize for not calling you. In no way do I minimize what happened between us the other night. But before we go any further, as friends or anything else, you need to know a few things. If I don't tell you these things now, you'll just end up hating me, or being pissed that I can't always match what you're feeling.

"Had we met 14 months ago, under the same circumstances, a lot more than that kiss might have happened. I know it always sounds empty when one person tells another: don't take this personally. Still, I will tell you: don't.

"I've spent all day wondering how I could explain this. Here's what I've come up with: let me presume, based on our interaction after class, that you've been emotional over me, because for one night we shared an intense connection. Well, imagine sharing a connection like that with a person for over a year. And then the person moves to NY for his job and, within a week, stops calling you and he emails you that he's smitten with someone else. How would that news make you feel?

"That's my situation. And I don't know whether I can involve myself with another guy just yet – maybe not until I'm finished with college.

"I hope we can keep hanging out. –Shelagh

I stuffed the letter into my jeans pocket and tried to focus on what my first words on the radio would be. But there was only one phrase on my mind: "…as friends or *anything else.*"

To the 22-year-old Zinsky, *anything else* was the chance of a lifetime.

The 30-year-old Zinsky still has this note. It's tucked within the pages of a 1997 *Guide*, a memento of what his life was like when it involved so much more than the evaluation of athletes.

* * *

The next few weeks of my last semester moved quietly. I saw Shelagh in class but our interactions rarely went beyond exchanging waves. At the radio station I never saw her. I continued playing basketball and participating at WCNB, developing rapports with Kris Holley and Jimmy Calipari, a thick-haired history major who wrote sports for the University *Daily*, and who also happened to be from Long Island. My intramurals squad, which Jerod had dubbed *Me and Mine*, went undefeated. In the finals we beat the *Daily* squad, on which Jimmy was the starting point guard.

The first papers for Am Lit were due in mid-February, a few days after Valentine's. Holding out hope for *anything else*, I used our deadline as an excuse to reestablish contact with her. My idea was for us to proofread each other's papers. So in writing mine (on *Gatsby*) I took extra care, hopeful she might read it. Not wanting to call or email Shelagh – I hoped to spare myself the annoyance of waiting for replies – I left a note in her radio station mailbox on the night of the 13th.

"Shelagh, Happy Valentine's Day! Well, it's been a few weeks, and I think I'm ready to hang out with diminished expectations. In addition, I was thinking we could proofread each other's papers for class. I'd understand if you don't want to meet up, but you really have no idea how happy just your friendship would make me. Sincerely, Ari."

I stood by her mailbox, proofreading the note for the nineteenth time. And then I felt fingers on my forearm, the touch jolting my entire frame with heat and energy. I didn't know what to say. "Happy Valentine's Day eve," fell from my mouth as I handed her the note. She read it as I continued: "I was just leaving this here for you so you'd get it tomorrow."

"Oh, Ari, that's so sweet," she said, reaching up to hug me. She threw her arms around my shoulders, and for a few seconds she latched on to me, like a knapsack worn on the front of the body. "I think this is the only Valentine I'm going to receive," she said.

"That's surprising."

"Not really," she said. "So – do you know what you're doing your paper on?"

"*Gatsby*. I did it already. You?"

"*Winesburg*," she said. "I did mine too. So how's the sports show going?"

"The guys are great," I said.

"Why don't we proofread each other's papers tonight?" she asked. "That way we'll have it done before the weekend."

In our jackets and hats we walked over ice patches and through chilly breezes down Thompson Street to South Quad. She scampered up the stone steps and entered her first-floor residence. Through a window I watched her move through a common room brightened by multiple halogen lamps and into what I guessed was her bedroom. I stifled my panic over whether she intended to stay inside. Soon enough she emerged, having changed into University of Michigan sweatpants and clasping in her black gloves an essay of several stapled pages. "I printed out a new one so you could mark it up," she said.

We were silent on the walk to my apartment. It was a full-mooned night in the upper twenties, the type to which every Michigan under-grad becomes inured. Filthy snow piles surrounded us on the lamppost-lit sidewalks. As soon as we turned onto Washington Street the wind shifted from our backs to our faces; Shelagh's paper rustled in her hands, flapping loudly like a miniature fan.

In my apartment I found myself explaining – again – why the living room floor was strewn with football cassettes. Shelagh nodded. Everything made sense to her. "You really do have a passion for what you do," she said, removing her boots at the door.

She picked up *10/12/96, Michigan State 42, Illinois 14.* "That was a breakout game for Derrick Mason," I said, removing my boots.

"Is he one of your favorite players?" she asked, sitting on the beat-up yellow upholstered couch, placing the cassette on her lap.

"You could say that," I said. I went into my bedroom to retrieve my *Gatsby* paper, expecting Shelagh would remain on the couch. But she followed me. "Holy shit, you have *more* tapes in here!" she exclaimed. She kneeled to the floor and scooped up two of them. Eyeing me coyly, she said, "They're such beautiful cassettes," playfully sliding one along her tanned cheek, still sanguine from the cold. "It makes me sad be-cause I've never seen such – such beautiful cassettes before."

"Very funny," I muttered, handing her my paper.

She sat at my computer, from which I'd recently sent out my *Guide* newsletter. "So this is where it all happens, right?" she asked. "This is where you write your football books?"

"Yup," I said.

"Okay," she said, rolling up the sleeves of her pink button-down shirt. "Then this is where I want to read. Maybe I can catch some of your passion." She flattened my *Gatsby* paper on the desk and began reading.

Here's an excerpt:

Nick Carraway wants to play Matthew to Gatsby's Christ, penning a hagio-graphic version of another man's life story. But Nick is no ordinary Matthew; he is a Matthew bent on asserting the accuracy of his Gatsby-Christ gospel, all the while insulting the accounts of Mark, Luke, and John. Not five pages go by, it seems, without Nick introducing documents – train-schedules on which he records party guests, Gatsby's boyhood notebooks, Gatsby's medals from the war – to persuade readers that Nick's version of Gatsby's life and death is the only verifiable one. All other accounts, proclaims Nick, "were a nightmare – grotesque, circumstantial, eager and untrue" (171).

In short, Nick seems paranoid about alternative versions of a history to which he's hardly an objective observer. He becomes a spin doctor of Gatsby's legacy. Wit-ness his erasure of an obscene word scrawled on the "white steps" outside Gatsby's house (188). (Incidentally, Professor Dalrymple: I believe Nick's erasure scene is the literary ancestor of Holden's attempt to erase expletives from the walls of Phoebe's school in Catcher in the Rye. *And I must say: The action of erasing an obscenity seems more plausible coming from a wide-eyed youth like Holden than it does from Nick – unless Mr. Carraway is not as world-weary as he'd have us believe he is by the book's end. And Nick wants us to believe he's weary: For he goes out of his way, twice, in this novel, to announce that he's 30 years old (143, 186), as if des-perately trying to impose his numerical maturity on the reader.)*

As Shelagh read I stared shamelessly at her, catching the profile of her breasts as she inked remarks in my margins. Soon she caught me peeking. "Are you reading my paper?" she smiled, before turning back to my essay.

I retreated into the world of Shelagh's paper, with its page numbers on the lower left and its solemn Palatino font. She compared the lan-guage and imagery of a *Winesburg* story called "Hands" to that of Ger-trude Stein's *Three Lives.* I was about halfway done reading when she said, "Okay, are we ready to talk about these?"

"I never would've thought to connect "Hands" and *Three Lives*," I said.

"You're too kind," she said. "I searched for a connection because we had to write a paper. But your essay seems totally...*unforced*. It's amazing. It's better than Dalrymple's lecture. I feel like my essay scooped the ocean floor and found a few flounders. Whereas yours – is about the wetness of the ocean. Does that make sense?"

"Don't give me too much credit," I said. "My mom's an English teacher. I've read *Gatsby* a dozen times."

"I'd do a lot to have your brains."

"I'd do a lot if you wanted the rest of me," I said.

Silence.

"Where's your bathroom?" she asked.

She left. I rolled onto my back and drifted into a fantasy of Shelagh returning naked and joining me on the bed. I fancied what life must have been like for her ex. I wondered how any man could dump her.

"What are you thinking about?" said Shelagh. She sat Indian style on the bed beside me, her odorless thick black socks inches from my nose. Then she lay on her side so that she faced me, our heads on the same plane. "Tell me what you're thinking," she whispered. Her cola-colored eyes floated within their whites like brown buoys on a milky surface. I stroked her light brown hair with my trembling fingertips. "Can I tell you something?" she whispered. "I don't want to go back to my room tonight," she said.

I leaned closer to her. Her mouth greeted mine with closed lips. I sensed her hesitation and though it hurt me, I was too elated about kissing her again to mourn the relative dispassion of the clench. This was the second kiss of my life and for all its shortcomings it still felt like the pleasurable culmination of a thousand once-buried wishes.

My right hand moved from her hair to her shoulder. Shelagh grabbed it there. "Would it be all right," she whispered, "if we just shut the lights and talked?"

I nodded. She found the light switch and returned to my bed. Mellow rays of lamppost light shone through my blind-less window. We kissed again; or I should say: she let me kiss her. My tongue treaded within her inert mouth. Her tongue did not move in sync with mine, so much as it met and supported, provided assurance through mere presence. Her hands were on my back now, over my sweater. We continued to kiss, she half-heartedly, I with about six hearts.

To this day I don't know why what happened next, happened next. It was as if someone – not me – flipped an off-on switch inside Shelagh. In two deft motions she unzipped my jeans and shoved down my boxers. Her robotic alacrity shocked me – not so much her possession of quick moves but her rapid decision to abandon her resistance. In turn I reached for her sweats, hoping to seem smooth and certain. In hooking her waistband I inadvertently snared her panties but she didn't stop me. Next we removed each other's tops and she was on me – and I was *in* her: without a word about contraception. With intense forearm pressure she squeezed my head against her collarbone. I sought kissing her but she wouldn't lower her mouth; I sought sucking her nipples but she held me firm to her neckline. Of course, it wasn't difficult subordinating these niggling concerns to everything else racing through my mind: how the inside of her felt like a warm bath within an endless glove; how her ass cheeks were almost too muscular to grip; how I was having sex – a hallowed act of matchless significance, according to everyone and everything – yet my mind and body, for all they *did* feel, had yet to feel wholly new or transformed; and how I was, in point of fact, fucking, though my mind was too preoccupied processing the moment to surrender to libidinal pleasure. Throughout – for all thirty or so seconds – I was unable to lose myself in ecstasy, for fear Shelagh would reverse her off-on switch and dismount. I felt like I might get caught trespassing. All this while I was cozy and erect inside her.

I gasped – giving vent to primal spasms, the unexpected pleasure of bursting into a warm body, rather than my hand. It surpassed the agonizing release of standing ejaculation. For here was flesh to clasp during those long, wrenching shrieks, a heated vessel absorbing my groans and shocks. I loved Shelagh more than anything at that moment. She was there for me as my body erupted and emptied and fell weak with joy and relief, surrender and gratitude.

And then it was over. I had slept with someone. And I could not believe I had slept with *anyone*, let alone Shelagh. And all because of – my note? My essay? Whatever had flipped her off-on switch, I had no idea. I was flabbergasted and confused: so women could fuck without kissing – what did that mean for my father's pronouncement about sex as a sacred female act?

In the aftermath Shelagh seemed disturbed – I tried kissing her and she kept her lips closed. And I felt no spark from her lips – it seemed as if she'd gone from half-hearted to vacant.

I grabbed her hand and kissed it several times. I guided her palm to my muscle-less chest, her fingertips pulsing life through my nipples. I pressed her hand against my sternum, hoping to squeeze the neutrality from her clinical fingers, because her indifferent hand was better than no hand at all, and because I wasn't certain when, or whether, she – or another woman – would touch my chest again. She said: "Ari, I'll keep my hand there, but I don't want you to get the wrong idea about my ability to commit. And I don't want you to wind up hating me if I don't stop to talk to you in class or I can't be with you again."

"Just please keep your hand there and don't worry about the rest," I whispered.

"I think you're getting attached," she said.

"I'm not. And if I am, it's my problem. You've given me the disclaimers."

"Fine," she said. She curled onto her side and pressed her head into the crook of my left arm. We lay naked and silent for several minutes. Finally, I spoke up. "What are you thinking about?" I asked.

"I'm thinking, where's your blanket?" she said. A thin beam of lamppost light cut through the celery green of her lower back's tattoo. My blanket was wedged between me and the wall. With a series of graceless kicks and shakes I spread it over both of us. "How many women have you slept with?" she asked.

"None," I admitted. Honesty had gotten me this far – and I was still too stunned about what had taken place to dissemble.

"But I can tell you've been hurt," she said.

"How can you tell?"

"You have some of my symptoms. I've never seen a guy who does what you do."

"What do you mean?"

"You bury yourself in activity and you don't even realize it. Your whole lifestyle is a display of self-medication."

"Do other guys hold your hand to their chest?"

"That's unusual too. But I don't know, actually. You seem to think I'm so experienced. Nick – that's my ex – is the only person I've slept with."

"Wow," I said.

"Tell me what you're thinking," she asked.

I considered saying the following: "I'm thinking about whether you'll ever kiss me again." Or: "I'm thinking I wish you were here every night."

Instead of saying those things I said: "I'm wondering if – as my life goes on – I'll just look at each sexual chance like a poor family treats a meal at a restaurant. You know, that it's special, just because you're not cooking it yourself, and you don't know when it might happen again."

"I don't know, Ari. I think if you spent less time on football and more time talking to freshmen women, you'd do pretty well." I wanted to debate that point but opted for silence, rather than risk saying something that might make her remove her hand from my chest.

When I woke the next morning she was gone. And so was my virginity.

*　*　*

Shelagh all-but-ignored me in class. She waved upon seeing me but kept her head on her notes and sped away when the lecture ended. When it became apparent I wouldn't see her before Spring Break, I nearly lost my mind. One night, after the radio show, and after an hour of basketball with Jimmy Calipari, I sought her out. Instead of heading home for a shower I went directly to South Quad. Peeking through the front window into the halogen-lighted common room, I saw Shelagh watching CNN, eating baby carrots from a plastic baggie, sitting Indian style, shoes off, on a black leather couch. On the coffee table in front of her, I spotted *two* navy blue mugs.

I tried remaining calm and rational. The second mug might belong to a roommate; or perhaps both mugs had been there for days, no one bothering to bring them to the sink.

Yet Shelagh's positioning disturbed me. She was next to the left armrest, even though the television was aligned closer to the right. And she wasn't dressed like someone who was home alone: she wore black stretch pants and her white sweater.

Then the mystery was solved: Shane Carson, a purple bandana surrounding his dyed-blond hair, entered the living room bearing a plate of brownies, which he placed between the mugs before sitting on the couch's middle cushion. Standing outside in the cold, I wanted to call out: "Hey Shelagh! I love gay men too! They're the greatest!"

I removed my basketball from my gym bag and dribbled it all the way home.

* * *

Meanwhile, students all over campus planned their Spring Break escapades. Jerod and Tim Nover and all my teammates from *Me and Mine* wanted to spend the week in Cancun. I had no desire to accompany them. Despite my physical success with Shelagh, her ensuing indifference made me revert to the boy I'd been only months earlier: the ugly boy for whom female encounters were synonymous with rejection; the forlorn boy whose unoccupied hours led to suicidal musings. I wanted no part of a Spring Break trip with the guys. Just *anticipating* the tacit pressure to get laid – which always exists in companies of men – made my decision easy. Consistent with my history, I pleaded financial hardship; and when Jerod offered to subsidize my travels, I told him I needed to remain in Ann Arbor because I had to work on the *Guide* – specifically, I'd decided to sell advertisements in it. "You have to be shitting me," he said, as we dined one night at the Student Union's Taco Bell, our gym bags resting on bright red chairs beside the table.

"Thanks for understanding."

"Listen," he said, fingering a plastic packet of hot sauce. "Don't think you're kidding me about why you don't want to go. I'm not going to pressure you. All I'm going to do is email you the phone number of our hotel. If you change your mind – and I don't care if it's only one day before we get back – you call me and I'll buy your ticket. I don't care if it costs a thousand – "

"Jerod, you'll have fun without me," I said, pouring some sauce inside my bean burrito.

"Don't be a bitch, Zinsky," he said. "I don't want my memory of senior year to have a Spring Break without you in it."

"Let's just say, for argument's sake, that I didn't have this magazine to bang out and I *could* go," I said. "I'd be a drag. I'd be depressed over the fact that Shelagh was running around in a bikini somewhere. You know that."

"I do," he sighed.

When my mother asked about my Spring Break plans, I told her I was going to Cancun with my teammates. At last, her wishes of 1995 would come true: her son was leading a normal life. He was not the insular, masturbating freak she feared him to be.

Barbara told me she expected a phone call upon my safe arrival in Cancun. I told her: no problem.

* * *

When the time came for me to phone Barbara, I was in my Ann Arbor apartment, watching the college basketball tournament with the volume down.

My stepfather picked up on one ring. "How's Cancun?" asked Neil.

"Just got here," I replied. "Mom wanted me to call once I landed safely."

"You're in the airport?"

"Yup," I said. "They got televisions hanging from the ceiling."

"What's on?"

"Sports," I said uneasily. To my relief he didn't press me and fetched Barbara, who said, "I'm happy you're there, but it's too bad, in a way, that you're not going to be around. We're moving some things into the West Egg house."

"Already?" I said.

"We didn't want to tell you," she said. "Knowing you, we figured you'd use it as an excuse to come back and help us instead of going away with your friends."

"Good point," I said. "So – are you just going to move all my stuff, from my closet and everything? You know, my stuffed Freeman McNeil football player and my first supermarket paycheck and – "

She chuckled. "We have movers, honey."

"I see," I said. "So – when's the official moving date?"

"They're not going to lose any of your stuff, Ari," she said. "Relax. Don't let this ruin your vacation."

"I won't," I said. "But I'm just curious because I might need to give the registrar a new address, update certain forms – "

"Ari, don't worry," said the scratchy voice.

"I'm not worrying," I said, irritated. "I'm just wondering when we will no longer be official residents of the Townsend Avenue apartment we've inhabited for more than two decades."

She sighed. "May 1, officially. But we're hoping to be functioning from West Egg by April. So there'll be an overlap. I can't believe you're in Cancun and you want to discuss this."

"Jesus," I said. The prospect of my mom explaining Freeman McNeil to my stepfather was embarrassing.

"What's wrong?" she asked.

"It doesn't matter. Anyway, I should probably go, the guys are standing here giving me the folded arms treatment."

"Have a great time. And don't worry."

I spent the next hour watching basketball. During a timeout I switched channels to MTV's coverage of collegiate Spring Breaks. I was wondering if I'd see Jerod and Tim in Cancun or Shelagh and Shane and Kris in New Orleans or Jimmy Calipari in Miami. As it happened, I'd tuned in to the live concert of a rap star I didn't recognize. On my TV screen I watched as two dozen bikini-clad women boogied and clapped and stared lovingly at this particular performer holding a microphone. He was a short stout black man who moved awkwardly on the stage. He crooned a hip-hop tune about how he'd risen from a squalid childhood in the projects of Atlanta.

I fancied what my life would be like if I had an adoring girlfriend: someone who was enchanted by the mating call of my own life story, even though I lacked the ability to set it to music or get on stage and dance to its awkward and arbitrary syncopations.

Chapter 8 – Goodbye, Townsend Avenue

Typically my Ann Arbor apartment buzzed with a strange mixture of ambient acoustics: the bangs of shoes on the stairwell; the screeches and honks of cars on Washington Street; the humming of my PC against the hardwood floor. But with the student body gone, my residence was quiet. I put on a CD – Bruce Springsteen's *The Ghost of Tom Joad*, a recommendation from Jimmy Calipari – and I lay on my bed with one of my yellow legal pads. When *Tom Joad* ended I put on *Ready to Die* by the Notorious B.I.G., which was a favorite of Nicole's and Jerod's.

I made a list of *Guide*-related tasks, since the NFL draft was only weeks away. I needed to print out 200 copies and ship them to my subscribers; buy plane tickets to NY so I could attend the big event; upload the final version of the 1997 *Guide* to ZinskyQuintessential.com; and compose my final promotional email.

In the midst of these solitary reveries my phone rang.

I hesitated to pick up, fearing somehow that Barbara and/or Neil had learned of my Spring Break hoax and were calling to reprimand me.

But I felt lonely in Ann Arbor and after three rings I answered: "This is Zinsky."

"Your mother said you were in Cancun," said the moist voice of my biological father.

"I came back," I said, curious how he had my Ann Arbor phone number. I was also surprised to be hearing from him at a time other than Christmas. "Were you trying to reach my voicemail," I asked, "or did you actually want to have a conversation?"

"You know how it is," he said.

"I guess you're stuck with me," I said. "So what's up? How's your real family?"

"What can I say," he said. "I love Sandra, and I still love Cam, and I can live with the fact that she's not crazy about me anymore, as long as the excess devotion goes to Sandra."

"But you haven't tested Sandra's character yet, have you? How can you love Sandra until you see how she responds to a nice kick in the gut?"

"Ari, don't give me guilt over how I treated you, okay? Seriously. You sound like those Indians on reservations that are still pissed at the American government. It happened. Life is brutal sometimes. Get over it."

"Why are you calling?"

"I've got a conference in Chicago the weekend before Memorial Day. So I figured I could drag my family with me and we could swing up to your graduation. You'd finally get a chance to meet them, and vice versa."

I was taken aback. My dad, like many successful businessmen, used pragmatics to broach emotional issues – that, I was accustomed to. But ending our 13-year détente because of a conference? "Why are you really coming up here?" I asked. "I mean, I'm happy to meet your family and all. But you can't blame me for wondering."

"No, I can't," he said. "And you can't blame me for trying to reach your voicemail."

I sighed. "See you soon, then."

"Bye, son. I won't tell your mom you're not in Cancun."

*　　*　　*

Daily I wandered through Shapiro Library. Professor Dalrymple's references to Whitman and Dostoevsky had flown over my head and I wanted to familiarize myself. But instead of checking out *Leaves of Grass* and *Crime and Punishment*, I preferred leaving the books in the library and visiting them everyday. I was alone on campus and didn't mind leaving my too-quiet apartment.

At night I went to the CCRB and I played full-court one-on-one games against myself: attacking one basket, I pretended to be the then-34-year-old Michael Jordan, pivoting and popping 15-foot jumpers, saving my drives to the basket for times of team need. Attacking the other basket, opposing Michael Jordan, I was the then-24-year-old Jalen Rose, a lefty like myself, and a Michigan man like myself. Rose was not quick enough to drive on Jordan but he was long and crafty in the post, ducking and feinting until the overzealous Jordan, perhaps eager to prove his vast superiority to the upstart southpaw, leaped to block Rose's shot. At which point Rose calmly floated a lefty jump-hook over the outstretched fingertips of the sinking superstar.

After basketball I dined at the West End Grille on Liberty Street. I ate rapidly and lingered over a dessert as I pondered my readings. I was dying for Shelagh to return so I could share with her my theory on Raskolnikov, the protagonist in *Crime and Punishment*. My theory was that throughout the novel, Raskolnikov was tacitly ruminating on suicide. And for all his philosophical, Nietzschean prattle, it was this – the prospect of his own imminent, anonymous death – that emboldened Raskolnikov to the action of murder. For Raskolnikov had nothing to lose by committing a crime in a world he intended to exit.

But Shelagh was in New Orleans. So my imaginary date for the evening was my waitress. With the rest of the student body away for Spring Break I was often one of the only customers – my unoccupied waitress frequently circled my table and refilled my water. Her excessive attention contented me, especially when my refills came with smiles or personal questions about my status on campus. Was I a basketball player? Was I staying in Ann Arbor to complete a senior thesis? Such affable concern for the cost of an entrée! To this day, I believe a starving man prefers the attentions of a waitress to those of a prostitute. Grinning upon your arrival, kneeling or crouching to reach your eye level as they take your order, focused on your comfort in a way that seems sincere – where else but a restaurant can a solitary man with ten bucks receive such satisfying service, such cooperation from young women eager to gratify?

On the Monday morning class resumed, I spent a full hour pondering what to wear to Am Lit. I believed Shelagh would talk to me after class, if only so she could share the narrative of her Spring Break in New Orleans.

But Shelagh did not make it to lecture that day.

After my shifts at the business school and the dining hall I emailed Shelagh about her absence from class. To my surprise she replied promptly:

Hi Ari. I'm back safely, thanks. A little messed up, is all. I'll be in class Wednesday. But don't worry if I'm not. Hugs, Shelagh

I was concerned about her, but I knew better than to follow up with pressing questions. I focused on the positive news: a sign-off like *Hugs!* Progress, was it not?

The next day passed in a blur. At midnight I went to the WCNB studios. Following the show, Kris asked me to wait for him while he finished some cart recording. I waited around, proofing the 1997 *Guide.*

"So how was New Orleans," I asked, as we exited through the double glass doors, stepping out onto breezy, lamppost-lit Thompson Street. It was a spring night, frigid only during sustained winds.

"This isn't easy to tell you," he said. "I'm just going to come right out and say it: Shelagh flipped for this Harvard soccer player. I'm pretty sure she slept with him. She was at his hotel room day and night."

I grabbed Kris by his jacket collar and threw him to the ground. In a flash my right hand clamped this throat and my left fist was cocked. "Don't fuck with me about her," I shouted. I dug my knee into his chest. He was frozen. Before long I realized it was I who was gasping for breath. I rolled off Kris and sat on the sidewalk, stunned and embarrassed by what had overcome me. "Oh fuck, Kris, I'm so sorry," I muttered.

"What's wrong with you?" he shouted, dusting himself off. "I thought long and hard about whether to tell you and now I think I made a mistake."

"I'm so sorry," I repeated. "I – do you know what she means to me?" I asked. I got to my knees, content to let Kris hover over me.

"You're fucked up, Zinsky," he said.

He walked off, hands on his hips, sighing audibly; I trailed him by a few strides, hoping he'd turn and forgive me. We walked quietly for several blocks — we were in shock, two privileged young men regrouping from a rare trip to the land of subterranean emotions. It was after 1:00 a.m., when on quieter Ann Arbor streets you can hear the traffic lights clicking as they change from green to yellow to red.

"I'm so sorry, Kris," I repeated.

"Stop apologizing already," he said, still walking ahead.

"Will you hate me forever because of this?" I asked.

He stopped. "I might fear you forever," he said.

"If I let you punch me can we call it even?" I asked.

"Ari, stop it," he said. "You haven't even heard the rest of the story."

"What if I buy your beer for the rest of the year?"

He paused. "Just shut up and listen," he said.

At an Irish pub called The Earle Kris finished his tale:

"Shelagh," he began, "was doing all this on the assumption that they'd keep in touch, see each other over summers, and eventually work in the same city. And this guy goes along with it. And on our flight back to Detroit, Shelagh is the happiest girl I've ever seen. Even happier than when she was in love with Nick."

I sat on my hands, pressing them into the cushioned barstool. So Shelagh had lied: the excuse of needing time to recover from Nick was total bullshit. My position in relation to Shelagh — a friend with benefits, to use the colloquialism — gave me some right to protest her fib, but no right to challenge her lascivious actions. But doing either would only endanger my procurement of what I really wanted: her. And if I couldn't have her exclusively, I wanted her as many times as I could have her anyway. "I can't believe she fucked another guy," I said.

"Drink your beer and let me finish," said Kris. He resumed: "From the airport we all shared one of those minivan-limo things back to campus. Shelagh and Tina invited everyone back to their apartment for an official farewell-to-Spring-Break pizza dinner. We got inside and the red light on her answering machine was flashing. Shane drops his bags and runs over and hits play. Shelagh starts jumping in place as soon as she hears, "Hi, Shelagh, it's Preston," in this deep-ass baritone voice. Now she and Shane and Tina are holding each other, living and dying with every syllable coming from the recorded Preston. So Preston says, 'Look, now that I'm back at school, I just don't think I can swing the long-distance thing. So call me if you're in town or whatever, but I'm really sorry. I know I said some things I probably shouldn't have and – anyway, I'm sorry. Take care, and maybe I'll talk to you soon.' Click."

"Serves her right," I said, though in my mind I felt terrible for her. If Preston's nonchalance had leveled her the way her nonchalance had leveled me – then Shelagh was in a wretched state of mind.

"So after the Preston call we're all silent," continued Kris. "Until Shane, after like five minutes when the girls are still crying, says, 'Well, are we still getting pizza?' Which I find so hilarious I curl up on the couch laughing. And soon Shane is in hysterics too. It was insensitive as hell, but if you heard how Shane deadpanned the remark – like, he was hungry and seriously curious if we were still eating together – you'd have laughed too. Then Tina says, 'I think you two assholes better excuse us.' So Shane and I got pizza by ourselves, and we let the two of them just stay there and dyke out."

"Dyke out?"

"It's Shane's line," said Kris. "He uses it all the time, whenever Tina tries to hog Shelagh all to herself."

When I got home to my apartment I lingered in the foyer for a moment, waiting for Kris to disappear along Washington Street. Once he was gone I stepped out again – bound for South Quad, eager to espy the activity within Shelagh's living room.

Though it was past 2:00 a.m. she was awake: curled on the couch reading *The Professor's House* for Am Lit, wearing a loose flannel pajama top and snug beige long johns. I considered knocking on the window; instead I scaled the steps and entered the superheated South Quad foyer as another student exited. My forehead began perspiring but I kept my hat on, wanting to preserve a non-bald appearance. I rang her buzzer and listened for her twang-less voice on the intercom. "Hell-eau?" she said, fighting a yawn through sonic static. "It's Ari," I said, my voice echoing through the vacant foyer.

The buzzer's shrillness was startling. She opened the door and hugged me. "I just left you a voicemail," she said.

"What'd you say?"

"I wanted you to come over," she said, playfully pinching my arm.

"Really?"

"Yes. Don't be so flattered, Ari. You never seem to believe I like you."

"I wonder why," I said.

She looked into my eyes. "Ari, you know I'd talk to you right now about what's saddening me if I could, don't you?" she said, deftly changing the subject. I was hip to her tactic but lost the spine to demur once she latched to my shoulder, moistening my neck with her eyes, clasping her warm hands around me.

"Tell me what happened," I whispered, stroking her dark hair.

She led me to the couch, where her paperback lay bookmarked. In those tight long johns she strode throughout the apartment shutting off the lights – first the kitchen, then the corner of the living room where there was a halogen. My arousal level escalated: there was perhaps an inch of flab on her bottom. Was I about to spend the night with this woman? Oh, how could her duplicity upset me if my silence earned me another night with a body like hers?

Into her darkened bedroom I followed her. The first thing I saw was a digital alarm clock with luminous green digits reading 2:51. There was a small rectangular window with an open shade, giving entry to slashing diagonals of moonlight and lamppost brightness. Against one wall was a queen-sized bed; against the opposite were dressers and a bookshelf. The bookshelf held not books but glass candle holders. Shelagh withdrew a match from the top dresser drawer and started lighting. In the candlelight I saw she also held several incense sticks. She lit these and balanced them flat on the bookshelf, giving the room an aroma I'd only known from various subway stops and street-corners at which I'd encountered tabletop scent-vendors.

But then I wondered: had she lit incense and strutted around in tight long johns for Preston? I remained standing. "What's the matter?" she asked.

"Nothing," I muttered, sitting tentatively. Somehow in the dimmed room she observed enough of my bodily hesitation to say, "Don't worry so much, Ari. I want you to stay here tonight."

I dove towards her and kissed her: warm, wet, and open. I pressed my tongue through her initial resistances. I seized the back of her head with both hands and pressed her lips onto mine. My cock snapped up against my waist like a triggered mousetrap. I stripped her and pushed her onto her back, clawing and groping and sucking with a beast's ferocity. Within five minutes I was finished, mulling when my powers of recovery would permit me once more to attack her.

*　*　*

"What are you thinking about?" I whispered, much later. The bright green clock read 4:31.

"You," she said.

"Can you be more specific?" I asked, stroking her cheek.

"I'm thinking you'll take for insulting what I mean as a high compliment."

"It's okay," I said. "You can admit you're only in this for the sex."

She chuckled and slapped my arm. "Did you brush up on your post-coital material while I was gone?" she asked.

"Did you?"

She paused. She wiped her eyes on my sleeve when she said, "When can you ever trust someone, Ari?"

"Tell me what happened," I whispered. "Who messed you up?"

"Just some arrogant, heartless Harvard snake," she sobbed. "Let's not talk about it. What were we talking about?"

"I asked you what you were thinking and you said you, meaning me."

"I think about you a lot."

"Like what?"

"Like I wish we met before Nick. Or that we could meet when we're in our forties and past the bullshit of careers and ambitions. Kind of like how you describe your mom and Neil. A no-nonsense companionship."

"I'm ready for that now."

"You're just saying that because you like me," she said. I withdrew from our embrace at her backhanded reprimand. She clasped the back of my head and pulled me back. "You're like a big turtle," she whispered. "One harsh comment and you need to be cajoled out of your shell."

"Just when the comments come from you," I said. "I've got thicker skin for the slings of others."

"I do like you," she insisted. "I'm very drawn to workaholics. I feel like they're the only ones who understand me."

"Bullshit," I said. "Why can't you just level with me about your hesitation, instead of attributing it to Nick?"

"I should've done more hesitating in New Orleans," she said, her eyes lambent in the slashing moonlight. "What are you thinking about?" she asked, her warm fingertips stroking my bald head.

I nestled my head below her breasts. Her heartbeat thudded in my ear. I raised myself up to kiss her. Her tongue was languid. "Kissing is nice but I want you to talk to me," she said. "Tell me why you work so hard," she whispered.

"So I don't think so hard," I said.

"Think about what?"

If she wanted to understand why my mind needed constant occupation, she needed to understand my suicidal ideation, dating back to age nine. I wanted to share it with her. But it seemed a bit much to get into with someone whose actions rendered specious her bedside claims of interest. She was more concerned about my inner workings than Charlene Chiu had been, and she was more concerned than any waitress had ever been; but she was not as concerned as I wanted my lover to be.

"Think about what?" she repeated.

"Like you give a shit," I said.

"You don't have to turtle up on me," she replied.

"Yes, I do."

"Why?"

"Because who can you ever trust, Shelagh?"

"Me."

"Don't say that to me."

"Why not?"

"Because we both know that you might not go for me when we're in our forties. You can't even say hi to me in class half the time."

"You know how I am in class," she said.

"I sure do," I muttered. I rolled onto my back, smelling the incense, watching the candles flicker in their glass containers. "How come you've only slept with one other guy in your life?" I asked.

"Two, now," she said.

The pronouncement floored me, even though it was not news. It's always a whack when you hear firsthand how a good-looking fellow in one night gets what you've toiled for weeks to earn. "So – how was he?" I asked.

"Ari," she admonished.

"Don't get prissy with me," I said. "I deserve at least that much."

She rolled her eyes. "Your pricks are about the same size," she said sarcastically. "Are you happy now?"

"What about our semen quantities?" I countered.

"Ari," she chuckled.

"I'm jetting the stuff of more arrogant republics," I said, quoting the Whitman I'd read over Spring Break.

She sighed. "I'm really going to miss you next year," she said. I reached for her hand and drew it towards me until it was stroking my chest. "I forgot that you like to get felt up," she whispered.

"So – why were you ready for a relationship with Harvard snake and not with me?" I asked. "I don't protest your decision; I just want to understand it. And please don't say chemistry. Say something palpable. And don't deny you're more attracted to him just to spare my feelings."

"Ari, I was stupid," she said. "Let it go."

"Okay."

"But before we switch topics," she said, "I want you to repeat the following."

"Fine."

"Shelagh Styne is physically attracted to Ari Zinsky."

"Shelagh Styne is physically attracted to Ari Zinsky, yet finds him eminently resistible."

"Resistible? Then why are you here?"

"Because I jet the stuff of arrogant republics."

She giggled. "No, but you turn me on when you get that verbal swagger."

"But Harvard boys really arouse you?"

"Stop it. Please?"

"Okay."

"We're never going to wake up for class tomorrow."

"I'll wake up."

"I know you will," she said. She dusted the edge of my hairless scalp with her thick smooth lower lip.

* * *

A few weekends later I flew back to New York to sell and promote my *Guide* at the 1997 draft. I recall waiting for a train and thinking how – for a change – I didn't ponder throwing myself in front of it to commit suicide.

My trip occurred while Barbara and Neil were honeymooning in Paris. In advance of their travels they had moved into the West Egg house, cramming my belongings into cardboard boxes labeled ARI'S STUFF in thick black marker. I did not wish to lodge in the West Egg house in my mother's absence. Instead, all my sentiments about the Townsend Avenue apartment compelled me to crash on its hardwood floor. Practically speaking, the apartment was still my mother's until the end of April. And my own financial condition – dead broke, after fronting the money to print 200 *Guides* – made staying in a hotel impracticable. So I would sleep on the cold stiff floor, blanketing myself with the Jets sweatshirt I'd packed as my draft-day wardrobe.

Before falling asleep I wandered around the dark, vacant apartment. The cream-colored oval kitchen table was gone. The television area was gone too: no couch, no ottoman, no TV, no VCR. I peeked out the window of the fire escape. The beat-up wooden chair was gone.

I stared at the dim, cobwebbed corner where my bed used to be. My bed: where I had read countless magazines and used innumerable yellow legal pads. Where I had phoned Charlene and Shelagh for the first time. Where I masturbated to them for the first time. How much sperm had I spilt in this bedroom? Assuming three years for simplicity, I could round to 1,000 days of self-love: 2,000 orgasms, since I generally pleased myself twice daily. Assuming two ounces per load, the orgasms yielded 4,000 ounces or 250 pounds of ejaculate over my bedroom's history. "Believe me, sweetie, I got enough to feed the needy," I said aloud, quoting the Notorious B.I.G., whose boasted-of fecundity I now recognized as kindred to that of his Brooklyn predecessor, Walt Whitman.

It was the bedroom that forever defined "bedroom" for me. It was the bedroom that nurtured me through my father's wounds and my mother's scolds. It was the bedroom in which my books were my breath and my box radio was my bloodstream. Yes, I recognized it was *just* a bedroom: one of billions the world over. But to see my precious space stripped bare – this was dramatic and worthy of lamentation. *Other* bedrooms were stripped bare. *My* bedroom, indisputably more poetical than the billions of others, was *strip'd*. My bedroom had been untimely rip'd, strip'd, and fleec'd from my life. And now? Within months someone else would move in, adorning the walls not with football posters but other decorations. And would My Room, inanimate, mourn my absence, or detect the presence of its new occupant? Smarter humans than I, surely, had debated the question of whether bedrooms possessed souls, auras, or spirits. Did bedrooms have souls? Or were rooms, like the busiest and comeliest of people, unfazed by loneliness, confident their attractions would preclude too long a solitude?

In the hollowed-out apartment, my voice carried further than it normally did. My footsteps echoed. Likewise the toilet, when I flushed it for no reason other than to hear its *whish*, possessed the sonic power of a thundercloud. So it was that my flush jarred me from my ruminations on the souls of rooms – or I daresay, the rooms of souls.

Chapter 9 – Crime & Punishment

In late April a global accounting firm – one you've all heard of – offered me an entry level job in Boston. I was hesitant, preferring to devote myself to the *Guide*. A compromise hit me: I could accept the offer, curry favor with my new employers, and then – after five or six months – announce my decision to leave, in pursuit of my entrepreneurial dream. In my ideal scenario, the firm would continue allowing me use of its resources – computers, printers, scanners, fax machines, copiers, phones, paper, pens, post-its – even after my departure.

Yes, the 22-year-old Zinsky was *that* naïve about the private sector.

My confidence was buoyed by my success at the 1997 draft: I sold 96 *Guides*, more than tripling the previous year's total. I also procured 141 email addresses from fans who didn't purchase the *Guide* but wanted my newsletter. (This was in '97 – years before spamming made people protective of their email addresses.)

I felt a connection between myself and my customers. It began when I sold my first *Guide* of the morning to a fan of the Oakland Raiders, who was excited his team would select USC's Darrell Russell with the first overall pick. I argued Ohio State's Shawn Springs was the better player. The sincerity and volume of our debate made me seem less like a gawky merchant freak and more like an earnest zealot out for an honest buck. Other fans, standing nearby in line for admission, caught something of our fervor and before I knew it I'd sold six more

Guides to my congregation.

In retrospect, I also believe there was something about *me* – a gangly, 6-8 young man dressed like a Jets fanatic, lugging around a gym bag of homemade glossies – that made all of these sports fans want to *help*. I wasn't selling them mere words on pages; I was proffering football *passion*, and they were buying it because my pitch was too genuine to be ignored. What took place on that April morning was not merely the exchange of $5 for a football magazine. It was something spiritual. And by the time the actual draft began at noon, I was so inspired about my life that I took out a yellow legal pad and wrote: *"To have not committed suicide all those years ago – days like this validate your choice. Envision a future where you are a terrific basketball player with a girlfriend who loves fucking you. You will make it happen. Know that your past would've snapped the spines of weaker individuals. Know, too, that the woman of your dreams will appreciate your backbone."*

Oh readers, I must confess – the naïve 22-year-old Zinsky still believed the pendulum of romantic karma would swing in his favor! He had a divination of deserving idyllic coupling because of all he'd suffered. Does it sound corny? Naïve? Or worse – typical? Perhaps I should have known better. After all, the entire strength of my attraction to Charlene and Shelagh had nothing to do with *their* biographies. Why did I expect different treatment?

*   *   *

My college pals had fixed their paths on advanced degrees and steady paychecks: Kris Holley was bound for NYU law school. Tim Nover was studying law too, at Purdue University. Meanwhile, Jerod had been accepted to med school at a discount in his home state at the University of Indiana. His ambition was to be an ob-gyn. His passion stemmed from an incident in high school when he'd impregnated a girl who swore she was on the pill. To defend his (and the girl's) abortion decision to his (and her) parents, he had to master the pro-choice side of the debate – small beer if you're from Long Island but borderline contrarian in the Wabash Valley. His aim was to found a national chain of abortion clinics – "a for-profit version of Planned Parenthood," is how he phrased it.

Only Jimmy Calipari wasn't going to more school. Jimmy was launching a journalism career as an intern with the sports section of *Newsday* – like me, he'd grown up on Long Island, and he felt a certain tug towards the sports section of Long Island's newspaper. So just like Kris, he was moving to New York. I wasn't certain how much of Kris I'd see on my visits home, mainly because Kris didn't play basketball and asked nettling questions about what I'd do for health insurance if I pursued the *Guide*. But Jimmy I planned on phoning whenever I was in town. Jimmy understood that fear can't drive every career decision.

Exempt from all this career news was the predominant non-senior of my campus existence. But something in the warming Ann Arbor air seemed to have affected her too. There is a species of junior who becomes unified with the grade above her; a junior who longs to graduate, to leave an institution not when she is supposed to, but when the respected elders who consecrate that institution take *their* leave. In this context, I daresay Shelagh Styne became pre-nostalgically attached to the 22-year-old Zinsky. She saw that she had only six, then four, then two weeks remaining on campus with him. She saw that the time of their bond, such as it was, was elapsing. She asked him to lunch on four occasions and thrice phoned for late-night booty calls. She even hugged him before and after morning lectures with Professor Dalrymple.

In hindsight, I perceive Shelagh's affection for what it was: a young girl with few deep friendships became flappable when confronted with a legitimate farewell.

But at the time? I felt she was warming to me.

We walked around campus with arms around each other's shoulders. In the dining hall, she'd leave her own seat and sit on my lap. At one of our lunches Shelagh asked me to Phi Alpha Delta's year-end formal. I spent the rest of the meal beaming. As we walked back to South Quad she asked me why I was so happy. "Because I'm going to a dance with you," I said giddily. She kissed me on the stone steps for a good five minutes.

* * *

The night of the dance I clean my Doc Martens in my bathroom sink and dry them with toilet paper. Smelling like a mélange of Gillette products, pawing and creasing a wrapped bundle of 12 pink roses, I walk to Shelagh's doorway, my mind a-tumble in anticipation of her appearance.

My blood jumps at the sight of her hips in a tight navy blue dress with low neck and high hems. Her dark brown hair is braided and two white pearls adorn her ears, matching a pearl necklace. Her legs and abdomen and backside seem trussed in the dress, which encases her body in a manner I've heretofore associated with soft knee braces. I feel ashamed of my comparatively baggy appearance, my open sports jacket flapping behind me like a curtain.

In the kitchen she pulls a glass vase from a cabinet, guns it with sink-water, thuds it on the counter, snips the stems, plunks them into liquid. Her actions are precise and polished. Her rote manner bothers me: deep down I want her to be awkward like me. I want this evening – already formative in my biography, before the dancing begins – to be an all-time highlight for her, too. Instead it's clear she's done this a thousand times. It reminds me of our first sexual encounter.

She brings the flowers to the coffee table. "What's the matter?" she asks.

"Do you hang out with me just to prove how unsuperficial you are?" I ask.

On her toes she clasps my bald head with her bare hands and takes a quick deft bite of my lower lip. "Would you still hang out with me if I were ugly?" she asks, grinning once more. My heart thumps.

"It's different," I say, completely derailed.

"I see," she says.

Tina and Shane emerge from Tina's room, primped for the evening. Shane wears a white tux, like an upscale waiter, while Tina sports a knee-length short-sleeved black dress. We greet each other with lengthy hugs.

Near the entrance to the Union Ballroom we stand at the rear of a swift-moving line. The music from within is a mix of contemporary hip-hop and 80s dance tunes. Shelagh and Tina hand tickets to a fresh-man sitting at a banquet table with a cash box. Inside, flashing red and yellow ceiling lights cut through the room's darkness. The music is ad-ministered by an undergraduate disc jockey whose only equipment is a CD player, a set of speakers, and a soundboard. The pounding volume relegates audible conversations to the room's quieter corners, where student-bartenders stand behind counters scanning IDs and selling drinks.

I want to seize Shelagh by the waist, to undam an ocean of energy onto the dance floor. But I'm too nervous. Shelagh leads me by the hand to what seems like the only vacant space. My eyes track her movements, which are in complete sync with the rapid cadence and punctuated rhythms of the Prince tune "Kiss." By contrast my shakings are a mixture of Shelagh imitation and stilted, conscientious wiggles. In fact I'm a disgrace to the participle dancing. I don't dance so much as lumber in place, performing an awkward Caucasian shuffle, my hips and legs lacking all fluidity. Mozart's "Adagio for Glass Harmonica" could be playing and my motions would be no different. Nevertheless, we dance for nearly an hour. During a slow song – Cyndi Lauper's "Time After Time" – I huddle close. We lock hands and complete a few graceless twirls.

After the slow dance I leave to fetch beers. When I return with two Budweiser bottles a curly-haired man is dancing with Shelagh. They are angled toward each other in a head-leaning manner. My sports jacket feels tighter around my shoulders. I hand one bottle to Shelagh, who acknowledges my return with a wave. Her insouciance, combined with the grinning assuredness of my thick-haired rival, make me seize his tuxedo collar with my right hand and wield the bottle as a club in my left. "Ari, chill out!" shrieks Shelagh. "Dude, relax, I didn't know she was spoken for," cringes my enemy. His blue eyes are watery to my glare. I relinquish him with a shove, eyeing him until he's crossed the room. I turn to Shelagh, who has stopped dancing. "Sorry I lost it," I say.

"You were really going to hit him," she says.

"Don't you ever want to hit that girl who Nick is so smitten with?" I shout. To my relief, she comes forward as I pull her by the hips. Her arms clasp my shoulders, the icy bottle in her hand chilling my neck. "I've created a monster," she says.

"You're like the ancient goddess Circe," I say. "You turn all men into monsters."

"You mean swine, not monsters," she says. Our cheeks and chests are touching. My sports jacket feels loose again.

"I was so scared," I say, kissing her cheek. One of her hands moves to my lower back. "You're the only guy I've wanted all semester," she says.

"At Michigan, you mean."

"You know what I mean."

"Do you think you could be my girlfriend just for tonight?" I ask. "If you say yes, this will be the greatest evening of my life."

"Yes."

We kiss, my brain whirring with ecstasies I previously believed were reserved for beautiful people. The pressure of Shelagh's tongue and the back-grasp of her fingers spike my blood and breath with reveries of returned affection.

My hands lose control. One floats up her flank and caresses her left breast. The other slides down and grabs her rear. Her stomach pulses against my own.

We leave Union Ballroom walking quickly back to South Quad.

*   *   *

By now Shelagh and I have our routine. Our first fuck is truly just mine: as if her body is nothing more than what it is – the object of my fantasies. From behind I ram myself inside her with savage ferocity. My tip touches her cervix. Within a minute I've exploded. Shelagh doesn't turn to look at me nor does she reach back to touch me. But as usual, I'm too grateful about fucking to split hairs over reciprocity.

After my feast I strap on my figurative hardhat and go to work: I dive toward her center, her exquisite blossom of liplike folds and pink-ish creases, swishing my tongue in and around the salty and sweaty juices. I caress her opening as if it's a mouth and caress her buttocks as though they are facial cheeks. Her cold heels rest on my mid-back.

My index finger swims inside and finds a small button. Soon her center is more salty than sweaty, my finger and tongue are wading within, plashing. Her upper thighs squeeze my ears. She screams and quakes as I lick and lap. And then it is over: she removes me and drops me on the bed, a discarded head of lettuce returned to the pile.

Intermission: bathroom breaks, cold drinks, frivolous conversations. Act II is what Shelagh and I term a *cuddle-fuck*: Multi-positional, empha-sizing sustainability rather than ephemeral gains. Sometimes she lets me kiss and suckle her during our cuddle-fuck, and sometimes she doesn't. Sometimes she blows me, and sometimes she doesn't. Sometimes she comes during our cuddle-fuck, and sometimes she doesn't. And strangest to me, sometimes her coming and blowing occur on the kissing occasions, and sometimes they don't. I can't figure it out. I care enough to ask but fear asking will set her mind on a calculus whose result is her refusal to fuck me anymore. I fear my pesky inquests will be like lifting the needle from a Mozart record – a mood-breaker from which only partial recovery is possible. So I limit my queries to simply *whether* she comes. She says, "No, but don't worry about it," about half the time. Her quakes on these occasions are not *quite* as seismic or wrenching or voluble as they are when she nods and says, "Oh yeah. Couldn't you tell?"

The cuddle-fucks culminate in *my* coming, either during a blow job or when I'm back on top and Shelagh has her arms around me. Her eyes are off to the ceiling; she's ready to "punch out" and adjourn to a happy hour of post-coital chat.

Strange to report: on this night I find myself going limp inside her. Greenhorn that I am, I try combating the limpness by watching Shelagh's jouncing breasts and redoubling my own pelvic thrusting. Yet nothing is working and I catch Shelagh glancing at her digital clock with its electrical green numerals. (It's 1:21.) I pull out, though by this time there's little to extract. All at once it occurs to me I should try harder; school is ending soon and this may be my last chance with Shelagh. But it's no use. I roll on my back hoping my posture will induce another blow job; I'm wounded when I see her hand scraping the floor for her panties. "What are you doing?" I ask.

"I'm cold," she says flatly.

"Don't you care that I couldn't come?" I ask.

"It's not the end of the world, Ari," she says. Her utterance of the truth bothers me less than her pedantic appending of my name.

"Aren't I supposed to be your boyfriend for the night, *Shelagh?*" I ask.

"What do you want me to do?" she asks, sitting up.

"Am I only imagining that you're less relaxed than you normally are?"

"The truth is, Ari, I'm amazed we've reached the point where we *have* a 'normally,'" she says. "You act like you own me."

"Why, because someone tried to steal you at the dance?" I say. I turn to face her. Then I'm up on my knees, straddling her legs.

"I'm not yours," she says, avoiding my glance.

I grab her chin and direct her gaze back to mine. "You're my *date*. Which means, sorry to break it to you, that you *are* mine for the evening. Nothing would've happened if you hadn't acted so tempted."

"I *was* tempted," she says.

I smack her face with a swift left hand. She rubs her cheek, glaring at me in disbelief. Her wet-soil eyes moisten at the corners. Without a word she nudges me aside and gets up, leaving her room without a backward glance, leaving the door open behind her. I hear the shower running in the bathroom. She returns wearing a red robe I've never seen before. "I want you to leave while I'm in the shower," she says with calm that unnerves me. "If you're here when I get out I'm calling campus police. I'm tempted to call them right now, to be honest." She disappears. I hear her footsteps in the common room, the bathroom door shutting.

*   *   *

When I got home I phoned Jerod. He spent ten minutes lecturing me on my lack of control and maturity. Finally, he answered my original question: "She won't call the police, don't worry," he said.

"How do you know? You've obviously never – "

"No, but Nesby did, and the girl never called. But Ari, even if she does call – what's going to happen? One slap, given the circumstances – you're still going to graduate. The worst thing would probably be probation, for a clean record like yours. And you think Shelagh wants to explain the story nine times to some campus cops who've seen worse? Trust me – it takes a lot for a woman to press charges."

"I've emailed her and called her and left a note at the radio station," I said.

"Just don't expect to see her again," he said.

"I just hope she replies," I said.

"You need to get it off your mind," he said. "Let's play ball or get drunk. I've been studying glycolysis all night and I've had it."

Over beers that night at my apartment, as we watched late-night basketball highlights on ESPN, I told Jerod my story, so he could understand how I'd reached the point of being a young man who slaps young women. "It's no excuse," he said when I was finished. "But I knew your shit ran deep." I appreciated his affirmation and welcomed the tale of his own troubled childhood. "My dad didn't touch me but it's all the same," he said. "One way or another, you get kicked in the head."

"But you still plan on having kids," I asked.

"Hell yes," he said. "It was just the wrong girl at the wrong time, and she lied about the pill. And once she was pregnant, it was like *she* had all the rights, though I did nothing wrong."

"Other than trust her."

"Right," he said, downing his bottle and grabbing another from the six-pack on the couch. "Still, the law is bullshit. Our society is bullshit, in this way. There should be circumstances where men have equal rights over an unborn child."

"Nover can work on it," I said. "Or Holley. One of those law school clowns."

"It'll never happen," he said. "Find me the politician who'll vote against women on this one." He took three giant gulps, his Adam's apple bobbing as he arched his neck and tilted the bottle vertical. "Now," he said authoritatively, as if by finishing the bottle he'd also finished with this particular subject. "You put all this shit about your dad in your notes to Shelagh?" he asked.

"Yes. I mentioned one incident."

"Good. She'll forgive you. Now the next step is forgetting about her."

"That'll never happen."

"It will, if you come to Europe with me and Tim this summer. You'll get your dick sucked just for being American."

"I can't," I said. "I have a big meeting in June. One of my readers thinks I can get the *Guide* distributed in San Francisco if I make a strong pitch to a 49ers marketing guy."

"Do what you gotta do," he sighed. We both turned back to the television.

* * *

I continued leaving notes, voice mails, and emails for Shelagh. Three days passed. Then she answered with an unsigned email: *You don't deserve a reply. I am too busy with finals to devote even five minutes to you. Please don't contact me again. Take care.*

It was around this time I pondered a life-theory called "The Incidences of Incidents." I can best explain it by asking: if you write one article, does that make you a *writer*? If you prepare one meal, does that make you a chef? No and no. Yet there are incidents in life where a one-time incidence can label you forever. Raise one child and you're a parent. Cheat once on a spouse and you're an adulterer. Plagiarize one article and you're a plagiarist. Kill one person and you're a murderer. Everything depended on the *rarity* or taboo level of the act. I had slapped one woman one time but I was finished: I was henceforth and forevermore a *slapper*. Shelagh would tell Tina and Shane and Kris and none of them would talk to me again.

My sleep was terrible. I dreamed of waking with an unquenchable thirst and walking to campus police headquarters and dropping to my knees in Raskolnikov style and confessing to the detective tracking my case:

It was I who –

"Drink some water."

I wave aside the Evian and speak distinctly: *It was I who slapped the hot young women, Shelagh Styne, with my bare left hand, on the night of the Phi Alpha formal.*

Campus police rush in from all sides.

Zinsky repeats his statement.

*   *   *

Nothing happened. Not only did I remain unpunished, but Shelagh – from what I could ascertain – didn't share our incident with anyone. The next time I spoke to Kris Holley I nearly cried when he innocently asked, "How's Shelagh?" For it was clear in his eager intonation that *he didn't know*. He was under the illusion Shelagh and I still were seeing each other. Subsequent interactions with Tina and Shane confirmed my suspicion: Shelagh had kept the whole thing under wraps.

Still my guilt lingered, knowing firsthand the harm of a slap's receiving end. For all I was experiencing, wasn't Shelagh's plight a thousand times worse? How was she supposed to trust another man again? I longed to write her another note expressing this view. But I heeded her email and kept to myself. In the days before my family visited I grew grateful that they would not discover my behavior.

Chapter 10 – Family Reunion

The last time I saw Shelagh Styne on campus she wore a v-neck t-shirt and cutoff denim shorts and didn't make eye contact with me. It was the afternoon of our Am Lit final. Her face was fixed on the inside of a light blue exam booklet. Upon finishing my essays I penned *Ariel Zinsky* on the cover. I twisted in my seat to gauge how Shelagh was doing. Professor Dalrymple raced to my desk and seized my booklet. "Have a nice summer," she said and soon I was in the hallway.

I spent the rest of the afternoon in my bed, depressed about the fate I'd brought upon myself: no more sex with Shelagh, no more staring at Shelagh, and all because I'd lost control. My solitary suffering was no more bearable for being deserved.

That night I went with Jerod, Tim Nover, and Jimmy Calipari to a baseball game. I tried to rally my spirits by listening to *Ready to Die*. But I was still depressed in the backseat of Jimmy's red Taurus, en route to the stadium. Jimmy played the CD in the car, despite his disdain for rap music – and for the recently deceased Notorious B.I.G. in particular. "I'm sick of everyone waxing elegiac over this guy," he said. "People are talking about B.I.G. as though he's JFK." He ran a hand through his jet black hair.

Jerod cracked a Budweiser and passed cold bottles to me and Tim in the backseat. I took a sip. "Maybe B.I.G. is bigger than JFK," I said, belching for emphasis.

"Ari, you can't compare a *rapper* to the president," said Jimmy. "Especially to a man who was president when people cared. When people still voted, and believed in change, instead of just staying home and watching HBO."

"Jimmy, if President Clinton died tomorrow, his death would not impact me – and I daresay, a lot of America – as much as B.I.G.'s death. Do you have any idea how brilliant *Ready to Die* is? It's better than many Beatles albums I could name."

"So compare him to other dead entertainers. Not the last president people believed could change the world. An entertainer changes nothing. He moves you, emotionally, spiritually, but ultimately he's an entertainer. He's a luxury, not a necessity. The best politicians, Ari – they do stuff. They feed people. They punish criminals. They *help*."

"Well, I have yet to meet the politician who's done a thing for me," I said.

"And what do you *need*, other than a girlfriend?" asked Jimmy, reaching back for a beer even though he was driving. Jerod and Tim laughed.

"If you want to make this socio-economic, Jimmy, you've got no argument," I said. "JFK: silver-spooned and handsome. B.I.G.: obese and from the ghetto. Maybe you should rethink your grandstanding about luxuries and necessities."

"Your looks are not the world's political problem," said Jimmy.

"I'm just saying, Jimmy, that the world is filled with one-thousand B.I.G.'s for every one JFK. We are the first generation of college students for whom history books have acknowledged this – that *history*, such as it is, is as much about the actions of the poor and ugly masses as it is about the doings of the rich and comely."

"Well, wake me up when B.I.G. gets Castro on the phone," said Jimmy.

*   *   *

In bed that night I lay awake, pondering whether to call Barbara for Shelagh-related sympathy. My distress blared within me like a dozen alarm clocks. But I thought back to Jimmy's perspective of emotional luxuries versus necessity-driven actions. And I concluded my emotions were not reason enough to wake someone like my mom, who needed to work the next morning.

On a yellow legal pad I wrote: *Suicides, despite the embarrassing stigma, still receive more pity than those whose mental toughness prevents their self-*

destruction. And this is because the world only pays attention to actions, even though inactions are often more intrepid. This is why recovered addicts get more attention then those who are tough enough not to lapse in the first place.

Will I spend the rest of my life seeking to match the ecstasies Shelagh provided, aiming to redress the heartache she caused? Or will I reconcile myself to lesser feelings, terming such a settlement "maturity" or "reality?"

*   *   *

When my apartment buzzer sounded the day before graduation a part of me wished it were Shelagh at the door. But the first woman I saw was my mother: a thinner Barbara Segal than the one I'd last seen, her newly lanky thighs flattered by a long black skirt. I recalled a boyhood when those thighs were at my eye level. I took her hand and led her inside. Nicole and Neil followed us to the yellow upholstered couch. Nicole's eyes were wide, a teenager processing the wonderments of a college campus. She glanced around, absorbing the details of my apartment. Neil reclined on the couch, propping his head on the armrest. Barbara removed his black loafers. "Neil was up all night doing research for one of his never-satisfied clients," she explained.

"Nicole...," mumbled Neil under a yawn.

"Yes, Nicole had a lot of homework too," acknowledged Barbara. Neil removed his glasses and placed them in his shirt pocket. "When's your father arriving?" she asked.

"Eight," I said. "So Neil's got time to nap."

"I hate to keep us all just sitting here, in your apartment," Neil yawned.

"Ari and I can walk around the campus and come back," offered Nicole.

So I gave Nicole a basic tour: down Liberty Street, past Ambrosia, crossing Central Campus to the CCRB, circling back to the student union, finally WCNB on University Street. On we marched to Shapiro Library, climbing the stone steps, reaching the slim shadows of the entrance's corrugated pillars. It was a bright, balmy May afternoon with a mild breeze and clear skies. "All these places mean so much to me today," I said as we sat on the steps. "But maybe I get too attached to places. Like my bedroom at home – someone else is probably already sleeping in it. I guess college is the part of life where you learn not to get so emotional over places. Or people."

"You had a great four years though, didn't you?" she asked.

"I suppose."

"So speaking of emotional over people, did your mom tell you," she asked, eager to segue, "that I kind of have a boyfriend?"

"No," I said.

"Well, we've only fooled around twice. Nothing serious. But he's around all summer and we'll probably become official after we hook up next time."

"Is that how it works?" I mumbled, looking at the library.

She put her hand around mine. "You okay?" she asked.

"I can't stop thinking about this girl," I said. "Can we just stop by her place, really quick, before we head back? I just – I need to see her," I said.

When we reached South Quad I peeked inside the large front window. Tina was on the couch watching TV. Tina looked shocked to see me, let alone to see me with a high school girl for a sidekick. After greetings and introductions I asked whether Shelagh was in. Tina's expression turned sympathetic. "Ari, she didn't tell you?" she asked.

"Tell me what?"

"She's back home, in Berkeley. She wasn't sticking around for graduation. She left, like, two days ago."

The news that she'd left relieved me: for much of my agony had stemmed from the belief that she was on campus but ill-inclined to see me. Her unannounced departure eliminated the prospect of another encounter with her – and probably gave me more closure than I'd have gained from a face-to-face farewell.

I lamely tried salvaging the visit by inquiring about Tina's summer plans. She smiled affably and we chatted for another five minutes before wishing each other luck.

On the walk back to my apartment Nicole – when I explained to her the relief I felt – touched my back. "It'll make your mom so happy just to see you relaxed," she said.

* * *

When we got back to my apartment Barbara Segal and Robert Zinsky were sitting on the yellow couch, each smoking a cigarette, sharing a Coke can for an ash tray. It was the first time anything had ever been smoked in my residence.

I hadn't seen my father in 13 years, but he looked almost the same at 52 as he had at 39. He was still slim; he did not occupy his section of the couch, as thick men do. Rather, the couch seemed to surround him on all sides: there was room enough for two pillows behind him and beside him. His black, curly hair was saltier than I recalled, as was his goatee. The lines on his still-chiseled face didn't seem any more pronounced; but that might've been because when I'd seen him last, at age 9, I wasn't looking for them.

Playing a card game on the hardwood floor, at the opposite corner of the room, was a slender woman in a white blouse and pinstriped pants, who looked to be in her early thirties but whom I knew to be about 43 – for I knew Cam Clark was all of 26 when my father ran off with her. Cam's playing partner was a small blond girl in a denim skirt, pink t-shirt, and sandals. Sandra Clark, 6, looked exactly her age.

This was the first time I'd ever seen my stepmother and half-sister. They were absorbed in their rummy game, staring at their hands, adding to the discard pile. They were not distracted by our entrance, and I divined that today was a larger social challenge for them than it was for me.

Barbara said: "Cam, Sandra, this is Ari and Nicole." My stepsister and I waved. Nicole straightaway excused herself to check on Neil, now napping in my bedroom. As she departed I saw the wandering gray eyes of Robert Zinsky checking out her ass – an action for which I felt a mixture of empathy, humor, and disgust. Nicole closed the door to my bedroom and Robert said, "What's her mother look like?"

Barbara rolled her eyes and Cam, snatching up Sandra's discard, said, "Maybe you should ask Neil."

"Give me a break, Cam," said Robert. "I waited until the door was closed."

Cam added a ten of hearts to the pile. Sandra took it and triumphantly dropped her hand to the hardwood. "Gin!" she exclaimed. The young girl slid on her butt, around the card pile, and toward her mother's lap. "I beat you again!" she said. "Three in a row." Sandra pointed to her winning collection of tens, fours, and sixes. "Wasn't it obvious I was collecting tens?" she asked. She leaned back on her mother's lap and tilted her head up at Cam. Mimicking Sandra's clipped, dulcet voice, Cam said, "*Ob*viously." And then Sandra emphatically repeated, "*Ob*viously," and giggled.

"Can I play?" I asked, my voice cracking.

The Clarks looked up at me, surprised. "Of course you can play," said Sandra. "You're my brother."

"We're playing ten-card rummy," said Cam.

"*Gin* rummy," said Sandra.

After a few hands I glanced at Robert and Barbara, still smoking on the couch. As the link between the gathered parties, I felt a certain need to integrate them into a group conversation. "Did I mention who's speaking at graduation tomorrow?" I asked. "It's Tim Flagler – he graduated back in '87, and he started a software company that Microsoft just bought for $90 million."

"They couldn't get anyone higher profile?" said Robert.

"He's no Robert Zinsky, but the students know who he is," I said, drawing laughs from the assembled. "He gives a lot of money for renovations. They named a refurbished dorm in West Quad after him."

"Do you think you'll be like that after you've made your millions?" joked Barbara. "Returning for homecomings, giving speeches?"

"No," I said flatly, as if Barbara were truly grilling me on the subject. "When I make my money, my charities will be real causes. Diseases. Poverty. Not a university, which already makes millions in annual revenues."

I was hoping my sermon's emphasis on revenues would lasso Cam the accountant into the conversation. But she focused on the hand Sandra had dealt her. Meanwhile my parents puffed away.

Neil emerged from my bedroom, Nicole at his arm. "Look who I found," she said.

Neil and Robert shook hands. "Neil Segal."

"Pleasure," replied my father, dropping his cigarette nub into the can.

"Dad, smoking is retarded," said Sandra.

"I know, sweetie," said Robert. "I'm retarded about a lot of things."

Sandra burst into laughter, rolling onto her back, leaving her hand of cards exposed. She pointed at Robert, eyed me conspiratorially, and said through her giggles, "He said retarded." And she started laughing again.

Cam said flatly, "Sandra, we're going to dinner soon."

Sandra sat up, piped down, and we resumed our card game.

*   *   *

The restaurant was crowded with other graduates and their guests. The host led us to a long rectangular table, which was actually three square tables-for-two squished together. To excise myself from the tacit jockeying over who would sit where, I departed for the men's room, passing through a tiled hallway featuring black-and-white photos of the restaurant's founders on some stony Tuscan street.

I rolled up my sleeves and stood in front of the urinal, convincing my bladder it had work to do. And then Robert entered, positioning himself at the urinal next to me. For half a minute we were dry and silent.

I did what men sometimes do under these circumstances: I spied Robert's cock, noticing it was only slightly larger than mine. I recalled my younger years with him – showering at the beach, pissing at the ballpark – when I'd routinely observe his prick. How utterly immense he seemed to me then!

Robert backed away from his station without flushing. After washing he glanced at himself in the mirror, resting his moist hands on the black marble counter. We were alone in the men's room and I recognized an opportunity. I stepped toward him, shoving him between the two sinks, until his back was against the mirror. My right hand clasped his throat, my thumb on his Adam's apple. For the first time in my life, he was under my control. I could have done anything to him. His arms were inert by his side, as if in recognition of my power; he behaved like I had as a boy, resigned to a physical defeat that resistance would only forestall. My left fist smashed his nose. Blood spurted over his lips and dripped onto my tensed forearm, landing on his light blue dress shirt. Evidence. Proof to everyone at our dinner table that I'd swung and connected and avenged myself, though none of them would know what for.

I felt a quick, singeing sprinkle of wet drops on my face. My father had switched on a sink, pooled hot water in his ready hand, and splashed it in my direction. I released him and stepped back. Rather than pursuing me, which I'd have welcomed, he faced the mirrors and tended to his nose, running paper towels under the faucet and pressing them to his face.

Clamping his nose, he said with a voice both nasal and clear: "I'm astonished, Ari, that my presence still has the power to prevent you from pissing. I have no doubt that you could beat the hell out of me. My God, I see so much of myself in you. I've been married to Cam for what, more than fifteen years now? And for all that, I think that sometimes – maybe it's the father-son genetic stuff, maybe it's because we're both men – I think I sometimes I feel closer to you than I do to her."

"How poignant," I said.

"We'll tell them I got a nosebleed," he said, moving to practical matters. "You got me pretty good there. But I tell you, my son, I'd rather get socked in the bathroom than stay out there and watch as Cam intentionally sits next to Neil or your piece-of-ass stepsister. At least now I can come out of the bathroom and sit wherever they want me to sit. Which is hopefully next to your mom. She's better conversation than Cam, anyway."

"Cam doesn't seem too bad."

"I didn't say Cam was bad, I said Barbara was better. Your mom – I'd still be with her if she kept giving a shit about me after she'd had you."

"Now *you* sound like those Indians on reservations," I said.

"All right, let me tell you the real reason I came to your graduation," he said, twisting a sink knob, triggering a new water flow. "I want you to visit us, out in Albuquerque, sometime in the next year or so."

"Why?" I asked. The "year or so" seemed peculiar. He replied, "I'm not going to get into why, Ari. I'll just say that, in one year I might be as bald as you, and in two years Cam and Sandra might have a lot more money."

"Since when are you so oblique?" I asked. He dried his hands on his khakis.

"Since I don't want anyone but my lawyer to know the truth," he said. "I don't want or need the fake attention, Ari."

"And isn't that what you'd be getting from me?" I asked, looking straight at him.

"You can stand here and keep doing that pretend-to-hate-me thing," he said, his hands ministering to his nose. "But you're a better, tougher man because of me."

"Whatever helps your self-esteem," I said.

"Listen, Ari – can I trust you not to tell anyone I'm dying?"

"Yes," I said. "But I'm not promising I'll visit."

"Good enough," he said, discarding his wad of moist and bloody paper towels and grabbing some fresh ones. "Well, I'm gonna head back to the table. I'll tell them you're still on the can."

Needlessly washing my hands, I attempted to digest Robert's news, and my promise to safeguard it. A part of me hoped he'd die soon. For the sake of closure, our bathroom encounter couldn't be topped. And his death – well, it wouldn't be the death of much, other than an annual phone call. How alive is someone whom you haven't seen in 13 years? And how bereaved can you possibly be – or anticipate being – over someone you've never loved?

I longed to share the news with someone who could appreciate its particular insignificance to me. But not even Barbara was capable of that. I mused on how an ideal girlfriend would react to this news: she'd be familiar enough with my biography to comprehend how momentous, yet distinctly non-tragic, was the news of Robert's demise.

I leaned on the sink where he'd been sitting. My mind lapsed into gory fantasy:

I am bashing the head of Robert Zinsky, the God my father, into the marble tile of the bathroom wall. I treat his tumor-filled skull like a coconut, ramming it into the wall until I crack it. Bloody cranial liquids seep from the gash. Tissue from his cerebral cortex spills out, onto the black and white hexagonal floor tiles. I bash and bash and bash his head. With each bash, with each pulpy, mucous-colored drop of ooze, I keep asking him one simple question, a question I have learned from listening to rap music:

"What's my name? What's my name? What's my mother-fuckin' name?"

Leaning against the bathroom sink, bearing my weight on my arms, I felt heavier than I wanted to feel, given the wine glasses that would be raised and the applauses that would be clapped out in Ann Arbor that weekend.

I returned to the table and sat between Barbara and Nicole. Our first and last meal together as a family passed without incident.

End of Book the Second

Book the Third: Zinsky Gets His Chance

"Amid the seeming confusion of our mysterious world, individuals are so nicely adjusted to a system, and systems to one another, and to a whole, that, by stepping aside for a moment, a man exposes himself to a fearful risk of losing his place forever. Like Wakefield, he may become, as it were, the Outcast of the Universe."

— Nathaniel Hawthorne, from the last paragraph of "Wakefield"

"...anon, he heard a voice shouting afar, and fancied that it called his name....Poor Wakefield! Little knowest thou thine own insignificance in this great world! No mortal eye but mine has traced thee."

— Nathaniel Hawthorne, from the fifth paragraph of "Wakefield"

Chapter 11 – Zinsky the Waiter, Zinsky the Thief, Zinsky the Romantic

Six months after quitting my entry-level job at the accounting firm, I was broke. I owed $27,000 on nine separate credit cards, mostly from *Guide* expenditures. I was so desperate for cash I started working as a waiter at Stevie's Joint in Boston's South End. I had six dinner shifts a week. The nighttime hours allowed me to perform *Guide* duties all day. And I saved countless dollars because I got free dinner each shift, and brought home leftovers for tomorrow's breakfast and lunch. On Sundays I rested, watching football at home and eating cereal and phoning my mother and Jerod and Jimmy.

The *Guide* became a year-round endeavor. For not only did I have the annual yearbook and monthly emails – there was ZinskyQuintessential.com. Surely you recall the business climate of the late 90s: investors treated web sites of all stripes like rivers bearing gold. Many sites had negligible revenues and zero profits – yet they were established, hyped, and sold for millions to prospectors who feared missing out on the next century's California.

All a web site needed for marketplace viability was *stickiness*, to use the parlance of that era. Stickiness was a term relating to how many people – or eyeballs, as they were called back then – regularly visited a site. And for those eyeballs alone, many sites were appraised to have multimillion-dollar values.

So I attempted, in my first few years out of college, to lure eyeballs to ZinskyQuintessential.com. And I continued collecting email addresses from all the football fans I could find. By March, 2000, ZinskyQuintessential.com was boasting more than 15,000 monthly visitors – something to brag about, back then. How did it happen? A football journalist named Joel Pollack crossed my path at the ideal time.

He was the editor of *Pigskin Prattle*, the glossy football monthly at which I now preside. And though *Prattle* had – and still has – wealthy corporate owners, Joel ran it on a shoestring. He was the only employee. Everyone else was freelance. *Prattle* was one of two dozen magazines in the stable of Becker + Fliess A.D., a Berlin conglomerate that also owned a record label. All 24 books operated out of the same building in Manhattan.

Joel spotted me peddling my *Guides* in a downpour at the 1999 draft and introduced himself. Though I dismissed *Prattle* at the time as a magazine for lay fans rather than diehards, I paid immediate attention to the svelte and handsome married man (he sported a wedding band) offering me space under his wide red umbrella. He handed me a business card with a football emblem in the upper left. I reached into my soaked gym bag for one my cards.

Set against the dim cloudy morning, Joel's thick brown hair looked as dry as dust, despite the rain pelting his parasol. It was combed forward fashionably, rather than out of an urge to cover baldness, and the effect was a hairline that seemed to be rushing toward his thick bumpy nose, rather than receding. His errant blue eyes bulged forward too, seeming overlarge and wayward and not at all set within their sockets, even when they focused up at me and he said, "So you live in Boston? This might surprise you, but I went to Harvard." So began my first conversation with him. *Prattle*, he told me, had only recently established its own web site. And Joel was looking for low-cost ways to augment the site, so that he could compete with ESPN.com, TheSportingNews.com, and ProFootballWeekly.com. After our chat, he bought two *Guides* with a $20 bill (I was now charging $8 per pop) and suggested I put the change toward galoshes.

One week later he phoned. He asked if PigskinPrattle.com could "link" to ZinskyQuintessential.com. I was floored. Within a month, based solely on importing Joel's loyal readers, I had amassed 10,000 regular visitors. That number held steady until March of 2000 when, with fans eager to read about the next draft (in April), we reached the 15,000 mark. So now Joel's readers were exploring my site and receiving my monthly emails. I got regular emails from *Prattle* loyalists commending my lists and articles.

Regardless of the accolades, my site – and my entire operation – remained swamped in red ink. Even my income from waiting tables could not set my lifestyle at breakeven. I had no health insurance or dental coverage, I never bought new clothes, and on three occasions my phone service was axed because of late payments.

So I continued on as a waiter to improve my cash flow. My manager at Stevie's Joint, Patti Kinkade, happened to be a football junkie herself, a single mom who watched New England Patriots games with her twin 10-year-old boys. I considered her my mom-away-from-mom, and brought Barbara and Neil to see her during their annual visits.

Patti's sons, Otis and Art, lingered around the restaurant, doing their homework at vacant tables as their mother seated patrons and monitored the staff. My first interaction with them came during my first week on the job. Having cleaned out my cubicle at the accounting firm, I found myself with spare pin-ups of my favorite athletes: basketball star Jalen Rose in his Michigan uniform, football star Mo Lewis in his New York Jets gear. I gladly gave these posters to Otis and Art, who pronounced my name "Air-Yell" and begged to look at my "football book," which was the *Guide*.

By its fourth year, the *Guide* was no longer an assemblage of black and white photocopies, slapped together at Kinko's. I had upgraded, and now my *Guide* was replete with color photos and streamlined charts, all of which I produced on the accounting firm's scanners, computers, printers, and copiers. And how, you might ask, did I access this equipment, after quitting the firm and losing my privileges?

I became a thief.

First, I devised a way to enter the firm's ten-story building at night without use of my electronic key. From the inside, I had unlocked an unused first-floor window, which had been shut and shaded because it belonged, strangely, to a room where spare computer equipment was stored. One night, while I was still employed there, I tested my method by sneaking a small table outside and mounting it to reach the sill. The window slid open. I tore my shirt and scraped my stomach on the brick exterior as I pulled myself up. I hooked one arm, then the next, and fell head-first into the building, toppling a stack of empty cardboard boxes in the storage room.

I took the freight elevator to the ninth floor, where I'd worked and gained familiarity with the equipment and office layout. The computers were password protected; but I had cannily obtained many usernames and passwords from the IT department, words they had used to troubleshoot problems on my terminal. During these late-night biweekly burglaries I created an electronic template for both my newsletters and the *Guide* – with a professional-looking layout and color photos I stole and scanned from other magazines. I made frequent printouts for proofreading purposes; and in early March I emailed my final template to a local printer of glossy magazines, who within two weeks – slower printing gave me the discount rate – shipped thousands of copies to my basement apartment in Boston's North End. From there I printed my own mailing labels. I contacted UPS when it was time for my subscribers and advertisers to get their copies.

So you see – early March became like Christmas to me: I sent *Guides*, rather than cards, to everyone I knew.

My father didn't get a visit, but he always got a *Guide*. Nearly three years after his dramatic pronouncement at my graduation, he was still alive – running his software company and phoning me each Christmas. "When are you visiting?" he always asked.

"Never."

"You promised."

"I expressly did not."

"Isn't the fact that I paid for half your education worth something?"

"You told me you had one year to live. It's been almost three. Let me know when it's really one. Maybe I'll change my mind. But I probably won't." And then I hung up.

I sent Shelagh a *Guide* each year too, to her parents' address in Berkeley. Whether she received any of them I never learned. She never replied. I invariably enclosed a business card with a personalized note on the back:

1998: *I hope your senior year is going well. I always think about you and daily yearn for your forgiveness.*

1999: *I wish you could read my mind and see where my heart is when it comes to you. Good luck in law school, if that's where you've wound up.*

2000: *I wish you well and hope one day you'll again seek my friendship.*

I also sent *Guides* to Jerod, Jimmy, Kris, and Tim. Jimmy – but not so much Kris – I saw on my New York visits; while Jerod phoned me from Indiana every Sunday.

March and April, as a rule, were my toughest months. Printing 5,000 copies of the 128-page *Guide* and its updated *Late Edition* cost me nearly $17,000. Shipping the magazines set me back another $3000. I paid for this by taking cash advances on all nine of my credit cards, and by restructuring my University of Michigan loans to permit lower monthly payments over a longer time period.

In a context of vast, immediate debts, you dismiss smaller, remediable ones. As a result, I typically went without phone service in April and May because of unpaid bills. I regularly incurred my landlord's wrath for not paying rent until the 15th of those months, by which time I'd finally accumulated enough cash to pay him from tips at Stevie's.

I also developed a knack for finding persnickety savings/earnings opportunities: For example, I swiped all discarded bottles and cans from Stevie's Joint and recycled them; I thieved toilet paper and paper towels from the Stevie's bathrooms, so I'd never have to buy my own. I also found numerous blood centers throughout Massachusetts giving $50 to eligible donors. I routinely violated codes forbidding two donations in a 56 day period. Nary a fortnight passed without a needle in my left elbow.

As it happens, I still have several of my blood donor cards – they're in a desk drawer in my apartment. On the back of one of them is the phone number of a woman named Cara O'Sullivan. The front is dated 3/23/2000, and states that I have B+ blood. Ah, Cara – what hope she filled me with, for a two-day span! It was an unseasonably warm morning at a clinic near Chinatown. The nurses were dressed in skirts or short sleeves, and my 25-year-old mind drifted from debts and deadlines. In an instant my motives in donating were not fiscal: I longed for a lass to spy my bloodletting as a moment of unrehearsed altruism and on that basis become smitten with me.

I'm sitting on a beige leather seat; a thick plastic straw pierces my elbow skin, diverting my blood to a whirring device with rotating spindles. My red juice spins through the machine before leaking into the clear plastic sack. My left hand intermittently squeezes a rubber ball. An attractive brunette about my age – Cara – sits in the chair beside me. And I assume off the bat I have no chance with her. For three solitary years as a Boston bachelor have eroded my confidence. All my fears regarding Shelagh – that she would be the best and only sex I ever knew – have come true. I firmly believe I'll never fuck again. So despondent am I that I console myself with a thought that is nothing but a positive, motivational spin on my chaste self-prophecy: "Don't worry about women *yet*," I routinely muse. "Worry about them *after* the *Guide* is successful."

I tape handwritten reminders of my rationalized stoicism within the kitchen cabinets of my apartment. Every time I fetch my cereal I see – in indelible black ink on yellow legal paper – classic lines such as DON'T EVEN *THINK* ABOUT WOMEN, ZINSKY. YOU CAN'T *FUCK* THE *GUIDE* TOWARD SUCCESS, CAN YOU? In another cabinet, closer to my refrigerator, I post another note: GET BACK TO WORK, ZINSKY. YOU CAN'T *EAT* THE *GUIDE* TOWARD SUCCESS, CAN YOU?

Heedless of these motivational tricks, I flirt with Cara as she sits beside me in her skirt, her smooth fingers clasping her own foam object. Instead of inquiring about *her* activities, I ramble on about mine, certain that *she* will be the woman seduced by my *Guide* endeavors and my life story. At length I ask if she'll have a drink with me some time. "Sure," she says, and I pen her phone number on my blood card.

She never returns my repeated calls. And I tell myself what I always tell myself: "It doesn't matter. I'd never have burnt for _____ as I did for Shelagh, so any romance was bound to fail anyway."

But my desire for female validation does not disappear. If anything, it redoubles, especially when I sneak into my former office or write a singularly eloquent phrase about a quarterback. For all my efforts, I want – nay, deserve – recognition; and *sex!* After all, I am a risk taker, gambling my fiscal future on a dream project. I am as bold – nay, bolder – as any young director of independent films or longhaired composer of acoustic guitar ballads. But who is noticing *my* art? Where are *my* screeching, adoring, female groupies?

So desperate am I for figurative breast milk that I ponder trekking to New York to visit my stepsister, who seems like the only woman left on the planet who finds me appealing. I send an email in advance of my visit, seeking sympathy for my *Guide's* struggles, seeking intimacy by requesting she keep such struggles a secret from our respective parents. Nicole's reply moves me to tears: *I believe in you* is the subject line of her email, the body of which reads, *Your career choice inspires me more than you know. Just stay true to yourself and don't let the pressures of this world make you stray.* The next paragraph, of course, is a lengthy rundown of all the boys she's hooking up with at Columbia University, where she's now a sophomore, long past her first serious boyfriend, whom she'd mentioned at my graduation. In the weeks to come I cancel my New York visit, citing time constraints and financial hardship.

One Sunday evening a few weeks later I attend a yoga class at my neighborhood gym. Exercise isn't my purpose – if anything, the stretches and twists expose how inflexible I am, despite weekly five-mile runs and basketball games. No, I'm in class because – while idly walking home, in the aftermath of a jog – I've spotted dozens of young women in tight pants entering the gym, and like a dog I intend to follow their rears until I'm shoed away. When the class ends, I'm exhausted. I remain seated on my moist mat as the spry women hurry out. I panic and literally shout out: "Would any of you like to have dinner with me?" Most of them keep walking. Three of them smile before returning with intensity to the packing of their belongings. Meanwhile, the instructor rolls her eyes. She has ignored me throughout the class, refusing to adjust my execrable form.

In the shower I ponder my solitude and curse my fiscal condition. I need $1500 in six days if I want UPS to ship the *Late Edition* of my year 2000 *Guides*. Waiting tables won't even get me halfway. Then it dawns on me: I have so much sports knowledge – why aren't I using it? I get dressed and spend Sunday night bouncing from bar to bar in the Boston area, looking for a bookie who'll take a wager on a pro basketball game.

Inside the dimly lit Gridiron Lounge in South Boston I'm eyed wearily by a double-chinned, gray-haired man on a stool. He squints up from his newspaper when I ask, "Are you Upshaw?"

"Name and phone number," he says, as if I'm ordering a pizza. "You got a drivers' license?"

I peel out my New York license – which still has my Townsend Avenue address on it – and he sighs. "This is no good. Look, just tell me your address. No, fuck that – you a student?"

I tell him I work at Stevie's Joint on Columbia Street. "Look, Ariel, I'll be frank with you," he says. "You lose this bet I'm coming to Stevie's to collect. If you can't pay you will get hurt. Are you prepared to pay me?"

"Are you prepared to pay *me*?" I retort.

Upshaw cuffs his barstool neighbor on the shoulder. "Hey, Sweeney, tell this kid I pay my debts."

"Always," mutters Sweeney, before turning back to the big screen television. Sweeney is about my age. He has thick, parted blond hair, and his cheeks protrude over his lower face, as if on the verge of avalanching.

Not about to question Sweeney's objectivity, I declare $750 on a match between the Golden State Warriors and Vancouver Grizzlies. The Warriors stink but there's no way they're losing by nine in Vancouver.

When Vancouver wins by 12, I spend the next day in hiding, arriving early at Stevie's under the pretense of helping Patti Kinkade slice fruit for a catering job. "I had it down in my planner," I tell her, when she insists she had not assigned me to the event.

I wind up playing tic-tac-toe and hangman with Otis and Art. Half an hour before my shift begins, Patti disrupts my diagramming. "Your friend Sweeney is outside," she says. I nod – this is what I've feared – but worry little about anything gruesome befalling me on pedestrian-packed Columbia Street.

Sweeney is flanked by two white kids, younger than I, both of whom wear gray hooded sweatshirts and have the crew-cut appearance of boxers or weightlifters. To my consternation the street is nearly empty – where are all the cars racing for green lights, the yuppies walking their dogs? "This can be easy or hard," says Sweeney. The young man on his left, to my amazement, has a pair of brass knuckles, a weapon which to that point I've never associated with real life.

I've prepared my speech and I deliver it calmly. "If you guys can come back after my shift tonight," I say, "I'll have the money. I'm about a hundred short right now."

"Unacceptable," says Sweeney. He kicks me in the nuts and in a flash his henchmen have thrown me to the concrete sidewalk. I cover my face, fearing the brass, but in fact the be-knuckled soldier is groping my jeans. I'm still on the ground when he's extracted my wallet. His colleague helps me up. We follow Sweeney and Knuckles to a nearby ATM booth. One by one, we insert my plastic cards into the machine and extract the cash as I blurt out my pin numbers. I'm so stretched to my credit limits I need five cards to reach $750. Then the four of us are alone in the cramped room. Knuckles tosses my wallet back to me. I drop it; my hands quiver as I retrieve it from the filthy floor of gray tiles. "Sorry for the trouble, guys," I say, wondering if they'll ever leave. The three of them stand at the counter; Sweeney is smoothly shuffling a pile of deposit slips. He says, "I'll be in the car," and departs. The henchmen walk me back to the restaurant.

Outside of Stevie's, just as I think I'm off the hook because there's a roller-blader and two skateboarding teens across the street, Knuckles splits my left ear with his metallic fist. As they run off I stay flat on the sidewalk, lest by rising I incite their return. I use my shirt collar as a poultice, pressing it to my aching jaw. My mind scrambles: how will I explain my blood-spattered shirt to Patti Kinkade? Will I have enough time before my shift to staunch my bleeding with paper towels?

Soon there are no paper towels left in the restaurant bathroom; my ear won't stop spouting. Inspecting myself in the recently Windexed mirror, I realize I may need stitches – there's a small tear where my ear lobe should meet my upper jaw – and my skin won't close, it won't stop gushing. Do hospitals accept credit cards, I naively wonder?

Holding the restroom's last wad of paper towels to my left lobe, I find Patti talking Spanish with our chefs and dishwashers, all of whom hail from El Salvador, half of whom are in America illegally. They behold my condition and go silent – the only sound is the sizzling fryer. "Oh, Lord," says Patti, rushing up to me. She's on her toes, removing her reading glasses to inspect my ear. "I got in a fistfight with Sweeney," I calmly explain. She dashes to her office and phones a cab. "Should I call your mother?" she asks upon returning. "It's no big deal," I say. We hear a honk outside. "We'll discuss this later," she says, escorting me by the arm to the waiting yellow vehicle. Within thirty minutes I'm numbed and stitched and released from the local hospital, having promised my nurse I'd go home and take it easy. But by dinnertime I'm back at the restaurant in a clean shirt – my return cab stops first at my apartment, where I change clothes. I pilfer $20 from the register to pay the driver, pledging to deduct the sum from my tips once the night is through. As for the hospital bill – it is something I'll deal with when it arrives.

Later that night Patti pulls me aside. "Is what happened today something I need to know about?" she asks.

"No," I say. "It won't happen again."

"If it does, you know I have little choice but to do something I'd rather not do."

"I know. And I'll deserve it."

"Okay," she says. "You're sure you're okay to work the next few days?"

I nod. And just then, my favorite customer enters and seats herself at a window table. "Your remedy," Patti mutters.

*   *   *

The first time I saw Sandy Appleton it was my third day on the job: March 16, 1998. She wore a red Kangol hat to cover her baldness, but her face alone was riveting, a tanned, diamond-shaped symmetrical ideal, smooth and sleek and with a nose profile so perfectly triangular yet slightly curving, it could've been the sail of a ship, with her blue eyes crisp like swimming pool water. She set her crutches down on the floor beneath her table. Within seconds her glasses were on, her laptop was out, and she was swallowing pills straight from a plastic orange container. Later, when I read the name on her credit card – a casual Sandy, as opposed to a form-letter Sandra – I had a name for my new favorite customer, my new crush, the sympathetic slender woman who tipped me 20 percent despite the slow service I'd provided while still learning my way around Stevie's.

She was sexy, but she was sick too. Of that I was certain. In my first year as a waiter she hobbled on her crutches and never bore weight on her left leg. She always wore one of four furry Kangol hats – red, beige, white, or black – to cover her baldness.

By my second year her blond hair had returned and the crutch was gone. Soon her limp was gone too and – to my infinite delight – she wore skirts in the summertime.

Yet the pills remained, as did the plastic orange container.

By then Sandy Appleton appeared like a typical customer in our upscale establishment: possessed of general health and a lucrative office job.

But I remembered her secret history.

And I pined that one day she'd be privy to mine.

*   *   *

I approach Sandy's table with a menu. "I know what I want," she says before I arrive. "The turkey on sourdough, Russian dressing on the side please, with a water and a Diet Coke with lemon." I grin and turn away. This is her usual order and I know it by heart, even if she doesn't know me from Abraham, after my three years at her service.

She swallows a few pills with ease, tilting her slender neck back. Her Adam's apple pulses. The water I've brought her goes untouched. She removes the lemon garnish from her cola and eats it, wrapping the rind in a napkin. I watch her from the kitchen counter while tucking sliced bread onto soup plates. The chef, Hector Perlera, toasts Sandy's sourdough and spoons her Russian dressing into a ramekin. "*Tu amor?*" he asks.

"*En mi sueños,*" I sigh. Hector works a double nearly every day and typically naps between shifts. That's how I learned that *sueños* is Spanish for dreams.

Sandy's hair is like a teenage boy's, tapered in visible layers, as if freshly barbered. Her face, with the blond hair, reminds me of the actress Mary Martin in the movie version of *Peter Pan*, which Barbara had taken me to see as a boy at the West Egg Public Library. Sandy seems to be in her early 30s. She wears tight, pinstriped pants and a thin wool sweater top. The top is not tight, but it holds back ample breasts – not as protrusive as, say, my stepsister's, but possessed of a greater circumference.

By the time I deliver her sandwich her laptop is on the table. She holds her prim, bespectacled visage, with its clipped blond coiffure, about an inch from the screen. And I wonder: What's she reading so intently, with her snapping blue eyes behind their glasses?

I am stunned to see that of all things, she is digesting a *New York Times* article relating to the 2000 NFL draft. Is she a football fan? A diehard, even? Is it possible, then, that she might know *who I am?*

I forget the pain in my jaw and in my ear; I forget my worries over how on earth I'll afford to ship my *Late Editions* or pay the hospital. And in an instant I unlearn every tenet of waiter-customer etiquette I have mastered. My belief in romantic karma is rekindled for the first time since Shelagh destroyed it. My heart races and I reach for Sandy's hand. My legs give out; I fall down sideways, in a heap, my entire frame overcome by a down-dragging rigidity. I fall swift and stiff like a tree, and on the way down my forehead slams the edge of the table and snaps back.

I next remember sitting up in Patti Kinkade's office, with Hector Perlera attending to me. For the second time that day my shirt is spattered with blood. I finger my left ear, relieved that my pricey stitches are still intact. "You faint," declares Hector. He and I are limited to the present tense in each other's languages.

"*Quien trabaja para me?*" I ask, wondering who's served the customers and wiped the tables in my absence.

"Nobody," he says, his mustache lifting at the corners. "Very slow tonight."

Only one hour has passed. I drink a glass of water and return to the floor as if nothing has happened, waving off my overfriendly coworkers, jesting that they are more concerned with hogging the tables – and the tips – than my recuperation. "That nerdy blond tipped you 20 percent," the hostess informs me. "She must have been concerned."

"She doesn't even know my name," I reply.

By the end of the night I've sworn my coworkers to secrecy: They can't tell Patti I've fainted, because I can't afford to lose my job. I can't even afford to lose one shift.

And at the end of a long day – a day when my body has bled and collapsed – I do not head home to sleep. No. I board the subway and go to the downtown offices where I used to be employed. And why? So I can continue toiling on the *Guide* that will give Sandy Appleton, if she ever learns my name, reason to believe we belong together.

Chapter 12 – Hey Diana

It was usually ten at night by the time I scaled the brick wall of the accounting firm's office and pushed through the unlocked window into the storage room. So on almost all occasions the building was empty. And I was free to mine its resources (paper, pens, staples, printer ink) and plunder its technology without getting caught by security or a late-shift employee.

Imagine: the 25-year-old Zinsky lurking in the dark, vacant office, his matted clothes smelling like French fries, his waiter's apron still stuffed in his jacket pocket. He is slouched over a Xerox copier-cum-scanner the size of a small piano. Tonight's mission? Printing four copies of the *Late Edition*: one for myself to proofread, one for Otis and Art to toy with, one for Joel's feedback, and one for my printer to assess costs of full-scale glossy reproduction. *The Late Edition* is shipped exclusively to my 372 "platinum" members, updating the 200-page annual *Guide* that all subscribers receive.

The only persons I've ever encountered during my late night frolics are the trio of Spanish-speaking janitors – also from El Salvador – who vacuum floors and dump trash and wipe windows. They suspect nothing about me. They recognize me from my days as an employee, unaware that I'm now an outsider. I smile as they dust the three never-used smaller copiers, which stand in the shadow of the marvelous machine I'm using. I'm hoping my grin eases their frustration – since my presence at the alpha Xerox prevents their task completion. Too bad for them – it takes 20 minutes to print four *Late Editions,* and I'm not going to lose that time should a janitor accidentally push the "stop" button during overzealous dusting.

On this night I can tell from the bleach-scent of the bathrooms that the janitors have come and gone. The office corridors are dark in their wake. Lights shine only from the copy corner. Within minutes the alpha Xerox spews the *Late Edition* and I'm at my former cubicle leaving *Guide*-related voicemails for Joel and my printer. My soul is alive! I'm seizing my fate – my dream – by the horns and making it happen, by hook or by crook! My blood races with an elation I am certain – certain! – no honest nine-to-fiver can ever feel. I am bucking the system and getting away with it! "Zinsky," I tell myself, "you were, and are, correct! You are different from all the rest! If a typical child's fantasy is roaming unbound in a toy store or confectionery, then yours – all grown up – is to be untrammeled in an office! You have not survived a wretched childhood in vain! You are decidedly not a well-adjusted nine-to-fiver! Let the Jerods and the Jim-mies, the Krises and the Tims, have their risible road trips and their den-tal plans and their two-week vacations and their trips to the movies. Let them take the safe route. You shall gun for a one-time jackpot, rather than 20 years of gradual gains!"

A successful *Guide* could make me the Dickensian hero of my own life – could provide indisputable evidence that all my beatings and suf-ferings and subsequent musings had amounted to something: I'd have risen from my circumstances and triumphed. I'd have earned the right to guiltlessly share my story as a tale of valor. For if a poor person and a rich person have lived the selfsame lives prior to the rich one's for-tune, it is the rich one who enjoys the luxury of sitting fireside and spinning biographical yarns. The poor one sounds like a complainer, even if his story, up to a certain point, is identical to the fireside ramble.

The *Guide* could deliver me from my past. If professional mountain climbers got depressed upon returning from skyward journeys, ex-changing peaks and valleys for streets and sidewalks; if superstar ath-letes dreaded their boring retirements, with nothing in Monday-to-Friday life matching the intensity of championship competitions; then

I, too, was in a lofty category, battling an inner discontent that would never die until I'd returned to the astronomical lust levels Shelagh had established. For my life had featured 20 years of solitude prior to her arrival; and she was my Mount Everest, my Super Bowl, my World Series. And rather than writing off the ecstasy as a generic youthful experience, rather than getting past it as the inevitable by-product of an imbalanced tryst – I became driven by a desire to lead my life in such a manner as to recapture that ecstasy. If a first taste of ice cream is all you need to crave it forever – well, you're in good shape if your first flavor was vanilla, or some other variety that's not hard to find. But to attain the flavor I sought – only a jackpot would procure it. Gatsby purchased a West Egg manse just to live across the bay from Daisy Buchanan. I too would use commercial means to justify romantic ends.

But for me there was no Daisy – no former flame dreaming of one last romp within my chambers. I would never get Shelagh back – for I had never truly had her in the first place. Shelagh had left me with the scent of a Daisy but not a single flower. And maybe that was why I had slapped her all those years ago, and why for all my whimpering I didn't entirely regret it.

*   *   *

The cubicles were set up mazelike, surrounded by a rectangular perimeter of darkened offices with glass doors. As I left my voicemail for Joel I saw a light go on in one of them – and my heart nearly stopped.

I hung up and feared for my entire enterprise. I shut down my computer and sprinted to the freight elevator, jabbing the button several times in rapid succession. It was then I realized my four *Late Editions* were still printing at the Xerox. Reasoning rapidly that I'd be incriminated if I left them behind – so the risk in fetching them was necessary and proper – I hustled to the copy corner, from where I peered back to the lone lighted office. Just then a familiar face emerged and shrieked – she'd spotted me. "Hey Diana," I said with a strained calm, raising my hand in greeting as if it were high noon and we were still coworkers. She had frozen in place but now looked quizzical. "Is that – Ari? What – wow, this is a random surprise."

I had met her during my first few weeks at work, when she had provided me and three other hires with our orientations and briefed us on benefits and sexual harassment policies. She assisted the human resources head, Amy DeSilva, with whom she shared an office. I was flattered Diana Kennedy had remembered my name and was relieved it was she and not Amy emerging from the office. For Amy had reprimanded me twice for using firm resources for *Guide* purposes. Still, redhanded was red-handed: I settled on my method for earning Diana's clemency and proceeded forthwith.

"You'll never believe what I'm up to," I said.

"You scared me," she said. "How'd you get in?"

I admitted my means and handed her some pages I'd intended for Otis and Art. "So – this magazine is how I make a living now," I concluded. "But the truth is, I'm losing money to produce it, and sneaking around like this and waiting tables is the only way I can stay in business. Please, please, please don't bust me, Diana. If you only knew how badly I want to make this magazine work. My site gets 15,000 monthly eyeballs."

She laughed. "Do you really think I would bust you?" she said. Only then did I relish the fact that she was in her twenties too – and though her human resources position gave her a type of authority, she was likely predisposed to favor an individual's quest over a corporation's coffers. She hinged fluidly at the waist to tie her low-cut sneaker, and rose again. "What brings *you* here?" I asked, now that I was off the hook.

"I had yoga, so I was in the neighborhood, and then I wanted to see if I'd gotten an email from Harvard," she said. "But no word yet. I applied to business school. I don't have Internet at home."

"I did yoga once," I replied. I told my tale with certain omissions. We sat in her office and caught up on our two-and-a-half year separation. I was comforted she'd come from yoga – for even if I reeked of canola oil and mixed marinades, she was probably too self-conscious of her own odors to think ill of me. At length she shut down her computer and slung her yoga bag over her shoulder. Something in the gesture alarmed me. I fought an urge to exclaim, "Please don't leave me here!" I suppose it's hard not to feel abandoned when someone intrudes on your solitary activity and seems relatively indifferent to it, skipping off to their next appointment. I rarely felt lonely or isolated, working diligently in the office on the *Guide* – but Diana's arrival and imminent, dispassionate exit clued me to the emotional realities of my nightly condition.

I racked my mind for excuses to accompany her to Cambridge, where she had mentioned she lived. I said, "Why don't you wait up for me? I'm actually meeting up with a pal who goes to Harvard Law."

Diana teased me – the late hour made her believe I was coyly describing a booty call. All at once, I was as nervous as I'd been when she first found me in the building.

*   *   *

The Red Line subway train rumbled out of the city. A strand of her straight red hair bounced jauntily along the black shoulder strap of her yoga bag. "What happened to your ear?" she asked, pointing to my bandaged left lobe.

"Shaving mishap," I said on the spot. We rode on silently until I worried our non-chatting would doom me to never seeing her again. "Look," I said, gesturing at the river view beyond the train's window. The Charles was an impressionist painting, lemony reflections of city lights streaking shapelessly across the black surface. She nodded. "I bet it gets kind of old for you," I added, amending my astonishment. "Still," I continued, "maybe you should enjoy the view now, because when you're at Harvard you probably won't be crossing the river too often."

She glanced out the window before turning back to me. Her eyes were a stony, misty color on the blue-gray border, like a wet baby elephant. I sensed she was put off by the intensity of my comment – reflecting, as it did, that I was thinking a little too much about her river crossings. It was then I knew: I burned enough for Diana to become irrational. Not irrational like I'd been for Shelagh or like I could be, in fantasies, for Sandy Appleton. There was security in Diana. If Shelagh had been an inferno and Sandy could be a conflagration, then Diana was a fireside. Maybe, in the diminished heat, I'd be comfortable reciting my stories.

I reminded myself that I had no evidence for Diana's attraction to me. I ditched my chatty sycophancy for churlish skepticism. "So – what do you think Harvard's going to do for you?" I asked. "Are there better ways to spend $60,000?"

She bopped my bald head with her yoga bag. "Not everyone wants to wait tables every night, just to run their own business," she grinned. I noticed, for the first time, that she wore a necklace with a silver cross on it, the pendant shining against the coal background of her sweatshirt.

The train jerked to a stop at Central Square. Diana stood. I stood too. "You're getting off here?" she asked. For Harvard was one stop away. "Yeah, my friend lives on Magazine Street," I lied.

I couldn't stand for her to walk away. I felt an urgent need to blurt out something before she unceremoniously departed and what came out of my mouth – of all the things a jittery young man could possibly say – was: "Did you know I have a stepsister named Nicole? She almost went to Harvard but didn't get in. She – would it be all right if I walked you home?"

"Sure," said Diana, grinning. I walked alongside her, leery I'd already spoken too much of myself. "I have an older brother, Tom," she said when I asked. "He's 30, married, and owns his own place in Hingham. My parents worship him. I think *that* – to answer your question – is my Harvard factor. Them. If I go to Harvard, they'll be off my back for two years. I know that seems like a stupid reason to do something. But the firm is paying a third of my tuition and my dad promised he'd pay the rest if I got accepted. So what's the harm? For me, it's not really a question of squandering $60,000."

"I see," I said.

We reached her house. I stood a yard away from her, my back against a lamppost. At that distance she had little reason to anticipate a quick-strike kiss. I ached to hold her face but feared my own despondency in the wake of a rejection. The risk of a failed kiss – and therefore never again seeing her in a romantic context – frightened me as if my life were in the balance. Whereas saving my lip-lock attempt for a later night – or rather, simply gaining consent to call her for a future date – would infuse my life with hope, or the necessary illusion of it, a lottery ticket purchased days before the drawing.

I stepped off the curb and into the street, leveling my height with hers. She was a little over six feet. Length pervaded her features: her neck seemed elongated, the throat soaring high above the collarbone;

her arms gave a slinky impression of reach and extension, stretching upward in imitation of a yoga pose she must have done earlier in the evening. The lamppost light shone down on us, our lanky shadows pinstripes on the pavement – black, faceless, mimes without their masks. "Oh anonymous shadow," I wondered, "How can I possibly be of use to this other slender shadow, which seems to have everything a slender shadow could want?"

"Diana," I said, "Thank you so much for being cool about my sneaking around. I – you realize on some level my life is in your hands. This is an extraordinary blackmail opportunity for you."

"I admire what you're doing," she said.

It took all the strength I had left not to move forward and embrace her. "I hope you keep checking your email at the office," I said.

"Oh, I'll be back tomorrow," she said. With this she turned and walked toward the dark green triple decker. A porch light switched on, revealing two wooden doors with peeling red paint. At the steps she turned and said, "Thanks for walking me home." Then she was inside.

Later that night I lay awake, despite several seminal discharges. My heart and mind and groin pulsated. I donned my navy blue Michigan bandana, my baggy Michigan basketball shorts, and set off for a jog. And wouldn't you know it? After 45 minutes or so, I found myself at the lamppost in front of Diana's triple decker. The lights were off and all seemed quiet. I lingered for a moment by her front steps, then continued running.

Chapter 13 – Diana's Acceptance

The next night was like any other: after waiting tables, I scaled the brick wall of my former office building and pushed myself through the first-story window. My leg cramped upon landing and I sat stretching on the floor beside boxes of paper for a good five minutes. I pondered what I'd say if I saw Diana again.

If she likes you, she likes you. I repeated the phrase to myself as I ascended in the freight elevator. I recalled my early feelings for Shelagh: When the strength of my lust was so powerful I'd have overlooked her cruelty just to savor her company. Distilling the lesson to my dealings with Diana, I lectured myself: *Zinsky, have the balls to be yourself with Diana. If she likes you the way you wish to be liked, then your actions and answers – short of brutality or overt racism – will not be deal-breakers for her. And if she does not like you the way you wish to be liked, then your time is better spent on the* Guide.

I was sitting at my former cubicle, dialing Joel Pollock, when Diana appeared in the light of my computer monitor. Her red hair was down and her silver pendant was tucked inside her maroon sweatshirt. "Think tonight's the night?" I asked, hanging up.

"I'm nervous," she said. "That must mean something."

"Do you want me to leave the office while you check?"

"Don't be silly," she said.

"Well, shall we?" I asked.

Inside her office I spied her fingers as she typed her username and password: *DKennedy* and *cupcake*, of all things. As the asterisks hiding *cupcake* appeared on the screen she said, "I have the lamest password of all time."

"Don't reveal it to a burglar like me," I said.

"I can always change it," she said.

"Mine was *Jalen*," I said. "He's my favorite basketball player."

"I remember that, actually," she said, sitting at her desk.

"You remember my *password?*"

"No! Just the name Jalen Rose. Don't you remember, during orientation?" she said. "At the end I asked if anyone had any questions. You raised your hand and asked if we were allowed to put posters in our cubicles. Everyone started laughing but you were serious. And the next day, I admit it, I wanted to see your posters. And one of them was of Jalen Rose."

I was processing whether to rejoice over her memory of Jalen Rose when she shrieked. "I got *in*, Ari! I got *in!*" She leaned forward, her face close to the monitor. She had enough presence of mind to print the congratulatory email before shoving away from her desk and moving toward me with three quick bunny hops. She threw her arms around me. "Whooooh!" she shouted. She led me by the arm to the copy corner where ten copies of her acceptance message were waiting. She held the printouts close to her face, re-reading several times. "Is this the greatest moment of your life?" I asked.

She looked up at me. "It's up there. I'm so happy right now, I almost don't know what to do with myself."

"Call your folks. Call Tom out in Hingham."

"They're in bed by nine," she said. "I'll call my housemates." She scurried into her office and called. They agreed to meet at a Cambridge bar called The Cellar. She invited me to come along.

And I held my breath, believing this could be one of my life's greatest nights too.

She saw me wincing as we descended steps to the subway platform. I was sore from the previous night's jog, having surpassed my typical 45-minute limit. "Are you okay?" she asked.

"Running injury," I muttered.

"I didn't notice it yesterday."

"I didn't have it yesterday."

"I never imagined you were such a jock," she said, sliding her pass through the reader and pushing through the turnstile.

"Sometimes we do things just to combat the initial perceptions others might have of us," I said. The train arrived and we boarded. We were quiet for a while, sitting in the hard rattling seats. "So – it bothers you to be perceived as *not* a jock?" she said.

I stole a glance at her slender, muscular legs in their black yoga pants. Her legs slanted diagonally outward from her waist, forming a triangle with the grimy subway floor. I mused for ten seconds on how to reply. Then I began: "Women," I said, "have good reasons for being picky with men. But when women reject you – you still take it personally. It makes you want to tweak your appearance or personality in a way that will beautify your mating call, and make women respond to it *like* they respond to jocks, or to the lead singer of the band with his long hair and acoustic guitar. At bottom, my drive in sports is rooted to a yearning for female acceptance. Or a belief that such acceptance will arrive when I've changed enough from the geeky unathletic boy I was for the first 20 years of my life. Because girls didn't come *near* that boy. They ran like I was the elephant man. And I don't care how much love I receive for the rest of my life. I will never unlearn my lonely boyhood. Never."

I imagine Diana exerted some discipline to maintain eye contact with me for the entire sermon. I was embarrassed to have wound up holding forth about my life on a night that belonged to her. "I'm so sorry," I said. "You touched a nerve but it's just uncool for me to ramble on like that when we've got things to celebrate."

With her yoga mat she lightly tapped the top of my head: the softest, slowest touch, an onomatopoetic *tap* like a raindrop, leaving you to wonder if you indeed felt it or if your skin's experience was driven by imaginative apprehension. "No worries," she said. "I'm the one who asked the question. I'm glad I did, before we meet my roommates and become part of a group conversation."

"Right," I said. I looked out the window at the glimmering Charles. I held back with what I really wanted to look at, and what I really wanted to do. At length I reached for her pendant, no longer tucked in. She remained still while the cross rested in my palm. My heart pounded. "Are you religious at all, Ari?" she asked.

My answer hid honesty and diplomacy behind a reworded cliché. "I'm very faith-based without being theistic, if that makes any sense," I said. "My faith in the *Guide* is what sustains me." The train screeched to a halt at Central Square, saving me from further reply.

She walked beside me on the breezy street, offering a profile of her face in the refulgent streetlights. A dangly red tendril fell past her prominent cheekbone; she brushed it aside but it fell again and she left it alone. "How religious are you?" I asked.

"Not as religious as my parents. Or as Tom is turning out to be. But I go to church on Sunday, if that's what you want to know."

"With your family?"

"No, but usually my roommate Lori comes with me. You'll meet her tonight."

"I haven't ever been to church," I said. "My mom's Protestant and my dad's Jewish. But neither of them really gives a shit."

"You're welcome to come with us sometime," said Diana.

Recognizing a chance to get her phone number, I reached inside my jacket for my outdated Palm Pilot – a corporate gift Diana had presented to me and the new hires – and dropped it to the sidewalk. "I don't think I have your digits," I said, kneeling to pick it up, disappointed our scene would not play out like a dopey movie in which Diana, too, would crouch to retrieve my Palm, and the two of us would wind up necking on our knees.

She gave me her number and it took all my grit and restraint not to hold her hand as we continued walking to the bar.

*   *   *

While Diana got drunk with her roommates Lori and Harper, I stayed sober and excused myself after one hour, citing the fatigue of my restaurant shift. In reality I had determined that I would not get any more one-on-one time with Diana. I also had to put some finishing touches on the *Late Edition*, which was shipping in four days – but only if I came up with enough cash to balance my accounts with UPS, which were still in arrears from the *Guide's* shipments one month earlier.

I hawked my Palm Pilot on eBay for $35, after uploading its contents to my desktop; I worked double shifts at Stevie's, begging my coworkers to cover for them; I took the subway to two suburban blood banks where I had not yet donated.

I remained hundreds of dollars short. So I did what anyone might have done with hundreds of loyal magazine readers depending on him: I wrote a check for the entire amount, trusting UPS would ship my *Late Edition* rather than holding them until my check cleared. My check would bounce, of course, but by then the *Late Edition* would be in subscribers' hands, which was all that mattered to me. The bank would charge me an overdraft fee, but so what? The *Late Editions* would ship.

There was a stack of 372 *Late Editions*, all of which were packed in labeled envelopes and piled in the first-floor hallway of my apartment building, where the UPS driver could reach them. I departed for Stevie's Joint and trusted the magazines would be gone when I returned later that night.

They remained.

When I called UPS customer service I was shocked by the explanation. "Your checking account has been frozen by the Massachusetts Department of Revenue," said the phone rep. "It says right here, *Failure to pay state taxes.* We phoned in your routing number to our collection service and this is what came up."

"But that makes no sense. Taxes aren't due yet," I said. "And I filed early this year. They owe *me* money."

The UPS talker had no more specifics; she urged me to contact the state. When I did the next morning, I learned that the Commonwealth was investigating my enterprise. "You've filed as an LLC for three straight years," explained an employee. "But according to our records, you've been employed at Stevie's Joint for over 40 hours per week, and you haven't been declaring all your tips."

"But what can I do *right now* so I can still use my checking account?" I screamed. "For the LLC I'm running, which I assure you is not fictional, and which you can learn about at ZinskyQuintessential.com, I need to pay UPS by day's end. How can I do that? And if I can't, what's the soonest I can do that?"

I was told I'd have to wait until the State recouped the thousands it was missing in unclaimed tips. Meanwhile, my paychecks at Stevie's would be garnished and my checking account frozen.

In haste I moved my *Late Editions* back into my basement apartment, stacking them on the floor. I spent the rest of the morning composing a mass email to the 372 Platinum Members, assuring them they'd get their *Editions* in one week's time – still three or four days prior to the actual draft date in late April. I explained that the delay was occasioned by a need to gather more breaking news.

In the afternoon I mollified all the grumbling Platinum Members who'd replied to my email. I also brainstormed for ways to ship the *Edition* over the next seven days.

When I got to Stevie's Joint – after stopping back at the hospital to get my stitches removed – my timecard was missing from the wall-bound slots. I thought nothing of it; Patti Kinkade had forgotten me several times through the years, as it was her habit to put our names to the cards by memorization, rather than by consulting a payroll list. But when I went to see her she closed the door to her office and sat me down. "You used to seem like the most honest kid I ever met," she said. She was holding a clipboard, on which she'd written the restaurant's supply needs. "Now I don't even know if I want Otis and Art playing with you."

"It's a bureaucratic mistake, Patti," I said. "I paid my state taxes. I – "

"You misunderstand me, Ari," she said. "I have to report to the owners of this restaurant that your wages are being garnished. Even though you've been a solid employee for three years, even though until the other night when that thug came by I had no reason to question you – this is a sign of trouble. Do you know who generally gets their wages garnished?"

"Noble small business owners," I muttered.

"Don't joke with me," she said. "It's deadbeat dads missing their child support payments, is who."

"You know that's not me."

"I do. But now if something, God forbid, goes wrong during one of your shifts, I look like an idiot for not reprimanding you. So, I don't want to waste your time, and I don't want to mislead you, because I do consider you a friend and I've looked your mother in the eye and feel responsible to her. But after talking this over with Stevie himself – and you've met Stevie, you know he appreciates you – we've decided to let you go. You can come back in one month if you still want to work here."

I stood. "I'll prove you were wrong to do this," I said.

She grimaced. "Wrong? Ari, I'm not in the business of bloody ears. And I can't work with anyone who isn't honest."

"When have I been dishonest?" I shouted.

"Why didn't you tell me you fainted?" she said. "Why did I have to learn that from Hector? And that you borrowed from the register to cover cab fare – what's next, borrowing to cover your taxes? You seem so responsible. You are one of my best waiters. But you don't have *twenty dollars* to spare for a cab? And now the state is garnishing your check? What would you do, in my shoes?"

"The same," I said, moving to the door. "I'll see you in one month, Patti. I know your heart's in the right place. You'll soon see mine is too."

*   *   *

There was a time in my life when under adverse circumstances I would call my mother for advice and support. That time had come and gone since my graduation.

The sticking point had been my refusal to stay in the West Egg house. "It's not my residence," I told her. "I just want to be my own man."

"You sound like a stubborn child," she said. "Your business is hemorrhaging cash, and you would rather sleep at a hotel than come home."

"First off, I'm crashing with Jimmy, I'm not staying at a hotel," I said. "Second, I don't see where it's written that stepsons have to sleep in their stepfather's houses. It makes me uncomfortable. It makes me feel unduly indebted to Neil. And I'd rather not feel that way to anyone, let alone him. I enjoy dining with you guys. And I think with Nicole we make a terrific quartet. But Neil is not someone I'm going to act like a son towards. I respect him as your husband and provider, but that's where it ends."

"Can't you just fake it? For me?"

"No."

She sighed. "Well, tell me what you've been reading lately," she said. And from there our conversation would drift to innocuous topics. We wouldn't let our dispute become a schism. But over three years, we had drifted, to the point where I began phoning Jerod or Jimmy or Joel in times of emotional need, rather than phoning my mother and getting an earful about the familiar familial topic – combined with her nagging concern for my enterprise. "How many credit cards are you using now?" she would ask. "I tried phoning but got a busy signal – was your phone disconnected again?" They were harmless and heartfelt inquiries, but to me they seemed like inquisitions.

In the aftermath of my sacking from Stevie's Joint I knew it would be foolish to phone Barbara. In fact, I felt too humiliated to phone anyone. The State was garnishing my revenues; I had been fired from a restaurant; and I had failed to deliver my product to my subscribers. I had failed, period. That was the awful truth of it. As of April, 2000, I was a complete and abject failure as an entrepreneur. About all I had in my favor was that I'd yet to declare bankruptcy or get evicted.

When I got home, I went to a kitchen cabinet to grab a bowl for cereal and beheld the following note: GET BACK TO WORK, ZINSKY. YOU CAN'T *EAT* THE *GUIDE* TOWARD SUCCESS, CAN YOU? I heeded the note and replaced the bowl, refusing to budge from my apartment until I'd determined how to ship my *Late Editions*.

All I could come up with was applying for a tenth credit card, awaiting approval, advancing cash on my line, and using the cash to pay UPS, since I no longer had the power to write a check. But that would take at least two weeks.

By nightfall I surrendered. The *Late Edition* simply would not ship on time. That was the end of it. I had borrowed, borrowed, and borrowed, and now the reckoning was here. What did I expect? Did I think that *I* – just by dint of being *me* – would somehow be exempt from the financial rules governing everyone else? That America was in such dire need of another football magazine, especially one authored by a sports geek from Long Island, that tax officials and credit organizations had no choice but to brook my deficit spending?

It was a setback. I had had them before. I would just have to deal with it and hope to keep my magazine afloat.

I penned YOU HAVE FAILED on five separate sheets of yellow legal paper. I taped the sheets to the refrigerator, the oven door I never opened, and the outside of my cabinets. And then I got more depressed. For what did it matter *where* I put these signs? I never received visitors anyway, save for Barbara and Neil once a year.

My thoughts turned to suicide, then to the realization that it would take weeks for someone to find me dead in my apartment. My most effective suicide, if my goal in self-murder was sympathetic publicity, would be shooting myself outside Stevie's Joint. Or perhaps I could wait until the NFL Draft, the following weekend. Like a crazy fan I could bound upon the stage at Madison Square Garden and fire a bullet in my mouth. Joel Pollock would notice, as would all my subscribers, as would the entire football community. And perhaps my Platinum Members would ease their ire over the *Late Edition's* delinquency.

My college pals had it so much easier.

Jerod was finishing medical school and had his choice among residencies at big-city hospitals. He had a steady girlfriend named Emily, also a med student. He cheated on her regularly, whenever her duties detained her overnight. In my next life I pledged to be a doctor, which seemed to rank third behind only rock star and film director in terms of its power to lure mates.

Jimmy was a star political reporter at *Newsday*, and though I was proud I was jealous too: Of his looks, as always, but also because Barbara often mentioned how probing his articles were, profiling this mayor or that alderman.

Kris and Tim, for their parts, had finished law school and were earning six-digit salaries. I was struggling to make rent; they were planning down payments.

And I had no one but myself to blame.

So it was that I shut all the lights in my apartment and crawled into my bed. By my side I held the Freeman McNeil football player I'd constructed as a third grader. (Barbara had brought him back to me, during one of her annual visits.) I wiped my face on his Negro fabric and tried consoling myself through self-reminders that – bleak though I was – I was happier now than I had been when I had created this huggable felt person.

Taking Freeman by the hand I strolled to my closet, where in a milk crate I kept my past's sacred mementos, items I had retrieved during visits home: my triangular glass shards, from old Yoo-hoo bottles; old yellow legal pads with football lists; scorecards from baseball games; cassette recordings of the *Mike & the Mad Dog* radio program; recordings from my own radio days in college. I sifted through the legal pads until I found one from three years earlier, which I had associated with inspiration:

To have not committed suicide all those years ago — days like this validate your choice to keep living. Envision a future where you are a terrific basketball player with a girlfriend who loves fucking you. You will make it happen. Know that your past would've snapped the spines of weaker individuals. Know, too, that the woman of your dreams will appreciate your backbone."

Did Diana appreciate my backbone? In the context of bleak business prospects, she had given me cause for optimism, reason to cherish my existence. I dialed her number, doubting she'd be home on a Friday evening. At once I feared losing her: she was likely at the Cellar in her tight workout pants, luring leers from Boston College jocks, inviting *them* to church, tapping *their* heads with her yoga mat. "Please pick up, you have no idea how much I love you," I said aloud as the phone kept ringing.

Before I knew it an answering machine had beeped and I was saying: "Hey Diana — and hi Lori and Harper, it was nice meeting you the other night — anyway, Diana, I just wanted to chat. Normally I'd beat back that urge, but hey, things lately — "

She picked up. "What are you doing at home? Football stuff?" she asked.

"Yeah," I said. "What about you?"

"Oh, I don't know. Reading. Watching TV. Screening calls. Deciding if I should rent a movie. I love Lori and Harper but it's nice to have the house to myself."

"Maybe I'll head your way," I said. "I'm tired of having a house to myself."

"Why don't we just meet up and get a movie?" she said. Just like that I was due at her door in 30 minutes, watching a film with a woman for the first time in five years, when it was Charlene Chiu and *The Shawshank Redemption.*

Diana's wet hair shimmered in the porch light's glow, like a sunken new penny in a brilliant fountain. Her pendant cross rested on her bare chest between open buttons of a black dress shirt. Her skin was so white, to see it between the parting black apparel made me think of piano keys.

The early spring weather was cold and windy. I wished I'd brought along my wool Jets hat, if not for myself, then to cover the wet hair and reddening ears of my tall, elegant companion as we walked to the video store. Her arms were crossed; yet she did not remark about the cold, and I admired her for it. Over the years, on so many occasions, I had overheard too many people lamenting the frigid Boston weather – as if they were required by law to reside in New England. I loved that Diana kept her discomfort to herself. On this basis alone, I was convinced she was the toughest woman I'd ever met.

At the shop, Diana remarked that I struck her as a Woody Allen fan. Her comment nettled me, as it again overlooked my athletic accomplishments. On these grounds I protested. "I should've realized that," she said.

"I'm joking," I lied, afraid she'd now perceive me – accurately – as someone who took himself too seriously.

"No, you're not," she said.

She had me. I kept quiet. In my head I kept chastising myself: "Great job, Zinsky. Now she will never like you. You have exposed yourself as narcissistic and dramatic."

Back inside her large, warm apartment we made dinner. On the kitchen counter Diana laid out eggs, vegetables, butter, milk, and bread. She cracked and beat eggs while I – having inserted bread into toaster slots – buttered a pan. Next she sliced and grated an aromatic rainbow of veggies on the white cutting board. I stood with my hands in my pockets. She rejected my claims of gender bias in the chore distribution. "It's because I'm hosting," she said. "Or is it *hostess-ing*? Whatever. You can chop veggies if we're ever eating at your place."

The promise of a future interaction pleased me. I had been in Boston for nearly a thousand days, consuming nearly three thousand meals – and now, for the first time in that period – for the first time *ever* – a friend and I were truly making dinner. It was a commonplace domestic undertaking, elevated to event status through its scarcity in my adulthood. Had Diana looked up from the cutting board, I'd have attributed the moist corners of my eyes to her mincing of onions.

She dumped the vegetable pieces into a simmering pan, where the omelet proper had already formed a waiting bed of yolk-yellow sheets. She said, "I need plates and silverware," grinning to take the edge off her command. Her teeth were evenly spaced and perfectly white.

My eyes roamed cabinets and shelves, uncertain which contained what. Diana stepped back from the stove and opened the correct one for me. "Aha," I said meekly.

She dished our omelets while I stood with my hands in my pockets. "I want some red wine," she said. "Or is white better for omelets?"

"Well, white's cold," I said, spilling the extent of my Dionysian discernment. Stevie's Joint did not have a liquor license.

"We keep red in the fridge too," said Diana. "We're quirky like that." I opened the heavy door and searched the fogged plastic shelves and thin grid racks. I handed her a bedewed green bottle. With case Diana knifed open the wrapping and inserted the corkscrew with a deft wrist twist. And again I became a charlatan as Diana poured. "Can you believe there are people in this world who'll pay $200 for a bottle of wine?" I asked. "I mean, is the grape quality *that much* better?"

Taking our plates, she led the way to the living room. I followed with a wooden tray bearing glasses of water and wine. No sooner had we sat – Diana on a chair, leaving me alone on a wide couch – than Diana rose to shut the lights and resumed her place.

We had chosen a romantic comedy called *Some Kind of Wonderful* – I had never heard of it, though Diana had termed it "a classic" from the 80s. My ignorance of it made her all the more insistent we rent it. She was quiet throughout the movie, save for periodic chuckles and one remark about the buttery smell of our eggs. The house was hushed, except for the film itself and the clanks of our dishes and silverware.

The plot involved two comely high school boys and two comely high school girls in a love diamond: the artistic middle class boy pines for the popular girl, who has just broken up with the rich athletic boy. Meanwhile, a musically oriented girl pines for the artistic boy – pines for him so much, that she is willing to help him attain the popular girl. Eventually, the artistic boy realizes the musical girl is the one for him. The credits roll.

How different this drama was from *my* high school reality! Even at age 25, I could not sit back and accept the données. I thought: "How am I supposed to empathize, nay, root for, any character who finds lust in high school?" By the movie's end I hated all four protagonists. I wondered whether Diana's affinity for the film signified key differences between us – differences I longed to ignore because I was in no position to reject any woman who welcomed my advances.

Her socked feet were up on the armrest, so that her knees were at the level of her shoulders. Viewed from the side, her body formed an exquisite "N" shape on the chair. I kneeled beside her chair, leaning over the armrest, and guided her face toward mine. My shoes clanked loudly against the plates stacked on the floor. We wedged together on the chair, kissing and adjusting and readjusting and kissing until she was on my lap and my hand was between her blouse buttons, beneath her bra, pawing her strawberry-sized breasts, her nipples pointy like chocolate chips in my palms.

It was my first kiss in years and I forgot my fundamentals. First my lips closed as hers opened; then vice versa, my tongue painting the front of her teeth. But at length we were in sync. "Sorry my boobs are so small," she whispered once my head had dropped to her chest. How a woman of Diana's caliber could possess physical insecurities was baffling to me. "Diana, you are so hot," I whispered back. "You're talking nonsense."

"Maybe we should slow down," she said.

I wondered at this request, since our belts were still buckled. I began buttoning her blouse. She stopped me. "You don't have to do *that*," she laughed. "I just want to talk for a while." I thought we were going to share the chair and chat. But Diana took my hand and led me up creaky wooden spiral stairs to her bedroom. We left the plates and utensils on the floor.

She hung her black shirt in the closet. Her long spine was defined and hollowed out, like a riverbed between the banks of her bony white back. She shut the lights and her room was dim, save for a crack of light coming from the outer hall. I sat on her bed in my jeans and socks. When she approached, she put her hands to my chest, massaging the flesh around my ribs and sternum. I breathed heavily. She kissed my hairless chest and sucked on *my* nipples. When her kisses moved from my chest to my collar to my shoulders she caught me wiping my cheek. "Wow," she said. "Are you *sad* right now?"

"No one's ever kissed my chest before," I said, voice cracking. She stroked my head and we just lay there for a while. "What are you thinking about?" she asked.

"I'm thinking, Why do you want us to slow down? Are you afraid of me?"

"It's not you, sweetie, it's not you," she said, and I could not believe that a female other than my mother had called me sweetie. But I had also heard, "It's not you," before, and I had my hunches about what it really meant.

"Why is that hard for you to believe?" she asked presciently.

"Because I'm ugly," I answered, holding her hand to my chest.

"You are *not* ugly. I think you're gorgeous," she said.

"Why?"

"Ari, there's no *why*, I just *do*," she said. "I noticed you on your first day. I was like, Who is *that one*? You were tall, and most guys are too short for me. And then I knew we'd get along when you asked about the cubicle posters."

"This is astonishing," I said. "I had no idea."

"Well, I was dating someone at the time," she said. "And I wasn't sure about dating a coworker. But I really regretted not staying in touch after you left. Especially once I broke up with Albert."

"Was he your first serious boyfriend?" I asked.

"I'm a virgin," she volunteered.

I was shocked – both at the declared fact, and at her non-sequitur assertion of it. Then I became flattered – she obviously took me seriously, if she felt not another second could pass before revealing such crucial information. Nonetheless, all I could say in response was: "Why?" Like any inexperienced man, I found it hard to believe that someone who *could* savor copious fucking would opt not to. I instantly associated her chastity with her cross pendant.

Her answer was not the rehearsed speech I expected. Her tone was casually philosophical, as if discussing a switch to vegetarianism. "Why? Because – well, I was raised Catholic, but that's not what it is. Tom and Miranda *totally* had sex before they were married. I guess what I'm saying is, I was raised to avoid premarital sex. But based on my own experiences, I think abstinence is smart. I see how women become blinded to the men they're having sex with. And I see how emotional I get over *just* foreplay."

"There's something we have in common," I said.

She laughed peremptorily before resuming. "And the other thing is – I'm completely pro-choice, but I could never see myself getting an abortion. And this is one easy way to make sure I'm never in that situation."

"I still love you," I said, shocked that the phrase had escaped my throat. I watched her expression for backlash at my use of the four-letter word. Her pink lips spread elliptically over her gums. "That's sweet of you to say, but you don't have to be afraid of walking away from me," she said. "I won't think badly of you if you don't want to be with me anymore."

"I dream about you," I said, burying my head in her chest and embracing her.

"Besides," she said, "there are other things we can do." Her head dropped to my waist.

* * *

The next morning I went downstairs to make coffee. Diana's roommate, Harper, was snuggling on the couch with a bearded blond man. Their repose in watching Bugs Bunny cartoons couldn't but make me feel intrusive. Harper's light brown hair, wrapped in a purple bandana, rested on her man's muscular thigh. The man's hand was down the neck of her t-shirt, while her hand squeezed his thick calf. I felt as I often had during my youth, tiptoeing through the television room so as not to disturb the broadcast-assisted intimacy that Barbara and her boyfriend-de-jour were enjoying.

The posture of Harper and her hirsute boyfriend – who, if he shaved, could have starred in *Some Kind of Wonderful* – indicated an uncertainty as to whether life existed outside of their assured union. I hadn't heard them come in the night before – did they sleep at *his* house? Why were they here now? Would Harper remember me from the Cellar? I clomped loudly down the final few wooden spiral steps and proclaimed, "Good morning!" They did not budge. They just kept watching TV.

To disrupt them, to remind them that couples do not rule the world, or even the apartment, was my instinct, despite *my* overnight status change from single to taken. The 25-year-old Zinsky could not forget his solitary years. How many Friday nights had I spent alone, with no one to hold but my stuffed Freeman McNeil doll? How many phone numbers had I collected – on the back of blood donor cards, or of my own ZinskyQuintessential.com business cards – only to have my calls go unreturned? How much porn had I rented, in the absence of real-life fantasy material, especially when weeks passed without a restaurant appearance by the pill-popping Sandy Appleton? Yes, you could take a young man out of Shawshank, but the scars of his confinement remained. I was institutionalized by the events in my life to abhor couples: to reject their jocular reciprocity, their so-called connection, as a personal circumstance that a twisted soul like mine could never attain. One blessed night with Diana wasn't going to change any of that. I wondered whether one month, one year, or one decade with Diana would be enough to reverse how organic the solitary condition had become to my worldview.

When Diana came downstairs – marching wordlessly past the couch cuddling as if she saw it every Saturday morning – she found me in the kitchen with my coffee reading the sports section of the *Globe*. She wore an ankle-length black skirt that elongated her already significant bodily length. A white crewneck sweater hid her cross and highlighted her bony, sanguine cheeks. She sat beside me and we kissed, openly and heated. My head fell to her chest, whose thudding invoked a sincerity I'd felt only once before.

I studied her face, the pointy parts of her Irish physiognomy, her slender neck and taut jaw. In the shady kitchen her eyes assumed the color of weathered jeans, a muted tone complementing the silvery gray of her necklace. I wondered whether a less attractive woman would be so audacious as to uphold her virginity. Less attractive women might not lure boyfriends *unless* they spread their thighs.

Perhaps an hour later, when Diana rose to go to the bathroom, I watched her hips and butt twitch beneath her skirt. Was this woman, whose rear I'd normally be shifting seats just to stare at, planning to come right back and sit beside me? My gratitude over her affection pushed aside my deeper questions. All I felt was luck. It was clear to me that some ugly Ancient Greek must have invented both Hephaestus, the patron saint of the hideous, and Cupid, the demi-God whose arbitrary arrow-slings seemed as likely an explanation as any for the mystifying science by which females selected their gross objects of affection.

Chapter 14 – Inevitable Comparisons

When Diana saw my apartment she was aghast at its condition. No sooner had I pulled open the brown wooden door than she muttered, "Oh my God." She doffed her odorless white running sneakers and treaded softly within, taking stock. I cracked my knuckles, panicking internally over what Diana was thinking as she beheld:

- My 372 sealed, undelivered copies of the *Late Edition* stacked on the kitchen's patterned linoleum floor, concealing black-trimmed squares of sullied white.
- My jar of Vaseline and besotted t-shirts atop the ottoman in my living room.
- My two-seater white leather couch – bought through generous store financing on impulse when I foolishly believed bloodletting Cara O'Sullivan might visit – covered with unpaid bills, early drafts of the *Late Edition*, my Freeman McNeil doll, my own running sneakers (muddied and reeking), and a yellow legal pad.

And all over my apartment, wherever Diana strolled, were signs on yellow paper reading YOU HAVE FAILED. She ripped them down in a fury, not stopping to remove the leftover tape, and marched toward me. "How have you failed?" she asked. Her voice was soft and beseeching, as if she were teaching a kindergartner to say please. She stared up at me, her eyes heightened and almost circular. Her long, bony hands gripped the thin pile of pages, which she crunched into a ball. Her head was tilted diagonally. She pushed aside the couch's accumulations and led me to a seat. She crouched facing me.

"Just don't leave me," I sobbed.

She sat beside me, stroking my back, as I told her about my sacking at Stevie's, my taxes entanglement, and my failed deliveries. When I was done she let me rest my head in her lap and look up at her. She took hold of the yellow legal pad and flipped to a new page. "Let's take these one at a time," she said. "You need your waiter job back. That's *going* to happen, right? As long as you show up and act contrite – "

"Right."

"Okay. And that will take care of the Commonwealth, because then you'll have paychecks that they can garnish. Right?"

"Right," I said.

"So it seems like your big failure is really just not having the liquid cash to ship these magazines. UPS won't negotiate with you?"

"No."

"Have you called FedEx? Or DHL?"

I jumped up from the couch. I knew in an instant her solution would work – whereas UPS had grown weary of my non-payments, *a new* shipping company would gratefully open an account without scrutinizing my history. For all my fiscal ineptitude, I had yet to miss a credit card bill, always sending along the minimum; so my overall standing was still good enough to skirt any perfunctory checking. I turned on my computer and sat at my desk. Diana rubbed my shoulders. "You're a lifesaver," I said, squeezing her hand.

"I'm always happy to propose the obvious," she said.

"How can I repay you?" I asked.

She whispered, even though we were alone in the apartment.

*   *   *

During the next few months we could not share tabletops or train rides without succumbing to the tug of kissing. Predictable and significant changes ensued: she replaced Barbara as my chief source of fashionable clothes, usurped Jimmy and Jerod as my chief confidante (except when the topic was she), and took me grocery shopping, so that cereal and milk ceased to be my main source of calories.

And as Diana predicted, my other troubles soon disappeared. By the time I got my job back at Stevie's Joint, the State had cleared me of tax wrongdoing, having determined ZinskyQuintessential, LLC, to be a plausible tax entity and the sums of my tip declarations passable for my 40 weekly restaurant hours. So I again had a steady income, especially when combined with ad revenues from *The Guide* and *Late Edition*, which trickled in 60-90 days after their publication dates. I picked away at my debt, devoting the surfeit of each month's earnings toward paying down my nine cards.

Summer arrived, and with it came a sight at Stevie's to which I'd grown pleasantly accustomed: Sandy Appleton in a short skirt, carrying her own bottled water or iced coffee into the restaurant. As usual, she crossed her legs, tilted back her head, and gulped her pills straight from the plastic orange container. I wondered anew what the medicine was for. I had always associated it with her convalescence; but now she walked without a crutch, and her blond hair had reached shoulder length. A linear striation of muscle appeared in her lower thigh, emerging from beneath her flower skirts and vanishing at the tan, shaven knee. She was not only healthy, but fit.

I had resigned myself to never learning why she'd read about the NFL draft on her laptop. I couldn't bring myself to ask. There were boundaries in my profession, and I felt obliged to them in deference to Patti Kinkade for rehiring me.

I wondered why I never saw Sandy with a boyfriend – or a girlfriend, for that matter. During my first time waiting on her after my return, I watched her closely from the kitchen. After she swallowed her pills she cast a spanning hand over her menu and gazed toward the hostess's desk – her signal of readiness. I approached with pen and pad, giddy and hopeful. Surely she would remark upon my absence – or my presence. But no: "Turkey on sourdough, Russian dressing on the side please, with water and a Diet Coke with lemon," she said, opening her laptop and staring at the square gray keys.

Nothing had changed. It was as though I'd never fainted by her table, as though I'd never been sacked from Stevie's. I could have been *any* waiter or waitress on the staff – or in the universe. I was to her what the UPS and FedEx drivers were to me.

And why did that bother me so much, now that I had Diana?

I phoned Jerod one Sunday to discuss it. I began by confessing Diana's policy of non-sexual relations, which to that point I'd kept hidden for macho reasons. "So she's cautious," he counseled. "Even if she was giving it up, it wouldn't change anything."

"How long before I can ask her to reconsider?" I said.

"She's not gonna reconsider," he said. "She's already considered all the angles, probably long before she met you. But – "

"But what?" I asked. I lowered the volume of my television, which was broadcasting a Red Sox game. Freeman McNeil was watching beside me.

"Some chicks who want to save themselves – they'll let you in the ass," he said.

I had no idea. "Ever do it?" I asked curiously.

"Every time Emily comes over," he said.

"Does *she* like it?" I asked.

"*Now* she does," he said. "It takes a few weeks to loosen up."

I felt as I had nearly ten years earlier in the West Egg Public Library, when I'd accidentally found myself a voyeur to a sexual act I'd only heard about but never truly pondered. This conversation with Jerod was my life's first evidence that anal sex was practiced, nay enjoyed, outside realms of pornography and prostitution. I wondered whether Sandy did anal; I wondered whether Shelagh *would have* done anal; I wondered if Diana would *ever* do it, and how long would be proper to wait before asking. Jerod's advice – "two or three weeks" – seemed like too little time, especially because all the women he'd ever asked had already consented to conventional intercourse.

"Here's the real problem," said Jerod, after indulging my questions. "Diana wants to get married. Have three or four kids. Send them to Harvard. That's not you. But you're having too much fun to fess up."

"I'm having as much fun as a guy can have without – "

"No sex isn't the problem," he insisted. "You'd see that if you had any experience. But she's your first girlfriend, so you're tripping like Romeo, because she buys your shirts and butters your toast."

"If I were so trippy, I wouldn't be so concerned with Sandy."

"Only someone tripping would date someone who's not fucking," he said. "Plus you're nervous about asking to hit the ass – another sign. Case closed."

*   *   *

(505)-555-0119. I recognized the New Mexico area code on my cell phone's display but didn't have time to pick up. I was rushing to meet Diana for lunch.

I met Diana two or three afternoons a week, using the occasions to model whatever clothes she'd bought me. I write *model*, not *wear*, because in addition to supplying the garments Diana offered advice on how best to don them: which shirts to tuck in or out, how many buttons to undo, a t-shirt underneath or not, which shoes with which belt, whether bandanas or baseball caps were acceptable accessories – so in preparing to see her I fussed for 15 minutes, primping and double-checking my raiment with a list of rules I'd jestingly jotted on yellow legal paper during her first fashion lecture. By the time I was ready to depart I was inevitably in danger of being late. Our first fight had occurred weeks earlier when I suggested my tardiness was her fault, since it was she who cared so much about my style. And so despite my curiosity about (505)-555-0119, I didn't pick up.

The blazing afternoon sun was hidden behind a series of low, chalky clouds. I hastened down a redbrick path along Boston harbor, passing quickly from dock to dock, from wharf to wharf. Commuter ferries and whale-watching boats and tourist catamarans were anchored, their white hulls lolling above calm brown waters. On benches along the path sat perspiring men in rolled up shirt sleeves and loosened ties, eating drippy sandwiches and pizza slices. Pigeons trolled for crumbs. Scents of garlic and fresh bread commingled with wafting saltwater and brine.

My armpits were soaked. The white linen top I'd consciously donned without an undershirt clung to my chest and ribs, well nigh revealing them through a moist diaphanousness. I waited on the hot gray steps of the Custom House, my feet adhering to their designer sandals. Suddenly on my neck then down my spine there was a slick, frigid sensation; Diana was behind me, giggling, her fingertips clasping the next ice cube she intended to wedge down my shirt. I seized her wrist and wrestled it behind her back. Thus began our playful, open embrace, culminating as we sat inches from each other, holding hands and sharing every detail of our mornings. "I think my father's dead," I said.

She pressed down on her light blue skirt and pushed closer to me. "Think?"

I mentioned the circumstances of avoiding the phone call, hoping she'd not view the truth as a passive-aggressive reference to our first fight. "So I'll call them back later," I concluded. Half my tuna sandwich was in my hand. I took a large bite, savoring the mayo-soggy bread and swallowing hard.

"Well, call me at work either way," she said.

"I might be too busy popping champagne," I said.

"Oh, Ari," she sighed.

I dropped her hand and stood up. "You know, when I told you about how he treated me, I did it so you could understand me – and not just at a time like this," I declared. "You wanted to know why I cry when you rub your chest on my back, why I don't attend Red Sox games, why I sewed Freeman McNeil, why I asked if *your* dad taught Tom how to shoot a basketball – and I told you. And this whole time I felt so happy because I thought you understood how it affected me. And now you're going to respond to my champagne comment with bemused disapproval? What is that?"

"Sit down, sweetie," she said softly. She stroked the top of my foot with her cool fingers. "You're totally over-personalizing my reaction."

I did as I was told and tried to be calm. "No," I said. "You don't understand the magnitude of having an asshole parent. You love your parents so much, you can't comprehend how someone could hate theirs."

"It's not rocket science, Ari," she said, sipping her Diet Coke through a straw. "I get it. But the idea of popping champagne over a death – sorry, it's a little extreme."

"What if that dying person is a serial killer or rapist or child molester? What if that dying person is *Hitler?*"

"Your father is none of the above," she said.

"You don't understand hate," I said. "I can't believe we're even debating this. You should support my feelings just because they are my feelings."

"Ari, you are overreacting," she said. "I get why you'd want to pop the champagne, I believe you deserve to pop the champagne, and I would be thrilled to drink it with you. I'm sorry I had the wrong expression at the wrong moment." Her hand crept up my calf to my knee, which she pushed toward her mouth. She pressed my kneecap to her chest. I felt her racing heart.

I wondered whether she was playacting and whether I could be utterly honest with her. If I confessed about never planning to reproduce, or if I told her I had slapped Shelagh – these truths, too, might lead to an adverse reaction. And if I raised the question of anal sex, right there in front of the Custom House – what would her reaction be *then*? Were we both concealing our deepest honesties in the interest of mutual harmony? And why were we concealing? Probably because it is a rare and precious thing to have a friend who eats lunch with you and squeezes your kneecap. "I'm sorry I overreacted," I tell her, and I mean it: all at once, the thought of *not* having her makes me want to humble myself. She's the Helen who makes it all possible. The momentary thought of life without her forms tears in my eyes' corners. "I wish we could just play hooky all day," I say, lifting her fingers to my lachrymal lashes. And our lunch concludes as it began: With an embrace we'd rather not reach the end of, a parting no less sorrowful for the shared knowledge of its brevity. I am Romeo, indeed.

*   *   *

On my voicemail there was a recorded female voice I didn't initially recognize: *Hi, Ari, this is Cam – your father's wife. I need to talk to you as soon as possible.* She had left her office number and urged me to phone back before noon "mountain" time.

I had work to do and I ignored her.

I set to drafting an article for ZinskyQuintessential.com, a speculative essay on which late-round selections had the best chance to become starters during the 2000 NFL season. The safest bets were Shane Lechler, the punter from Texas A&M drafted by the Raiders; I also liked the Texas Tech running back Sammy Morris, who was joining a Buffalo Bills squad bereft of incumbents. And my heart, of course, was with all of the Michigan alumni: defensive tackle Rob Renes, quarterback Tom Brady, and linebacker Dhani Jones. It had been a strong Michigan class, and maybe I'd allow myself to write about it under a heading of admitted subjectivity. Or maybe I'd create a new web page altogether, calling it *alma mater*, and using it for alumni analyses of *all* major schools: Michigan, Penn State, Tennessee, etc. I rotated in my swivel chair, away from my computer monitor, and flopped onto the couch, where Freeman McNeil and my yellow legal pad were waiting.

I was mulling metaphors for Brady's ability to make quick defensive reads when my phone rang again. It was Joel Pollock, who often called in mid-afternoon to shoot the breeze. I answered professionally – "Ariel Zinsky," I said – though our friendship transcended our business partnership; he discussed his wife Berit and I discussed Diana. But I wanted to maintain airs of corporate formality with Joel, since he knew bigwig publishers who might acquire the *Guide* and its web site and make me rich. Joel, to his credit, recognized my motive, and spent most of his time trying to crack my punctilio. "If you ever sell the *Guide*, then I want fifty percent of any after-tax profits," he told me.

"I'll certainly evaluate some kind of remuneration," I replied.

There was a pause. I went back to my computer, saved what I was working on and paced the apartment in preparation for his harangue. "Ari," he said, drawing in his breath, "you are a gullible neophyte, a naïve cygnet in a business world of hawks!" he shouted. "It's *your* magazine. The magazine is proprietary of you. The monthly emails *are* you! You are the Pavarotti of college football player analysts. You are the magnate of a magazine that people happily pay for and actually read! For 15,000 people, including myself, you make the world a better place. And for this, some stuffed-suit muckety-mucks might reward you. And you say you'll evaluate rewarding *me*, when it was you, you, and *only* you standing there in the rain at seven on a Saturday morning, selling your *Guides* on a street corner like a pretzel vendor. Ari, the next time you offer to do something that generous – which is to say, that stupid – I will no longer be your friend. Because my entire self-esteem is derived from not befriending the stupid. For you to offer me a piece of what's legally yours is on par, for stupidity, with people who attribute violence to rap music or people who believe that prayers get answered."

His little prayers comment was an attempt to tease me about Diana. I wasn't biting. "You want to see this piece I'm doing on the Michigan rookies?" I asked. "Should be ready tomorrow."

He chuckled. "Sure, why not," he said.

Just then I had a call-waiting. Joel seemed as surprised by the clicking sound as I was. "Who the hell is calling you?" he asked.

"I'll tell you tomorrow," I said, clicking goodbye and greeting the new caller with: "Ariel Zinsky."

"Ari, this is Cam Clark."

I kept in glad-handing mode, though I instantly wondered whether *her* calling meant my father had already passed. "Cam, I'm sorry, it's been a – "

"Ari, how long have you known your father is sick?" she said sharply.

Sick. That meant he was living. But he still wasn't phoning, which meant he was probably on the ropes. In my head I suppressed a joke about keeping champagne on ice. I also divined that Cam had learned about my father's graduation confession, and was interrogating me for explanations rather than information. So I tried helping her, though I knew too much levity had crept into my tone when I replied, "Cam, do you always believe what my father says?"

"Answer my question, Ari. Please."

Again, she was sharp with me. As if I were culpable for anything. As if I could be blamed, under any circumstances – even cancerous ones – for ignoring common protocols. Further, I had had only one conversation with Cam in my entire life – did she think *that* gave her the right to cross-examine me? I checked my watch, saw I had 45 minutes before I had to be at Stevie's Joint, and in a flash I grew testy. "Cam, before this conversation becomes the last one you ever have with me, you're going to have to lose that hectoring tone," I said, quite hectoring myself. "I'm not your employee, I'm not your child, and most days I don't consider myself a child of your husband."

"I apologize, but I'd think you could forgive my tone given what I just learned."

"Fine. The truth is, Robert said something to me at my graduation."

"Graduation!" she yelled.

"Yes," I said proudly. "And if you think I've been callous not to mention it, then you know too little of my history with Robert."

"Ari, there are nights he cries himself to sleep over what he did to you. But never mind him. This is between you and me. And it's me, as a mother and an adult, telling you that you used bad judgment by keeping your father's secret from me, even if he ordered you to do so. That's all I was really calling to tell you. I'm upset at you, but you're too young and I'm too old to hold a grudge about it."

"So what's the scoop?" I asked. "Another three years to live? Or is it urgent?"

"It's going to get him within the next six months," she said. "The door is always open for you to visit. I can tell you he'd really appreciate that."

"Can I bring my girlfriend?" I asked.

"You have a girlfriend?" she said.

* * *

Late that night I ran my fingers through Diana's sweaty hair and said, "You're the best thing that's ever happened to me." We palmed our slick faces and kissed slowly. Then I pinned her to the bed, my hands clamping her wrists to the damp orange sheet, which had popped from its corners. I rolled her onto her stomach and aligned my center with hers, inserting myself within her pale muscular butt cheeks and pushing between them, until I was inside *something*. My tip was probing. But I was not *within*. And yet, there was a kind of insertion going on. I was not in the house, but I was not outside either. I was in an anteroom, a foyer. "How's that feel?" I asked Diana.

"Not bad, actually," she whispered.

"I want to go inside," I said, my lips pressing her matted hair to her moist neck.

"Stay there for now."

In a few minutes I whispered, "Can I come?"

"Yes."

"How did that feel?" I asked when it was over.

"I need some toilet paper," she said. "I've never had a come-wad up my butt before."

"But I wasn't *inside*," I reconfirmed.

"No," she said.

I rose to get some toilet paper. When I came back she laughed. "I didn't need it *this second*," she said. She rested her head against my chest and kissed my nipples. "It's very clear you were raised by a woman," she said.

I lay back, my shoulders sticking to the bare mattress. Our bodies were glistening, despite her bedroom's state-of-the-art air conditioner, with its lime green digital temperature display. Summer was still summer and sex (or not-quite-sex) was still sex. We were hot, perspiring primates doing what we were born to do. I licked the sweat from within her bellybutton and rejoiced quietly over my prospects.

*   *   *

My first night of actual anal intercourse: it was July 4, after an evening of watching fireworks at a beach in the Cape Cod town of Sandwich, where Diana's parents owned a summer home. Those selfsame parents had taken the holiday in Paris with her brother Tom and his wife, Miranda. Diana had bypassed Paris – where she'd been the previous year – to spend the weekend with me. "So your parents – they think we're staying here, but *not* doing it?" I asked. "I can't believe people like that still exist. Weren't they teenagers once?"

"Well, technically speaking, we're *not* doing it," she said.

"Thank heaven for compromises," I said. I held my cock by the base and wedged it within its new home. She gasped, gripping my shoulder tightly. With my free fingers I probed her in the manner she'd taught: slowly, then rapidly.

We had spent the day on the beach, sunning together on parallel towels, reading, drinking water, and reapplying lotion. I got so hard as she massaged the creamy oil into my lower back I nearly burst. We went to the water and, shoulder deep, our bodies hidden by the liquid dark-green-brown, I throbbed against her until I cried into her ear, my lips tasting the saltwater that had soaked her hair and flavored her skin. No one but Diana heard my wail: the rush of waves, the electric hum of distant motorboats, the surrounding shouts of children and their caretakers, the periodic whistle from a lifeguard, the thud of a flying football smacking the water's surface – all this muffled my pleasure so much that the Atlantic barely blinked at my labored moaning. I writhed in ecstasy and wrenched with supernatural spasms. Diana held me up when I was finished. I was quiet and appreciative. I felt the small stones piercing the bottom of my feet and the dark green seaweed caressing my shins. What Diana had just done for me – I swore to myself I could spend forever with her, if she kept on doing that, even though it was neither intercourse nor our gainful substitute. What Diana had just done for me – it was *exactly* what I had craved. She acceded without reservation. What she had just done was so purely, so distinctly for only my physical benefit – I had no idea what I might do in return.

The water lapped our backs and shoulders; we stood in a slow, rotating embrace. I eyed the cloudless sky and soon fell into a trance, pondering Diana's altruism, wondering whether it was distinct to her or if it could be generalized to her gender. Was Sandy Appleton this good to *her* boyfriends, or girlfriends? Did Jerod's and Jimmy's girlfriends do this for *them*? Was my mother like this with Neil? Was Nicole like this with her college sweethearts? Had Cam Clark been like this with my father, before they'd given birth to Sandra, and my father's mind had given birth to his mantis metaphor?

These were my thoughts as a 25-year-old man, hell-bent on twisting my fortune within a vortex of needless comparisons.

Chapter 15 – Death in Albuquerque

In layout, Robert Zinsky's residence reminded me of Diana's parents' estate on Cape Cod. A front foyer gave way to an expansive living room and kitchen on the right. To the left were a guest bedroom and bathroom. At the rear of the kitchen, a sliding glass door opened toward a wooden deck with umbrella-clad circular table and plastic chairs. The deck overlooked an oval swimming pool and three lounges surrounding it. Upstairs there were two bedrooms – each with its own bathroom – and an immense study with two desks: one, I gathered, for each adult.

Cam Clark led us to the pool, wearing a red sweatshirt over a black one-piece swimsuit. Robert reclined on a lounge wearing a white bandana, a Hawaiian shirt of the Tommy Bahama brand with three open buttons, and a bikini swimsuit, which was not as unflattering on him as it might have been on other men over 50. He was reading the *Wall Street Journal* and he didn't look up until we were standing in his light. "Hey," he said, soft and listlessly, as if we came by every day. He glanced at the paper, as if to resume reading. "I think I'm the only man on the planet not buying Internet stocks," he said. "But it makes no sense to me. I'm reading here that Amazon.com is now worth more than IBM. At this rate, it won't matter that I'm gonna kick the bucket, because my net worth is crumbling by the day. You like my yarmulke?" he said, tapping his bandana with the newspaper. "I have a few weeks left, at most," he continued. "There. Now we don't have to talk about it. You two want to go swimming?"

Diana and I shared glances and nodded. Led by Cam, we retreated to the guest room, where our packed bags lay on the bed. "I can't believe your folks are letting us sleep in the same room," said Diana, as soon as Cam had disappeared up the steps.

"Technically speaking, we're not sleeping together," I said.

"Are you trying to tell me something?" she said.

"Maybe."

"I've been thinking about it too," she said. "But let's talk about it tonight. For now we should probably get to the pool before they get suspicious."

We changed, went outside, and lotioned each other before jumping in. "You been sun-bathing, Ari?" asked Robert. "Your skin has always been whiter than this."

"Ari goes running without his shirt," offered Diana.

Robert didn't put much energy into his ensuing laugh, but I could tell he found Diana's declaration hysterical. "Oh, that's the East Coast for you," he said. "I've lived out here so long I forgot runners sometimes *wear* shirts. You look decent, though, Ari, you really do. You got some muscles on those legs. And, uhm – "

"Diana," she volunteered.

"Sorry," he said. "I have cancer and Alzheimer's too, apparently. Anyhow: Diana, you don't look so bad yourself. Those triceps look like yoga triceps. Cam has triceps like that. Sandra probably will too by the time she's ten, with the yoga Cam drags her to."

"Thanks, I guess," said Diana.

"So what does Ari say about me?" asked Robert. "Don't worry about offending me. I'm just curious. And Cam will kill me if I ask these questions when she's around."

Diana floated at the edge of the pool, her skinny white arms resting on the sunned concrete as she pondered how to answer. "I know you guys went to baseball games. Ari says you were kind of cheap with the soda and candy."

Robert chuckled. "Well, come on now. Ballpark sodas were like, what, two bucks back then? And it costs *them* maybe three cents to pour each one. The margins on stadium concessions are ludicrous. If I'm an entrepreneur in my next life, I'm not doing soft*ware*. I'm doing soft *drinks*. Heck. I still can't believe zillions of people pay a buck each day for a can of Coke."

"So when you go to a bar," sallied Diana, "do you order drinks, or do you go nuts about how it would be cheaper to pour it yourself?"

Robert continued: "I don't doubt 'cheap' is a word Ari uses to describe me. But everyone has their pet peeves. I'm sorry if I can't sit back and get ripped off like the rest of the country. If you find my views offensive, then I doubt you want to know my feelings on business school."

"It's just your opinion, Dad," I said. "There are a lot of people, just as smart as you, who've deemed business school an acceptable use of their time and money."

"More than a lot," he sighed. "But what else, Diana? What has he said about me?"

"That you're a math whiz. That you taught him long division on a napkin in a booth at McDonald's when he was four. And that you drilled him on the multiplication tables, one through 20, but always omitting the easy ones, like the twos and fives and tens. And the sevens, which were easy for Ari because of the touchdowns in football."

"Sixteen times seventeen," said Robert.

"Two-seven-two," I snapped. "Don't insult me."

"All right," said Robert. "Diana, forgive me if I ignore you for a few minutes so I can ask some questions about Ari's mother. Despite what you may have heard, I have an interest in how she's doing. But my wife gets pissed if I get nosey, so I gotta ask now."

"No worries, Robert," she said.

"Excellent," he said, shifting ever slightly in his lounge to my direction. "So. You've told her I'm dying?" he said to me.

"I've told her you might die tomorrow or in a few months."

"And she knows you're visiting."

"Yes."

"Excellent," he said. "She knows you're here with Diana?"

"Yes."

"Excellent!" he proclaimed, somehow finding the strength to sit up a bit. A small grin revealed his uneven, lemony teeth. "And how's Neil? Still obedient?"

"Seems that way."

"And when was the last time you saw your mother?"

"She and Neil visited in February."

"And has she met Diana yet?"

"No."

"Wow," he said. "I really hit the lottery here. So what's going on? Am I to infer something has *happened*? You're calling her every week, I hope."

"I am," I said. "The deal is, I refuse to stay in Neil's house. And we're quietly fighting about that."

"You're not fighting," he said. "You're still talking. She'll get over it if you act meek for a while. Don't sweat it. You gotta stand your ground with women." He realized, anew, that Diana was in the pool, and he said, "No offense intended, Diana. But you know. A guy just can't cave in every time, or he's finished."

"Well, that's true in any circumstance," said Diana, who'd crawl-stroked in my direction and now stood by my side. "I don't know that it's solely endemic to male-female relations."

"Ya," said Robert, his remark morphing into a yawn. "Oh," – he yawned again – "I can feel it coming. I'm gonna doze in about fifteen seconds. Well, before I do, let me just say some things before Cam comes back and I lose my first amendment rights. Diana, my son is a catch. Handsomer, you can find, but otherwise – stick with him. Also, Diana, don't think I hate Ari's mother. It may seem like I'm asking questions and keeping score, but that's what you do when – well, you both seem to know what I'm driving at." He adjusted himself, minutely, on the lounge, and let the newspaper fall over his eyes. Within a minute we heard snoring, Robert's breaths muffled by the *Journal* covering his face.

For dinner that night Cam prepared chicken teriyaki in a shiny silver wok that was so big and concave, it reminded me of a colossal cereal bowl that was a recurring figure in my teenage dreams. Skillful Diana sliced green peppers and minced onions, while the barefoot Ariel helped Robert climb to his upstairs bathroom for a pre-dinner bath. "Still some dignity in bathing," he said, sitting on the edge of his tub, his gray-haired big toe beneath the spigot. "But in a few weeks Cam will be soaping my back, too."

"There are worse women for the job," I said.

"Think Diana would do this for you in thirty years?" he asked. "I don't."

I could – and at the same time, could not – believe what he had just said. I could believe it because, of course, my father was prone to speak his mind. I could not believe it because we were alone together in a bathroom, and I had it in my power to injure him. Was he fearless of injury because he was so close to death? Or was he fearless of injury because he did not fear *me?* Did he still think I was a meek nine-year old, unable to hit back? In the five seconds of silence following his re-mark, I pondered all this, until my father said, "Oh come off it, Ari. It's not the end of the world. So you're banging a girl who's not addicted to you. Better you know it now. You have to *screen* for it, you see, because once you're married it's too late. This way – "

I smashed his solar plexus with my left fist, instantly disrupting his wind and power of speech. He fell backwards into the tub with a small splash, his robe falling open. I seized his hand and pressed it into the metal spigot, twisting the hot water knob. I relished a momentary scowl on his face, his eyes slamming shut, the tip of his nose flaring down-ward. For those few seconds I burned him good. He couldn't breathe, he couldn't cry for me to stop. But stop I did, when the scalding water leaked down to my wrist and proved too painful for me to hold on. Robert leaned back against the pink tiles, the inch-deep water plashing his legs and soaking his terry-cloth. On his hand there was a square shaped pinkish blotch, a cookie-cutter-like imprint from the spigot. I adjusted the water to its previous temperature and climbed into the tub, pulling the wet robe from his shoulders and hanging it atop the curtain rod. "If I had any strength I'd bite your nuts," he muttered once he caught his breath, his lips almost touching the back of my knees.

"But you don't have any strength, and soon you're going to die, which is why you shouldn't insult someone who has the power to hurt you," I lectured.

"It's nice you can finally hit me back now that I'm sick," he said. "I might have respected you if you took a swing at me *before* I was dying."

"I might have respected you if you took a swing at me *after* age 15," I said.

"You're too sensitive, Ari," he whispered. "Can't you see – I'm trying to help you. Diana is – she likes you, okay, but I can see she's not *addicted* to you."

"How can you see that? She loves me."

"She may. Ari, women – women love *cats*, okay? It's all very well that things seem reciprocal to you right now. But trust me – trust me because I was burned by two women who I thought loved me – Diana's love – it's real, but it doesn't strike me as lasting-thirty-years real. That's all I'm trying to tell you. And so you sucker punch me and crank the hot water like I'm a fucking war criminal."

"You're worse than a war criminal," I said. "You act like I did this because of what you said about Diana, and not because of the shit you did when I was a kid."

"You don't see me crying, do you?" he said. "I'm just trying to plant a seed in your head. You are naïve about women. You don't understand that they are *just as piggish as men*."

"Fuck you," I said. He looked away, his gaze falling on the water splashing down from the spigot. I left him there, shutting the bathroom door behind me.

*   *   *

Sandra Clark, now nine, attended day camp each morning and took an intro-to-Spanish class in late afternoon, a free course that Eldorado High School offered to the brightest youngsters. Sandra propped her elbows on the unset dinner table, studying vocabulary flashcards, her legs still short enough so that she crouched, rather than sat, on the wooden chair. I placed silverware, napkins, and plates all around as Cam and Diana prepped the meal on the other side of the king-sized kitchen.

I tested Sandra on the difference between *ser* and *estar*. She said, "*Ser* is like, permanent. *Ser* is for *what* you are. You would say, *Soy largo*, which means, I'm tall. *Estar* is temporary. It's more like *where* you are.

You would say, *Estoy en la cocina*, which means, I'm in the kitchen."

I paced while Cam went upstairs to check on Robert. I realized I could be jailed for my actions; or worse, in my 25-year-old view, I realized Diana might dump me on the spot if she learned what I had done. I whispered that I loved her as she heaped some sizzling chicken onto a serving dish. I turned around and suddenly asked Sandra: "So, do you think you're too young to be studying Spanish over the summer? Don't you just want to – I don't know, go swimming all the time or watch television?"

"Depends," she said. "It's annoying to have tests over the summer. But I'm not too young. In Sweden they start learning other languages in first grade."

We were quiet for a few seconds, and then Sandra asked both me and Diana, "Want to play cards?" She pointed to a deck of bicycles, resting by her flashcard pile.

Sandra, Diana, and I were in mid-rummy-hand when Cam and Robert came downstairs, her arm around his waist. He wore khaki shorts and a white t-shirt with a blue pyramid logo on the right breast, the word ACUITY – Robert's most recent software enterprise – stenciled in blue beneath the shape. She settled Robert into the seat next to mine before beginning food distribution. I almost clapped, so relieved was I that Robert seemed to have reciprocated the code of silence which I had granted him for decades. "I've never seen Ari so relaxed," said Robert, as I gaily circled the table with a water pitcher and filled glasses. "Are you this chipper when you wait tables?" he asked.

"I sure am," I said. *"Por eso me pagan."*

"What's that mean?" asked Cam.

"For this, they pay me," said Sandra.

"Or, colloquially, *that's why they pay me*," I amended. "My coworker, Hector, gives me Spanish lessons," I added.

Sandra wanted our rummy game to resume. But Cam took the cards and stacked them atop the refrigerator, mixing our hands with the discard pile. "You can't take those cards away, Mom," said Sandra. "We're not done playing."

"You'll finish after we eat," Cam said.

What stood out during dinner was Robert Zinsky's slowness and smallness of appetite. By the time Diana and I had each polished our plates Robert had taken perhaps six bites. Rather than eating, Robert spoke to Sandra non-stop. At first I attributed his interest in rudimentary Spanish to a late-blooming selflessness, a hackneyed pre-death rededication to family interests. But no: judging by Cam's reaction, Robert was socializing in the hope the guests would overlook his rationing. Cam, whose plate was half empty, said, "Stop asking Sandra questions. You've eaten *nothing* today."

"Scrambled eggs and toast is nothing?" replied Robert.

"That was 12 hours ago."

Robert shrugged. Sandra placed her hand by her mouth and whispered, in a blatant aside to me and Diana, "They have this conversation *every* night."

After dinner and cleanup, Robert, Cam, and Sandra filed upstairs, bidding goodnight to the guests. Diana and I adjourned to our room, where we read in snuggled silence. I pondered the day's events, in light of what Diana and I had planned to discuss. Watching Cam minister to my dying father certainly made a case for marriage, which is to say, avowed lifelong unconditional support. And yet, I still didn't grasp Diana's need to avoid conventional sex until marriage. For all I understood about my girlfriend, I still did not get that. I knew every nuance of Diana's competitive history with brother Tom; I could recite key dialogue from every historic battle she'd had with her parents; I could write a dissertation on why she felt closer to Lori than to Harper but still loved Harper albeit more in a roommate way than a best-friend way. But why wasn't my girlfriend giving me everything?

Though we had pledged to discuss it, we were keeping quiet, perhaps mutually aware that to have the discussion here might ruin an otherwise enjoyable getaway. At one point Diana said, "Don't you want to call Barbara before we go to sleep?" Diana had phoned her mother upon landing in New Mexico but I had yet to phone mine. I dialed West Egg, only realizing that it was past midnight on the East Coast when a groggy Neil picked up. "You make it out there okay?" he yawned. He handed the phone to Barbara before I could reply. "How is he?" asked Barbara.

"Pretty sick, I think. This could be the last time I see him," I said.

Barbara paused. "Do you have the address out there?"

I gave it to her and then summarized our day. Diana held my hand as I spoke. When I hung up, Diana shut the light and we lay in silence. Then Diana said, "I don't want you to think I'm avoiding a certain topic."

"We don't have to discuss it," I said. "I want you to be my girlfriend. I accept the terms and conditions."

"But I want you to like the conditions, and to understand them. Not to stoically accept them as part of the job."

"How can you expect any guy to like it?"

"I expect a guy to understand it. I don't want to torture you."

I lowered my head to her stomach and said, "With what you give me, with our sacred and precious compromise, how could you possibly think I feel tortured? It's just that – I don't see what harm could come from conventional sex, at this point."

She pulled my head up to hers and said, "Do you actually think I don't want to sleep with you?"

"How can't I think that, on some level?"

"How can you? I want you every time I look at you. Every time you talk. Every time you stick up for business school in the pool." She stroked me intently, and I lost my train of thought in the upward rush of ecstasy. I reciprocated in kind. And then, lying awake, our breaths calmer, we resumed. "I had a scare with Albert, you know," she said, referring to her previous boyfriend. "We were fooling around in his bed, and before I knew it he'd stuck himself inside of me. I pushed him away, he apologized profusely, and I couldn't sleep all night. I bought three kits the next morning and tested negative on all of them. And that whole scare has a lot to do with this. I'm not ready to have a child. But I would have one if I got pregnant. And I'm so scared, that even if I were on the pill, even if we used condoms – I can't even think about what I'd do."

"I didn't know you had a scare," I said.

"I know you didn't," she said. "And I realize how I can make you feel like you're somehow disposable to me – how, because I would lose you over this, you can feel as though it's the weakness of you and not the strength of this. And I just don't want you to feel that way. I really don't think you realize how much I love you. Maybe because you're a guy you think no sex means less love on my part. But it doesn't."

And with that we ceased talking. I realized Diana did not perceive me accurately: she believed, above it all, I was a sweet boy, caring, sensitive – she would probably struggle to believe I'd socked and singed my father only hours earlier. All this time, all my life, I'd spent so much mental energy musing on getting a girlfriend who'd know and appreciate my life story – and all this time, I had been incorrect. If Diana knew my life story, she'd despise me. It was far better for me – in terms of sustaining my relationship – to be perceived falsely. If I wanted a girlfriend, I would have to spin-doctor my personality so that she only saw the scrappy entrepreneur with the pounding heart, and not the unavoidable flipside, the violent daredevil who'd not hesitate to hurt people for his own satisfaction.

It wound up being one of those nights that boyfriends and girlfriends, and presumably husbands and wives, sometimes have: neither Diana nor I slept well, and each of us doubtless wondered whether the insomnia was triggered by the other or by a latent, and possibly unrelated, restlessness within.

*   *   *

The following afternoon the five of us piled into Cam's gray Ford Explorer and rode to a dude ranch: a tourist trap a dozen miles southwest of Albuquerque proper. There were dirt roads and sawdust piles. According to its pamphlets (which I still possess), it was where films like *City Slickers 2* and *Texasville* had been shot. If your movie required cavalcades of horses, cows or buffalo, swinging saloon doors or shiny sheriff stars or wide open terrain, then the Sierra Del Norte ranch was your place.

We shared a humid hayride with a dozen other perspiring visitors, exploring every saloon and horse-pen and crinkling our noses at the periodic wafts of manure drifting in our direction. After the ride, Cam and Robert, their foreheads moist, strolled off to lay together on one of several hammocks attached to the shade trees outside the sheriff's office. Sandra tagged along with me and Diana. We spent a half hour at the air-conditioned souvenir shop. I bought a black cowboy hat for Sandra, who pulled the brim down over her head until it covered her eyes. As we walked along the ranch's main path, lined with straw and hoof prints, Sandra extended her hat to passersby and called out, "Spare change, pardners?" She caused several laughs and even collected a few nickels.

For myself at the gift shop I purchased four postcards, intending to mail one each to Barbara, Jimmy, Jerod, and Diana herself, who would naturally appreciate the surprise upon returning home.

I filled out three of the four postcards – all but Barbara's – while having a pint of Budweiser in a saloon. Nearby Diana and Sandra played a video game wherein sheriffs gunned down outlaws. As I observed Diana, in her denim cutoffs, gripping the game's plastic pistol and shooting moving images on the monitor, I was aroused and charmed and ready to put last night's insomnia behind me. And yet: what was really going on in my head, as my father took one of his life's final naps and my girlfriend dallied with a half-sister I barely knew? As I readied myself to write to Barbara, I realized I was in no mood to send her four sentences of jocular bullshit, on the flip side of a glossy card reading "Greetings from Albuquerque." I still hated my father. And to whom could I confess this lack of sympathy? Who would appreciate this confession at this stage in my life? Who could best comprehend my hatred? It was Barbara. The only problem was, she had never known about his beatings. Why not start now, I wondered? Maybe, through my confession, she and I could bond again – our conversations could be less about the books we read and the places we visited and Neil and Nicole and Diana…and more about us.

I kissed Diana on the cheek and told her I needed to get some air, I'd be back in ten minutes. Then I was back in the gift shop, where I purchased a Sierra Del Norte pen and a spiral notebook with the actors from *City Slickers 2* on the cover. I sat on a wooden bench outside the shop and wrote the following:

My dear Mother: please forgive the crassness of all that follows. You're the only one I can trust with the toxic material of my mind. Please too forgive the longstanding secret I've never told you, herein divulged (see paragraph 2). It took me 25 years to realize you're the one who'll most appreciate the truth of my early life. Love always, Ari

ROBERT ZINSKY, 55, ENTREPRENEUR AND HOME-OWNER, PASSES AWAY

Robert Zinsky, a software magnate living in Albuquerque, NM, died yesterday of a cancer type that he and his wife refused to specify, even to Robert's own son, Ariel Zinsky, 25, of Boston. Zinsky the Elder's death concludes a 30-40 month battle with the uncharacterized malady, and also concludes a 25-year-old 'relationship,' so to speak, between the father and Ariel. Robert also leaves behind (with no small fortune) his wife, Cam Clark, 46, and daughter Sandra, 9. Ari, as his intimates call him, is the product of Robert's first marriage, to Barbara Segal (née Pratt) of West Egg, Long Island.

The Frugality of Shylock, With About as Much Respect for the Concept of Mercy

Neither Barbara nor Ariel discussed Robert's history of beating them. "It's not like my family to get specific about things that suck," said Ariel. But Ariel's girlfriend, Diana Kennedy, and his confidantes, Jerod Wilkins and Jimmy Calipari, say that Robert's repeated brutality toward the 6-, 7-, 8-, and 9-year-old Ariel was formative to the young man's psyche, the chief source of his rage against anonymity, and accountable for his reluctance to form bonds with his stepfather, lest the world – as if it gives a shit – would thenceforth view Ariel Zinsky as an ordinary stepson, affable and eager to create and vaunt family attachments. "Ari is thrilled the old man is dead," said Wilkins. "If he's faking sadness, it's so Diana doesn't think he's heartless – which he is, mainly because of the old man."

Love or Sympathy?

Also difficult to ascertain was whether Cam Clark's attention to her husband, in his final weeks, stemmed from sincere connubial love or routine sympathy for the terminally ill. Ariel questioned the heart behind Cam's attentiveness. "In two years, she'll just marry someone else, and probably be more in love with him than she ever was with Robert," he said. "And Sandra – because she was not beaten as a child – will eventually embrace her new stepfather too. There'll be a new man in charge at the Albuquerque manse that used to be my father's. All that will remain of Robert are snapshots and memories that no one works too hard to preserve."

Never Taught Son to Throw a Ball

"To this day," groaned Ariel, "I cannot gloss over my inability to throw a tight spiral. It's only because of my work ethic and devout fear of failure that I've molded myself into a solid basketball player. Baseball – if you consider my height and left-handedness and lack of footspeed – is where I could've and should've made my mark. I should also mention, while I'm holding the microphone, that there are other things Robert never taught me:
• To ride a bicycle
• To shave
• To knot a dress tie

Whither Ariel and the Clarks?

Will Ari keep in touch with Cam and Sandra? Should he? Would they even want him to? Would they suspect him of too blatant an altruism, or too great a desire to preserve a bond that never existed? Will the inevitable arrival of a new *dominus domus* obviate whatever need, if any, Cam and Sandra have for Ari to remain in their lives? A more relevant question may be: why, on earth, would either Clark ever contact Ari of her own accord? And why would he, unless desperate for a game of rummy, contact them?

Bleak House, Bleak Thoughts

If Cam suddenly died, would Ariel be compelled to step up and raise Sandra? No. He would pray Cam had affluent relatives to pick up the slack. If Robert had died during Ariel and Diana's recent visit, would Ariel be happier than if Robert died a week later? Yes. For he'd be spared the hassle of a second trip to Albuquerque (though he'd not be spared the social courtesy of assisting Cam with funeral logistics). If Ariel were truly secure about Diana's love, would he hesitate sharing these pigheaded thoughts with her? No. She would understand a dead father is a buried enemy.

I wrote all of this in about 20 minutes. I went back to the saloon and Diana and Sandra were gone.

When I found them, by the hammock with Cam and Robert, Diana fixed me with a stolid, embarrassed glare. "There he is," said Sandra, her cowboy hat over her forehead. "What'd you buy?" she asked, seizing the *City Slickers 2* spiral – which still included my mock obituary – from my hand.

She eyed the cover, its picture of horseback actors brandishing lassoes. I wanted to snatch it back from her, but held still lest I appeared too nervous. Diana approached and said, "Trouble finding the gift shop?"

"Sorry," I said.

"Trouble rising to the 'social challenge?'" she asked at a lower volume.

"No. I – "

"We'll discuss it later." She raised her volume again. "Sandra was saying we should just leave you here overnight."

"I was not," said Sandra. "That's what you were saying." Sandra turned to me. "We were talking about whether you could ride a horse all the way home."

I grinned, too concerned with regaining possession of my letter to Barbara to retort. Robert, sitting up on the hammock, was helped off it by Cam, and the two of them walked towards us, slowly, their sandals kicking up small patches of dirt. We walked, petty-paced, back to the Explorer, not wanting to make Robert feel even more self-conscious about how slowly he moved.

Before climbing into the car Sandra handed Diana the notebook. She read everything I wrote during the air-conditioned ride back to Albuquerque as Cam initiated a discussion about what we should do for dinner.

*   *   *

I was certain my relationship with Diana was over. I had to talk to her, to explain everything and seek forgiveness. But she wouldn't let me. She kept herself close to Sandra throughout our dinner of delivery pizza and homemade iced tea. We dined on the deck, sitting on sticky plastic chairs, cooled by the black shade of the large umbrella. After the meal I asked Diana if she wanted to take a jog. She declined, speciously citing the heat and a need to pen her own postcards.

I couldn't look Robert in the face after she said this.

When I left the deck to fetch my sneakers, I saw Diana had left the

City Slickers 2 spiral open on our bed. I gratefully picked it up and re-read my letter to Barbara. On the following page Diana had written a note:

Ari,

1. If you had shared these thoughts with me, I would not have been mad at you.

2. You are not heartless and you could never make me believe you are, no matter how many pigheaded thoughts you include in a letter to your mother.

3. I understand your hatred of your dad. For some reason, you seem bent on defining me by my lack of understanding this. But I get it.

4. I'm only pissed that you snuck off to write this and stranded me. How does that make us look to your family?

5. While it hurts me that you have confidences with your mom – and maybe with Jerod and Jimmy – that you don't share with me, I can't be too upset. I have confidences with my mother and with Lori and Harper. I hope one day you will trust me completely. I won't condemn you for your thoughts, my dear friend.

So much, I thought, for my plans to spin-doctor myself to Diana as an all-around sweetheart. And yet – she wasn't upset. Not for the content of the letter, only for my greed in stealing time to write it.

I stuffed my fake obituary into an envelope and dropped it in the mail, along with my postcards to Jimmy, Jerod, and Diana. I found some extra white space on Diana's card and wrote: "Wish you were out jogging with me right now."

After an hour's run, I returned to the house, dripping with sweat. All the lights were off. I went around the back and found Robert and Cam squeezed onto a lounge together. Cam's hand was inside Robert's shorts, and her blond head rested on his slender chest, with its salt-and-pepper sprinkling of hairs. Robert spotted me, tapped Cam lightly on the shoulder, and said, "Hey there." Cam withdrew her hand and sat up, concealing chagrin with a mannered smile. She said, "Diana took the car into town with Sandra. They went to see a movie and get ice cream. Do you need to get inside?"

I nodded and Cam walked me to the sliding glass door. I said, "I'm sorry about interrupting. I should've just walked away."

She said: "I'm so concerned with him that I forgot you were out running and might need to get in. I could probably use a run myself."

I showered and sat up waiting for Diana. Despite her note, I worried frantically she intended to dump me. I tried reading in bed but I could not concentrate. I skipped back and forth between *Moby Dick* and Diana's *Poisonwood Bible,* which she'd purchased in the airport. Not a sentence went by without my drifting into a series of worries over whether this was my last night as her boyfriend.

And yet – how important was Diana to me? In my 25-year-old way, I made a game show out of my emotions and wondered: if forced to choose between Diana's eternal love and a lucrative, prestigious, successful *Guide* acquisition, which one would I choose? They both meant so much to me. But only one of them had been in my life for the past six years. But both of them, it seemed to me, could make me feel as though I'd rendered fruitful the solitary detritus of my childhood.

But the *Guide* wouldn't help me have an orgasm in the Atlantic. The *Guide* wouldn't make me dinner and rub my back and write me notes calling me a "dear friend." I reread the note Diana had left me and wept at the thought of losing her.

As soon as Diana came into the bedroom I threw myself onto her and began kissing her cheeks and hands and arms and hair, showering her with distinctly non-sexual gestures of affection. She giggled throughout, asking, "What's gotten into you?" when I'd kissed her right hand fifteen straight times. I replied, "I can't deal with how worried I get when you're mad at me. I just get scared you'll wish your boyfriend was the type of guy who loved romantic comedies and didn't have issues with his parents."

"Honey, we're traveling together for the first time, and we're going to fight," she whispered, stroking my head. "You're not on trial with me. I'm not Shelagh. I promise you I'm not going anywhere."

"I'm sorry I didn't come back to the saloon in ten minutes."

"It's okay, sweetie, it's okay," she whispered.

"I love you so much, Diana," I said, wiping my eyes on her t-shirt.

"Me too, sweetie," she said. "I'm curious, though, why you're scared to tell me what you wrote in the notebook."

"I was afraid you'd minimize it because my dad isn't Hitler," I said.

"I can see how you'd think that," she said.

"I won't think it anymore," I said. "You trusted me with your pregnancy scare."

She kissed me softly and soon we went to bed, sleeping far more soundly than we had the night before.

*   *   *

On the fourth and final night of our visit, I found myself alone with Robert in the living room, watching a baseball game between the Arizona Diamondbacks – in their third season of existence – and the San Francisco Giants. Following our dinner of homemade goat-cheese ravioli, of which Robert had two squares, Diana and the Clarks wanted to make brownies for dessert. This spontaneous decision required a run to the supermarket for certain ingredients. The women left Robert and me alone in the house, and I realized, all at once, that I was maybe having my final conversation with him.

"So," I ventured, when the ballgame adjourned for a between-innings commercial, "are you getting any wiser in your final days? Any profound insights about love, life, death, or God?"

"Nothing I hadn't figured out already," he said, reposed on his black recliner, hands behind his bandana-clad head. "First off, God doesn't exist. I'll tell you that right now. Love is bullshit too. Love is simply physical attraction plus mental dependence. It's nothing sacred. As for life, it sucks without money. But you seem to understand that. Death? Nothing sacred either. We die just like bugs get crushed and squirrels get smashed on the road. The body parts stop working. There is no soul." He struggled to shift his frame in the chair, so he could face me. With both hands, he pulled on the armrest, swiveling himself on his butt until his knees pointed in my direction. He continued: "I wish I could tell you there was a God. Or a soul. All my life I've wanted to believe in those things. But I really think, after 55 years of life, that humans are just animals. We die, and that's it. The rest of it is just biblical bullshit, stories told so we have a reason to believe."

"Or a reason to behave," I rejoined.

He sighed. "There you go again. Had to get in your last whine before I croak."

"I suppose."

"Well, that seems consistent. You obviously don't find yourself softening towards me, now that I'm dying. You want to attack me again?"

"Yes," I said. "But my religious principles forbid violence."

He flashed his tobacco-stained teeth. "The witty one, over here,"
he said.

"You're not worth the jail time," I said. "I've come too far with the
Guide to risk getting in trouble over you."

"So you're practical, not religious."

"You know the type."

"You didn't seem to care about the *Guide* in the bathroom the other
day," he said.

"Oh, I did. That's why I stopped."

"What I mean is, I provoked you by insulting Diana."

"You're right, she's not addicted to me," I said. "The truth hurts,
okay?"

He nodded – he put both hands back behind his head – he seemed
as satisfied as I had ever witnessed him to be. I waited for the game to
resume. An inning or so passed before I spoke up. "What do you think
Cam saw in you?" I asked. "Besides money."

"Same thing Diana sees in you."

I shrugged. "I can't figure it out."

"Sperm, Ari. It's like I've been telling you forever. Sperm is all they
want. Some of them just don't know it yet. But some of them do. It's the
big female conspiracy. Capture the sperm, then become indifferent to its
source. Like a praying mantis. Mate with the male, bite his head off."

"Cam hardly seems indifferent to you."

"Took her long enough," he said.

"You'd be in a lot worse shape right now without her."

"I don't deny it. But enough about Cam. Gimme the dirt on Diana.
She give good head?"

"Yes."

"Smart girl. And you? Are you munching carpet?"

"What do you think?"

"I think you are, because you're an obedient kid. And you're fair."

Our conversation was interrupted by the entrance of Sandra, clamoring to learn the score of the game. She sat on Robert's lap, and the three of us watched television quietly as Diana and Cam baked.

A few innings later a chocolate smell came a-wafting from the kitchen. Robert said: "Those smell ready."

"Are you finally hungry?" I asked.

"No, I'm just saying they smell ready."

"I'll take them out," I said, leaving him and Sandra to the ballgame.

Uncertain whether slicing the brownies would encroach on Cam or Diana's territory, I went to the guest room, where the latter was laying on her left side in her denim cutoffs. I slid next to her and put my hands on her hips. "Is it okay if I cut the brownies and try to feed Robert?" I asked.

"Stay here a few minutes," she said.

We made out for a while, confining our gropes to our upper bodies. "I'm glad you came here with me," I whispered, stroking her cheek. "You should know that I want to meet Tom and the gang whenever you'd be ready for something like that."

"I feel like they already know you," she said. "I talk about you so much."

"What will surprise them about me? I mean, besides my jump shot."

"That you haven't dumped me yet," she said.

"Stop."

"It's true. They think that you're going to dump me because Albert dumped me after six months and Patrick after five."

"What logic."

"You know how parents are," she said. "They take the first instance, and that becomes the archetype. Until I'm married, they'll pretty much expect me to have a few wonderful months that amount to nothing."

"Is that what you expect?" I asked.

She nodded. I stroked her copper hair and whispered, "Why would I do that?"

"Because you want to fuck. Because I'm not as hot as Shelagh. Because you're more comfortable sharing risqué things with your mom than you are with me."

"Di," I said, "you can't honestly believe I'm not devoted to you."

"I'm sorry. I guess I'm fishing for compliments. What have you and

Robert been talking about in there?"

"Baseball," I said. "Just balls and strikes." We kissed once more and she smacked my butt as I left the room.

When I was in the kitchen, slicing the brownies, Robert called out from the living room, "Did you have a quickie or something? Sandra and I have been waiting five minutes on those fucking brownies." His curse provoked raucous laughter from Sandra.

"I thought you weren't hungry," I replied.

He groaned. "I'm not. I just want that chocolate taste in my mouth," he said. "Can you bring them here?"

"I'm slicing them."

"Ari, just bring me the whole thing. Please."

I bore the warm, weighty platter in front of me, a clear rectangular dish of gooey brown, partially gridded by my unfinished slicing. Robert stuck his fingers into the center of the batch, clawing a cakey fistful and stuffing it into his mouth, a chunk falling from his lips to his lap, on which Sandra still sat, giggling over his antics, scooping up the wayward chunk and eating it. Robert, for his part, chewed slowly and deliberately. I imagined he was forming the brownie into a chocolaty cud, a toothsome reserve he could store like tobacco between his cheek and upper gums, extracting flavor when he needed.

When Robert finished chewing, he said, "Take it away. That was all I needed." And he waved me back into the kitchen, where Cam stood, puzzled by my transport of the batch with its gorged-out middle. She took the pan from me and set it down. "I guess your father has no room for dinner and plenty for dessert," she muttered. She proceeded to slice four brownie squares, placing each on small plates, and topping each with a scoop of vanilla. At length all of us (except Robert) ate a la mode in the living room, watching the conclusion of the ballgame. Before long Robert had drifted to sleep, and had to be coaxed from his chair before Cam could guide him upstairs. Sandra followed them, and Diana and I went back to the guest room, where we lay in the dark holding hands and discussing how quickly our time in Albuquerque had passed.

The next morning Cam drove us to the airport after bringing Sandra to day camp. She pulled over and parked, with blinkers flashing, by the baggage check. Robert lacked the strength to get out of the car and stand on the sidewalk. With the door open, he swung his legs to the side and leaned forward, his butt on the edge of the leather passenger seat. He was like a young boy atop a daunting playground slide, teetering but unable to slide forward. I hooked my arm around his back and helped him down. He extended his arm to the car door for support, wanting to look as if he were casually leaning but betraying weakness through his posture's strenuous rectitude. I gripped him tightly for the first time in decades. Robert placed his hands lightly on my shoulders, balancing himself. I waited for him to whisper something to me, to utter a dramatic and profound final bon mot. Maybe he was waiting for me, too. But neither of us said a word. And so, after our tongue-tied, ten-second embrace, I lifted him back into the Explorer. Cam, chatting with Diana through the driver's window, started the ignition. Robert and I clasped each other's hands. "Bye," I said, and I released him, waving to Cam and stepping away from the door.

Chapter 16 – The Leech

Six weeks after Diana started at Harvard I got tossed from my own apartment. My lease expired and my landlord only offered me a renewal at $1500 a month – double what I'd been paying, but an amount he argued he could obtain on the open market. I was at a loss. Diana saved me once again by proposing the obvious, which as usual I was blind to: if I took a bedroom in Lowell and commuted to the city, I'd save on rent. I could also crash at Diana's apartment and stay there for days on end, whenever the *Guide* required my putting in more extensive hours at Harvard Business School (whose resources I now leeched in place of those of the accounting firm).

Relying so much on Diana's kindness made me uneasy, since we'd had our quarrels as the summer bled on. In August, she had offered to pay airfare for us to attend Robert Zinsky's funeral. I refused, even telling her to go by herself if Cam's and Sandra's opinions meant so much to her. To which she replied: "You act as if *I'm* the one with reputation issues over this."

"You are," I said. "Why else would you care?" We had just taken a jog, and were walking back to her house on a bike path by the sun-reflecting Charles. Our shirts were soaked, our arms were glistening.

She stopped walking. Grabbing my hand, she pulled me over to a stone railing overlooking the water, sandwiching my wrist between her hip and the stone. "There are just times in life when decency requires being a little phony," she said. "I know it doesn't come easily to you. But there's going to come a time when you finally meet my parents, and one of them is going to challenge you. And when that time comes, I'm going to want you to play the game. For me."

"And I will. I just don't want to play it for Cam and Sandra."

"Well, I think you should get over yourself," she said. "I'm not minimizing that your father beat you. But just because that happened, you don't get a pass on decency."

I freed my hand, peeled my sweaty shirt and wrung it out on the stone. "Would you say my father was an abusive parent?" I asked.

"Yes," she said.

"And so you're saying it's indecent to skip an abusive parent's funeral?"

"Not quite," she said. "I understand why you won't go. I'm saying, if you did go, that would be an act of decency and virtue, especially because Cam knows why you'd rather skip it. If you don't go, then Sandra's going to ask Cam why you're not there, and that puts Cam in a tough position."

"Who's to blame for that?" I asked.

"I'm not exonerating your father," she said. "I'm just telling you that I would go if I were you. It's as simple as that."

We resumed walking. It was the last time we discussed the issue.

The funeral came and went. We spent the weekend in Cape Cod.

So my father was buried, and I hoped the subject of honoring his passing was too. And it was, in terms of our openly speaking about it. But over the next few weeks Diana found reasons to postpone my chances to meet Billy and Connie Kennedy, her brother Tom, and sister-in-law Miranda. In these postponements I felt a passive slap at my brazen non-bereavement. But it was difficult to accuse her: Harvard projects and social gatherings kept her legitimately busy and provided feasible-enough excuses for her cancellations. Also, she tended to go skiing or golfing with her family, which automatically eliminated the prospect of my presence; for I didn't know how to ski or golf, and had neither the time nor the money to learn.

Then came one weekend in late autumn when she planned to visit them without me. Not golfing, not skiing, just an ordinary visit in their Lincoln home. "Are you embarrassed I'm your boyfriend?" I asked. It was the night before her visit. She had just picked me up from my shift at

Stevie's Joint in her car – her brother Tom's discarded blue '89 Camry.

"Why would I be?" she said as we stopped at a red light.

"We've been dating for half a year and you won't take me to the parental Estate."

"I have an exam tomorrow. I can only stay for two hours. It's just not worth it."

"It seems to me like it would be an ideal introduction for that reason," I said. I ran my index finger between dusty grates of a small AC vent.

"We disagree, then. Apparently you know more than I do about how my parents receive significant others."

"Do they know I work at a restaurant?"

"Yes. They also know you run your own publishing business with an Internet component."

"Do they know I have a room in Lowell and don't have health insurance?"

"We're not having this conversation," she said. "You're a college educated man who works 80 hours a week and you think my parents might believe I'm slumming?"

"I'm just plumbing for reasons we haven't met yet," I said.

"What's the rush?" she asked.

"You know – you're right," I said, too abruptly changing my mind. I'd been blind to the implications of my line of questioning. Wanting to meet her family signaled a matrimonial intention on my part. And though I could not foresee dumping the only girlfriend I'd ever had, seeking an introduction to Billy and Connie and Tom and Miranda was misleading: for I still did not want a wife or a family. I just wanted Diana to keep being my best friend. And I feared her hesitancy to introduce me jeopardized that. Once our conversation assured me I was secure in my elevated station as her top non-familial priority, I conceded. But respect for my late father's assessment – that Diana was not addicted to me – lingered. I wondered if my entire appeal to her *was* her non-addiction. In the same way I was more comfortable with her than I'd been with Charlene and Shelagh, perhaps Diana too was willing to sacrifice chemistry for security – for a boyfriend who'd carry on like a committed chum, unlike her previous flames.

"You're going to give up, just like that?" she asked. We had crossed the bridge into Cambridge, our butts bumping in our seats from the potholes of Massachusetts Avenue. We were a few minutes from her apartment. "I kind of like it when you ask about meeting my folks," she said.

"You've convinced me you still like me and I have no need to worry," I said. "Plus it's not like you've met Barbara yet, so we're more or less even. I know I'll meet your folks eventually. In the meantime I can rehearse 'playing the game.'" She giggled, and content with our in-joke we transitioned to frivolous Saturday night topics such as where we'd eat the next morning and the latest love-life sagas of Harper and Lori, which were, naturally, melodramatic and juvenile compared to ours.

Our typical weekday was like this: we went to Harvard in the morning. Diana went for classes, and I for the elaborate computer lab, with its high-backed ergonomic chairs and rapid Internet connections and flat-screen monitors. After Diana logged me in, I wrote football articles all morning, communicating with Joel via my cell phone. At noon Diana returned to the lab to check her email, after which we had lunch together, discussing what we'd done in the morning. In the afternoon she stayed in the Baker Library and evaluated her case studies. I returned to the computer lab where – I must confess – my chief joy was utilizing streaming video to watch football players. Such activity was neither discouraged nor frowned upon by the graduate students surrounding me, since – for all the lab's bells and whistles – most of them used it merely to check their email or surf sports and entertainment sites. Like Diana, they seemed to prefer doing homework on their own laptops, toting them to their dorms or apartments or any of the campus's cozy wireless hubs. With my cell phone constantly ringing – it was either Joel or one of my advertisers getting back to me or one of my Stevie's Joint coworkers seeking shift coverage – I felt like the only person at Harvard who was actually working.

At 3:30 p.m. I left for Stevie's, logging off the Harvard network so Diana could use it the rest of the day. I didn't get home – which is to say, back to Diana's triple decker – until eleven, by which time Diana was in bed. The upshot was, we had only three time slots together all day: our morning drive, lunch, and bedtime. We were aware that this scheduling represented American normalcy for most couples; but for

Diana and me it was difficult, because our earlier days had been leisurely by comparison. My hiatus from Stevie's had coincided with her lame duck status at the accounting firm, and the result had been a pleasurable avoidance of bedtimes and other structures.

Still, we were content. We chatted wonderfully at lunch and climaxed regularly before sleeping. What else could a hardworking couple seek? We respected each other's work ethic and never begrudged each other the occasional all-nighter, impinge though it might on the nightly orgasm. We always – always – had lunch, and in the shared meal came all the frivolities of intimacy. I can still rank Diana's favorite beverages – Fresca, followed by Dr. Brown's Diet Black Cherry Soda, followed by Raspberry Snapple, followed by lemonade of any brand.

There is no one else in the world I have ever been able to do that for.

*   *   *

It was during Diana's first semester that the Internet bubble began popping: prominent stocks plummeted in share price, and statistics showed decreasing amounts of investor capital flocking to unprofitable startups like mine – even though by this time I had 20,000 loyal web readers and 1,000 loyal print subscribers. My ad revenues were paltry. Visitors to ZinskyQuintessential.com simply read the articles and left, rather than "clicking through" to my links for sites offering affordable stock trading. So I earned zilch in commissions. The advertisements in the *Guide* and the *Late Edition* generated real income for me, but it was small: each issue had three-dozen full-page ads, for which I got $300-$600 from various businesses targeting male sports fans: Fantasy Football sites, retailers of authentic jerseys or collectibles, nationally syndicated radio shows, even a web site specializing in sports nonfiction. My stated rate was $600, but I negotiated downward to $300 for the sake of closing deals. I preferred adding satisfied customers to my stable, who could ultimately become third-party authenticators for the *Guide's* viability, in case a potential acquirer began conducting due diligence.

All told, though, my annual advertising revenues were roughly $6000, a figure I'd need to quadruple to break even – unless I found a way to further lower my costs. I was now balancing my debts among 15 credit cards. I made a list of my expenses and all of them seemed irre-

ducible: rent, cell phone, toiletries. It dawned on me I was renting a
room I never stayed in: I arrived at Diana's late each night and left in
the morning, rotating a supply of clothes I kept in two of her drawers.
If I got a post office box for mail and ceased paying rent, I'd save $500
a month, which I could put toward my solvency.

With one phone call to my surprised landlord I made it happen. By
the end of the month I'd sold my television and furniture and was
without a proper address. I donated my spare clothes to goodwill and
crammed the rest into my two drawers at Diana's.

And I did all this without Diana's knowledge.

I didn't regret the action until one night when Harper was having a
house party for all of her friends at WMUR, a volunteer radio station
affiliated with MIT. Diana didn't begrudge her roommate a night of
revelry, but for the sake of our sleeping she suggested we adjourn to
my place. I agreed and spent the rest of the week mulling what to do.
At length I drove us to a hotel suite at the Radisson in downtown Boston, in which one night cost almost as much as the rent I'd hoped to
save. Diana protested on these grounds, knowing the cost pressures I
was under. But I told her Joel had gotten me a discount through advertising connections; and we went to our suite and didn't leave it until the
following afternoon.

So I had dodged a downfall, but I told myself I'd find a room again
as soon as possible, since I'd care not about pinching *Guide* pennies if
Diana dumped me for my deceit. But after a few weeks, I remained
homeless on paper, as my fears of being found out gave way to my
business's craving for liquid cash. Then came one Saturday evening
when Diana and I were returning from a day in the Berkshires. Her
parents were visiting her early the next morning, and she preferred my
spending the night in Lowell lest her parents – who sometimes arrived
at the triple decker as early as 7:30 a.m. – discover me fleeing from her
back window. "And it's not that I don't want you to meet them," she
insisted. "But they would *flip* if they knew we practically lived together."
I agreed, and when we came to my former residence in Lowell I kissed
her goodbye and charged up the front steps, as if I'd never left. She
watched from the car, waiting for me to get inside. I had kept my spare

key on my chain, and it worked: I opened the door, stepped inside the foyer, shut the door, and watched her blue Camry roll away.

When she was gone, I pondered where I might spend the night. The foyer was risky. My former landlord might return home and see me. Harvard Business School was risky too. Security wasn't tight, but a potential discovery would be disastrous for the *Guide* and Diana's reputation. Stevie's Joint was an option, but Patti had her ways of finding out about things. She was already irked I'd taken Saturday off to go to Tanglewood with Diana.

I decided to explore Harvard's undergraduate campus – which was a safe distance from the business school. I hoped to find a warm library with a soft couch to crash on. If the setup was anything like the University of Michigan's, then all the libraries would close at a certain time, during which it would be my duty to hide while staff combed the stacks for sleeping students.

I had spent so many consecutive Saturday nights at Stevie's Joint, it was enjoyable simply *not* to be there. In the stacks I found the fiction section and sat at a dusty wooden desk that looked as if it had been moored to the dusty tile floor for centuries. A window provided a view of the lamppost-lit campus, which was enlivened with students moving in vociferous groups from dorm to dorm. Inside the stacks, all was quiet. Whenever someone got up to leave, I heard the squeak of their wooden chair on the tile, the clacking of their footsteps, the elevator door squeaking open and clapping shut.

The house lights remained on, which told me it wasn't safe to sleep yet. I stayed at my desk, rotating among the six books I'd gathered and brought to my carrel: I had browsed among the B, C, and D authors, coming away with *David Copperfield, Augie March, Robinson Crusoe,* and *David Levinsky.* In the mold of all four I fancied myself a pitiable protagonist, and pondered how I might one day pen the story of my own life, or the life of a character I imagined. Would it be in the first person, like those four books? Or would it be in the third person, like *Crime and Punishment?* And what were the ramifications of this decision? In terms of style, these books were such a far cry from the football articles I churned out almost every day. But if there ever came an era when I wrote football no more, and my free time needn't be devoted to income or *Guide* management – well, maybe the story of my life would be a project to consider.

After an hour or so of likening myself to the heroes of the classics, I heard a light crisp chime, a ping, followed by squeaking from the elevator doors and feet stomping quickly in my direction. Before I could look up an obese, bespectacled man in a buttoned navy security uniform shouted brusquely: "Library's closed. Come back tomorrow at eight." I gathered up the books. "Too late to check out," he said. "Tomorrow at eight."

It was a cool star-filled night in the high forties, jackets helpful but not necessary for short distances. Mine, a thin dark brown polyester cotton Barbara had bought me at the Gap, remained unzipped, and I hoped, in fact, to use it as a pillow rather than a garment. By dint of my age, I reasoned nothing could be made of my curling up beneath a tree and falling asleep; I doubted campus security would wake me and ask to see my student ID. So with my folded jacket cushioning my head I lay back and shut my eyes. Students traversed the surrounding paths, while hip-hop music blared from nearby dorms.

I'm not sure how much time had passed when I felt a hard rounded wooden edge prodding my ribs. I had rolled onto my side and compressed my left arm to the point of pins and needles. My prodder was another campus official, a black man dressed much like my library persecutor. His accent, tinged with French, signaled Haitian origins. "Do you want to sleep in your own house, sir," he asked me, as I sat up. I nodded and stood. "What house do you live in?" he asked.

"Wentworth," I said quickly. The name was in my head as *something* on the Harvard campus.

"There is no Wentworth House," he said authoritatively. He took my arm, as if I were five years old, and led me to a gate facing Massachusetts Avenue. "You'll be arrested if I see you again," he said.

I crossed the street to the Coop bookstore, under whose prodigious awning there slept a half dozen homeless. Here I lay me down, my jacket again serving as a pillow. As non-religious as I had always been, I found the words "Thank God," coming involuntarily to my tongue, as my gratitude for not having to rest my back nightly on such hard concrete. It was 3:14 a.m. according to a lighted clock perched high atop a nearby bank; and to my thinking none of my homeless bedfellows were awake to hail my arrival. But just as I had shut my eyes the man closest to me said, "Welcome to the Hotel California, kiddo." I twisted my neck around to view him. He was sitting up, and all I could make out of his face was a long gray-white beard. A crusty gray blanket wrapped his body and a white woolen cap covered his hair. "Got a cigarette?" he asked.

"Sorry, man," I said, staring up at the dark awning. I truly dreaded his presence more than I dreaded the lack of bedding.

"Your wife kick you out or something?" he asked. He mulled this for a moment before bursting into a loud throaty laugh, which awoke the black man sitting across from him. "Shut the fuck up, Morty," said the black man. "I got a big day tomorrow." This had them both in stitches. I chuckled politely and waited for the hysterics to subside. I felt my pockets, confirming the presence of my wallet and keys, and knew then I'd probably not sleep soundly until the next night in Diana's bed. But at least I could lay here for a while, before sneaking off to the triple decker to shower while Diana and family were at church.

"Your wife kick you out or something?" repeated the man identified as Morty.

"Yeah, that's pretty much the deal," I said. The moment struck me as humorous: Where *now* was my pressing need to share my life story? Faced with Morty for company and the street for a bed and an awning for a ceiling, it didn't bother me so much to provide a redacted history of how I'd gotten where I'd been.

"Welcome to the Hotel California," said Morty.

* * *

I woke up galvanized. I felt like the worst entrepreneur in the history of America. After nearly six years of the *Guide*, I was sleeping on the street. So I had 20,000 loyal Internet readers and 1,000 magazine subscribers – how was that relevant? Was I an author, or was I an entrepreneur? I was both, of course, but the question was how I could transform readership into dollars.

And so, after a discussion with Joel, we transformed

ZinskyQuintessential.com into a subscribers-only site: you could read it, but you had to pay a monthly fee of $5. "It's elementary, rudimentary, and fundamental," said Joel. "On the front page of the site you announce you're going to go bankrupt unless you start charging. Then you shift gears and proclaim you're for the common man – so much so that you openly state the mathematics: if each subscriber pays $60 a year, you have 20,000 times $60, which is – actually, that's a lot of money. Don't write that. Just stick with $5-a-month."

By the end of the day on ZinskyQuinteesstial.com I'd posted the following:

Sports fans:

Favor me with your attention for seven statements:

1. Granted: you love ZinskyQuintessential.com because it is a frivolous, enriching break from the nonstop business news and political shenanigans passing for 'current events.'

2. Alas, some business news is now encroaching on our splendid non-reality reality, after our six years together in the football playhouse.

3. Because none of you click on my ads, ZinskyQuintessential.com doesn't generate revenues.

4. I need more revenues to keep this site going – especially if you want me to join the 21st century and add high-speed streaming video of our nation's pigskin warriors.

5. So starting immediately I must transform ZinskyQuintessential.com into a password-protected site – hence these seven commandments, rather than the football stories you've come to expect.

6. Passwords – which you can get by clicking <u>here</u> – cost $5-per-month, and can be automatically billed to your credit card.

7. Think of all the money you waste on bad coffee, bad newspapers, bad pornography, bad weed, bad food, bad housing – isn't *good* football content worth $60 a year?

And do you not reach points in life – with friends, lovers, employers – when you ask this selfsame question? When you proclaim to the woman or man or job of your dreams: am I not worth at least *this much* to you? I beg you all to consider the nadirs or crises you must reach to merely pose this narcissistic interrogative. It is like the Declaration of Independence: you have experienced a 'long series of usurpations' and you are at the proverbial breaking point. Yet you are content to carry on, *if* your partners offer a *de minimus* show of faith.

Five dollars a month is all I need, folks. If most of you can give me that, then I can keep doing what I'm doing, which will hopefully be enough to gratify you for another six years. And ponder: how boring would your workdays be without the Internet? And how boring would the Internet be without *the only site that updates its NFL draft-related content every fucking day*?

Come on, sports fans. Is it not precious that this is the only sports site capable of using *fucking* as an adjective, and bragging about it?

There are times in life where your American boat reaches Normandy Beach and you can't hesitate, you can't guess – you just jump off the boat and start shooting Germans. That time is *now*, my patriots. <u>Buy that password</u>, and don't think twice: it's just $60 a year, for Allah's sake. And if you have any gripes about my slandering of Allah or my minimizing of the so-called Greatest Generation…

…or if you have questions about this business transition, or the financial specifics compelling it…

…please email me at <u>Zinsky@ZinskyQuintessential.com.</u> Links to non-virus-spewing porn sites are encouraged but not required. Until then, I am,

Your headstrong, but needy, founder, publisher, head writer, friend, and fellow sports fan,

Ariel Zinsky

Over the next few weeks the money rolled in: nearly 9,000 of my subscribers paid up. From their fees alone I had nearly $45,000 in recurring monthly revenues, even though I'd lost the other 11,000 site visitors in the process. Joel and I were stunned. "After six years," he said, "You no longer have an expensive, time-consuming hobby. You finally have a business."

All I had to do was keep it going. With a daily audience of paying members I felt more pressure than ever to write compelling football stories. For I feared my new fans would cancel their subscriptions – and mar my newly established fiscal credibility – if I delivered anything less. I was thrilled to be emerging from years of red ink and to be recovering my seemingly lost dream of an acquisition. But the pressure I'd always felt in April, when the *Guide* was due to ship, was now a daily rigor: I forced myself to compose three new articles every day.

So I wound up spending seven days a week at Harvard Business School. I got so caught up in production that I worked until 4:15 p.m., only making it on time to Stevie's Joint because my cab drivers ran red lights at my bribing behest. Invariably I was distracted during my shifts. Even when Sandy Appleton came in and swallowed her pills, my mind rarely veered from the three new articles I had to post the next morning.

Arriving ten or fifteen minutes late became a norm: I recall one week when my punch-card read 4:44, 4:41, 4:47, 4:46, 4:42, 4:39 in computerized red ink. I was required to show up at 4:30 but officially began serving at five, so my dereliction went unnoticed – until Patti Kinkade handed me this particular punch-card and sat me down in her office. She awaited my explanation as she traced her pencil along the clipboard on her corduroyed lap. I was silent. "You got nothing to say?" she asked. "Do you still want to work here, Ari? Or are you just covering your debts again?"

I hesitated to brag about ZinskyQuintessential.com's new revenues. If anything, that would make her point, give her fuel to believe I was increasingly indifferent to my restaurant income. At the same time, her reprimand disturbed me. I had worked there for more than three years. Could she not begrudge me one week of sub-par performance?

Now that I am 30, I recognize my absurdity in thinking this. But when I was 25, I felt enraged that Patti, after all I had done for Stevie's, could not offer me lenience. "I guess you think I'm interchangeable with anyone you could hire off the street, right?" I asked. I stuck my hands deep within my apron pockets, fingering a butter knife.

"Spare me the self-pity, Ari," she said. "Don't insult me by pretending I just insulted you. You're constantly late and distracted and I want an explanation."

Her use of the word *distracted* set my mind to a football tangent. One of the articles I intended to draft the next morning was about Oakland Raiders rookie kicker Sebastian Janikowski, and whether his scrapes with law enforcement officials would prove to be a distraction to his play. I focused on Oakland's draft history. The last time one of their early selections had been a disappointment was 1994, when Louisiana-Monroe linebacker James Folston couldn't crack the starting lineup. The point was: good players were good players, and if your ability to throw or kick or tackle was compromised by an off-the-field distraction, well – then you weren't a good player. Janikowski was a good player. But was I? I looked at Patti, whose hands were tightening her spongy hair band. "I mean – you think I'm a good waiter, don't you?" I asked.

She chuckled. "There's no separating tardiness from your job performance. I need you here at 4:30. It's that simple. I thought – based on how long we've worked together – that you might have something going on, so I wanted to give you a chance to explain why you've been late. But if you're just going to sit there with your hands in your pockets and ask *me* if I think you're a good waiter – when you know I do, and when you know that's irrelevant – I don't know what I can do, other than tell you: don't be late again, or I'm going to have to do something I'd rather not do."

"Okay," I said. I stood up and left her office – and the restaurant – without a backwards glance. It was the last time I ever saw Patti Kinkade.

The next day, on the instinct, I left Harvard Business School in late afternoon. It was only after I had reached the subway station that I realized I had no mandatory afternoon destination. No longer needing the income of Stevie's Joint, I had chafed under the basic obligation of employment. But what would I do now? It was my first free weekday afternoon in Boston in more than three years.

It was early October; brown leaves covered the sidewalks of Harvard Square, which were filled with hustling undergraduates, lugging backpacks and spiral notebooks. Oh, what a whirling and shocking world it was. Less than one month earlier I had been in the selfsame neighborhood, seeking a place to lay my head! Now I was practically a rich man, spurning my job of three years to wander the redbrick streets like a young dandy.

I strolled along a concrete path on the raked college campus – two miles away from the Business School. Why such distance? So there was no chance Diana would discover my absence from work. And why didn't I want her to? It was probably because my restaurant work had given my unconventional lifestyle some credibility. There was gravitas in working nights. There was gravitas in being physically tired. And this gravitas made me guiltless about crashing at Diana's – and probably made Diana more willing to help me. I felt less leeching and more *boot-*

strapping. I no longer needed to bootstrap, but I wanted Diana to continue *perceiving* me that way. And why was that? I couldn't figure it out. But I knew it to be true.

A pigeon wandered meekly in front of me, the path's gray concrete setting his rubbery pink legs in relief. $45,000 a month. It was staggering. It was an income almost bound to lure prospective acquirers. And it was mine. All mine. As long as I didn't fuck it up, as long as I kept delivering my three articles a day, I would be out of debt by year's end. It was great news. If I couldn't tell Diana, I at least had to tell Jerod and Jimmy. I left a voicemail with Jerod and reached a relaxed Jimmy at his *Newsday* office. "Shouldn't you be serving iced tea to yuppies right about now?" he asked.

"I quit," I told him, and explained why. He congratulated me before admitting he'd not yet purchased his own ZinskyQuintessential.com password. "But it sounds like you don't need *my* money," he said.

I told him my reluctance to reveal the news to Diana. "Well, as usual, you're giving yourself way too much credit for being complex," he told me. "See, you *like* where you're at right now. If you tell Diana, everything might change. She's going to ask what you're *doing* every evening while she's studying her ass off. And if you say, well, I was lounging on the Harvard campus with my cell phone, shooting the shit with Jimmy – now that's something you have every right to *do*, but it's not easy to confess to a busy girlfriend that *you've* been relaxing. She might ask you to hang out with her Harvard friends, or to take her car to the mechanic, or to move her bed to the other side of the room. Now, these are things a devoted boyfriend would love doing for his girl. But you, Ari – let's not pretend, okay? In your life, you've grown accustomed to doing whatever you want, whenever you want. And it's gotten you this far. But it's also spoiled you. For a girl like Diana, who you know is way too good for you, you should be willing to inconvenience yourself – if you're serious about her. For all these years, your insane lifestyle has given you a bulletproof excuse to be greedy with your time. But that's not reality. And if you want it to be reality, well – good luck."

Jimmy was right. Entrepreneurship gave license to the solipsism that had steered me from a lonesome youth and turned me into a productive adult. It was hard to turn my back on that, especially now that my egoism had finally yielded a fiscal Valhalla: a profitable *Guide* combined with ample free time. Had I not toiled on the *Guide* for nearly six years, braving legal and fiscal risk, in pursuit of an epoch such as this, when the magazine I loved producing could finally support me, when my passion had genuinely become my vocation, my path to legitimate subsistence, recognition, and even fame?

So I continued concealing my financial turnaround – and my quitting as a waiter, and my homelessness – from Diana. I wanted my time still to be my own, not hers. I could use my free afternoons on other *Guide*-related tasks. I could proactively *seek* acquirers, place feelers with dealmakers, and bolster my subscriber totals by marketing my wares to the millions of sports fans to whom I was still an unknown. And I could do what I had not done for years: I could fuck around, reading novels, playing basketball, or even – I grinned and laughed aloud at the thought – watching televised sports in bars. I might – could it be? – begin having fun on weeknights. No wonder the rest of the world seemed so content with their nine-to-five existences! There was so much joy, so many entertainments – sports, books, movies, television, music, Internet sites, magazines – all constructed only so the masses could savor and embrace their leisure time. And didn't I, the 25-year-old from Long Island, deserve a break as much as anyone?

Chapter 17 – Truth & Consequences

So the *Guide* became successful; and every month I received checks from MasterCard and Visa and American Express and Discover totaling nearly $45,000, less processing fees. My mother was not as impressed as I'd hoped. "How long till you're out of debt?" she asked.

"How about 'I'm proud of you, son?'" I replied.

"I'm proud of you, son," she said. "How long till you're out of debt?"

"It depends on interest rates," I said. "One year, max, if the dough keeps coming in. But I've got to get rid of it soon, or no one will want to acquire me."

"*Acquire* you? That sounds pretty serious. Want Neil to get you a lawyer?"

"Mom, do you think I've been running this business in my *sleep*? Leave him out of this. I can find a lawyer if I need one."

"I want you to make an effort to befriend him this Thanksgiving," she said. "Enough is enough. You're going to know him for the rest of your life."

"You're right," I said. "I can play the game a little."

"It won't be so difficult," said Barbara.

"But I don't want to stay in his house."

"Ari, it's *our* house, not *his*," she said. "And if you're bringing Diana, you must consider staying here. What sort of impression do you think you make, not wanting to stay in your mother's house?"

"Fine," I said.

It was on the previous Thanksgiving that Neil and I had had our biggest quarrel. It was a shouting match occurring when he benevolently wondered why I didn't disband the costly print magazine portion of the *Guide* to focus solely on the Internet. "Like *you* know anything about business," I seethed.

"Ari, you don't have to attack me," he said. "Maybe if you tried, instead, to attack my *suggestion* – and that's all it is – you'd see there's nothing wrong with it."

"It's the problem with white collar professionals like you," I continued, in flagrant defiance of his rhetorical tip. "*You* approach advice-giving as if the only factors are measurable financials. What *you* fail to see is that the whole magic to the *Guide* is *intangible*. The whole reason people love it – both the magazine and the site – is because *I* am more concerned with spreading the football gospel than with slamming ads in their faces every three seconds. If *you* knew anything about sports, you'd know sports lose charm the instant they *seem* commercial."

"You can't live on credit forever," he warned.

At which point I pushed out my chair and left the table, though the four of us were in the middle of turkey and cranberry sauce and sweet potatoes. "Ari, you're being immature," said Barbara.

At the front door I looked back at the three of them. "Even if you think my business is an illusion," I shouted, "you should know enough about me, and enough about humans, to let me enjoy that illusion until it bursts. I hope one day you put forth half the effort I'm putting toward the *Guide* toward anything. Maybe then you'll understand where I'm coming from, why I'd rather die than retreat on the *Guide*, and why the tamest thing I can possibly do at this moment is *this* – "

And I slammed the door behind me, walked to the West Egg train station, and spent the night crashing on Jimmy Calipari's couch, reading the *New York Post* the next morning while he and his girlfriend humped loudly in his bedroom. I went back to Boston that same day, after borrowing $35 from Jimmy for my bus ticket.

I never apologized to my mother or Neil or Nicole for the incident; I was 24 at the time, and I felt it was they who owed me the apology, for deigning to inquire about the feasibility of my lofty ambitions. The next time Barbara and I spoke, it was like it had always been: books, jobs, significant others – everything but the innermost truth of our rapport was on the docket.

My postcard from Albuquerque changed all of that. I told my mother the stories of Robert's beatings, including the ones occupying the first part of this book; and she confirmed my suspicion that there had been no others for her, save for the time he'd whacked her with *Night*. And with this exchange of heretofore hidden pasts a forthright quality seized hold of our chats. Now she unabashedly criticized my iciness to Neil, and to his home. She insisted regularly that I stay in the house, that Neil would welcome me and forgive all, and that Diana too was welcome to stay whenever I was ready for such a thing. I, in turn, confessed to Barbara about all I'd kept hidden from Diana regarding my newfound success and resulting lifestyle.

Barbara admonished me for my concealments to Diana. The admonishments became reprimands as the weeks went by. Then one day came a scolding: "Don't you see, you're only making it worse, the longer you hold out?" she screamed. "What kind of man doesn't have his own apartment?" I held the phone further from my ear.

Barbara knew my counterarguments: chiefly, that I believed I was always one day away from finding my new apartment; and if I did so, I could fib to Diana that I had simply *moved*, rather than gone homeless for a short time; and this fib of moving would spare me Diana's anger, and coincide with an announcement about my *Guide's* fortune and my quitting as a waiter.

But each day, I wound up writing my *Guide* stories all morning, and reading novels at some Boston or Cambridge hangout – one where Diana would never find me – all evening. I read all the novels I'd found in the Harvard library during my vagabond night. Then, continuing alphabetically by author, I read *Daniel Deronda* by George Eliot, *Tom Jones* by Henry Fielding, and *The Tin Drum* by Gunther Grass.

So I procrastinated the problem of finding my own apartment. Diana, in whose bed I still slept, remained under the impression I was slaving away at Stevie's Joint.

I also got back into the radio business. My interest was having my own sports talk show, as I had in college, to promote my *Guide* and myself as a leading brand of football expertise. And I hoped that the radio station, itself, would give me a place to crash whenever Diana needed a night by herself. So I sought a volunteer position that would earn me some keys to station headquarters. This position was – to be blunt – a monkey's job. Two nights every week, from midnight to three a.m., I simply sat in a wooden chair and played the station ID every hour on the hour, a recorded stentorian voice saying, *You're listening to WMUR Cambridge.* This was while WMUR broadcast a nationally syndicated blues show called *Lafayette Lightning.* At three a.m., I switched us over to another syndicated program, *Punk in the Trunk.* And then I slept on a peeling dark green chair in the studio room while another volunteer, a tall gay man named Ryan Shields, played the station ID at four, five, and six. Of course, WMUR had technology to automate the station ID function. But getting new volunteers in the fold was central to the non-profit station's mission; the overnight shift was invented as a means to gauge aspirants' desire.

Ryan was a huge baseball fan who worked in sales for a software firm specializing in architectural design. We became fast friends – as two people in our circumstances usually will – and enjoyed many conversations about sales and sports. Out of necessity he became privy to the circumstances compelling me to sleep at the radio station; together we plotted to overthrow WMUR's syndicated programming and replace it with our own late-night sports-talking tandem. We joined the WMUR sales team as commission-only mercenaries; we left voicemails with prospects during our dead hours, hoping to enhance our standing by increasing station revenues.

Armed with WMUR as a new obligation in my life, I finally gathered the nerve to confess to Diana about the lie I'd been leading. For I could embellish my story so that Diana would continue perceiving me as a nonstop worker – rather than what I had become, a grown man who wrote football articles all morning and read novels all afternoon. I didn't yet have a new apartment, but I didn't think it mattered, if I made my confessional correctly: I fancied myself deft enough as a storyteller to convince Diana my apartment-dumping had come during a desperate time; and that I was slow to rectify the situation only because – now that I had money – I'd hoped my next apartment would be a purchase; so I had to be picky.

That was how I imagined my explanation unfolding.

We were in downtown Boston on a cloudless, windless Sunday evening in the high 30s. We passed through the Public Gardens with its changing foliage, and on to Boston Common, with its Frog Pond ice skating rink. Diana proposed some impromptu skating. I'd have appreciated the idea, had it not been for the fact that I didn't know how to skate. But I was eager to prove myself game for elite winter sports. The previous weekend, Diana had gone skiing with brother Tom and his wife Miranda, and I'd once again felt left behind by my lack of training. So I said yes and before I knew it we'd rented skates and were sitting on wooden benches, squeezing them on.

It took me about five minutes to ram my left foot into its size-17 holster. When I knotted my laces loosely, not yanking to compress the heel and ankle, Diana sighed. "You've never done this before, have you?" she asked. I shook my head. She grabbed my skate and tugged the bottom-most laces so tight I could feel a pulse in the blood vessels of my foot. Eventually I hobbled behind her toward the small rink. Dozens of other couples were skating around the oval, holding hands, their expressions bedazzled by all the precocious, helmeted six-year-olds veering around them and grinding to dramatic, slashing halts. And there I was, being led around the rink by my redheaded chaperone, my blades clunking over the ice, stepping rather than gliding, my gloveless hand gripping hers so tightly, so nervously, that perspiration threatened to loosen my grip and send me thudding downward. At one point Diana said, "I know you've never played much baseball. But do you know what my dad used to tell Tom, when he was teaching him to play? He'd say: 'You can't be afraid of the hard ball, Tommy. Pretend the pitcher is throwing a *cupcake.*' And he'd say the same thing when teaching Tom hockey. 'Just pretend the ice is a *mattress*, Tommy. And pretend the boards are covered with pillows.' My point is you'll never skate well – or ski well, for that matter – if you're afraid of falling. So next time around the ice I'm letting go of your hand. I'll be right behind you."

"Don't let go, Diana," I said.

She smiled and released me. I clacked on the ice for two or three strides but kept upright, my hands waving in front of me as if I were blindfolded, until the time came for me to make a rounded left at the oval's edge. Unable to slow my momentum, I smacked helplessly into the curved white rink, avoiding a fall but not the embarrassment of nearly mowing down a pair of legging-clad teenage girls who were leaning against the wall, chitchatting. Diana raced up behind me and apologized to the girls: "Sorry, it's his first time," she said in what struck me as a conspiratorial, we're-all-women-here tone. The girls skated away and Diana said, "So, did you recognize what happened there? You were afraid you'd fall if you turned too sharply."

"I would have fallen if I turned too sharply," I said. I had snapped at her and I quickly said, "Sorry. I – I have a lot to tell you tonight, and it's stressing me out. I wanted to wait until we were eating, but I think – "

She led me off the ice back to the bench where we'd laced our skates. "Tell me *now*," she said.

I couldn't look her in the eyes. I looked down at my skates, resting on the sticky-soft black canvas, the rusty blades sprinkled with ice shavings. I listened to the jaunty 80s pop music playing on the rink speakers – the song was "Karma Chameleon" by Culture Club. Sharing the bench with us were two blond teenage boys who looked like brothers, splitting a warm pretzel and dipping it in mustard. I recall the salty smell of their food, and I recall fearing Diana might get up and leave me once I unbosomed myself of my secrets; so I memorized how everything around me smelt and sounded and felt, believing these were my final moments as her boyfriend.

"Just say it," said Diana, the breeze blowing her red hair over her forehead.

"Have you visited the site lately?" I asked.

This caught her off guard; given my preface, she took the question as an accusation. "No," she said. "Why? Is that something you'd like me to do? I feel like you update me on it every day, so I guess I don't read it myself."

I explained my subscription initiative, and how it had made me rich almost overnight. "So," I concluded, "I'm reaching the point where I can quit the restaurant, move back to Boston, and rent an office space, instead of using Harvard computers."

"That's amazing!" she said. She hugged me right there. "But there's a 'but' coming, it sounds like," she added.

"The 'but' is, I already quit the restaurant, I already gave up my place in Lowell, and I've been crashing at WMUR whenever I'm not at your place," I said. "I've been spending my afternoons reading the great books in Starbucks. I've been living this way in secret from you since September, basically. Why that is, I don't know."

She protested. "What about that time after the Berkshires, when I dropped you off?" she asked. And I explained. She was looking out at the rink, repositioning her red winter hat over her forehead. "What are you thinking?" I asked.

"I'm thinking, you and I have made no progress since Albuquerque," she said. "Let me guess: your mother, Jimmy, and Jerod have all known about your career activity from day one, while you kept me in the dark. True or false?"

"True," I said. "But you're using confidence as a barometer for intimacy. And life doesn't work that way. You have secrets from your parents. It doesn't mean you're not close to them, it just means you're scared the truth will hurt their feelings."

"Well, that's what I don't get about your behavior," she said. "What did you think, I'd yell at you for reading novels all afternoon?"

"Yes," I said. "And what would your parents think if they knew that was how I lived? I wanted to keep impressing them – and maybe you – by working 80-hour weeks."

"You disgust me sometimes," she said. She left me on the bench. I watched her skate, around and around the rink, for five or ten minutes. Every now and then one of the rink guards, wearing flashy yellow jackets emblazoned "GUARD" on the back, would eye her slender figure, her rump in particular as she decelerated into curves and sped up on the straightaways – and I felt glum, wondering anew how I could've chanced dishonesty with a prize like Diana. Of course, I knew how: the *Guide* was competing with Diana as my love interest. And I flocked to whichever one I was in danger of losing.

At length she returned, and I thought it was to reconcile: She sat next to me and smiled and I leaned in to kiss her. But she turned away. "And let me get this straight," she said. "You *don't have a home* right now?" I nodded. She went back to the ice and skated for what seemed like an eternity. My eyes wandered throughout the lamppost-lit Boston Common. Couples, it seemed, were everywhere: holding hands while sitting on benches, carrying shopping bags while traversing the park's crisscrossing concrete paths. At that moment I didn't know if I were part of a couple, or back in the land of the single. If Diana refused to kiss me – it meant, on some level, I had little power over her. If her desire for me were strong, she'd never deny me a kiss, no matter how poorly I'd behaved. This had to be true: for nothing Diana could do would ever make me turn from *her* kiss.

And yet she had turned from mine. She had every right to be angry – but did she have a right to do *that*? If she were fearless about doing that, then Robert Zinsky was correct: she was not addicted. It didn't mean she didn't love me. I was certain she did. But it was conditional love. As she skated round and round the rink I wondered if my violation was fatal or temporary, *ser* or *estar*. A half hour passed and she remained on the ice. I had three articles to write the next morning and grew tired of waiting. I returned my skates, donned my sneakers, and sat on the bench, scanning the circling throng of skaters in search of her slender bedenimed figure, her red hair flapping in the breeze behind her red hat. But I could not find her. Apparently, she had departed too – and quickly. I dialed her cell and got no answer. Without leaving a message, I hung up and began walking to my new home: WMUR, Cambridge. I hoped that the radio station was equipped with a computer and a high speed Internet connection. For I'd no longer just be sleeping there, if Diana – and the Harvard Business School – were no longer a part of my life.

Chapter 18 – Thanksgiving with the Kennedys

For the next three days I slept at WMUR and did ZinskyQuintessential.com work on the station's computer. I did not change my clothes; I did not shower or shave; and I did not hear from Diana until the fourth afternoon. "Where have you been?" she asked.

"At the station. I have work to do," I said.

"You make it sound like I turned you out. You're the one who left me at the rink."

"What are you talking about?" I shouted. I was alone in the studio, and my voice resounded through WMUR's vacant hallways. "You went off and skated on your own for twenty, thirty minutes. You expected me to stick around?"

"Yes, I did," she said.

"Well, I'm sorry I didn't," I said. "It didn't seem like you wanted to be my girlfriend anymore."

"What makes you say that?"

"Because you wouldn't let me kiss you."

"Oh God, Ari," she said. "I was so angry. How could you keep all that from me?"

"It was an innocent mistake at first. Then a few weeks passed. So I stayed silent because I figured something like this would happen."

"Well come home already, will you?" she said. "What clothes are you wearing? The same ones I left you in?"

When I got to her doorway we faced each other for the first time in days – after having faced each other every day for the past seven months. I reeked of body odor, my socks were damp, my feet were itchy, my face was stubble, my teeth were stained, my mouth was dry and cakey. She looked pristine, with her hair up and her loose light blue jeans and navy blue v-neck sweater. She stepped toward me and I stepped back. "I'm not sure you want to touch me," I said. She stood on her toes and scooped my unshaved face in her hands and drove her tongue down my throat. I leaned back against the door for balance. "You think I don't want to kiss you?" she said.

She stepped into the shower with me, and before long we were writhing on the wet floor, our bodies sticking to the mat. Soon I was inside her mouth and it was all I could endure not to explode, having gone celibate for the past three days. I tapped her on the shoulder and she looked up at me assuredly. "Be right back?" I asked. She nodded, and I scrambled dripping to her bedroom for condoms and lubricant. I settled beneath her and held the base of my cock as she sat atop me. She moaned as I pushed myself within her rectum. It was snug and fiery and I came immediately, softening in a matter of seconds. In her bedroom I licked her for nearly half an hour, until she pulled me up to her face and held me tight and said, "So, would you rather be doing *this* all afternoon, or reading your novels?"

"This," I said seriously, gazing into her eyes as if she'd asked me to marry her.

Before long we went back to the bathroom, where she sat me on a stool and shaved my face. The next day we went shopping for clothes we could wear for Thanksgiving, when we were to meet each other's families.

* * *

The Kennedy house was an immense three stories painted all in white save a crimson door. It sat behind a trimmed, pathless lawn that seemed darker than a typical green – more spinach than parsley, as if the gardener had injected the soil with chlorophyll enhancements. Beside the house was a vast tar driveway, wide enough for four cars, to the rear of which stood a basketball hoop with a shining glass backboard.

We wore hats and gloves and white puffs came from our mouths as we approached the door, advancing up the driveway so as not to trample the grass. A trio of purple corn cobs hung beside the gleaming silver knocker, below which KENNEDY was inscribed on an elliptical silver plate. "They might ask us to sleep over," said Diana.

"I'm quite prepared to do so," I replied, "because of the 49 times you've mentioned that this week."

"Sorry," she said. Her gloved index finger pointed toward the bell, but she hesitated. "Ari, my parents aren't the bonding type. Tom can be intimidating. And – "

"You've been telling me this for weeks. I'm ready."

"Maybe we should drive into town and get wine. So we can bring something."

"To your parents?"

"They're judgmental like that."

"Well, let them be. Of both of us. We're both subsistent adults in the world. What can they do to us?"

A tall, muscular young man – he was almost my height, and about twice as wide – opened the door and said, "Hey, Di. I thought I heard your voice." He stepped outside, letting the screen door slam, and hugged Diana. He stood about five inches above her, a mishmash of chili-flake curls atop his distinct diamond of a face: freckled, pointy-cheeked, and clearly hewn from the chopping block of Irish physiognomies. Tom's eyes were grayer than Diana's, the hue of a dull nickel. After separating from Diana he shook my hand. "Hi," he said, foregoing a formal introduction. He stepped back into the house and up a flight of stairs, shouting, "Di's here! Di's here!" through the corridors and up the steps.

We entered a white-carpeted living room with two burgundy leather sofas. A glass table between the couches shone our reflections. "We never sit in here," said Diana. To our left was a piano with its lid down; behind it there was a carpeted staircase, down which presently came a-thumping Tom's boat-sized black leather shoes, followed by the less discordant clops of a slender blond in black heels and pinstriped pants. Tom's right arm rested on the piano as the blond and Diana moved toward each other. "Hi, Miranda," said Diana. Miranda wore a tight salmon sweater, and on the expected finger was a transparent jewel the diameter of a pen cap, enclasped by six silver insect legs.

Diana led Miranda toward me. I extended my right hand. "Hi," said Miranda, about as eager to exchange names as her husband had been.

"Where are the Hapsburgs?" asked Diana, referring to her parents. Tom and Diana had bestowed their sires with this arbitrary nickname ten years earlier. Sitting together at the dining room table one evening, doing their homework, Tom had asked aloud if his sister knew who the Hapsburgs were. Diana replied that they were a ruling family of some sort. In walked Billy and Connie Kennedy, searching through the week's stack of *Boston Globes* for an article they'd been debating. The siblings eyed their parents and exchanged glances. Moments later the Kennedys became the Hapsburgs.

"Mom's getting dressed," said Tom. "Dad's watching TV."

On our way to see Billy Kennedy, we passed through the kitchen, which had a shiny floor of black tile and a remodeled, black marble sink-and-counter isle in the middle. One kitchen entryway opened to the dining room. Another opened to the television room, where on a brown leather loveseat sat Billy: full head of brown hair, lanky and be-spectacled, khaki pants crossed at the knee, light blue dress shirt with sleeves cuffed and undone top button. The remote control rested be-side a scotch-rocks on a tray table to his right. The first football game had begun. Billy gazed at us and returned to the television. Diana approached and kissed his cheek, her fingertips on his jaw.

I extended my right arm to Billy and said, "Ariel Zinsky."

"Nice to meet you. I know who you are and what you do," said Billy. He gestured at the wide screen. "I got Detroit minus the points. Every Thanksgiving I bet for Detroit, against Dallas. I usually do okay." He went back to the game.

I stepped back and moved toward the others. "Does mom need any help setting up?" I asked, half-whispering, to Diana and Miranda.

"No, we're all set," said Miranda.

Tom, standing by the television, said, "Are you guys sleeping over?"

"Maybe," said Diana. "Are you?"

"Depends how much I have to drink," said Miranda.

"Because I was hoping maybe Ariel packed sneakers," said Tom.

"I didn't," I said.

"What size are you?" asked Tom.

I need not record what ensuing dialogue led to my borrowing a pair of Tom's old Nikes and joining him by the basketball hoop. Tom also lent me a maroon Boston College sweatshirt and he was impressed when I shunned his sweatpants in favor of baggy mesh shorts – it was a frigid, wind-whipping, cloudy day in the 30s. "You play high school?" he asked, dribbling the light-brown ball between his long legs, puffs billowing from his mouth as he spoke. "I sucked at sports in high school," I said.

"You're trying to get me to underestimate you," he said, passing me the ball.

"You already do," I said, bouncing it back to him.

He drove toward the goal and completed a righty reverse layup. "I love Miranda, don't get me wrong, but our marriage has absolutely killed my playing time."

"Already with the excuses," I said, puffing my own mouth steam for effect. "This is your home-court. You could probably fall asleep for 20 years, wake up, and make shots out here blindfolded."

We warmed up with a game of HORSE. Tom destroyed me. I had S before he had H. He knew every shot of this court, every angle. And I was distracted by how clean and clear the glass backboard was. Inside a gym, the only thing behind a backboard was a monochrome wall. Vision posed no problem. But behind this backboard sat the entire expanse of cloudy autumn sky, a grayish shade of white set in relief by the milky house. I struggled keeping the rim in perspective.

Between shots I warmed my hands beneath my armpits; I ran in place, trying to get a good sweat going beneath my wool hat. Tom's black hooded sweatshirt, by contrast, had a sewn-in sleeve for hands; and instead of a hat he wore one of those wraparound ear-coverers that skiers don, leaving his thick, cinnamon-tinted hair exposed in the wind.

Tom won the HORSE game and said, "Make it take it? To 21?"

I nodded. Tom drained a 24-footer from an imaginary top-of-the-key. We began.

Tom was quicker than I, so my defensive strategy was to allow jump shots and force him left. Tom took my allowing him the jumper as an affront; he took one dribble to his left, pulled up, and shot a brick. The rebound clanged right and I raced to corral it. Tom looked askance at me – for I had hustled a bit too blatantly for an uncontested rebound, as if our game's opening salvos had championship ramifications.

Yo-yoing the ball between my legs, I assessed Tom's defensive posture: lax. He wasn't just allowing me the jumper; he was defying me to shoot. I could not shoot from 24 feet, though – I needed to get to foul-line distance, about 15. I assumed my Jalen Rose post-up posture, backing into Tom, bumping him hard until he held his ground, about eight feet from the hoop. Despite all the shooting we'd done during HORSE, revealing my left-handedness, Tom was not defending me as a lefty. I spun, pivoted, and pump-faked until Tom finally bit and jumped for a shot block. At which point I banked an eight-footer from the left wing, a shot I could make blindfolded, even against a backboard with a strange background.

I did the same thing on my next four possessions and took a 5-0 lead. Tom said, "You really are a workhorse. When I get the ball back, I'm taking it to you."

Now that Tom expected me to back him down, he softened his face-up defense: he let me square to the rim, within 15 feet. I surprised him by taking, and making, a foul-line jumper. "Wow, you're lefty, huh?" he said, catching on.

He didn't defend my jump-shot until I'd made the next three for a 9-0 lead. At which point he finally awoke. He had doubtless begun to fear the embarrassment of my telling his wife, sister, mother, and father that I'd cruised to victory. Likewise, I feared the storytelling consequences of squandering a nine-point margin. I posted him up again. Finally aware of my left-handedness, Tom forced me right, assuming an absence of ambidexterity. Big mistake. I spun right and went baseline, going under the hoop for a righty reversal. 10-0.

On my next possession I did the same thing, but instead of reversing I finger-rolled, converting the basket despite Tom's hack at my arm. "And one," I said. "That's eleven-nothing."

"I know the score," he said.

For the first time, he challenged me on the outside, was belly-to-back with me as I dribbled 20 feet from the hoop. The key was patience. With the lead, I had more patience than Tom. If I kept dribbling in place, he'd feel more pressure than I to make a move. Sure enough, he attempted to steal the ball, at which point I yo-yo'd by him for my Jalen Rose one-handed floater. Soon I was up 14-0.

I tried convincing myself our game was scoreless, so I'd remain dogged. But I was giddy. Borrowed sneakers, foreign court, inferior genetics, and I was up 14-0 on The Natural! Winning this game had the potential to crack my life's defining moments. Diana could have dumped me at the Thanksgiving table, and I'd have recalled fondly: "She broke my heart, but at least I whooped her brother." I almost had to miss now – basketball players, once cognizant of their special days, usually lose an ounce of concentration. Tom decided to allow my jumper again. He was a little winded, his hands resting on his knees. I focused and made four more foul-line jumpers: 18-0.

But then I missed. And Tom was far from fatigued. He'd merely been saving his energy for offense. And I hadn't played defense since the game's opening possession. Tom posted me up, elevated, and banked in five consecutive turnaround jumpers. I was still winning, 18-5, but I had begun to panic – for Tom could jump much higher than I. To prevent him from shooting was physically impossible, despite my height advantage. I had to hope he'd miss, or I was finished.

I got the ball back at 18-13. Tom had figured out how to defend me: tightly inside of 20 feet, never leaping in response to my fakes. I resorted, now, to a gag Jerod used to pull on me: I intentionally aimed the ball off the backboard, so it would ricochet to a certain spot. I beat Tom to the spot and converted a finger-roll. "That was an asshole thing to do," he said.

"You left me no choice. I can't rely on conventional methods anymore."

"You tried to show me up."

"I was just trying to score, Tom," I said. "We all know you're better than me. You've been able to score your entire life. You have to think about how you'd play if you lacked natural ability."

"Check the ball," he said. I bounced the rock in his direction and he heaved it back to me, hard, at my chest. I caught it with ease and yo-yo dribbled as he stared me down. I gestured as though I planned to ricochet the ball off the glass again. "You wouldn't dare," he said.

"I might," I said, faking one last time before I bounced the ball through his open legs, raced around him, and finger-rolled my way to a 20-13 lead. "Point," I said, checking him the ball.

He guarded me so closely, I feared I couldn't take more than two dribbles without losing the ball. I turned my back to him, but he kept me a good 15 feet from the hoop with swift sidesteps and hard hand-checks. I had no idea how I'd even attempt another shot. At length I raced directly away from the basket. Tom closed on me quickly and, in a panic, I fired an off-balance 19-foot fadeaway from the left wing, knowing instantly I'd shot the ball too strong and at the incorrect angle. But the shot caromed high off the glass and into the basket. Game over. 21-11, Zinsky. "That was lucky," I admitted, feigning sportsmanship but internally relishing how much better the turkey would taste, having the entire family recognize my victory.

Tom eyed me and said, "You're smiling like you just got laid or something."

"You have no idea."

He chuckled. I imagined he knew about Diana's celibacy. The question was whether he respected my obeisance to it. Had he – or had Billy – ascertained why I was dealing with it? Did they believe my intention was marriage? Or that I was so smitten I'd accept anything? Or that all-but-vaginal-sex with my beautiful best friend was preferable to solitude? I wondered whether Tom and Billy had sized me up in this manner. Or were they waiting for further interaction – or just the passage of time – before drawing conclusions?

"Best of three?" said Tom.

We played two more. He defeated me 21-13 and 21-17. In keeping these games close I surprised myself. My only intention was sustaining a semblance of effort. I dug deep, struck a defensive posture, and worked hard on offense. But my mind wasn't in it.

Tom and I shook hands, clasping sweaty yet frigid digits. Then we went inside, both smiling like we'd recovered precious pieces of our childhood puzzles. Tom ran upstairs to his room, and I was left standing by the piano, my cheeks and kneecaps thawing. From the kitchen came the metronomic banging of a knife against a cutting board. A tall but plump woman in a black cardigan, with hair the tint of ginger ale, hovered high over the island countertop, slicing two baguettes at once into inch-long segments. Was it from this woman, whom I presumed to be Connie Kennedy, that Diana had learned her mincing skills? I wanted to introduce myself, but I reeked of perspiration, and I was certain my dried sweat had formed salty lines on my face.

Connie finished cutting and placed the slices into a wicker basket lined with a green napkin. She brought the basket into the dining room and upon returning to the kitchen spotted me lingering. "You are tall," she said. She turned to a stack of pots and pans in the island sink and began scrubbing with steel wool. "Been out playing with Tom, have you?" she said.

"You have the most amazing driveway court I've ever seen," I said. "Where'd you find a glass backboard?"

"Billy found it somewhere," she said. "One of those sports megastores."

"It was so – clean," I said. "I could see the house and the sky right behind it."

"We actually take a ladder, climb up there, and Windex that thing every few months," she said. "Well, not 'we.' Tom does it once every few visits. It was one of his chores growing up."

"How often do he and Miranda visit?" I sallied.

"Almost every weekend."

"Wow."

"Wow? Well, I guess that must be 'wow' to you, with your mom in New York and everything. Do you ever think about moving back there?"

I wondered how I was supposed to answer that. "Only if your slender daughter comes with me," was what I felt like saying. I said: "Why would I move back there?"

Connie laughed heartily at this. Something in her easy risibility messed with my values – made me feel like I was somehow provincial for not living within 50 miles of my relatives.

"How old are you?" she asked.

"25. How old are you?" I rejoined, grinning.

"Never you mind," she said.

"Have you been to New York?"

"Oh, sure," she said. "I went to Barnard. I went back for my 30th reunion not long ago. Billy had his at Columbia the same weekend. We visit New York three or four times a year. One of Billy's pals from work gets us cheap Broadway tickets."

Billy was an executive with a New England banking colossus; that much I knew. "What did you major in?" I continued.

"English. Not that I ever did anything with it. I was an admin at the state house when Billy started at BancBoston. I got pregnant with Tom in less than a year, and that was that. When Di started college, I considered working part-time, but Billy talked me out of it. Di says you're a rising star in the publishing world. Are you enjoying yourself?"

"I can't complain. Late hours, but that's how it is, you know?"

She looked down into the sink, giving a pan a few final, vigorous scrubs. Then she turned back to me. "I can't believe you played out there in shorts," she said. "Tom's sneakers fit okay?"

"Yeah," I said. "He's a terrific athlete. I'd kill for an eighth of his ability."

"Don't sell yourself short," she said. "I saw you making quite a few shots."

"You watched?"

"Diana and I watched. You can see the basket from her bedroom window."

"Well, I don't suck," I said, before catching myself. "Excuse my language. I mean – I'm a capable shot-maker. But Tom – I've played with great college basketball players, and he's got a dose of what they possess. If he solely dedicated himself to basketball, he'd have been a player somewhere."

"Williams and Amherst recruited him. But he didn't want to go to school 'in the boonies,' he used to say. He preferred baseball anyway. He walked onto BC's team, then quit after a year because he wasn't starting. And you went to – Michigan State?"

"University of Michigan," I corrected. There was a dash of impatience in my tone.

Diana came into the kitchen, stroking her mother's back. Her copper hair contrasted with Connie's ginger and her lankiness with Connie's knobbiness. Diana winked at me, and I approached her and kissed her briefly on the mouth. Diana, to my surprise, didn't curtail the kiss in Connie's presence. In fact, she seemed pleased with it. She turned to Connie and said, "See how he is?"

"Funny and self-deprecating, as you described," said Connie.

"But in definite need of a shower," said Diana.

"Get him one of Tom's shirts," said Connie.

"He has his own," said Diana.

"I was just telling mom what an athlete Tom is," I said, eager to learn Diana's perspective on my victory before hitting the showers.

"He said you caught him sleeping and took one out of three," said Diana.

"Pretty much," I said.

Diana dismissed herself to fetch towels for me and I went to the living room to check the football score. Billy napped in his chair. Miranda had swiped the remote and switched to a movie channel showing *Fargo*. "I've seen this about twenty times," she said. I nodded, and just then Diana returned with towels.

We went to the guest bedroom, which had a bathroom in it. "Here's where you'll be confined for the evening," she said.

"Take a shower with me," I whispered. I seized her, not without force, by the small of her back.

"Behave," she said. She removed my arms and glanced out the door, toward the kitchen, from whence came the whacks of Connie's cutting. She returned to me, undid the drawstring of Tom's shorts, and reached inside my boxers. She held me for a few seconds and whispered, "Think of this while you're in there." She looked into my eyes. "I love you," she whispered. She bit my lower lip and released me.

* * *

The Kennedy dining room had a dark cherry wood table rimmed with silver. At each seat was a white cloth napkin folded into a triangle. The napkins rested between two wine glasses. As for the seats themselves, they were high-backed, cushion-less, and of the same cherry wood as the table.

We each stood behind our chairs. Billy, at the head of the table, had looped an eggplant-colored tie around his collar. He thumbed through what appeared to be a prayer book, with a black leather cover and gilded pages. Connie stood directly opposite him. Tom and Miranda were on the kitchen-side of the table, and Diana and I faced them. Tom and I sat closer to Billy; the ladies closer to Connie.

My girlfriend had changed into fitted black pants and a white blouse; her brother wore a dress shirt with blue stripes and a tie with a swirling red and black pattern. His wet hair was combed straight back but starting to dry, the mishmash beginning to break free from his mousse-assisted efforts at stylization.

A wine key lay at the center of the uncovered table, beside a bottle of Pinot Noir and a silver ice bucket, tongs straddling the rim. Inside the bucket, resting diagonally in the ice, was a chardonnay called Hanzell. "Okay, Tom," said Billy, his eyes fixed on a prayer book page. Tom reached for the red bottle and wine key. He uncorked it in seconds with a rapid series of movements. His grip and motions were unconscious; he gave them about as much thought as the average person gives to how he holds a pen when he writes. He placed the cork on the table and passed the bottle to Miranda, who passed it on to Connie. The matriarch poured for herself and then for the two ladies, all small amounts. After which the bottle returned to Billy, who poured first for himself, then Tom, then me, finishing the bottle on my glass. Meanwhile, Tom had passed the opener across the table to me. I looked to Diana for instruction. Her eyes heightened, a gesture telling me to open the white wine.

I yanked the green Hanzell bottle from the ice bucket, scattering three ice cubes along the cherry wood. "Shit," I said, before covering my mouth. Diana leaned over to gather the cubes. I tried replaying in my head exactly how Tom had used this instrument to open the bottle. What was that twisting wrist action he'd used to unsheathe the foil and stab the cork? I felt the heat lamps of ten thirsty Irish eyes, and said, "Someone else at this table is probably more qualified for this job than I am."

"Give it to me," said Billy. Within seconds, the bottle was opened and back in Connie's hands for a second round of ladies-first pouring. "Is this all some old Irish custom?" I asked.

Diana suppressed a giggle but Billy and Connie and Tom and even Miranda seemed taken aback by the innocent question. Diana muttered, "Ari, there's no talking before grace." The scolding expressions now went in her direction.

Billy raised his glass of red and said, "This method of opening and pouring is not an 'old Irish custom.' I don't know how you could even speculate that it was Irish, seeing as Thanksgiving is an American holiday. My family is Irish, as is Connie's, and both of our families came to this country in the 20s. This wine procedure, as far as I know, began at my maternal grandparents' home when they were celebrating their first Thanksgiving in this country. At the time, they were living with three other couples in a small apartment on M Street in South Boston. I regret to say I don't know why or how this procedure developed. I just know that I've seen it at the Thanksgiving table since I was a boy. One way or another, it's a tradition. One I intend to continue."

Only now did I realize that the rest of the table had raised its red glasses. I picked mine up, trying to gauge whether Billy's sermon was a reprimand or a speech his family had heard before. Their expressions were pokerfaced. They awaited Billy's grace. "I've been thinking all day of what I wanted to say right now," he began. "I kept coming back to how this is the third year Miranda has been with us; and how nice it is that you and Tommy live close by. Maybe next year we'll have a grandchild at our table. So, what I want to say is this: we live in a world that is chaotic and dangerous. You don't realize just how dangerous it is until you have children, and have to deal with letting them out of your sight. I cannot express to you, Tom and Miranda, how wonderful it makes me feel that you're on your way to becoming young parents. You don't yet realize how brave you're being; but I do, and this year, I am thankful you've found, in our home, a comfortable place for yourselves and hopefully for any beings you bring into this world."

Everyone at the table said, "Amen," and sipped. Now Tom announced tersely that he, too, was thankful for Miranda's comfort with the family. Miranda announced she was thankful for the same. Connie expressed gratitude for our collective health. Diana reiterated the health wishes. It was my turn. I said, "I want to thank all of you for having me as your guest tonight. You have such a beautiful house. Thank you."

Billy uttered a formal grace, verbatim, from the gilded book. We sipped from the white this time. Then Connie, Miranda, and Diana went to the kitchen. Miranda returned dispensing bowls of cheese-topped French onion soup. Diana followed her with two bowls of salad. The five us heaped salad on our plates but waited for Connie to return with several 2-liter cola bottles before eating.

To Billy I said, "I'm sorry if I showed any disrespect towards your family's traditions. I honestly didn't know. My family just shows up and eats."

"I figured as much," he said. "You gotta improve with that wine bottle, though. This will be a trying life for you if you don't." I chuckled, and under the table I felt Diana's heel rubbing my shin.

Soon all of us had finished our wine and Diana retrieved two more bottles. She opened the red herself and the white she handed to me. "Time for a lesson," she said. Following five minutes of instruction, I unsheathed the bottle. But in twisting I broke the cork, half of which fell into the tinted container. "Give it here," said Billy. He poured the wine into his glass, the liquid slapping the sides awkwardly because of the cork-impeded flow. He tasted it, and said, "It's a hassle to pour, but still okay to drink." Billy rose from his chair and went around the table with the wine, pouring for everyone, kissing Miranda, then Connie, then Diana on the cheek as he did so. He emptied the bottle on my glass and proclaimed: "This time, I'm fetching four more bottles. It's my mission to make sure everyone is too drunk to drive home tonight."

We proceeded to eat and drink together, moving along to a main course of turkey, mashed potatoes, baked carrots, and squash salad. The conversation focused not on our lives but on world events, such as whether the Red Sox would surpass the Yankees next season, or whether any candidate would have had a chance of unseating Clinton if the Arkansas stud, blow job and all, had had the constitutional authority to seek a third term.

At one point Connie, who'd by my count downed five wine glasses, said, "So you spend all day using the Harvard computers, huh? Do you plan on making an alumni donation if your magazine hits the big time?"

I understood she was drunk, I understood Diana wanted me to be sycophantic rather than combative, and I understood Connie had a right to protest my leeching. But I was not about to have my ethics or ambitions questioned by a housewife who'd been supported by others almost her entire life. What did she know about defying the vast odds of small business failure? For that matter, what did Billy or Tom know about it?

Still, I had promised Diana I would behave. So I responded to the pleasant part of her inquiry and ignored the criticism. "My life is all about making the impossible come true," I replied.

This drew laughs from the inebriated table and a foot-stroke from Diana, whose facial expression indicated severe remorse. So the Kennedys knew I was a leech; now that it was out on the table, and now that we were drunk, it didn't seem like such an embarrassing confidentiality. In the next instant a smiling, drunken Diana asked, "Why don't you elaborate, Ari, on how you've made the impossible come true?"

"Oh, spare me," said Billy. "Everyone your age is starting companies and selling them. It happens way too often to be remarkable."

My composure snapped. "You're not the only one who's paid your dues, Billy," I said, shifting in my chair to face him. "How many businesses have you started?"

Billy looked straight back. "You're nothing special," he said.

"But you are?" I fired back. "Why? Because you have two healthy children? You're telling me that doesn't happen way too often to be remarkable?"

"Settle down," said Connie, turning to me. "You haven't answered my question."

I rolled my eyes. "I'm never giving a penny to Harvard. And I feel just fine about leeching off Diana, if that's what you're driving at," I said. "In a few weeks I'll buy my own office space, which she'll be welcome to use anytime she wants," I added.

"One day you're mooching, the next day you're buying real estate," said Billy.

"It's a remarkable story," I replied.

"And probably a boring one," said Billy.

"Indeed," I said. "It all began in a small apartment on M Street."

This line had the entire table, including Billy, in hysterics. I was especially pleased to see him laughing; perhaps his bluster had only been a test of my spine. Billy turned to his wife and said, "See, I wasn't being obnoxious, Con. I'm trying to acclimate our guest to our family's style of humor. And he clearly understands it."

"Oh, I understand it, boss," I said, reclaiming a tone of parental reverence.

Miranda came to my rescue by asking when I had been at Michigan, and whether I knew so-and-so from her hometown of Cohasset, Mass. From which I transitioned to the topic of Massachusetts towns and their pronunciations: not the commonly mangled ones, like Worcester, Gloucester, and Peabody, but other towns that I was only just learning in my fourth year of residence: Billerica, Haverhill, Leominster.

And so the meal passed, with no more Zinsky scrutiny from the Kennedy family. Following dessert, Billy and Tom remained in their seats while I rinsed dishes and handed them to Diana, who placed them in the dishwasher. Miranda wiped the table and swept, while Connie stuffed leftovers into containers and crammed them into the fridge.

We reconvened at the cleared table, the cherry wood moist from sponging. Billy said, triumphant, "So – all of you sleeping over?"

The four children nodded.

"Terrific," he said. "Now who wants to watch a movie?"

We nodded again.

"Con?" asked Billy.

"It's okay with me," she said.

And into the living room we spilled, the six of us. Billy bestowed on Con the power of movie choice. "Oh, I don't care," she said. "Whatever the kids want to watch."

Tom and Miranda shuffled through the Kennedy collection of VHS cassettes. This was, I remind you, the year 2000, so the phenomenon of DVD ownership had not yet begun. "Oh yes," declared Tom, pulling out a rectangular box for Miranda's inspection. "The best sports movie ever," he said. "I've never seen it," countered Miranda. Tom said: "You did. Two years ago. It was snowing like crazy and we both came home from work early. It was on cable."

"What is it, already," shouted Billy.

"*Slapshot*," said Tom. "Right, the one with Paul Newman," added Miranda.

Diana and I had a couch to ourselves. We held hands, the way couples do when they know they won't be getting naked together anytime soon: our hands, already naked, performed their own little mating ritual. Fingertips kissed fingertips. Knuckles intertwined. Palms slid and squeezed. About halfway through the movie, Billy and Connie announced their intention to retire. Fatigue, apparently, overcame any parental anxiety about a ménage-a-quatre ensuing among the deserted semi-adults. As soon as Billy and Connie left, Miranda leaned back into Tom's lap.

When the movie ended Tom and Miranda simply said "goodnight," and went upstairs. I promptly moved in on Diana, pushing her down on the couch and rolling on top of her. We made out for a few minutes, and then she whispered, "If we don't stop now, I'm going to go crazy. I think I have to take you to your room now."

"They won't get pissed if they don't find out."

"They'll find out. They're not sleeping yet. They're reading the *Globe*, they're waiting to hear me pitter-patter up the stairs. They know the pitter-patter of how I go up the stairs versus how Tom tramples. They know we're down here alone, and that we're probably not watching a movie."

"It's amazing how just foreplay would piss them off. I mean, aren't Tom and Miranda probably fucking up there, as we speak? It's a double standard."

"What can I tell you."

"So your folks never slept together as undergrads? They never kissed goodbye at those Columbia gates on 116th? Do they really think we aren't fooling around?"

"It's not the fooling around, Ari. It's the fooling around in their house. You don't understand how they're going to just look at me accusingly tomorrow, and make me feel like I'm a whore. My mom is probably irate you kissed me in the kitchen."

"You liked that though."

"I did. But okay" – she wriggled out from beneath me – "I have to go upstairs now. I'll come to your room tomorrow morning. Maybe you can borrow Tom's sneakers again and we'll go for a run."

"Kiss me goodnight," I said. She leaned in and we necked for a few minutes.

* * *

It was six a.m. the next morning when Diana entered my room in her maroon Boston College sweatshirt and running sneakers. She was carrying a pair of Tom's sneakers. As soon as I saw her I pulled her next to me. Within minutes we were gorging ourselves to compensate for the prior night's missed meal.

When we finished, Diana pulled her gear back on and urged me to do the same. We cuddled in sweats and sneakers, prepared to spring up and feign imminent departure should Billy or Connie come down the stairs. "It was so hard to sleep without you last night," she whispered, her hand on my chest.

I replied: "Zinsky: Can't sleep with him, can't sleep without him."

She removed her hand from my chest and rolled onto her side. "Hey," I said. "What's this about?"

She was sobbing. "You know how I feel about this topic, Ari. It's not negotiable. If you wanted to break up with me over this, I'd be devastated and probably hate you for a while, but I would, on some level, understand. You – you have no idea how terrible you make me feel when you even joke about this. I know it bothers you, okay? Doesn't it seem like I do everything else I can to make you happy?"

I apologized, reiterated that I was only joking and was quite satisfied with all she gave me, and let the topic rest as we lay still for a few minutes. When we heard some stirring upstairs, we donned our hats and gloves to jog the quiet streets of leafy Lincoln.

Diana's prominent cheeks were flushed by the cold air. Her white sweatpants hugged the contours of her hips; and my cardio condition allowed me to sneak glances at her without compromising my pace.

Around us, red and yellow leaves seemed pasted to the sidewalks, a shimmering minority among raked, rusty, desiccated browns. Houses rose up among vast lawns and driveways; and I wondered what sort of Thanksgiving scenes were going on within them. I was running, sweating, with a girl I loved, in a serene setting. I reminded myself that there were worse things to be doing on a holiday. I found myself softening, sympathizing; energy became enervation. So I wasn't having vaginal sex, I thought. I was still getting some great ass, wasn't I? And my girlfriend — just having the right to use that phrase, my girlfriend, still gave me glee.

After the jog we were where we'd stood less than a day earlier: on the threshold of the Kennedy household, before a large door with a trio of corn-cobs on it. There was a looseness in our frames that hadn't been there yesterday. Our shoulders were relaxed; we were on our heels not our toes; our knees were slack rather than stiff. And I wondered if we'd retain our droopy carriage once we went inside.

The crimson door swung open, revealing Billy in a terry-cloth bathrobe of the same color. "Who wants eggs?" he asked.

We joined Billy at the marble island in the kitchen, sitting on stools with navy blue cushions. Connie, buttering a pan, wearing a baggy gray sweat suit, stood behind the island, like a bartender prepping concoctions. "For cheese I have Swiss, feta, American, cheddar, mozzarella, provolone, and goat," she called out. "For veggies I have tomatoes, onions, broccoli, mushrooms, green peppers, and red peppers." We each put in our orders and waited, breathing in the smells of simmering butter and brewing coffee grounds. "Some water for the marathoners?" asked Billy. "I'll get it," said Diana.

Just when Connie pulled up a stool to eat, Tom and Miranda entered the kitchen, dressed for the road. Tom wore a pink dress shirt and khakis, his wife a long black skirt and matching sweater. Connie slid off her stool and said, "I'm making omelets."

"Sit down, Mom," said Diana. "I can make them."

"You're not done eating," said Connie.

"You haven't started eating," said Diana.

"We'll make our own," said Miranda.

"But you're all dressed up," said Connie.

"Mom, sit," said Tom.

Eventually the six of us were seated around the island, munching eggs. Diana, upon finishing, placed her arms on the counter and rested her head. "You tired?" I asked.

"You were up awfully early," said Billy. I stared at my plate.

"Want more coffee?" asked Connie.

"You better have some coffee, if you're going to drive today," said Billy.

"Actually, I'll be driving to New York," I said. "Diana can nap in the car."

My statement hardly set the Hapsburgs at ease. They were silent, and I wondered what about my personality – in the few hours they'd been exposed to it – made me seem the untrustworthy driver.

Miranda, again, came to my rescue. "How many cups should I pour?" she asked, wielding the steaming pot.

"At least two," I said.

After the meal Diana and I excused ourselves to shower for our trip. Tom and Miranda said farewells and drove north to Hanover, NH, the weekend home of Miranda's parents.

When Diana and I said our goodbyes, the eyes of Billy and Connie Kennedy kept making me nervous. They eyed me as if I were taking their daughter parachuting. Sensing all of this, Diana said, "We'll be fine. We'll call as soon as we get there. Okay?"

"Okay," said Billy.

The red door closed behind us and we walked to the Camry. The windows were frosty. From inside, as I checked my rearview, I spied Diana, her index finger tracing a clear circle on the otherwise white window. I leaned across from her and poised my finger by the pane. "AZ + DK" I wrote within the loop. "Who loves you?" I asked.

"A lot of people," she said.

I nodded – it was the answer I deserved – and started the engine. I wondered at which point in our trip we'd discuss our rift; and I wondered, too, if my mother planned to house us in separate bedrooms.

* * *

My bed for the evening was a pull-out couch in the basement of the

West Egg house. Diana slept upstairs, and I was too tired from turkey to protest the arrangement, which came at Barbara's behest.

Also in the basement was a storage room containing my boxed-up childhood keepsakes. I pondered opening the boxes and examining which possessions were worth taking back to Boston. My radio colleague Ryan Shields would appreciate my old *Sports Illustrated* issues. And perhaps they could provide grist for *Guide* writing.

In the midst of these thoughts the 55-year-old Barbara Segal descended the basement steps. Her pair of sweatpants, the first thing coming into my view, were a faded charcoal color, attributable to decades of launderings. How many times, when I was a boy, had the machine-washed cotton of those sweats caressed my unstubbled cheeks? Now the sight of them prompted me to roll onto my side, like a Labrador signaling for a belly rub. Barbara sat on the pullout. I rested my head on her soft thigh, my palm inert on her knee. "It's good to see the nouveau riche still need their mommies," she teased.

"Are you disappointed in how I've turned out?" I asked.

"No," she said, stroking my head. "Why would I be? You're all I brag about."

"Including my athletic and romantic conquests?"

"I do bring up Diana on occasion. But why would I be disappointed?"

"I don't know," I said. I lay back down and rested my head on her thigh. Barbara rose and circled the bed, beginning the formal tucking, ensconcing me within blanket and bedsheets. "You don't strike me as completely smitten with Diana," she said.

"What are you talking about?" I asked.

"I didn't mean it that way," she said. "Sorry. What I mean to ask is — well, what is your aim with her?"

"My aim? I don't know. Just to be her boyfriend and hang out with her and buy her flowers and write her long emails."

"You think that's what she's after?" asked Barbara. I had no clue what Barbara's aim was, with her line of questioning. There was no way Barbara could know — or even intuit — that Diana and I were not having conventional sex. "What do you mean, what she's after? Are you implying my body and soul aren't enough for her?"

"No. I'm just wondering what your aim is."

"Look, mom, I know she wants a husband eventually. But I'm not prepared to do that. I might never be. But what can I do? I'm not going to dump her."

"And all of that's very nice for both of you. All I'm trying to communicate, Ari, is that Diana's going to want a ring sooner or later. And if you've already decided that you're not going to step up, then you should exit soon. Difficult though that might be. It's easier to split up now than it'll be a year from now."

"What do you mean, step up?" I said. "Why is marriage the pinnacle? When did you become a wholehearted Judeo-Christian? You make it sound like I'm some straying gigolo unless my intent is to wed."

"Not a gigolo," she said. "But, more so than you realize, you're leading her on. Implicit in your being a guest at her Thanksgiving, and her being at ours, is the idea that you have long-term intentions."

"I do have long-term intentions. I will never dump Diana."

"Well, I've said my piece," she said. "You can believe me, or you can continue to think she's pleased with indefinite girlfriend status. I'm not saying you shouldn't have your fun, Ari. Believe me, I'm the last who'd suggest you marry before you're ready. But I just – I don't like the way you sound, over the phone, when you call me up all brokenhearted over some girl. And I'm only raising these questions to prevent you from going through that again."

She squeezed my hand and kissed my forehead. "Goodnight, Ari."

"Goodnight, mom." Softly she ascended the carpeted steps and shut the light.

End of Book the Third

Book the Fourth: One Child Left Behind

For, what with my whole world-wide wandering,
      What with my search drawn out through years, my hope
      Dwindled into a ghost not fit to cope
With that obstreperous joy success would bring, –
I hardly tried now to rebuke the spring
      My heart made, finding failure in its scope.

So petty yet so spiteful! All along,
      Low scrubby alders kneeled down over it;
      Drenched willows flung headlong in a fit
Of mute despair, a suicidal throng:
The river which had done them all the wrong,
      Whate'er that was, rolled by, deterred no whit.

Which, while I forded, – good saints, how I feared
      To set my foot upon a dead man's cheek,
      Each step, or feel the spear I thrust to seek
For hollows, tangled in his hair or beard!
It may have been a water-rat I speared,
      But, ugh! it sounded like a baby's shriek.

—   Robert Browning, verses IV, XX, and XXI from "Childe Roland
     to the Dark Tower Came"

Chapter 19 – A Reunion and a Breakup

The heartbreak my mother predicted befell me three years later. By then I was long past waiting tables and leeching. I owned my own office overlooking the waterfront near Boston's North End. It was two blocks from my new one-bedroom apartment.

Diana, for her consulting work, used the office as much as I did; and I was tempted to trumpet this to Billy or Connie Kennedy, who continued their grudging acceptance of me.

I was of two minds about their standoffishness. On the one hand, I understood it. If I were they, I'd certainly have preferred to see Diana dating a stable robot of the workforce…someone who aspired to fatherhood and family-building…someone like her brother, Tom. But on the other hand, I was Diana's boyfriend of three years. If I was good enough for her, why wasn't I good enough for them? I was a college graduate, and I earned more than Billy and Tom combined. By what standard was I lacking, other than in my non-intention to marry and procreate?

Diana didn't complain. And I mistook her silence for happiness. I never realized Diana wanted me to "step up" of my own volition.

We were still having fun: lunching every day, moaning every night, cuddling every morning. We had gotten past the issue of vaginal sex: the anal and the oral were good enough for me and I never complained or joked. Likewise, she never complained or joked about my dead father's relatives and how I only called them on Christmas. She stopped scrutinizing my wardrobe; and I stopped concealing the lazy parts of my schedule. If I wanted to screw around all afternoon reading Dickens and texting Jimmy and Jerod and Joel while drinking coffee at Starbucks, that was fine by her. She told me I deserved it – that it was great I was finally feeling guiltless about it. Whenever she said these things to me I almost cried with giddiness.

She enjoyed using my office while I was out of it. She advised corporations on their 401(k) plans. It was a fruitful consulting area, but its practitioners tended to be bootstrapping individuals with home offices. So for Diana to invite clients to a pricey downtown spot with plush furniture and wide windows overlooking the wharf – it lent her expertise an elegant gravitas consistent with her Harvard pedigree. She networked with the other professionals in the building, an affable group of white men with schedules like mine: they had work to do, sure, but the real loot was in the bank and in property. We all had time to say hello to each other and discuss sports – which, of course, was all they wanted to do with me, given how I made my money.

I'd become a minor celebrity to sports fans in the Boston area: Ryan Shields and I had copped our own overnight sports-talk show on WMUR. Boston had three full-time sports-radio stations but, incredibly, all of them switched to nationally syndicated programs after midnight. So if you wanted some distinctly Bostonian views in the early morn, you had no choice but tuning into "Shields & Zinsky." We aired twice a week, and our ratings were large enough (and small enough) to keep it that way. Joel Pollock was a recurring guest. So was Jimmy Calipari, who had transitioned at *Newsday* from covering politics to covering the New York Islanders hockey team.

At first, I didn't believe my office mates listened to my radio gig. They all seemed like the types who retired at ten and rose at six to golf or swim or read the *Wall Street Journal*. But they listened. Over time, they got to know Joel and Jimmy from their radio appearances. They even shouted hellos to Joel and Jimmy, sticking their heads in my always-open office door while I was on the phone with one or the other.

My office colleagues all knew I was dating Diana too: both from her frequent appearances and my narratives of our weekend getaways.

For the first time in my life, I was having a blast being alive.

And I loved acting like the office's party paladin: I organized Friday evening happy hours, Thursday night hockey games, and gambling pools for pro and college football. If I were heading out to lunch, I relished the chance to act as a courier. On my state-of-the-art handheld device, I noted my colleagues' orders with my stylus, clacking a venti iced vanilla chai latte for Arn Hurley the condo developer, or an eggplant parmesan and 7Up for Kevin Thompson the insurance broker.

One particular afternoon I entered the local Starbucks with my digitized list of seven drink requests and three pastries. The month of May: a crisp, fresh-breeze weekday in the 60s, my black sports jacket slung over my bony left shoulder. I thought: "Behold me, all ye reclining and underemployed Starbucks patrons, lounging on ye earth-toned upholstered chairs. Here I am, age 28, sensitive boyfriend, radio persona — and for all that, I will not hesitate to make a coffee run for the office."

Employees in green aprons made the drinks and stuffed them into cardboard holders; I stacked them within a capacious plastic bag with girded handles. On my way out patrons glared: I'd unwittingly disturbed their reading, writing, typing, or texting. One vexed customer, after turning her gaze from me, held her prim, bespectacled visage, with its clipped blond coiffure, about an inch from her laptop screen. My heart pounded upon beholding her for the first time in years. I spied on what she was reading so intently.

She fixed me with an angry glare; I sat beside her on the thickly cushioned maroon couch. "Something besides your looks is compelling me to sit here," I said. She kept glaring. I glanced at her half-finished scone, overturned on a crumb-laden plate.

"Do I know you?" she asked. There was no recognition in her wan wrinkled brow or bulging blue eyes. It was as if I never worked at Stevie's Lunch and she never dined there; as if six-foot-eight bald slender white guys roamed everywhere, their appearances indistinct from everyone else's.

"You ought to know me, if you follow the NFL draft," I replied. I'd waited three years to say this. I fainted the last time I tried – didn't she remember? Her hair was still tapered like a teenage boy's; again the actress Mary Martin came to mind, as did comforting memories of watching *Peter Pan* with Barbara at the West Egg Public Library. Sandy's garb – it was a look I now associated with Diana's sister-in-law, Miranda Kennedy: tan dress pants and chest-flattering designer sweater.

"I don't follow football at all," she said. "I do have a friend from law school who's in the sports agent business. He sends me articles about his clients."

"Who are they? His clients, I mean."

"Oh, I can't remember," she said. I begged her to search her laptop for emails. At length, she discovered a name: "Antonio Garay," she said.

"A Jersey kid," I proclaimed, clapping my hands loudly, as if we'd just watched Garay steamroll a few linemen. "Cleveland took him in the sixth round, 195th overall. He's a monster: six-foot-four, weighs about 300, and he played defensive tackle right here at BC." Her eyes heightened at my arcane display. Like a professor in the absence of student questions, I resumed: "His agent is – Farouk Caro, isn't it?" My hesitation in naming Caro was faked; I feared my encyclopedic recall would seem a little *too* savant-like for her comfort. At once I felt the need to emphasize that I had a job, girlfriend, investments, and things other than football to think about. I handed her a business card, plucking it from the front pocket of my sports jacket.

"Nice to meet you, Ariel," she said, reading the card. "I'm Sandy Appleton." She extended her right hand. We shook. "Looks like you have drinks to deliver," she said.

"I do," I replied, rising. But I didn't want the conversation to end without revealing my former life – and my knowledge of hers. "Don't you have a business card for me?" I asked.

"I can hang on to yours."

"Actually, the truth is I've been waiting for you to recognize me. I was your waiter at Stevie's Lunch. I brought you turkey sandwiches all the time, hold the Russian. You were there reading about the draft when I fainted so I've always – "

"Oh my God," she said. "I knew you looked familiar. I just couldn't place you. But now that you mention it," – she cuffed her forehead with her hand's heel – "duh! I guess it was such a context shock, seeing you here and not there."

I was too overwhelmed to react. She was happy to see me! But then she dismissed me with five fatal words: "It was nice meeting you." I grabbed my plastic bag and returned to the office.

*   *   *

One month later Diana announced she was moving to Portland, Maine. With three other women she was launching a 401(k) advisement firm called Dollar for Dollar. All four had their own client bases, and by operating under one roof they'd save costs. By combining resources, they'd easily afford the designer web site and marketing materials they all coveted.

Diana met her partners through Harvard contacts and through Arn Hurley, our office colleague. I recall the high pitch in her voice, the giddy warble, when she mentioned each partner to me: Gail Martin, 51, a mother of three, who already lived in Portland and had been in the trade since the inception of 401(k) plans in 1979. Then there was Katy Calhoun, Diana's age, who'd lived a parallel life to Diana (human resources background, and she had a married older brother) except her business school was Dartmouth (Tuck) and she lived in Hanover. Finally – and the one who made me most jealous – there was Loretta Gupta, a graduate of West Egg's North High School and, amazingly, a former student of my mother's. Gupta had been a standout softball player at West Egg North, moving on to Penn's Wharton school. She was only 24 but had started her consulting practice as a college sophomore; and she gave Dollar for Dollar an extended reach, out of New England and into New York and Pennsylvania.

Diana had introduced me (verbally) to Gail, Katy, and Loretta over a period of weeks. She had mentioned how powerful she believed a partnership could be; but I never thought she'd actually do it until she did it. And only then did I chastise myself for not asking more follow-up questions, for not inquiring more about her five-year life plan, her epiphanies, and her roads to ecstasy. What had she and I been talking about, all these years? Had I been so narcissistic as to believe that only I had dreams of vocational deliverance? And was this – her departure, with or without me – the price I paid for an egoistic belief that if Diana had something to say to me, she'd say it?

And yet, Diana put it all so fairly and gingerly. One Saturday morning as we lounged naked in bed: "I want to drive to Portland next week."

"To see Gail?" I asked.

"To look at houses. Unlike you, I can't afford what I want around here."

I hesitated. "You want to move to Portland?"

She hesitated. "I'd like us to move to Portland. You could do your job from anywhere. But I think Gail and I could make a nice team, especially if we brought in Katy and Loretta."

"Can't you be a virtual team? It's 2003. Partners can live in different states."

"Clients like visiting an office. An office makes you seem more established."

"Are you going to carry on like this?" I whispered. "Are you going to phrase all of this like it's a strictly business decision?"

She held my head to her chest. "Sweetie, I want you to come with me."

We kissed languidly for a few minutes. "I know you want me to come with you. But – just level with me. You also want me to – how do I put this – make a sacrifice for you. My moving would show you some long-term devotion in the absence of a proposal."

"You put it so clinically," she said. Her remark stung. I imagined her sharing it at lunch with Gail, Katy, and Loretta: "Oh, Ari was sweet, but so clinical. I asked him to move with me, and he responded like I asked for a home-equity loan."

Before I knew it I was bawling. "Look, don't act like I'm lacking in romance for us, okay?" I said. "You're dumping me. Gradually. That's fucking obvious. How am I not supposed to respond clinically?"

"Ari, I asked you to come live with me in a beautiful town. You can commute twice a week to do your radio show. You can do the *Guide* from anywhere. Do those seem like major sacrifices? Does an invitation to live with me seem like a dumping?"

I apologized and told her I loved her. We agreed to scout Portland together over the next few weekends.

*   *   *

Two weeks after Diana signed for her one-bedroom condo, I was still undecided. Something had prevented me from simply saying: "Oh, sweet love of my life; oh, only girlfriend I've ever had; I'd love to move away with you."

Maybe I was just a person who didn't like moving. I recalled flipping out, all those years earlier, when my mother announced her relocation to Neil's West Egg manse.

Maybe I wasn't ready to dispose of my Boston happiness: my office chums, my radio show, my jogging routes, my short flights to New York to visit Barbara and Joel and Jimmy.

Maybe I didn't feel comfortable leaving the town where I'd recently bought an office and an apartment. True, those investments wouldn't disappear, but I was not the type to treat real estate like real estate – I wanted to use the property. And I loved that my home and office were blocks from each other.

But the question was: did I love that more than I loved Diana?

*   *   *

We prepped for a long-distance relationship, planning visits and vacations.

She had purchased a one-bedroom, two-bathroom condo on the first floor of a two-story white-brick house. The bedroom was roomy enough for three king beds. The kitchen, which had a walk-in pantry and space for a dining room table, had a built-in microwave, glossy cabinets and polished counters. There was also a study which could serve as a guest bedroom. The living room was an open space as ample as the bedroom with a shiny hardwood floor. And the place had style: the ceilings were 15 feet high, and the previous resident, a graphic de-signer for *Yankee* magazine, had painted all the interior walls and doors various shades of purple: violet, lavender, indigo, orchid, plum, egg-plant, mauve, and iris. Each room was a variation on the hue.

We completed the move quickly – there were six of us, after all – struggling only to contort a trapezoidal dresser through the main entry and interior door. Billy Kennedy held one end and I held the other, as he barked out angles and grips. When we finally dropped the dresser in the colossal iris bedroom, I wanted to exchange high fives. But his quizzical gaze made me feel like I was about to become yesterday's news.

At last the six of us sat around the lavender living room, swigging cold beer bottles, our shirts moist with sweat. Billy stood and circled the apartment, as if scanning for absences or possible upgrades. "What about a nice new television?" he asked.

"I don't need one," said Diana. "I'm going to be busy."

"But you like to rent movies," said Connie.

"Well, I can get one if I decide I really need one," said Diana.

"You know a good place we can take you for dinner, before we all go home?" asked Billy.

"I'm not hungry," said Diana.

"Okay," said Billy, reaching in his pocket for his car keys.

"You don't have to leave, dad," said Diana.

"I'm hungry," he said.

"Do you have to return the U-Haul tonight?" Connie asked me.

"Technically yes, but if I don't, I don't," I said. "I'll just pay a little extra."

"I'm glad you can be so lax with your money," said Billy. His hands were in his pockets.

"It's more like, I prefer to be lax with my time," I said.

"Well, I don't. Con, Tom, Miranda – you all ready?" asked Billy.

The trio rose and made their farewells to Diana. Tom and Miranda filed out of the apartment. But Billy and Connie hesitated at the doorway, looking back in my direction. "You coming, Ari?" said Connie.

I looked at Diana. "You should really return the truck," she said.

"Okay," I said. I understood her need to dismiss me; I suppressed my hurt over her willingness to trample my feelings, not those of her parents. I put my hands on her shoulders and said, "Talk to you later." I left the apartment. Billy and Con remained in the doorway behind me.

I met Tom and Miranda outside by the Explorer. "Sucks to be you right now, huh?" said Tom.

"Shut up," said Miranda, punching her husband in the arm.

"What do you think they'd do," I asked, "if I just stayed here right now and refused to leave?"

"I think my dad would grab the phonebook and order a pizza," said Tom. "He'd eat slice after slice and wait you out."

Connie and Billy approached. I shook hands with the men and kissed the ladies on the cheek and climbed into the U-Haul. I waited for the Explorer to depart, but it did not move. I pulled away and drove to the highway; the Explorer followed me.

After 15 minutes on the road, the Explorer was still behind me. My cell phone, sitting in the passenger seat, began beeping. There was a text message from Diana: *Come back ASAP. XOXO.*

I reasoned it was only a matter of time before the Explorer grew impatient with my 50-mph ways and zoomed past. But no: Driver Billy remained behind me, the vehicle and its Massachusetts license visible in my side-view mirrors. After ten more minutes of driving I lost patience. I signaled and exited and watched with glee as the Explorer whizzed by, continuing on the Interstate.

No sooner was I back on the highway when my phone beeped again. *RU mad @ me?* was Diana's message.

When I reached her door she looked as though she'd been crying. Her cheeks had the same strawberry-milk tint as her lips. She held me tightly and said: "Don't leave. Stay here. We'll wake up early and you'll be back in Boston at a decent hour."

We lay on the new black couch, its tall armrests looming over our heads. Diana reached inside my boxers and whispered, "I want to go really, really slow tonight."

From our experience together I knew 'slow' meant Diana would want a thorough 30 minutes of cunnilingus, mixed at intervals with finger probes and insertions. On other occasions I'd tell Diana, "I really want to go fast," and she'd drop her head like an anchor to my crotch and have me screaming for mercy in 30 seconds. So I set to work, hindered somewhat by the armrests, but too bashful to suggest we abandon the couch and christen the iris room. Her perspiring, muscular thighs encircled my ears, tightening, tightening, and culminating in ghastly shrieks that seemed both louder and more lonesome because of the celestial ceilings and echoing wooden floors.

Our own sweat glued us to the couch, yet allowed our upper bodies to slither over and around each other. Diana said, "I feel so close to you."

"I can't believe we're here," I said.

"It's so weird, that feeling after you've moved in somewhere," she said. "It's like, Okay, I'm moved in. What the hell do I do now?"

"You'll be fine once work starts," I said. "You'll take to it. Before long you'll be logging 12-hour days."

"And then I'll come home and have no one to hang out with."

"You'll have happy hours with your coworkers," I said. "In the winter you'll ski."

"Do you think my folks know you're here?" she asked.

"They saw me get off the highway."

"Well, fuck them for making you feel like you had to leave," she said.

*   *   *

"Everyone was so accepting and flattering," said Diana as we discussed, via phone, her first day on the job. "My brain felt so *picked*. I didn't even have time to set up my office until seven o'clock. I got home at eight – there's no traffic up here."

"I want to see you *now*," I said. We'd been apart four days. We'd spoken every night for hours. We'd worked out a visiting schedule, whereby we'd alternate weekends staying with one another. I was driving up Friday.

"I want to pull you through this phone and hug you," she replied.

"I want to go back 200 years before cars and phones and trains and planes and all the other things that made it easy for people to move away."

In anticipation of my first visit I purchased a stuffed animal as a gift for Diana. It was a lanky bright red teddy bear, with gangly legs and loose shoulders. I had named the bear Lamar, for it reminded me, in its relaxed and elongated carriage, of a basketball player named Lamar Odom, whose team at the time, the Los Angeles Clippers, had scarlet uniforms very much like the bear's color. Like Jalen Rose, Odom was a favorite of mine because of his left-handedness.

I buckled Lamar in the passenger seat of the Ford Focus I had rented. The ride was an enjoyable, two-hour bath of air conditioning and sports-talk radio. But when I arrived at the apartment my girlfriend was not home; her Camry was nowhere to be found, and she did not answer her cell phone. I sat on the front step, periodically wiping sweat from my forehead, engaging in pretend-conversation with Lamar about where Diana might be. The scarlet bear speculated Diana was still in her office, or perhaps at happy hour with her cool new colleagues. In the midst of this mental play the Camry pulled up. Diana's expression was stern. I braced myself for a speech. But as I stood to greet her, she pushed me down on the step and sat on my lap and made out with me.

When we got inside she said, "I have a whole list of cool dinner places we can walk or drive to. You can meet my partners. We're — they're all meeting for drinks later tonight." She fetched a printout from her backpack. She read a series of restaurant profiles and asked which one I liked. "I like staying here and fooling around all night," I said. Diana bit on her lower lip. "Wrong answer?" I asked.

"Don't you want to see the city a little?" she said.

"Tomorrow. Tonight I just want to stare at you and play with your body. Let's just get drunk and fool around."

"Ari, I've been alone in my apartment all week. It's Friday night. You drove all this way. We should go out."

"Okay," I said, reaching for her back. Her muscles were tense. "But can we just stay here for an hour or two? You're tense, I'm tense, let's just neck for a while."

"Do you need time to steel yourself, before we face the public?" she asked.

"No, I'm quite prepared for the public," I said. I didn't quite understand why she was invoking my rhetoric of social challenges. So I let it slide and hoped a compliment would both assuage her and clarify my feelings: "It's just that I have not gone 48 hours without seeing your perfect ass in a very long time. I think you should let me examine it, stroke it, and kiss it for a good hour or so before you cover it up and we hit the streets."

"I'm sorry," she said, rising from the couch. "Work was tense today. Enjoyable, but tense. I really need a drink." At her fridge she cracked open two Sam Adams bottles. She handed me one and looked me over. I was wearing baggy khaki shorts and a white t-shirt, which had become moist in the back and beneath the armpits during my drive. She said, "I have something for you to wear." She led me to the iris bedroom. From her closet she withdrew a brand new white linen buttondown shirt. She turned me around and pressed the shirt against my shoulders. After I donned it, she undid the top two buttons, revealing my pale sternum and lack of chest hair; she also undid the *bottom* two buttons, exposing my gaunt midriff and a belt buckle of brushed silver. "Oh, you look so hot right now," she said.

"Then why don't you jump me?" I asked.

"Because I want us to have time for a nice, lengthy dinner. Then you can meet my new peeps at ten. Then we can come back here and I'll jump you."

"We've spoken on the phone every day this week, and you never mentioned anything about meeting your peeps," I protested. "I really thought it'd just be us two tonight."

"So did I," she said. "But you know how it goes in an office, sweetie. Sometimes you just make spontaneous Friday night plans. I've had a great week, and I really want you to meet everybody, especially Gale, who's been *so* nice to me."

"Do you want them to meet *me*, or do you want them to meet a guy in a linen shirt?" I asked.

"Where did that come from?"

"I don't know," I said. "Probably from the same place as 'steel yourself.' I'm sorry." I gestured toward the kitchen, where our open beer bottles sat glistening. "Maybe I could use a drink too."

She wrapped her arms around me and kissed my neck. We finished our beers and left the apartment, walking, hand-in-hand, to an Italian restaurant called Ribollita. The evening sun shone brightly, shadowing long and black on some streets, glaring harsh and hot on others. Diana and I plied the conversation to the safer ground of national politics. About a month earlier President Bush had announced that the major fighting in Iraq was over; and already the major newspapers had returned to their safe harbor, eschewing war coverage for stories about celebrity deaths: the actress Katharine Hepburn and the senator Strom Thurmond had kicked the bucket within one week of each other; and that their deaths received more attention than those of America's perished soldiers was an outrage Diana and I could agree upon.

Ribollita is a tiny, intimate place of eight tables; not having made reservations, we found ourselves waiting outside on a wooden bench on Middle Street. There was plenty to look at: Middle Street was very much a main drag, full of shops, restaurants, hotels, and historical buildings. Diana explained that it was also a hub of Portland's art district; and that it was near the "Old Port," along which there were yet more shops and hotels and restaurants. To judge by the Middle Street traffic, Portland had a population of diverse ages. Within minutes we saw several groups: high schoolers, grandparents, twenty-somethings, thirty-somethings, forty-somethings – all walking around, some bound for dinner, others just strolling. Everyone we saw was Caucasian.

I went into the restaurant to check on our table status. When I came back to the bench Diana was absorbed in conversation with a pair of forty-somethings who appeared to be husband and wife. The short, brunette woman had a boy's haircut and the muscular thighs of a biker or hiker; she wore short khaki shorts and a black tank top. Her stubble-faced, burly, gray-haired companion clasped his hands behind his back, leaning forward as Diana spoke. I clopped over to the group, and Diana promptly introduced me to Gale Martin and her "partner," Ira. He had something of Neil's admirable calmness and social earnestness. It was not a trial for him to exchange pleasantries with me and Diana. He seemed sincerely interested in learning who I was and what I did for a living. He followed Diana and Gale's conversation as if it were a riveting Joycean dialogue. And I? I was hungry, I was horny, and I was 28 – I felt slighted and affronted that my girlfriend was doing nothing to alleviate either state of need. Whereas Ira – there was no edge in his voice, not a sliver of impatience or crankiness to reach whatever destination he and Gale had in mind for the evening. How did he get like this? Was it a function of age? Was it a function of being sexually active for a few decades, of having shunted enough sperm into enough vaginas so that it was easier to forestall the satisfaction of one urge or another?

"Would you care to join us?" Diana asked. I seconded the request, though inside I was seething. Chirpily, I said, "Let me tell the hostess we've got two more," and I went inside. And at that moment a table for four happened to open up. I ordered a Heineken from a busboy. Diana flashed me a look when my beer arrived only seconds after we sat. I promptly downed half the bottle, all the while inhaling the scents of baked bread, olive oil, and mixed marinades that came a-wafting from the kitchen. When our waiter took drink orders, I excused myself, announcing my food choice (pan-seared gnocchi with prosciutto) lest the waiter return before I did. Before I even entered the bathroom I had text-messaged Jimmy: *Reporting live from Portland.*

When a few minutes passed and Jimmy hadn't responded I tried Jerod, who was down in Washington, DC, doing a stint at George Washington University hospital. His new career goal – having broken up with his girlfriend, Emily – was to network his way to a job at a hospital in Europe, both for the stimulus of travel and for the women he could attain as a tall black American doctor.

It was so hot in the men's room, which lacked the dining area's whirling ceiling fans and central ventilation, that I left the restaurant through a back exit and found myself facing a parking lot, leaning on Ribollita's redbrick exterior. "We've had this conversation before," said Jerod, who had five minutes to kill before reporting for his overnight shift. "I wish I could tell you something encouraging. But what you're experiencing is par for the long-distance course. The visitor and the visited bring completely different agendas to the table."

"Right," I said. "So what are you doing next week?" I asked. "If I fly down, can we catch a Wizards game?"

He laughed. "You should get back to dinner." We said goodbye and I discovered Ribollita's rear exit wouldn't open from the outside. I went around to the front and found the three of them savoring drinks at the table. Diana glared. I said, "I got a call, stepped outside, couldn't get back in." They all nodded in understanding.

During our meal I drank my beer like it was water and noticed more congruities between Ira and Neil. They both had a laidback way of holding forth. It might have been the unspoken confidence of men who've "made it" in life, that is, cleared the conventional hurdles of home-ownership, retirement moneys, college tuition for offspring, and – of course – a monogamous partnership. But their tranquility bespoke another, unnamable parallel, one I struggled to finger as I rapidly lost sobriety. I drank heartily, triumphantly, particularly after I contributed a sentence or two to the group conversation. I would say something like, "The problem is the electoral college *itself*," and then swallow my beverage, in tacit self-celebration that I could now go another few minutes without having to speak again.

When our meals were finished and our empty plates had not yet been removed, my inebriation got the best of me. Musing once more on the Neil-Ira parallels, and relating them to my own life, and pondering how I'd ended up dining in Portland with three fashion plates — I chanced to ask Ira, during an interval of silence, whether his black pocket t-shirt was from The Gap. "It is, in fact," he said. "I like it," I replied, hoping this addendum would minimize any harm done by my harmless question. I swallowed some beer and mused again on Ira vs. Neil. I thought to myself: "These men have all the money they'll ever need. But why is that a reason for calm, as opposed to jubilance, or constant misbehavior? Regardless, this Ira person is like the Maine version of Neil. What gives?" I studied Ira's face, tried discerning an ethnicity in his physiognomy. Then his possible commonality with Neil finally hit me. Interrupting Gale's dissertation on male t-shirts, I said, "Ira, are you Jewish by any chance?"

The three of them stared at me as if I'd just used the word kike. I understood their surprise. But I didn't see the harm in the question, especially compared to all that a drunken person could have asked Ira. I was reminded, too, that I was in Portland, not Boston, and certainly not New York, where it is commonplace among residents to be ethnically inquisitive, to ask whether a dark-skinned person "has any Spanish in her" or whether a Fawn-like man with dark curls "is part Sicilian." Ira's smooth forehead became a narrow landscape of four creases, and he replied, "Why do you ask?"

"I'm a native New Yorker," I said. "I guess we Manhattoes are just curious about these things."

"I'm Irish Catholic all the way," he said. I glanced at Diana, who stared at her empty plate. A fork, knife, and a creamy tuft of uneaten linguine rested on it. "Want me to finish that?" I asked her.

"I'm going to take it home," she replied.

Ira requested the check and before long we were on Middle Street again. Gale and Ira stated their desire to go home, to rest up for a morning hike up Bradbury Mountain. Diana mentioned a morning yoga class — the first I'd heard of it — and we said goodbye.

When Gale and Ira left, she said, "Let's just forget about meeting my other coworkers. I can't even speak to you right now." She started walking away from me.

I felt I'd done nothing incredibly wrong. I was tempted to follow her down the sidewalk, to shout and scream about how sorry I was and how much I loved her. But a part of me wanted her to apologize: for thrusting Gale and Ira in our path, for not being at home when I arrived, and for not giving me some head after my two-hour drive.

I sat on the bench and text-messaged Jerod. *Bitches*, I wrote. My anger mounted, from not only the evening's events, but also how Diana had literally walked away from me, rather than directly telling me what had pissed her off. I composed a long text-message to Jimmy: *For all the Mars-Venus tripe about men having poor communication skills, it is women who sit there, stewing, hoping in vain the man will guess the cause.*

I phoned Diana. *Ring. Ring. Ring. Ring. She did not pick up.* I wondered whether she went home or sought her new Portland pals. Or maybe she just went to a bar by herself, to flirt with guys who didn't ask ethnic questions to strangers, who didn't seek cell-phone refuge from group conversations, who didn't need coaxing to wear linen.

I lingered in the stores and shops of Middle Street. Part of me felt like pressing my luck in the bars, linen shirt and all. Maybe sobering up was stupid. Maybe, if I got even drunker, Diana would be less likely to initiate a serious conversation. I could just pass out and deal with everything in the morning.

But at length I returned to her apartment, alert and ready to defend myself. She opened the door and sat on the couch, where she was drinking bottled water and watching local news. Lamar, the red bear, was facedown beside the opposite armrest. "Do you want to break up?" she asked.

"No. Of course not."

"So why are you acting like you do?"

"Getting drunk after you railroaded our one-on-one dinner isn't acting like I do. But I'm afraid your railroading of dinner means *you* do — or at the very least, you're unconcerned about making this visit less enjoyable for me."

"Cut the crap, Ari. You admitted to taking a phone call during our meal. Who were you talking to? A client? You can be a wise-ass in front of my boss but then you leave the table for ten minutes to conduct your business? And now you come back here, one hour later, and pretend to be ignorant of your poor behavior? If I weren't so concerned about your driving drunk I'd really consider asking you to go home."

"How would you like it if, when you visit, I insist we hang out with strangers?"

"I'd prefer hanging out with you alone. But I'd be mature about the reality of our situation. Which I'm not certain you're capable of doing."

I lowered my head and walked to my backpack, which lay in the corner of the mauve room. Her eyes were on the television. I snared my paperback *Moby Dick* – three years after Albuquerque, and I was ready for a reread – and I toted it to her bedroom, where I lay reading with the door open.

Perhaps an hour later she clicked the television off and stood in her doorway. "I'm going to sleep," she said. "Thanks for a wonderful Friday evening."

"Sorry I'm the worst boyfriend of all time."

"I just wish you'd act a little older," she said. At her closet she changed into boxers and a t-shirt. Barefoot, she sauntered to the bathroom to execute her face-washing ritual. She returned looking fresh and crisp in her bedtime gear. "I won't ask you to stay on the couch," she said. "But I'm shutting the light, so if you want to keep reading, you should do it out there."

I flopped on the couch and clicked on the television. I was miffed Diana's cable package didn't include HBO, Cinemax, or any movie channel on which I could find female nudity. For there was no way I'd be able to fall asleep without jerking off. I slid down my shorts and boxers and began stroking myself to the videos on MTV. The cleavage shot of a teenage singer I'd never heard of set me over the edge. I came into my right palm, and wiped my residue on my shorts, chuckling quietly over the fact that Lamar, still face down by the armrest, had witnessed everything. Before I knew it I'd passed out, my bare, sweaty ass adhering to the couch's leather.

An hour later I entered her dark bedroom. I slept on the edge of the bed. Perhaps one foot of sheeted mattress separated us.

In the morning I struggled with my bearings: for there is an initial surprise, sometimes, upon waking and realizing you've not slept in a familiar place. At first I was in Boston; in the next drowsy instant, I bethought myself in the New Hyde Park apartment; one moment later, I was in West Egg. Next, I believed I was back in Diana's old triple decker. Only upon seeing the iris walls, mixed with rectangles of sunlight, seeping in through half-drawn shades, did I recall exactly where I was. All this confusion, mind you, took place in perhaps my first two seconds of awakening.

Diana slept on her side, the slender curvature of her flank shaped like an integral, or the clef-like carving etched into violins. I reached for her hips. She rolled away.

My entire frame became wrought with worry over whether her rollaway was permanent or temporary, *ser* or *estar*. I reached for her again. "Stop it, Ari," she whispered. "I have to think."

"Don't remove my hands from you while I'm still your boyfriend," I said. "Please just let me hold you."

She relented, and I caressed her cheek. "I know you've been good to me," she sobbed. "But I really have to think about whether we can continue like this."

"Please don't drop me yet," I said, and I was sobbing too. "Give me a chance. I – I've never been in this situation before."

"I know, sweetie, I know," she sobbed.

"I feel like it was only yesterday I'd never even kissed a girl," I said. "I was just this lonely guy who watched football games. And now I'm 28, an age when people make decisions like this. And I don't think I'm prepared."

We were silent after that, fading in and out of sleep.

At one point Diana rose and stuffed her yoga mat into a gym bag. She left the room and I presumed she was heading out. But an hour passed before I heard the apartment door click shut. Through the bedroom window I saw her climb into the Camry.

I crept out to the living room and watched sports highlights while eating a bowl of Grape Nuts. Then I crept back into bed.

When Diana got back she showered, then came into her room, one long towel around her body, and another around her head. She removed a pair of panties from a dresser and, without removing the towel, stepped into them. Donning denim cutoffs and a white tank top, she left the room and came back holding a spiral notebook. I sat up and said, "Want me to leave?"

"I want you to answer one question honestly: do you have any intention of either moving here or marrying me in the next six months?"

"I honestly don't know," I said. There was her answer.

"That's just what I thought," she said. "I'm not mad." She looked down at the notebook, then up at me. "Well, this morning I wrote down my thoughts before going to yoga. I just want to read them to you. Is that okay?"

I nodded. She began:

"Dear Ari. You are the best friend and best boyfriend I have ever had. But I have been through more relationships than you have, and those experiences tell me it's time for ours to end.

"I love you so much that I've been lying to myself about what I need and your ability to provide it. You possess a million great qualities I won't find anywhere else. But one quality you don't possess, as much as I tried telling myself that you did, is a long-term vision of us. And that's why we can't continue. It would be one thing if I loved you less; then I could tolerate an uncertain future, because I myself would have reservations about committing long-term. But I love you so much that your laissez faire approach to our future hurts my feelings. I keep thinking to myself: 'Why doesn't he want to live with me or propose?' I tell myself not to take it personally. I tell myself that your issues are rooted and psychological, that they have nothing to do with me and everything to do with your childhood. I tell myself that you'd hesitate to marry anyone.

"You're a logical guy, and you can't deny the logic of this: that if you weren't going to commit, then we were going to break up eventually, anyway. And if that's the case, then what's the point of continuing, now that I'm here and you're there? Implicit in any long-distance commitment, Ari, is the prospect of wedded futures. Without that prospect, what is the point?

"I admit I'm coming to this decision rapidly. That only days ago I was mentioning attending Kris's wedding with you, finally meeting Jerod and Jimmy, finally get-

ting a glimpse of Shelagh, things like that. But I think we'll only end up fighting more and resenting each other if we stay together. Whereas if we end this now, we can make an easier transition to friendship. And who knows? Maybe we'll come back to each other in a few years, when you can see the virtues of long-term commitment.

"I think we should go three weeks without talking and see how it feels. I will call you. Trust me. I will call. I am not Shelagh. I am a woman who loves you very much and, if you can believe it, it's going to be hard for me to not think about your feelings all day. I am also certain I'll be thinking about you on my wedding day.

"I don't want you to think I'm terminating three great years in one weekend because of your behavior last night. I've suffered worse and, overall, you're fairly broken-in for a guy your age, if I'm to judge by the Harvard cretins and Lori and Harper's horror stories about Scott and Lee. Point is, I've been thinking about all of this for a while. A few weeks ago you asked if I was forcing your hand. I was not forcing your hand, though, as much as I was making a decision about my future independent of you. And can you really blame me for that?

"Don't ask me whether we'd still be together if I'd found career bliss in Boston. It doesn't matter. All I know is, I need to get used to solitude again. I tend to enter relationships quickly, and I'm afraid I end them quickly too. When I knew I wanted to be your girlfriend, I knew; and it felt like we were a real couple after our first night together, didn't it? But now I'm not sure I want to be your girlfriend, and in my experience, 'not sure' means 'no.' 'Not sure' means maybe I'll soon be wishing I was at yoga when we're hanging out, because at least I know yoga will still be there for me in five years.

"I could summarize everything I've just written in two sentences: please don't interpret this mature, smart move on my part as a rejection or a dumping. You still have no idea how much I love you and how, as if you have invisible hands, you sometimes twist my heart." –DIANA

She looked up from the pad. I reached for her hand. She backed away and said, "I think you should go home."

"I want to spend the weekend with you."

"And I want to spend it with you," she said. "But it's not a good idea to keep smoking if you have to quit eventually."

"Why not just smoke because smoking is fun?"

"Ari, I've made my reasons clear to you. I know we'd both have a lot of fun today if we could just play stupid and keep fooling around while ignoring the larger questions. I just think you're more capable of doing that than I am."

"Can I keep that note?" I asked, pointing to the pad.

"I guess so," she said, handing me the entire pad. "What for?"

"Posterity," I said, walking past her into the living room and zipping the pad into my backpack. I put on my shoes and said, "This is a good move for you, Diana. You'll find someone handsome who'll marry you and take you skiing. I predict you'll be smitten within six months."

"I'll call you," she said.

"How can you just end us?" I said.

"Ari, how can you protest? Do you really think I'm being malicious?"

"Let me hug you one more time."

She paused. "Okay."

She approached me cheek first. We embraced and I made no effort to curtail. "Okay, Ari," she said, tapping me on the shoulder.

But I kept hugging. "So you'll call in three weeks?" I sniffled.

"It's in my planner."

*   *   *

In the gray Ford Focus I strapped Lamar into the passenger seat. Lamar. My big black buddy. My new riding partner. Jerod's substitute. The Jim to my Huck Finn. The Clarence to my Springsteen. The Red to my Andy Dufresne.

I began another play-conversation with Lamar: "Yeah, she was too good for me," I confessed to the stuffed bear. "Luckily," I continued, "her female subjectivity blinded her to that for three years. My time ran out, is all. You can't live at a resort forever, or you'll run out of money. Only jocks like you, Lamar, or rock stars like Springsteen get to stay at the resort forever. The rest of us, the normal guys, have to pay or go home. What's that you say, Lamar? You want to hear track 14 of *Ready to Die?*

> Bitches come and bitches go / That's why I get my nut and I be out the fuckin' door

"Lamar, that's not fair to Diana. She's no bitch. But I'll say this: I once read this Saul Bellow novel, *Herzog*. And this lawyer told the protagonist, Herzog: 'The bitches come and the bitches go.' And I was struck by this repetition between Bellow and the Notorious B.I.G. It reminded me of this parallel between Whitman and B.I.G. I discovered in college. And when I told Diana about these parallels, she appreciated it – you know? It's going to sound so silly, to say that of all the Platonic qualities I'll miss about Diana, it's her appreciation that I could observe parallels like that. Isn't that crazy?

"Sit on my cell phone, Lamar. Otherwise I might just call Diana and be obnoxious. Or tell her that I have so much more to offer. At least in the way of hip-hop's connection to high literature. In *Moby Dick*, Ishmael says that no ethnicity knows how to let loose and party like the blacks do. I'm not making that up. Check the book. Then you have *Gatsby*, in which Tom Buchanan smacks women in public and nobody protests. And we all know bitch-beating is seminal to hip-hop.

"Oh, man. What made me think Diana wouldn't dump me? Was I that far-gone, to believe she'd stay with me forever just because I know my classics?

"Yes, I was that far-gone. I still am. And I should be. For the life I've lived has been beyond belief. Simply the fact that I have dated someone like Diana Kennedy is incredible. I'll be damned if it's not as incredible as some other stories in bookstores. The ones about geishas, piano tuners, drug addicts, Irish immigrants, dying actors, and newspaper heiresses. Did any of those motherfuckers take a shit in a parking lot, masturbate to their stepsisters, or beat Tom Kennedy on his home basketball court?

"You want to read about their adventures, Lamar? Or mine?

"I know what Diana's answer would've been."

Chapter 20 – Ariel's New Guide to Life

My mother displayed her usual skills for balming my broken heart. Without Diana to visit anymore, I spent weekends in West Egg. I left Boston on Thursday afternoons and reached Neil's house by dinnertime. Nicole and Stephen, a second-year law student who was her new boyfriend, were usually there too.

In its own way, Diana's dumping made me want to behave better with Neil. For I realized anew the precious rarity of long-term commitments. Neil had committed to my mother. And for that I owed him my respect, rather than resentment. What right did I have to be brusque with him?

Yet brusque I remained. I often responded to his harmless questions about my drives down from Boston or my business with one-word grunts and silent nods.

My temperament needed improving. That much I knew. I had a notion to seek a marijuana lesson from Jerod or Nicole, if only so I could, by smoking, provide for myself and others the calm that those others deserved.

* * *

But until I became proficient with pot, I'd have to master my mood without narcotics. I resorted to old habits: within my brand new kitchen cabinets I posted the following reprimands:

• *Just because Neil didn't have a horrid childhood, doesn't mean you have the right to be rude until he pays homage to your childhood.*

• *So be grateful to Neil: he is family. And family by definition is more permanent than girlfriend. So start acting like his relative, and stop acting like someone whose ass he needs to kiss. Whether he gets you is irrelevant.*

• *So your dad beat you. It doesn't mean that everything you feel is correct or proper or deserving of immediate attention, just because you feel it.*

• *No self-pity for Diana: you could have relocated. Even those with horrid childhoods don't get a pass on the compromises adulthood brings.*

These were my new goals, my new epiphanies. At last I had stumbled upon the truth: Ariel Zinsky, compared to most of the world, had led a privileged life. Leaving aside the beatings and the baldness, I'd had it pretty good. So maybe it was time I did just that – left them aside.

Had I been stationed in Iraq? Had I lost someone on September 11? Had I been stricken by a serious disease? If I had been – if I had been forced out of my individuality by life's rough circumstances – then perhaps my newfound perspectives would not have been 28 years in the making. Only in the aftermath of Diana's dumping, of my newfound solitude and trips to West Egg pondering it, did I realize this – what Jimmy Calipari had been telling me for years, what I was content to ignore because in the ignorance I'd found motivation and self-medication and money.

Now I wanted to be worthy of the *man* moniker – man, as opposed to *boy* or *guy*. Physically, I had belonged to manhood for some time. And here were more signs: my frame, previously as hairless as my head, seemed overnight to sprout follicular wisps on the back and shoulders. There also came a change in bladder capacity. In years past I could down two Gatorades following an evening of basketball or running and sleep through the night. Now I woke to piss at four each morning.

There was one other bodily change, which my duty to truth compels me to report: my erections were still firm and powerful, but rarer now were the occasions inspiring a teeming, maximal rectitude. However, I continued masturbating twice daily to a variety of pornography and real women: mainly Diana and Sandy, but also Shelagh, as the upcoming occasion of Kris Holley's wedding gave me reason to consider her again.

The issue of my nominal manhood weighed on my mind. I recall walking to my office one summer morning, trotting a few steps behind a young mother carrying a toddler on her shoulder – the child's popping eyes were riveted on me. As I strode past them the toddler tracked me, whereupon the mother (who was about my age) smiled and asked her cooing progeny: "Are you looking at *the man*?"

The man. Ha! If only this mother had known that I was probably nothing like her dutiful and fecund husband, but rather a solipsistic loner who'd just spent 30 minutes of his morning jacking off to a mixture of exes, porn stars, and an older woman whose hair reminded him of Peter Pan.

I would never be a dutiful or fecund husband, but I did aim to be less solipsistic. And in this aim I felt myself change in relation to the books I was reading. I completely reversed myself on a passage in *Moby Dick* that seemed particularly apt in light of America's history, circa 2000-2003:

> And, doubtless, my going on this whaling voyage, formed part of the grand programme of Providence that was drawn up a long time ago. It came in as a sort of brief interlude and solo between more extensive performances. I take it that this part of the bill must have run something like this:
> "Grand Contested Election for the Presidency of the United States.
> "Whaling Voyage by One Ishmael.
> "Bloody Battle in Affghanistan."

I had viewed this passage as my justification for solipsism, for believing that the events of my own life's whaling voyage were as important as international relations – and therefore well worth chronicling. Wasn't inflated self-importance part of human nature? Yes, it was – but at age 28 I resolved to *fight* this aspect of human nature, to subordinate my ego and whims and become a better friend and family man.

In retrospect I realize: It is easy to get noble after you've earned your money, or after you've been dumped. Still: at the time, I was eager to pursue a new identity as a family man. So the visits to New York continued.

The most fun I had in the post-Diana era was my Friday afternoons with Barbara. She had no eighth- or ninth-period classes, so she could leave school by 1:45 and the two of us would grab a late lunch. We drove to Gatsby's house to sip coffee and chat. In sharp contrast to Boston, the West Egg area remained in visible mourning for 9/11. American flags were still – nearly two years later – draped all over town, in store windows and front porches and on wires hung above two-way streets. Several flags hung from the bridge next to the main branch of the West Egg Public Library, over which Barbara and I had driven on our way to Gatsby's.

We sat atop the trunk of my Ford Focus rental, occasionally strolling over the leafy grass to the water and standing by the shoreline. It was early September and though it was warm, the stirrings of autumn were upon us, in the form of fallen green leaves and waves that rolled in a bit faster and more frequently than you expected. On our third walk to the water my mother did something I never thought she'd do: She offered me a smoke. "I can't start now," I demurred.

"You want to smoke dope with Jerod and Nicole but with me you can't start?"

"Okay," I said, putting one in my mouth. She lit it and I followed her instructions to suck in and swallow. I expected to cough up a lung, but perhaps from years of watching Barbara I got it right the first time. "Ooh," I said, recoiling a bit, my forehead aching pleasurably. A rush of merry motes was hammering my skull from the inside.

Barbara held my hand. "Do you love Neil and Nicole?" she asked.

"You know the answer," I said. "But the answer isn't too relevant."

"That's my boy," she said. I was comfortable she said *boy* not *man*. Diana wanted a man and I wasn't ready. Did Sandy want a man? I looked out at the brown Long Island sound, whiffed its brininess, and tapped some surplus ash from my cigarette to the sand. Judging by my college friends, I wasn't the only 28-year-old opting for boyhood. Jerod and Jimmy were both single again, having broken up with their own lives' equivalents of Diana. Only Kris Holley was ready to settle down, and he had always been more of a by-the-book type – which was why I was better friends with Jimmy and Jerod.

"Do you know what I miss about Shelagh?" I said. My remark wasn't out of nowhere, but Barbara couldn't tell. "The hot sex?" she replied.

"I miss being of an age where all a girl wanted was a boyfriend, or less than that."

Barbara had no idea I had slapped Shelagh; as far as my mother was concerned, the harm was all on Shelagh's side, and I was the innocent victim of an emotional beating. So when she heard this answer, she got concerned. "Don't get your hopes up for Kris's wedding," she replied. "If something happens, great, but you should go without expectations. You should maybe even bring a date, to protect yourself."

I thought about whom I wanted to attend the wedding with.

On my drive back to Boston I told myself I'd go to Starbucks more often.

*   *   *

My affair with Sandy began on an unseasonably warm October day. She wore an olive-green skirt falling loose to her mid-shins, and a black blouse with only the top button undone. "Would you care to take a walk?" I asked, after we shook hands. She seemed amused to have bumped into me again.

We wandered to the waterfront, strolling along a pink-brick path, gazing at a cloudy horizon providing a dingy background to the harbor's light brown waters. Boat horns sounded periodically, marking the departure of commuter ferries to the South Shore. We turned a corner and reached a part of the path lined with black benches. We sat and she removed one of her black shoes, shaking a pebble from it. Inches from our feet, a trio of pigeons lingered on the path, their feathers resembling the sky's color, their necks jerking forward as they waddled.

I leaned in to kiss her. She anticipated the move and turned her head. I pecked the taut, warm flesh of her cheek. She shut her eyes and waited, fists clenched on her olive-skirt lap. She curled a finger around her black purse's shoulder strap. "You really don't know me very well," she said.

"I've been smitten with you since the first time I saw you."

"I was on crutches and had no hair."

"You wore a furry red Kangol and had one of the best bodies I'd ever seen. You still do."

"I have a boyfriend," she said, staring at the water.

"Is he as smitten as I am?" I asked. "There's no way."

"Let's walk again," she said.

I took her hand. We continued on the pink-brick path until we reached the city's aquarium. "Don't you need to get back to work?" she asked.

"I got in at seven," I lied. "I can hang for another hour or so."

Inside the aquarium we confronted a chlorinated, musty scent. We followed a winding ramp that rose from the basement to the roof, encircling a dirty-glass cylindrical fish tank. School children abounded, their faces stuck to the glass, mesmerized by the countless varieties of fish within. Sandy and I reached the top level and faced the tank, our hands still joined. My heart raced with these thoughts: "I may, if I play my cards right, have vaginal sex for the first time in six years. I may, if I play my cards right, have a physical experience that will make forgetting about Diana a little easier. All this with a woman I've pined about for six years."

Slender, inky moray eels and fierce-eyed barracudas streaked past us, followed by a pair of thick gray groupers. A green sea turtle floated daintily, exploring a mossy cave before passing to a sunset-colored coral forest. His eyes resembled black beans. "This one's my favorite," I said, squeezing her hand.

"She seems like an outcast to me," said Sandy. "She's the only turtle in there. You'd think the aquarium supervisors would find a turtle friend for her."

"But her whole charm to me *is* her aloneness," I said.

"She's less charming once you realize what a head case she is."

"In the fish tank, there's an unofficial freemasonry among the head cases," I said. "There are in-jokes and phrases they can exchange. Once you meet another freemason, hanging out with anyone else seems like homework." With my free hand I directed her face to mine and we kissed for an instant. "I better go," she said.

"This can't be the last time we see each other," I said, in front of my office.

"What are you doing Sunday?" she asked.

I had planned to be in West Egg, of course. But now my libido was in the game, and my family was on hold again.

*   *   *

Sandy proposed a nature walk through Winterbottom Park in the leafy town of Auburnfield.

When I reached her house she was on her cell phone. She wore flattering blue jeans and a gray hooded sweatshirt. I followed her to the kitchen, where – still on her phone – she stuffed water bottles and two paperbacks into a red backpack. The paperbacks were the same book; I couldn't identify the title but both volumes had apple-green leather covers. Meanwhile, Sandy's cat – an obese, spayed, de-clawed black-gray lump named Clinton – crept toward me and rubbed her ears and nose against my shins.

Sandy said, "Talk to you later," and clicked off her cell phone. Then she faced me. "Sorry," she said. "That was Anthony."

Anthony was her boyfriend, who lived in Boston. He was a British man whose job as an integrator of database software kept him traveling all over the world. He was in town probably 10 days out of each month, and Sandy was getting tired of it – or so she told me, during the one phone call she and I had shared at this point. During this chat I told all about Diana and the *Guide* but nothing about my past or my family. For I was trying to be a man and I was resolved: I would not make my next lover an emotional prisoner of my life's sordid history.

I learned Sandy had had serious bone marrow cancer in her left leg. First there were weeks of chemo, during which her hair fell out; then the doctors inserted steel rods into her leg. I also learned that the pills she swallowed from the plastic orange container were multivitamins, simple as that – not the painkillers I fancied them to be. I learned she was a lawyer – a midlevel associate at the local firm Ackerman & Alter.

She owned her own apartment. And when I arrived on her premises, I saw in the driveway a black Mercedes SL, which I assumed she owned too.

After a short drive the Mercedes pulled into one of the countless vacant spots in the paved lot of Winterbottom Park. There were three tar paths, each of which cut across a steep grassy hill. Sandy led up the rightmost path, along the hill's edge, then up the green slope. A moderate wind pushed our backs, aiding the ascent.

At the hilltop we reached another tar path, which crossed an expansive, leaf-strewn area of open woods. Sandy led into the woods, her brown hiking boots crunching the desiccated autumn leaves as we passed between the thick, peeling trunks of bare-limbed shady trees.

Now she withdrew the granny-smith-green paperbacks from her red backpack: Copies of the *National Audubon Society Field Guide to North American Wildflowers*. There were hundreds of luminous photos; detailed descriptions of appearance, habitat, and classification; and a glossary of terms with entries such as *pistil: the female organ of a flower, composed of an ovary, style, and stigma.*

I scanned the ground for plants and flowers and tried finding them in the book: if not by color group, then by cluster shape. Sandy gazed at the treetops. One squirrel chased another along a branch. I brushed some blond locks from her forehead, and she stepped away from me, leading us further into the woods.

We walked to an uncluttered patch of ground where there were wide spaces between the trees. The mid-afternoon sun, no longer eclipsed by protruding branches, shone directly through. Dry brown leaves, with a few of their red and yellow brethren, adorned the brightened walkway. Sandy stopped before a patch of pink flowers with a cluster shape. Hoping to find the exact picture, I hastily thumbed past mallows and geraniums, roses and morning glory, sorrel and smartweed. Whereupon Sandy touched my forearm and advised: "I believe the Echinacea cone-flower is under purple."

By the time I found it she was kneeling beside the coneflowers, which jutted from a patch of bifurcated, fish-shaped green leaves. From the head of each flower radiated perhaps 20 separate pink petals of nearly equal lengths, all protruding from the perimeter of a spiky central node of dark orange. The petals tended to droop downward, except on the smaller, nascent flowers, on which the central heads had yet to reach the full blown diameter of three inches. Sandy caressed the underside of the coneflower, supporting the flagging petals. "I've seen these flowers all over the place," I said. "I didn't know Echinacea came from them."

Sandy said: "They are common, but I'm always drawn to them."

Further up the path she knelt again, amidst a patch of Black-eyed Susan. I tried plucking one by the stem and my fingers received a mild prick. "Sharp?" asked Sandy.

"Not *sharp* sharp," I said. "More like stubble." I crouched closer and fingered the stem's stubble. The petals were multiple shades of yellow: a burnished golden, like Sandy's hair, closer to the central node; a brighter, amber hue toward the middle; and a brighter, watercolor smudge of banana at the petal's tip. "Question for you," I said. "Why do some of these Susans – like these, over here – have only eight petals, while these – right here – have more than a dozen?"

"I don't know," said Sandy. "I guess it just depends how nature cuts the corolla."

We came to a portion of the path winding along the damp periphery of a muddy, duck-filled lake. Several of our quacking friends feather-paddled to the water's edge and literally *leapt* from the liquid, popping up like toast, their orange legs dangling from their undersides like the ropes of a swing. They flapped forward onto the land and wandered in circles, pecking at the air.

Perhaps five yards back from the lake was an adumbrated region of the woods. The tree trunks were close together and the dim, leafy ground was moist beneath our squeaking shoes. Sandy stepped toward a dense cluster of pear-brown wildflowers growing out of a tall leafy plant – tall enough to reach her waist. The light brown petals had flecks of red, as if they'd been sprayed with salsa. Sandy seemed baffled; she flipped through her *Guide* and I awaited her verdict. "I've never seen impatiens here before," she said. "Though it makes sense, given the lake and the shade."

"Those stems are amazing," I said, probing their soft surface. "They look like tinted straws." I found the corresponding page in my *Guide*. "Why are they nicknamed the *Touch-me-not?*" I asked teasingly.

Sandy pointed to the center of the flower, where a jellybean-sized structure was nestled within the petals. "When that capsule opens up," she said seriously, "the fruit seeds, supposedly, come flying out of there. It's a sensitive capsule. You wouldn't want to trigger the seed explosion by touching the capsule."

"But would the capsule really explode?"

"I doubt it," she said. "But that's how the name originated."

I stepped toward her and we kissed for a few minutes. She stepped away. "Ari, I can't let this stuff continue," she said.

The 22-year old Zinsky might have pressed forward, begging for affection.

The 28-year-old Zinsky backed off. "You're right," he said. "You're seeing someone, and I just got out of something."

On the drive back to her house we exchanged the basics about our families and educations. Her parents and a fraternal twin sister resided in the Minneapolis-St. Paul area. She had attended St. Olaf's college – I enlightened her on the fact that Gatsby, himself, had put in a semester there – and then Harvard Law, where she'd met Farouk Caro, the sports agent. In discussing my college experience, I used this conversation as a chance to mention Kris Holley's wedding – not to invite her, per se, but to plant the seed in her head so that a future invitation wouldn't catch her off guard.

At her door she surprised me. "I need to think about whether this is the last time we can see each other," she said. "You understand why, don't you?"

I nodded. I told her I hoped otherwise, and would still seek her out. "Please do," she said, and she shut herself inside.

It was not yet evening and I was in no mood to go home and watch football, as I did every Sunday when I wasn't in West Egg. Though my rationale told me Sandy would see me again, my irrational mind became sad. What a great afternoon we had shared! And to not be able to hold her hand or embrace her as a nighttime culmination to such fun – it was hard not to feel sad under such circumstances. I wanted to be in Sandy's arms. Instead I was in my car, searching for a solitary, leisurely activity that could not possibly compare to being in her arms.

I found myself in a familiar location for leisure: Starbucks in Harvard Square, where I'd wasted many afternoons after hitting the jackpot with the old *Guide* and quitting Stevie's lunch.

I sat and read. Or I tried to. I rotated among *Moby Dick* and *Pro Football Weekly* and the new *Guide*, which Sandy had lent me. But none held my attention. Every time a slender young female entered the shop I leered longingly. And at a nearby table I spied a young couple, Harvard freshmen perhaps – squeezing each other's hands and whispering words like "hello" and "hey" to each other. It was all I could take. I phoned Diana. "I'm just thinking about you," I said. "That's so sweet," she said. Her voice seemed half-sincere and half-detached, like a stewardess wishing you good morning.

"You home?" I asked.

"Walking there. We all worked today, then had dinner and drinks at Sapporo." There was silence for perhaps three seconds, which she broke by asking, of all things: "So how's Nicole?"

"That's random," I said. "How's Miranda?"

"Fine."

"Are you really curious about Nicole?"

"Yes," she said.

"She's enjoying law school," I said, omitting her recent engagement to Stephen.

"That's great," said Diana. "So – where are you now?"

"In Cambridge, by myself," I said. "I'm looking at all these happy young people and wanting to puke."

She was quiet. I said, "Sorry about that last sentence."

"I should probably go," she said.

It was the last time we ever spoke.

*   *   *

And I told myself: maybe I didn't want Sandy to be a girlfriend. Maybe I just wanted her to be a friend whom I slept with. It was contingent on her seeing me again, her breaking up with Anthony, or her continuing to cheat on him. And was that likely? Wouldn't it have happened already, if it was likely? I felt rejected. Also looming in my mind was the prospect of facing Shelagh alone at Kris Holley's wedding. She was going to look gorgeous and available, while I was going to look ugly and alone.

I strolled through Cambridge for a while – the first time I'd done so in a few months. The redbrick sidewalks seemed no different for my absence. It was overcast and breezy. I found myself standing before the movie theater on Church Street, staring idly at the show times in the ticket window. A group of undergraduates, three boys and two girls, lingered nearby. They held their cell phones or Discmans – this was 2003, a few years before the iPod pervasion – and seemed so self-occupied with their technical devices. They appeared so much more smooth-skinned and youthful than Jerod or Jimmy or Kris or I could possibly have looked at their age.

I bought $10 worth of candy and a ticket for an unrated Italian film called *Restless Gabriela*, which seemed to offer the best potential for female nudity. I sat back in my theater chair and took a deep breath, feeling the felt against the back of my bald head. The lights dimmed, obscuring the faces of me and the eleven other single men whom I'd counted present on this forlorn Sunday night. None of us knew each other, but I could sense the relief that all of us felt as the darkness aided the anonymity with which we pursued our mild, cinematic perversion.

There is so much emotional safety in pornography. You get to disembody your fantasy from the actual, to divorce your pleasure from the precarious hope that you'll potentially fulfill it.

Chapter 21 – The World is a Wedding

Sandy and I begin sleeping together after a mid-afternoon Starbucks encounter. We leave the café and rush to my apartment, our heads ducking in the mid-November wind, her gloved hand in mine. In my bedroom we strip ourselves, rather than each other. On her pale left shin is a surgical scar, running in a straight line down from her knee. The scar is faded pink, the color of a fingernail. We kiss for a few minutes before I ask, "Should I get a condom?"

"It's okay," she says. She stolidly explains that she's infertile, owing to chemo she'd received six years earlier – treatment for the bone marrow cancer that had been in her shin. There's no emotion in her voice – I'm guessing she's given this speech before. I'm thankful when we finally resume our kissing, and some semblance of compassion returns to her fingers as she tugs me to her chest.

In the days following this fateful afternoon, her text messages to me become simple declarations: *stop by tonight; Anthony's gone till Tuesday; calling in sick 2mro.* My responses are just as plain: *b there in 15* is what I type, and then I race over. These booty calls are the main reason I purchase my own Ford Focus and secure, with Sandy's assistance, a sticker allowing me to park legally outside her house, in the affluent township of Brookline.

My sorrow over Diana – it remains, but it lessens every time I explode inside of Sandy. Within weeks Sandy knows all about Diana; and she knows she's giving me a sweet treat, long withheld, each time I'm inside of her. Sometimes she whispers, "Oh, sweetie," once I'm inside, and I wonder what cruel things Anthony has done to deserve this – or if Sandy's past makes her feel as if cheating on Anthony – or simply feasting on lust – is something *she* deserves. She comes easily in all positions; our oral exchanges are stimulating you-first reciprocities. This is enough – more than enough – so that I convince myself Sandy is the best thing that has ever happened to me. I've been longing my whole life for a dalliance like this. I long to tell her *I love you*. But I'm too wise at age 28 to voice this utterance, fearing it will doom us – for she already has a boyfriend and probably doesn't want another man for whom things seem consequential. Nevertheless, I ask her one night, as we soak in her bathtub: "So, of course I'm not complaining, but, you can't blame my asking – why do you cheat on Anthony?"

"He cheated on me once," she says. "I forgave it, since we do have long-term intentions. But I never forgot it. And a part of me just wants to enjoy sex with other guys before I settle down with him. But it's hard to find guys who can deal with the arrangement. Most of them say they can, but they get attached."

"So I'm not the first."

"You're the second. But you're probably the last." She turns around in the tub and kisses me. "I almost *want* him to catch me," she continues, "so he can understand how hard it's been for me, and so we can go forward on even ground."

Within weeks I secure her attendance at Kris Holley's wedding. She learns about Shelagh, and I learn about my predecessors; and I come to understand, in my 28th year, that so much of one's personal history *is* your lovers. I wonder why all biographies don't take the form of chronicling lovers – could a more straightforward window to a person's essence possibly exist?

I remain mum on the subject of my father. Sandy knows he's dead, but doesn't know the deeper truth. And in truth, I feel guilty sharing it, and seeking pity or sympathy for it: how can my past stack up to hers, cancer and all? How can what Robert did to me compare to infertility? My past makes me *want* to forego reproduction. Her past leaves her no choice in the matter.

So I carry on with Sandy, humble and grateful for what she can provide. I know our affair will end some day. And I know she only cares so much about me: for she doesn't ever *ask* about Robert Zinsky. Nor does she inquire why I didn't follow Diana to Portland. Which is okay. Because on some nights with Sandy – when my mind is bleeding with one theory or another about football or novelists or rappers, and Sandy seems so indifferent I could scream – I wonder myself why I so easily gave up on Diana, whose heart once beat so fast against my own slim frame.

*   *   *

Our relationship wasn't only sex. We hung out at each other's apartments and chatted, sometimes for hours, before the carnality commenced. We smoked a lot of weed. She taught me how to roll a joint. But despite the pot, despite the sex, despite the happiness – I soon felt a violent version of myself returning, and wondered then if I would ever unlearn my past.

It was New Year's Eve. We had smoked all night, watched the ball drop to 2004, had sex, and turned in. At four in the morning she was passed out and I was awake and dehydrated. I strolled to the living room to watch college football highlights with Clinton the cat by my feet and a big glass of water by my hand.

When I went to get the water I saw Sandy's flower *Guide* atop the refrigerator. But when I reached for it I felt a second book, a leatherbound volume marked JOURNAL and filled with lined pages, many of which contained Sandy's loopy, all-capitals penmanship. Oh, was I tempted to read this volume, in search of her innermost emotions! But I slammed shut the book and replaced it above the *Guide.* I feared discovery – perhaps Sandy positioned the JOURNAL a certain way every night, and she would be quick to detect a disturbance of its restful angle. Also, I was still intent on behaving like a man, rather than a boy: And there was no question that ignoring the JOURNAL was the virtuous path, the foolproof way to comport myself like an adult.

Soon I was relaxing on her couch in front of the television. Clinton jumped up beside me, purring as she rubbed her pink nose and black ears against my sleeve. After a few minutes she simply sat on the couch, blinking. What did she *want?* I wondered angrily. What audacity, to sit there blinking for no reason! My hands tightened into fists. With my right hand I seized Clinton's neck. With my left I smashed her jaw with a rapid upper cut. The cat sat stunned, for a half second, before leaping from the couch and scampering into Sandy's bedroom.

So much for my adulthood behavior, I thought, inspecting my knuckles.

One hour later I went back to Sandy's bed, under which lurked a blinking Clinton. I had no fear of her exacting vengeance as I dozed. It just wasn't in her nature.

*   *   *

Kris's wedding took place in Manhattan's Marriott Marquis hotel, in a room adjacent to the one where the NFL draft was held in 1995. There were no pews, only rows of squeaky white plastic folding chairs to the right and left of a central aisle. Three musicians – two violins and a keyboard – sat on their own chairs in the back, performing a jazz ensemble while the guests filed in.

Sandy and I sat beside Jimmy Calipari, who wore a tuxedo with a scarlet vest, even though there was no black tie mandate. He'd bought the tux years earlier for his brother's wedding, and now he wore it because it was the only suit he owned. The vest flattered his slender ribcage; the blacks and whites of the jacket and the shirt complemented his jet black hair. He looked even handsomer than he had in college.

Sandy, for her part, looked ravishing: her upper arms were toned and sleek; her cleavage, only hinted at in the mid-cut dress, was head-turning. The hem fell just below her knees, but ascended to her lower thighs as she sat. My friends stared and I was proud but also insecure. I wondered what kept Sandy by my side, as opposed to jumping on the most beautiful guy she could find. I got sad in a hurry: maybe my value to Sandy *was* my resistibility. It was like Shelagh all over again. But this time I was prepared. This time I'd be ready for a dismissal. Let her ditch me, if that's what she wants, I thought to myself. I didn't need her. I didn't need anyone anymore.

Meanwhile, the musicians had begun playing Pachelbel, and the wedding party – which included old pals Tina and Shane – began walking down the center aisle in man-woman pairs. Jimmy rolled his eyes as soon as the opening notes of Pachelbel sounded. How I still loved him so! I gave his arm a tight squeeze and arched in my chair, the back of which pressed into my middle vertebrae. Jimmy fingered the pages of his prayer book and whispered to me: "Pick a page number."

I replied: "24. Freeman McNeil, baby."

He attempted, it seemed, to open his book *exactly* to page 24. He landed on 31. "Within ten pages," he said. "That's a double. So I got a man on second. Within 15 pages is a single, within five a triple, and exact is a homer. Pitch."

"283."

Jimmy opened to page 250. "One out," he whispered.

So ensued my first game of prayer book baseball. Jimmy had learned the game as a 13-year-old on Long Island, where because of the heavy Jewish population, Jimmy had attended a Bar or Bat Mitzvah nearly every weekend in seventh and eighth grade. "I'm surprised you didn't learn it too," he said, knowing I too had grown up on Long Island. I reminded him that the best friend of the 13-year-old Zinsky was his stuffed Freeman McNeil doll. He smirked. "Yes, how could I forget your orphan-like childhood," he said.

Of course he still didn't know the half of it – he knew nothing of my father – and he was just taking his usual stance against my brand of solipsism. I thought about spilling my guts re: Robert Zinsky then and there. But I wondered: Was it worth it? Did Jimmy really need to know? And how could I just tell him? What would I do, write him a note? Email him? Whisper the whole thing while Kris and his bright-eyed bride exchanged vows? So I did what Jimmy wanted me to do: I shut up and kept playing. "143," I muttered. Jimmy opened his book and singled.

The bridesmaids wore dresses of shimmering indigo while the groomsmen wore tuxedos with black bowties and cumber buns. Kris and his bride, Tori, faced the preacher, their backs to the audience. The preacher implored them to always respect each other; to never raise their voices; to daily say 'please' and 'thank you.' These simple requests recalled me to my mother's wedding, and got me thinking about how the first wedding I ever attended *was* my mother's. Did Jimmy know how something like that felt?

During the exchange of vows, Tori sobbed. She gazed at Kris the way I once gazed at Shelagh; and Kris matched Tori's jubilant stare, and I wondered if both of them might just get through life without knowing the pain of heartbreak. I wondered how both of them could be so happy about an obligation like marriage. Did Kris worry that Tori might stop fucking him in a few years? Did Tori worry that Kris might forsake her for his career ambitions? This was a real wedding in a real hotel in the heart of real Manhattan, but the leading man and leading women grinned like grand performers in a Hollywood film. It was stunning. Was I the only person in the seats who needed a barf bag? I glanced at Sandy – she was grinning, her eyes riveted to the podium, her entire expression a mixture of awe and ecstasy for a bride and groom she'd never met. Jimmy and Jerod were also riveted – they shook their heads and uttered phrases like "Oh man," and "holy shit," and "look at Kris." Who were these people? How had we all befriended each other? Why did it seem like I was the only one not blinded by music and ceremony?

Shelagh had understood my skepticism – and if I could find her at this instant of the ceremony she and I might share a glance of mutual comprehension. But I couldn't find her. I put my arm around Sandy, who continued beaming as Kris and Tori exchanged rings. I was amazed my infertile, cancer-surviving pal had more romantic optimism than I did. Or did she? Perhaps she was just behaving like an adult – smiling out of respect for the ceremony. Was she imagining herself and Anthony swapping rings? I wanted to ask – but if Shelagh had taught me anything, it was not to question your non-girlfriend girlfriends – unless you were prepared to be dropped. Censuring my conversation was a small price to pay for canoodling a comely woman. It was, in other words, the same as it had been with Shelagh and Diana. You couldn't be honest. And the dishonesty that got you in kept you in – or you *feared* it kept you in, which prevented the cleansing confessional you dreamed about in those precious seconds after orgasm.

* * *

When the ceremony ended, I spotted Shelagh exiting from the last row of white plastic seats, stuffing the wedding program into a small brown purse. Her dress resembled the bridesmaid's gowns in its shimmer, though the color was more navy than indigo. A white pearl necklace collared her caramel skin; her light brown hair was up, braided, revealing two ears adorned with small silver hoops.

Later, during the cocktail hour, I saw her while I was transporting four glasses of cabernet to a circle including Sandy, Jerod, and Shane. She sipped her own glass of red while chatting with Tina and Jimmy. She waved at me and grinned. I smiled back but lacked the free hand to return the wave.

Soon guests filed into the banquet room, seating themselves at the elegantly set tables surrounding a parquet dance floor. Sandy took my arm. She said, "Are you going to play it cool and distant? She's a few paces behind us, so I decided to take your arm."

"I love you," I said, and Sandy squeezed tighter.

When the band, led by a goateed, pink-faced vocalist, invited all couples to the dance floor, I winked at Sandy, downed my champagne, and grabbed her arm. I found myself slinging her all over, to a medley of songs from the movie *Grease*, to Van Morrison's "Brown-Eyed Girl," to the Beatles' "Twist and Shout" — an entire lineup of up-tempo, Caucasian classics. We held hands, twisted, spun into and out of each other's arms; and at the conclusion of each song, I dipped her. When the band leader announced it was "time to slow it down," I pulled her near me, and she reached up and put her arms around my shoulders. "Who knew you were such a dancer?" she asked.

"Not I," I said, and it was true. Diana and I had never gone dancing; but somehow this miraculous improvement had happened, perhaps only because I *wanted* to be a good dancer on this occasion. On this night, everything felt right on the dance floor.

Until the slow dancing began.

Over Sandy's blond head I glanced at Shelagh's empty table. We twirled, and I saw Tina dancing closely with Shane; beside them, Shelagh was nuzzling with Jimmy Calipari. My shoulders tensed and I stopped swaying. "Relax," Sandy whispered, but I couldn't return to my previous mood. Within seconds I resumed dancing, but my eyes remained moored to the attractive pairing. I examined their distance from each other: minimal. Lower bodies: contiguous. Arms and hands:

wrapping and gripping, necks and deltoids and lower spines. Cheeks: touching. They were doing everything *but* kissing.

When the dance concluded Sandy and I walked back to our table, leaving Jimmy and Shelagh in the center of the floor. Sandy sensed my anger and said, "Don't even look, Ari. If Jimmy's going to do this, you don't want him as a friend anyway."

But I looked and, sure enough, rather than returning to her table for the cucumber salad, Shelagh simply grabbed her small brown purse. The two of them exited arm in arm, passing through a set of double doors.

I tried to be rational. *None of it will matter in twenty years.* I tried to be calm. *You have no claim on Shelagh.* I tried putting myself in Shelagh's shoes. *Why isn't she allowed to have some fun, and why isn't she allowed to have it with Jimmy as revenge for the slap?* I tried putting myself in Jimmy's shoes. *What straight guy could possibly resist a chance to be with Shelagh?* But none of it was adding up to Jimmy being a good friend – or a good adult. And worse, none of it was calming me. Jerod sat to my right, but between us was a seat with a white napkin on it – where Jimmy had been sitting. Jerod saw what had happened – *everyone* saw, it seemed to me – and he said, "You want me to go and break it up?" I was floored. I almost said yes. But Sandy intervened. "Ari, let them have their fun," she said, addressing Jerod as much as myself. "If that's who Jimmy really is, that's who he is. You don't know your friends until temptation comes along."

Jerod held up his big black hand, a stop sign, as if directing Sandy to be silent. "Ari, I'll break it up for you," he said.

"Sandy's right," I said. I wanted to add, "And she has some experience with sexual jealousy," but kept it to myself. Jerod nodded and turned away, angling himself to the right, where Tim Nover was sitting. "I'm losing my fucking mind," I said to Sandy. "If you weren't here *I'd* probably go after them," I added.

"I doubt it," she said. "We all have that urge, but to actually do it is different."

"You really don't know me very well," I said with a grin.

* * *

"You were a lousy friend tonight," I said, tapping Jimmy on the shoulder. He searched his pockets for the key card to his room.

"You been waiting here all night?" he asked. His scarlet vest was unbuttoned.

"Wouldn't you, in my shoes?" I shouted.

"Quiet down, Ari," he said. "Jerod and Tim are sleeping in there. You want to shout, let's go to the bar."

I grabbed his vest, one fist clenching each unbuttoned side. On the reflex Jimmy kneed me in the nuts. I went down in a heap. I was done for. I rolled onto my side. Jimmy hovered for a while, and I readied myself for a kick from his shiny black shoe. But he walked away. At length I sat with my back against his room door, my fingers resting on the rough and linty hotel carpet. When Jimmy came back he sat on the floor beside me. "You'll never forgive me," he muttered.

"So there's really no point in sitting here talking to you," I said. "You chose her over me. That's fine. I can't say I blame you. On your dying day, you'll probably remember your night with her, more than all our years of conversation and basketball. What more is there to say?" I got up and went to the elevators.

Jimmy called after me. "You gonna slap her again?" he said. I faced him.

So my secret was out. Whenever I had anticipated this moment, I feared embarrassment – for no guy wants to be known as the type of coward who strikes women. But now I didn't care. It was as if he had slapped *me*. "It's not her I'm pissed at," I said. "Maybe in twenty years, if we're still friends, you'll hear my side of the story."

"There aren't two sides of it. You slapped her. That was wrong," he said.

"Well, you always had your doubts about me," I said. "Hey, maybe one day you'll sleep with Diana or Sandy and learn even more about my past. But until then, Jimmy, I wish you luck. I hope you meet lots of sane, sanitary people."

"You're more immoral than I could ever be."

"You're right," I said.

I turned around and kept walking.

I heard his hotel door click open and clack shut.

It was the last I ever saw of Jimmy Calipari, my handsome adversary.

Chapter 22 – Dust Specks and Minor Miracles

How I then wished Sandy had brought weed to the wedding! I longed to sit drugged beside her, relaxed yet hyper-responsive to her soft touch. I expected to find her in bed, resting on her side as she always did, her inert arms forming an isosceles triangle on the sheets, her blond locks resting beside an angled elbow. Instead she was outside. The full moon shone, adding brightness to the balcony, which had its own yellow lightbulb, hanging tackily above the sliding door. A red winter hat held her growing hair in place, and her loose ends brushed her cheeks whenever the wind blew. The view beyond consisted of dark buildings; the view below was a lamppost-lit triangle of Manhattan sidewalk, partitioning the midtown traffic. Without looking back at me Sandy said, as if reading my mind, "Quite the scenery we've got, here in room 710."

I tucked my hands in my pockets. "The moon's okay," I said, gazing at the black sky's glowing Frisbee. "A shiny pita in an ocean of tar," I added, paraphrasing Romeo.

"The moon's overrated," she said.

"Why are you awake?" I asked. I massaged her shoulders.

She placed her hands over mine. "Let's just go to bed, my young friend," she said. She led me back toward the bed, sliding shut the door behind her.

Later we lay awake and I wondered why she hadn't inquired about me and Jimmy. "Why were you outside in the cold?" I asked.

She nuzzled her head against my chest – something she'd never done in bed with me, to that point. "In the morning I'll tell you," she yawned.

Her nuzzling comforted me, made me briefly forget our status as a non-couple couple. I was ready to tell her what I wished Jimmy had always known. "Can I tell you about my father in the morning too?" I asked.

Her fingertips caressed my face with a softness I hadn't felt since Diana. "Tell me what?" she whispered. "I have noticed you never talk about him."

"How come you never ask?" I said, and before I knew it I was sobbing, wiping my cheeks on her smooth body. "I swear I'm not getting attached," I continued. "But sometimes it just kills me, how you never ask."

"I never ask because I'm sometimes scared I'm getting attached," she whispered.

"So what if you are?" I asked.

And she was quiet.

I was quiet in return, and figured we'd soon be sleeping.

Then from Sandy: "Tell me about him, Ari. I'm listening."

When I finished I was happy; and as we fell asleep, her arms around me, her own confession still buried within her, I wondered whether we would ever again feel so close.

* * *

Her confession was that Anthony had broken up with her. "How come?" I asked, as we drove back to Boston. "Was the distance too much?"

"That's part of it," she said evasively. I was quiet, awaiting the other part of it. But she was silent, and I was content not to press her. We switched subjects to various legal cases she was working on, a mixture of local corporate mergers and media libel.

As we said goodbye that night at her door, she asked me out for Friday night. "Is this our first official date?" I asked, instantly worrying that the date would never happen, now that I'd called a rose by its proper name.

She looked worried. "You're sure you're free?" she asked. A shocking question — when had I not been free for her? We kissed goodbye and I told her I'd see her Friday night. In the few days between our meetings I turned 29; and Sandy was the only person who phoned me on my birthday besides my mother.

*   *   *

We walked down Harvard Avenue on a damp, chilly Friday evening, our gloved hands in our jacket pockets, our path filled with rain-soaked brown leaves adhering to icy pavement. On the two-way road there was moderate traffic. Vehicles splashed by at suburban speeds, most of them with headlights on. Sandy and I had just come from Hollywood Video, where she jestingly reproved me for wiping my wet shoe bottoms on the store's carpet. In recompense, I'd settled for *Singin' in the Rain,* her preference, instead of the Godard film — *The 400 Blows* — which my mother had recommended during my birthday phone call.

Sandy looked up at the road, waiting for a series of cars to drive by before she asked: "Ari, have you ever experienced a miracle?"

"A miracle? That's random," I said. "But, yes, I have. It'll make me sound so young to you, though. And you know how insecure I am about that."

"I still want to know," she said.

First I considered Shelagh: how ugly I'd been as a college boy, and how I had still managed to "get" her. Was that not miraculous? Next came basketball: how terrible I'd been, how competent I'd become. My victory over Tom Kennedy: a triumph for the ages! It was will over skill, desire over genetics, B.I.G. over JFK.

Sandy had grabbed my hand and was expecting a response. I had already told her about Robert, and I didn't want to rehash; the Shelagh answer might also suffice, but the wedding was behind us and I didn't want to seem too smitten with a non-ex ex. So I told her about my victory over Tom Kennedy. I finished by saying, "It makes me sound young and naïve, right?"

She ignored my question and replied: "So what if I told you a miracle had just happened to me?" We turned off Harvard Street and onto Vinal, where she lived. "I was two weeks late," she continued. "So I took a pregnancy test and it was positive. I went to my gynecologist and she confirmed it. So I'm pregnant."

"Are you kidding?" I said. I dropped her hand.

"Not kidding," she said.

"How is that possible?" I asked. "I thought you were infertile."

"So did I," she said.

"I mean, how is it possible?"

"I don't know, Ari," she said. "But it's real. And it's yours."

We entered her building. I pondered how to deliver my next batch of questions without seeming callous or indifferent to her miracle; but callous or indifferent I was – especially as she'd yet to mention the word abortion.

I wiped my feet, smiling as my shoes scraped the mat. She'd doffed her boots in the hallway, and from the living room she returned my smile and kept gazing until I, too, removed my shoes and stepped inside. Maybe this is the reason Anthony broke up with her, I thought to myself.

She retreated to the kitchen where she took out tea bags, sugar, and two mugs. Sink water slapped against the kettle's tinny interior. I sat at the table and looked at the top of the fridge, where her journal lay atop the *Guide*. Who kept a journal in the kitchen? I now wondered. Did a part of her want me to find it? "So how are you feeling about all this?" I finally asked, uncomfortable with her silence, uncomfortable with her comfort.

"I'm still processing," she said. "I'm in shock. The first thing I did was call my old doctor at Dana-Farber, and yell at him for telling me I was infertile."

"What'd he say?"

"He apologized. He called it a 'minor miracle,' and he said not to get my hopes up, because a miscarriage is usually what happens in cases like this."

"So what are you going to do?" I asked impatiently. It angered me that it was all up to her. But that was my fault, after all: I was the one having unprotected sex with a non-girlfriend. Faced with the common consequence, I was losing my mind. I was an affluent 29-year-old man reproducing with an affluent 34-year-old woman – and I was as desperate for an abortion as a poverty-stricken teenager. So derailed was I from my foreseen road to joy, which I'd worked my whole life to achieve – and which was, namely, to keep sleeping with a bright beautiful woman without fear of consequences. Her miracle had come along and ruined mine.

"You're not going to like hearing this," she said, "but I'm going to try having it."

"You are," I muttered. I couldn't look at her. I stared at the kitchen table, picked up the *New Yorker* off it, pursed my lips and made a sucking sound which I hoped would lure Clinton into the room. I had an immediate urge to cuddle and stroke the cat and make up for all the harm I had done. My eyes fell to Clinton's double-bowl setup on the black-tile floor. Both her water and food were filled, nearly to the brim.

"I am," said Sandy, dumping sugar in the tea mugs. "You can take whatever role you'd like to have."

"I don't want a fucking role," I said. "I mean, all I want is to be your boyfriend. Sandy – seriously – think about the time and money it takes to have a baby. Think about how arduous and relentless life can be, even without a baby. Leaving aside the fact that I, as the father, don't want it – how does having a baby make any sense for you?"

"Because it might be my only chance," she said. "And I have the money."

"So there's no way you're getting an abortion?"

"No," she said.

"And – not that I blame you, but I just want to be clear: my wishes, as the father and your good friend, are totally irrelevant to you?"

She hesitated. "More or less, Ari," she said. She put an arm on my shoulder and I pulled her to my lap. Just then a faint whistling began, growing shrill, and she rose from the chair and rescued the shrieking teapot.

* * *

We finished our tea and retreated to Sandy's warm bedroom to watch *Singin' in the Rain*. Afterward I lay awake, reading the *New Yorker* by a bedside lamp while Sandy slept. It was after midnight and the small, rectangular room was quiet, save for the humming of her humidifier and the occasional muffled rumble, heard through the closed window, of a vehicle on Vinal. Clinton lurked in the living room, on the couch; and I longed for her to come into the room and purr against my leg.

Sandy lay on her side in a midriff t-shirt and Harvard boxers, a dark green blanket by her ankles. I watched her pale stomach moving slightly with each breath. A part of me wanted to kiss and nibble on her tummy skin, wake her, move lower on her scrumptious body. But another part of me couldn't touch her anymore. Another part of me couldn't touch any woman, ever again.

I twisted off the bedside light and sat up on the bed, the humidifier huffing in the dark room. I doubted I'd get to sleep anytime soon. My unease was a part of it, but so was the simple fact that I had not ejaculated.

Was it vulgar to consider self-pleasure at a time like this? Not really, I decided. Wasn't self-pleasure, the need to satisfy an abiding biological urge, the ultimate motive behind Sandy's decision? Didn't most men and women rely on abiding needs – to ejaculate for men and to procreate for women – to drive most of their decisions?

I moaned with ecstasy as I released myself in her bathroom, my bare butt on her frigid toilet. I had unwrapped one of three heart-shaped purple soaps Sandy kept in a teacup next to her toothbrush holder, creating a foamy lubricant by scrubbing my hands under warm water for a minute. I had also left the door open a crack. And who should approach me then, perhaps in response to my moan, but the black-gray lump herself, gently padding, timidly escaping from beneath Sandy's bed and crossing the hallway and nestling against my calf. Clinton looked up at me, blinking, meowing several times. She rubbed her cheekbones against my shins, nestling her entire frame along my ankle, purring, melting like butter atop my sock.

I had seen Clinton behave this way with Sandy. I always believed these affections were intended to goad Sandy into offering food or water. But no! Here was a cat with two full bowls, still cuddling and cooing.

Clinton remained at my ankle when I went to the living room to watch basketball highlights. As I sat with the remote control in my hand, I longed for the time in my life when sports were the most important thing. I told myself that if I ever got through this crisis – it was a crisis to me, that I might have a child – I would rededicate my lifestyle to making sports number one, and everything else a distant second. And I set my mind to altering Sandy's decision. How could I make certain she didn't have this baby?

*   *   *

The next day Sandy went to her office. She and her fellow associates often worked Saturdays. I phoned Barbara and told her everything, making her swear that under no circumstances would she tell Neil or Nicole. "Why can't I?" she said.

"It's none of their business," I said. "They'll find out if they have to find out."

"You're right, she'll probably have a miscarriage anyway," said my mother. "You shouldn't really sweat it too much at this point."

"Don't sweat it?" I screamed. "Mom, my life is over if this happens. I can't be a father. I can't. No way."

"Well, maybe you're going to be. You can't blame her, can you? What do you want her to do, abort her only chance? Ari, I don't want to you have a child yet either, but this is your fault. And if she has the baby, I expect you to support it."

"I can't do that," I said. "I just want to watch sports and be left alone."

"Maybe it's time to grow up a little," she said.

"Maybe it's time for you to understand I grew up a lot when I was little," I shouted. "Why do you have to bust my chops over this? Just because I'm not naïve about the fact that having a kid ruins your life – "

"It does not ruin your life, Ari," she said. "It illuminates it."

"Bullshit," I said.

"You think that's bullshit?" she asked. "Well, fine. Maybe you'll find out."

Or maybe I won't, I thought to myself.

*   *   *

The logic of Diana's celibacy was so apparent now. The logic of Diana's mindset was apparent too. Oh, how logical everything was, when your sexual partner was a real true girlfriend! Why, why, *why* had I left behind my logical red-haired lover? Oh, sure – by now she'd have moved on, recognizing in *my* mindset the aversion to reproduction. But still: my imagination, my fancy, my daydreams, every ounce of my irrational mind began ruminating on Diana, wishing for her return, if only to tell her I now realized that the three years we spent together were the best of my life despite the absence of conventional sex. She was the only partner I'd ever had who'd met my parents; she was the only one who'd met Nicole and Neil; she was the only one who understood how I'd built my business up from nothing, gone from sleeping on concrete beneath the bookstore awning to a success. Sandy had known me afterwards; Shelagh had known me before.

Sandy seemed intent on persuading me toward active fatherhood. We talked everyday about our situation. But our positions did not change. One Saturday, about three weeks into her pregnancy, I phoned her at her office. "How are you holding up?" I asked.

"I feel like there's this little dust speck inside of me," she said. "I sort of felt it on the drive over here this morning. In the parking lot I stepped in a puddle, and was way too worried I'd catch a cold from the wet. Then I got it into my head I should start going to the gym, maybe try Pilates or yoga or something, just to get in better shape for this."

"So you're going to the gym later?" I asked.

"Yes – I think it would be good."

"Do you have a minute," I asked, "to hear how I'm feeling?"

"Of course I do."

"I guess I'm feeling like from now on, I'll have to ask you questions like that. Like my feelings are so utterly secondary to yours, or yours and the dust speck's."

She paused. "Don't feel that way, Ari," she said. "I want you to be a part of this."

"I know," I said. "I just – I'm not ready for a kid. And you – here you are, working every Saturday, you still owe thousands to Harvard – "

"There's never a right time, Ari," she said. "I have to make this work. Every ounce of me is urging me to nurture this dust speck."

"I feel little betrayed," I said.

"Why?" she asked.

"Because it's my kid too, and yet both society and natural law dictate I have no clout in the matter."

"Well, how do you think I feel?" she said. "I need your support, and every time we talk it sounds like you're praying for a miscarriage."

"You need to separate my feelings for you from my unease about having a child I'm unprepared to support."

"You won't need to support it."

"Well, what you're really saying is you don't need me to support it."

"I want you to help," she said.

"I need your support too, you know," I said. "I feel like I've been kicked in the head. You told me you could never get pregnant."

"I know it's not easy for you."

"We'll get through this," I said. But I wondered how we would.

*   *   *

I couldn't focus at work. I spent hours on the phone with Joel Pollock, begging him to help me find an acquirer for the *Guide* – I just couldn't do it anymore. I refused to divulge Sandy's pregnancy, insisting only that I was burnt out, that after nine years I finally needed to do something other than run my own publishing company. What I told Joel most often was: I needed a job more like his: Nine-to-five, football-related, predictable schedule, predictable tasks.

I took long lunch breaks by myself. I took long walks, navigating crowded street corners in Boston's financial district. Sometimes I believed – for several seconds – that I had happened upon Diana herself: I'd behold a redhead gazing at shoes in a storefront and my heart would race. In the moment's fancy I started to pine: perhaps Diana had driven down from Portland, her soul as lonely as mine, her heart eager to reconsider me!

But all the women I hoped were Diana turned out to be Diana mirages: other tall slender redheads whose facial structures – the high cheekbones, the pointy chins – marked their Irish descent. I invariably approached these lasses only to realize up close they lacked Diana's baby-elephant gray eyes or super-lengthy fingers. Oh, to have dated an Irish girl in the Boston area! Oh, to miss her badly! Oh, to wait on line at the deli counter behind a slender redhead, and to hope – for a forlorn second – you could wrap your arms around her without an objection! Oh, to wander past Boston's Frog Pond in midwinter, surrounded by dozens of women in their tight jeans and winter hats, and to think one of those protrusive cheekbone faces is yours alone to kiss!

Meanwhile, Sandy and I had not had sex since her miraculous announcement. Yet this lack of action hardly corresponded to our levels of affection. We stayed in the same bed every night, snuggling and kissing and groping and learning more about each other. It was during this period that Sandy began referring to Nicole and Neil by their proper names; I began mentioning Sandy's relatives too. I learned about her progress in yoga and Pilates; I learned how she liked her tea and began making it regularly, bringing it to her in bed, all the while taking responsibility for filling Clinton's dual bowls.

One night as we watched the ten o'clock news on her bed we began kissing. She gently pushed her thigh between my legs and I shifted away. "Please don't do that," I said. "It just makes me want to do something I don't think I should do."

"Why don't you want to sleep with me anymore?" she asked.

"Believe me, I want to," I said. "I feel so close to you. But I'm just not ready yet."

"I don't know if I believe you," she said.

"Would you still be my girlfriend if I couldn't sleep with you anymore?" I asked.

"How would you answer that question?" she asked. "How would you answer it if I'd asked it before the dust speck?"

"Different than I'd answer now," I said. "I used to think half the point of having a girlfriend was sex. I don't feel that way anymore."

"I believe you," she said. "I'm feeling a little rejected, though."

"Well, so am I," I said.

She put her head on my chest and I stroked her hair as we watched the news and waited for it to provide a new topic of conversation.

*   *   *

A few nights later as Sandy slept I sat in her kitchen reading her journal. Over the past few weeks she'd made numerous entries about herself and the dust speck. Time and the fear of getting caught prevented me from copying all of them down for my record keeping. It's my hope the entries I duplicated suffice to illustrate her mood:

1/14/04: This is my first entry as a pregnant woman. I am in a complete state of shock. Who knows how long this will last? I guess I was more upset about my infertility than I realized. Five years ago it seemed like a small price to pay for living, walking, having hair again. And now just the 20% chance I could be a mom has me on cloud nine.

1/18/04: I wanted to tell Ari at the wedding but I just couldn't, not after what Jimmy did and how I also haven't told him about Anthony's reaction. I wonder if Ari will react the same way.

1/26/04: It's taken me a while to process Ari's reluctance. It makes no sense to me. He's in a perfect position to support this child. He seems to like me a lot — even love me at times. He seems to have thought a lot about how a father should and shouldn't be. And he's not even that young. I guess some guys just don't want to do it, and that's that. They are still men, and they like their ducks in a row I guess. I just wish he'd be less negative in his vibe toward me. Doesn't he see I have to try this? He must.

2/2/04: I know his libido hasn't died — I can feel how hard he still gets. He's withdrawing his love when I need it the most. He still kisses me hard, like he did that first time by the impatiens in the park. You don't kiss someone like that un-less…but he doesn't want to be a dad, and that's that. He thinks he knows every-thing and he's not even 30. He doesn't see how much he might regret things at 40.

2/11/04: There's a living particle or granule inside of me. It's miniscule, like a needlepoint. Sometimes I'm not sure it's there. Or I only think it's there because I know it should be, like how your head starts itching when you think about dandruff. Today the yoga teacher asked us to block out all exterior thoughts. But this was so interior, I wonder if it counts. We did that tree pose where you balance on one leg. I balanced on my left leg pretty easily — I couldn't believe it. The instructor looked at me and said, "Stop hunching forward," kind of coldly. I wanted to say something to her after the class, about how I used to crutch around on that leg, how I had two surgeries to insert a titanium rod in that leg, so let me hunch forward, please, for at least my first few classes! But it's better she doesn't know. I'm actually happy she had no reason to suspect!

2/18/04: Today the yoga instructor ended class by saying something like, "Be grateful for this breath that you breathe; be thankful for your lungs, and your heart; be thankful for this pulse, this soul, this life, this energy." And all I could think about was, "How long will you be with me, Dust Speck? If I stay grateful for all the little things, will that prevent me from miscarrying?"

2/20/04: I don't miss Anthony one bit. I rarely think about him. He probably became peripheral to me as soon as he told me about his fling, but I couldn't admit it to myself. I was too eager to show how loyal and forgiving I could be. In reality I had mentally dumped him myself, otherwise would Ari even have been in the picture?

As I sat in Sandy's kitchen with Clinton purring on my lap, as I read this journal for the first time, I was in complete shock. Sandy's reaction to the pregnancy was radically different from mine. She had not devoted a single sentence – a single word – to the practical side of raising a child. Affluent though she was, wasn't she worried about the reality of expenses – for doctors, for clothing, for food, for education? Wasn't she worried about diseases, disasters, and drunk drivers? And wasn't she worried about never having time to watch *Singin' in the Rain* again?

I crawled back into bed with Sandy but remained awake. Thoughts scrolled through my head like movie credits:

Having sex with you was my miracle, Sandy. Lame as that sounds.

Can you appreciate it?

Do you realize how small I feel, considering how colossally insignificant my questions, my miracles, and my needs are compared to yours?

Yours and the Dust Speck's.

Not that I'm complaining.

Our priorities are in order, ovaries and offspring first. All's as it should be.

But I kind of liked it as it was.

You know?

* * *

At lunch the next day I spoke up. "You're not blind to the world's harsh realities," I said. We sat at her kitchen table. We drank tea and split the newspaper. "Aren't you scared of putting more life on this planet?"

"I'm scared of *not* putting more life on this planet," she said. "That's what I'm living for. If you want to live for football games and meaningless sex, that's your decision. It's your life. You've been through what you've been through, and I don't doubt that it makes you believe your view of the world is the most accurate one. But it's not the only view, Ari. There are plenty of people who make it through life very happy. Look at Kris and Tori. And you're discounting the fact that this may be my only chance. If you only had one chance to have a child, it might change your perspective."

I nodded and looked down at the sports section. A few minutes later, I watched as she swallowed her multivitamins from their plastic orange container. It was then I struck upon the idea. It was then I realized my only salvation was to commit an evil deed. Otherwise I'd have a child, and the carefree life I'd worked so hard to attain would disappear.

Chapter 23 – Sons & Liars

It was too late for morning-after pills. But it was not too late for the drug formerly known as RU-486. The question was: how could I get some? I phoned Jerod in Europe and explained everything to him; I wondered whether his loyalty to me – and to abortion, as a principle – would compel him to bend the rules governing prescriptions and international shipments. When he phoned back from London's Langley Hospital it was three in the morning. "So can you help me?" I asked. "My life is over if she has this kid."

"Nothing I can do," he said.

"Send me some RU-486 or whatever it's called," I said.

"You're crazy, Ari," he said. "A doctor has to administer all this."

"Bullshit," I said. "I've been reading. In Europe, women take these pills at home."

"Sandy's not in Europe," he replied. "And it's not a one-shot deal. First she takes mifepristone, and then there's a return visit for the prostaglandin two days later."

I hesitated. "Is the prostaglandin strictly necessary?" I asked.

"You could say it completes the job. Why?"

I hesitated. "Just curious."

"Curious my ass," he said. "Why'd you ask me that question?"

"I'm trying to persuade her abortions can be quick and painless."

"You better watch yourself," he warned.

"Fuck you," I replied. "Since when are you Hippocrates' standard-bearer? You know damn well these pills won't kill Sandy. Yet you're gonna sit back and watch my life get ruined – "

"I love you Ari, but I won't break the law for you."

I hung up. I spent the next day at my office scouring the Internet for black-market RU-486. There had to be some merchant-thief in Europe who'd ship the pills sans prescription. In the early afternoon Jerod phoned me again. "You going to help or not?" I asked brusquely.

"I'm going to save you from yourself," he said. "If you don't want this kid, then do yourself a favor. Renounce it. Leave town. Live in London with me. Sandy has given you the green light to escape. And instead of speeding through, you're lingering."

"I've come too far to be ruined like this," I said.

"And you've come too far to ruin *yourself* by breaking the law," he said.

"Have you said your piece?"

He sighed. "I think in a few weeks, you're going to call me back and thank me."

"We'll see," I said.

*   *   *

In my dream life, Sandy miscarries. I console her. We live happily ever after as friends and lovers. In my dream life, we spend our days as well-paid professionals. At night we have sex and watch television. In my dream life, it plays out like this:

Another frigid Friday night on leaf-strewn Harvard Street: Ariel and Sandy on their way to the video store. In his gloved hands Ariel holds a plastic bag of takeout Chinese food. Sandy is cramping: an achy period sort of discomfort, strains behind her lower abs and in her back. She has not had her period for seven weeks. She knows what's bound to occur; it may happen tonight, or the next day.

She says nothing to Ariel until they're back in her bedroom. The Chinese food is eaten, the chopsticks are in the sink, and Ariel is kneeling by her television, inserting The Producers *DVD. "I think I'm having a miscarriage," she says. She's cross-legged on her bed, in baggy jeans and a brown sweater.*

"What?" says Ariel. "How do you know?" He sits beside her.

"It feels like a period," she says. "It feels like I'm about to bleed."

She gazes into his brown eyes and spies a mix of relief and sympathy. She spies a young man who wants to tell her something kind. A young man too young to fake empathy worth a damn. "I'm sorry, sweetie," he says meekly.

"Start the movie," she replies.

They change into sleeping clothes during the opening credits. Then they lie down together, hands touching. Throughout the film Sandy's feet are inert – a marked change from the mattress-bopping her heels had performed during Singin' in the Rain. *"You okay?" he whispers.*

(The song "Springtime for Hitler" is playing.)

"Yeah," she replies. "But I don't want to watch anymore. Let's go to bed."

Soon the room is dark and they are under the same blanket. Oh troubled and unpredictable duo! Oh, former waiter and customer! How did you come to be bedfellows? The lonely sports fan from Long Island and the overachieving twin from the twin cities – a dad and a mom! Both try in vain to sleep. At one point he asks: "How awake are you?"

"Medium," she says. "You?"

"Medium."

The conversation stops there.

Early in the morning she sits on the frigid toilet, leaving the bathroom door open. It spills out from inside her, a warm discharge of blood, slapping the toilet water in a steady dribble. She stands and looks down at the water: bright red. It's a texture she's never seen before: pulpy and stringy, filmy and fibrous.

Ariel stands in the doorway. "You all right?" he asks.

"Take a look at this," she says. Ariel stares at the bloody toilet water, kneeling to get a closer look. "Jesus," he says.

"I can't take my eyes from it," she says. "What do you think that stringy stuff is?"

"It looks like – like tissue," he guesses. "Or membrane, or something."

"Go get a chopstick from the kitchen," she says. "I want to poke at it a little."

Ariel returns with a chopstick. She pokes and prods the bright red mixture, stirring the stringiness. She uses the stick to drag a portion of tissue onto the dry edge of the toilet, like fishing eggshell from a bowl of battered yolks. The tissue is scarlet, mingled with pale yellow mucus. She looks down at it silently.

Then she pushes it back into the tinctured water and flushes.

"You better not go into work today," he says. "Or yoga."

"Maybe yoga would help," she says, still holding the chopstick.

"Maybe I'll go with you," he says.

"Okay," she says, dropping the chopstick into a small garbage pail.

"Why'd you ask for that chopstick?" he says.

"I was just curious. It felt like I was in the middle of a ritual. I kept thinking that this has never happened to me before, and it probably won't happen again. So I didn't just want to flush it right down."

"Did you really think you were going to make it nine months?"

"No. But if I made it – what do you think you would've done?"

"I don't know," he says. "I just need a break from larger questions."

She nods. She washes her hands, then he does, and in her bedroom they crawl beneath the covers and quietly embrace.

*   *   *

In my real life, I wash my hands of the entire Sandy experience.

In my real life, I choose leisure over parenthood. And I sit in my Manhattan apartment writing my autobiography – a manifesto about *my* right to choose.

In my real life, I wonder: would anyone – having lived their first 29 years as I had – choose differently? In my real life, it plays out like this: Sandy tells me again that I can have as little – or as much – involvement as I like.

I decide I want no involvement. I decide to leave Boston forever – lest I spend one more second pondering how to poison her pill supply. So my evil act isn't the murdering of a fetus, through deception of the mother. It is simply the abandonment of a mother and child I'm able to support.

And why? I did not fight this hard for my freedom, financial and otherwise, only to lose it now. I did not *not* follow Diana to Portland, only to start a family with someone else. And after 29 years, I know this much: I would rather do *anything* with my time – watch football, smoke weed, read literature, rent porn – than practice fatherhood.

And did Sandy know enough of my life story to see all this?

I sure hoped so. I did not intend to make our final conversation a long one.

*   *   *

She had been in her office on a Saturday afternoon, and phoned me as she was driving home. "Are you coming over tonight?" she asks.

It's difficult to keep silent over the phone, to save my farewell for an in-person encounter. We're seated in her living room, with Clinton skulking along the coffee table. The muted television broadcasts a weatherman in his navy blazer and tie, pointing at a diagram-filled map of New England. "I'm moving to New York in one week," I say. "You know I care for you, and would like to be your best friend – but there's no getting around the fact that we're praying for different outcomes here."

Sandy extends an arm to Clinton, who jumps from the table to the couch and nuzzles beside her. She plucks some of Clinton's wayward black-gray hairs from her dark green sweater. As badly as I want her to be nonplussed by my announcement – or at least to act like she'll miss me – she stays focused on the weatherman.

I continue: "Let's not pretend, either, that you're madly in love with me. I'm not saying you have no feelings for me. But I know what it's like to be loved by a girlfriend. And even before the dust speck came along, you were short of that. There's asymmetry between us. So," – and here I stand up – "I'm just going to go now. Good luck with everything." I extend my hand and she shakes it; the gesture is appropriate enough, given that she and I now have the proverbial handshake agreement over my non-involvement.

I don't quite depart; I'm waiting for her final words as I button my winter jacket. But she's silent, staring at the silent television. I turn and walk out and shut the door behind me. And when I start my car and switch on the radio to sports talk – well, I must confess – I'm subsumed by a mixture of giddiness and relaxation, a sense that I am – for the first time in months – a human who is as free as a human can be, owing nothing to no one, under no obligations to fake sympathy or tenderness to friends, relatives, and lovers.

There is, of course, the possibility Sandy will renege on our handshake. But if that happens, I tell myself – well, I'm glad I have a friend in Europe I can hide with. A friend who is intent on saving me from myself.

I phone him to share the news. Then I phone my mother. But when she picks up – when she says, "Hey sweetie," with her oh-so familiar scratchy voice – something inside me breaks and I realize there's no way I can confess the utter truth of my dereliction. So I begin with a partial truth: "I'm moving to New York," I say.

She screams with joy and asks for details. "Sandy had a miscarriage," I continue.

"How is she?" asks Barbara.

"Sad, but not devastated," I say. "She knew it was highly possible."

And after these words, my mother and I shift to the easier topics: where I'll live and what I'll do for work and whether I'll sell my Boston properties.

The whole time I'm thinking: is a 29-year-old who still lies to his parents, qualified to be a parent? And is there some honor, at least, in a fibber's pitiful self-recognition, and his subsequent self-recusal from parenting?

Sure, I had some lingering fears Sandy would contact me in the coming months. But I doubted it. Sandy had her pride and, more importantly, her money and her beauty. She didn't need a father or spouse and, if she did, men would line up for the job.

It wouldn't take 20 years of solitude for Sandy to find *her* Neil.

Chapter 24 – Funeral for My Friends

By the time I turned 30 I had moved into my Manhattan apartment, sold the *Guide* to Becker + Fliess A.D., and replaced Joel Pollock as the editor-in-chief of *Prattle*. Joel and his wife, Berit, moved to San Francisco (closer to her family) and Joel became a football columnist for the *Contra Costa Times*. The distance – and the fact that we didn't work together anymore – eroded our friendship. There was no divorce, no falling out, just a gradual devolvement from daily communiqués to weekly, then monthly, then rarely.

My separation from Jerod followed a similar curve. He remained in London, and the distance exacted its price on our once-precious bond of shared sacred truths. At one point he emailed me to announce his engagement to a doctor named Alix Dunstl. But no wedding invitation ever came, and that was fine by me. He and I had had a great run together as black and white, Jim and Huck, Red and Andy, Clarence and Bruce. What would it accomplish to see each other again? We had no illusions of a tight-knit future. As a 30-year-old man, you recognize that your days of forging ironclad same-sex friendships are over. And you're rarely blue about it. For if there's one lesson you've learned, during your everything-is-precious days as a twenty-something, it's that most of the relationships you form *aren't* going to last. All that time and energy wasted, all so that a Shelagh or a Diana or a Sandy or a Jerod or a Jimmy could know your life story and your relationship could intensify accordingly – well, then one day you're 30 and none of your old friends is around. And your life story, precious though you believe it to be, becomes something you type in your solitary apartment for an audience of no one.

I type "solitary" apartment, but the truth is it wasn't so solitary during my first year in Manhattan. Nicole and Stephen visited frequently, as did Barbara and Neil.

One on occasion – a few weeks after Nicole and Stephen married – all four came together, and they came with paint and paintbrushes and the past week's *New York Times* to cover the floor as we stood on chairs and coated the ceiling. Barbara had chosen six blue hues from dark to light and had strategized about their application in my two rectangular rooms. "The short walls get the dark colors," she announced, lugging a Kelly-Moore bucket of midnight blue called "Evening Magic" to my emptied-out bedroom. The ceiling was to be a slightly brighter "Cascade Twilight" while the longer walls were to be a much brighter "Soothing Sapphire." The notion of one color, varied hues reminded me of all the purples in Diana's Portland apartment. But I kept such nostalgia to myself, bashful as I'd become about spouting tidbits of my life story.

Nicole and I spread newspaper along the floor while Neil and Stephen climbed ladders and began rolling the ceiling's perimeter. Barbara went back and forth between Neil and Stephen with a roller tray of Cascade Twilight, so each man could keep fresh paint on his roller.

It was the first time in my life I felt attended to by a family. I inhaled the pungent aroma of fresh paint and felt spoiled; I wondered if such attentions were a norm and a standard for Nicole and Stephen and the world's other well-adjusted adults. Certainly Diana's family had all shown up when it came time for her move to Portland. In contrast, I'd managed moves to Ann Arbor and within Boston all by myself. Did that qualify me for sympathy? Certainly not. But having experienced such transitional moments in isolation, rather than among loved ones, I felt a continuation of my childhood's solitary moments, of the applauseless aloneness, of the world's indifference to my fate, and of all the things that bothered *me* more than they bothered affable souls like Jerod and Jimmy and Nicole and Stephen. Isolation was still isolation: it hurt and it built character, regardless of whether you were born in poverty or a middle-class setting. And even if my isolation was finally over at age 30, there was no shaking its formative grip on my thinking – on my *appreciation* for the fact that four relatives of mine were donating their time to paint my new apartment. It was one way my life had improved.

While the men and Barbara colored my bedroom, Nicole and I spread newspaper over the living room floor, where three more buckets of blue awaited. When Nicole excused herself to take a call on her cell phone, I found myself lingering over a week-old *New York Times* story:

> Darfur's Babies of Rape Are on Trial From Birth
> By LYDIA POLGREEN
> GENEINA, Sudan -- Fatouma spends her days under the plastic tarp covering her tent, seated on a straw mat, staring at the squirming creature in her arms.
>
> She examines over and over again the perfectly formed fingers and toes, 10 of each, and the tiny limbs, still curled in the form they took before leaving her belly five days before, and now encircled with amulets to ward off evil.
>
> Everything about this baby, the 16-year-old mother declared, is perfect. Almost everything.
>
> "She is a janjaweed," Fatouma said softly, referring to the fearsome Arab militiamen who have terrorized this region. "When people see her light skin and her soft hair, they will know she is a janjaweed."
>
> Fatouma's child is among the scores of babies produced by one of the most horrific aspects of the conflict in Darfur, the vast, arid region of western Sudan: the use of rape against women and girls in a brutal battle over land and ethnicity that has killed tens of thousands and driven 2 million people from their homes.

At once I was nauseated; not over the plight of Fatouma's janjaweed, but over how it cast my own act of procreation. Did *any* American father have a legitimate reason to abandon his offspring? Yet I'd done what I had done. I hadn't contacted Sandy and she hadn't contacted me. For all I knew I was the biological father of a newborn who lived with his comely mother in Brookline, Massachusetts. And for all I knew Sandy may have miscarried moments after I departed.

Still I wondered: how would I feel if the *Times* just happened to write a feature about the plight of single mothers in America, and just happened to include Sandy in it? And what if Barbara discovered it – and thereby discovered not only that she was a grandmother, but that her own son had lied? It became clear to me now that I was ashamed of my selfish behavior: on one level my entire life story, thematically speaking, was all about how a boy can turn out when he's raised by a single mother. And now, for all my lamentations, I was potentially putting Sandy in the same situation as Robert had put my own mother.

Potentially, I thought, as Nicole returned to the living room. My stepsister divined my pensive mood. "Are you thinking about a girl?" she asked.

"No one new," I said. "I just miss Sandy a little, I guess." I peered into my evermore blue bedroom; Stephen and Neil and Barbara were painting and chatting, paying little attention to Nicole and me. "So how's married life?" I asked her, confident Stephen was out of earshot.

"Amazing," she said, as if he *were* in earshot. I wondered if I'd ever trade confidences with her again.

"I think about being the uncle to your child sometimes," I admitted.

"Aw, that's sweet," she replied. "I must agree with my dad though: I still think you're going to have your own."

Maybe I already do, I thought. And then I didn't want to think anymore. I reached for a bucket of "Bird's Egg" and began pouring it into a rolling tray. "Well, we should get started before they accuse us of slacking," I said.

*   *   *

A few weeks later the five of us dined at Eddie's. My mother looked more exhausted than I'd ever seen her. Her elbows rested on the checkered tablecloth, and bore an undue portion of her weight. I wanted to attribute her fatigue to the workweek's conclusion, but I feared it was something worse.

I wondered if she was secreting something from me too; something profound and puissant and life-altering and dreadful. When Stephen and Nicole left the table to play video games, I raised my hand, tacitly declining their invitation. "So you're an official adult now?" asked a grinning Nicole.

"I just want to catch up with my mommy," I said, reaching across the table for Barbara's hand. Nicole and Stephen left us. "Mom, you look you just finished a marathon," I said.

"It happens when you get old," she said. "First you lack energy for video games."

"Very funny," I said. "But no. I mean, you look beat."

"I'm saving myself," she said. "We'll see who has more energy after dinner."

I nodded and we moved on to other topics: my new job; whether I missed my radio show; and why wasn't I dating anyone yet. And Barbara's energy *did* improve as her diet cola performed caffeinated magic. By the time we got back to the West Egg house, she wanted to dance. Now Neil was tired. He reclined on the couch but grinned with joy – his perfect teeth on display – as his daughter danced with her husband and his wife danced with her son. Leaning into my mother, swiveling her hither and yon as one song bled into another, I felt her warm fingers caressing the back of my neck – it had been almost a year since anyone had touched the back of my neck – and I started crying when a particular song I'd grown up with, heard in the kitchen of our small apartment above the Watching the Wheels bike shop, came lushly through the speakers:

Oh when you were young,
Did you question all the answers?
Did you envy all the dancers who had all the nerve?
Look around you now,
You must go for what you wanted,
Look at all my friends who did and got what they deserve.

Wiping my cheeks on her blond-grey hair, I whispered: "We made it, didn't we, mom?" Barbara surprised me then, by holding me tight around the hips and pressing her head into my chest. Neil and Nicole retrieved their digital cameras.

We danced until the CD ended, at which point Neil and Barbara filed upstairs. I sat for a while with Nicole and Stephen until they went upstairs too. I slept in the basement.

* * *

So my New York City life became what I've already described – an adventure in anonymity: the morning jog in Central Park, where I was one of thousands sweating it out at dawn; a nine-to-five office job that rarely challenged me; evenings of pot and porn and televised sports. I recall one weekend when Nicole and Stephen, making a surprise visit a few weeks after their pregnancy announcement, happened upon a towering stack of soft-core DVDs. It brought to mind how I'd changed from my younger days – when such a pile would have been footage of football players (and would've been VHS cassettes). "Do you watch all of these in one night?" said Nicole.

"Sometimes," I said.

"Maybe you're next project will be a *Guide* to skin flicks," she kidded.

"My days of entrepreneurship are over," I quipped.

"I don't know," she jested, tipping the pile onto my coffee table. "You seem to have a teeming passion for porn."

"You're wrong," I said flatly, as if she was serious. "I'm just a consistent consumer. Passion would mean I was skipping work for it, or preferring it to real women. To say I was passionate for porn would be like saying someone was passionate for margarine. It's a convenient and affordable substitute, is all."

Stephen and Nicole exchanged glances. "I'm gonna use that line, from now on," said Stephen. Nicole sighed and looked up at the Bird's Egg ceiling. "Ari, it seems to me you *do* prefer it to real women."

"I have my reasons," I said. They took my hint and switched subjects, inviting me to join them at the Museum of Modern Art. Eager to prove my social functionality, I accepted. At the museum we wandered from floor to floor, separate and together. During one of our separations I found myself staring at van Gogh's *Starry Night*. It got me thinking about my *Guide* epiphany of 1995 – and how Charlene Chiu had laughed at it. Yet I'd made my dream come true: my idea had been a few lines on a yellow legal pad. And now it was a reality, because of me and only me. I had to admit: part of me still pined for an ideal girlfriend who could appreciate my accomplishments and cherish my dream's fruition – someone who would view me as something *more* than one of the thousands of anonymous Manhattoes who jogged in Central Park every morning. And I wanted someone who could recognize how serious I was about leading a life of frivolity: Someone who wouldn't weigh down our precious nights with grave thoughts of wedded bliss and reproduction.

What I wanted was Sandy prior to the dust speck.

I phoned her on my cell and reached her voicemail. I hung up – how could I make a case that I truly cared for her – or our progeny – after ignoring her/them for a year? And yet, why couldn't I make the case? Hadn't she forced my hand, by wanting the baby despite my wishes?

Nicole and Stephen found me staring into my phone like it had hypnotized me. These two young happy adults, a mother and father to be, a duo who'd invite me to every important event for the rest of their lives, a duo who'd probably bury me – and they had no idea what had taken place between me and Sandy. But who was to blame for that? Why was I so scared of being honest with relatives? Did I fear they'd drop me? No, but I feared they'd deem me a deadbeat: they, whose impregnation was so idyllic, so connubial, that they'd nary comprehend how a sensitive rich cat like me could opt out of a supposed blessing like fatherhood.

To understand that, they'd have to understand my *Life and Times*. And when I got home that night, I determined: I was done procrastinating. I'd make a project of setting down my life story, from the perspective that reading it would allow Nicole and Stephen and their unborn child to understand *how* I'd become *who* I'd become.

*   *   *

Yet I could not ignore the question: did I, myself, have an unborn child? I phoned Sandy again. Voicemail. But later that night came her email: *Our child is three months old. Don't contact me again. You had your chances.*

It was so condemning in its brevity that it confirmed for me why my next mission had to be composing the record of my life's events. Sometimes a criminal needs a jail sentence to set his pen in motion; this was mine: a ruling body had decreed me guilty of reprehensible behavior, but I still wanted *my* affidavit to be heard, seen, touched, smelt, and felt. If I was reprehensible, I wanted the world – and my child – to see *why* I'd been reprehensible. I wanted Nicole and Stephen and Sandy and their children to read my life story and believe: "If we had lived Ariel

Zinsky's life, we too would've slapped Shelagh, dissed Diana, and abandoned Sandy." I could call the book *The Life and Times of Ariel Zinsky*. I could call it *Zinsky the Obscure*. But perhaps the most accurate title would be: *Why I Abandoned My Progeny*.

After all Sandy and I had been through, she didn't deem me worthy of salutations. There was no "Dear Ariel" at the top or "Sincerely, Sandy" at the end. Just the three sentences, one for each month of the child's life. I didn't know the child's name or weight or gender. And in my ignorance I felt a mixture of freedom and regret, wistfulness and bliss. On one level I had come through: I'd dodged life's biggest bullet; I was free to spend my days and nights – and time and money – as I pleased, heedless of attachments and obligations and remunerations for my life's mistakes.

And yet, there I was: alone in my apartment, preferring to write an account of my own life than to actually lead it. Beginning in college, I had spent so much time and energy trying to escape the twenty-year solitude of my childhood. And though I'd met some great friends and lovers over the years, it seemed to me now that I was alone again.

*   *   *

So there was nothing to do but get down the business of writing. I printed out Sandy's email, and wondered how long it would take me to get to the part of my biography when I could include it. But first I had to share my thoughts with Sandy:

Some world we live in, isn't it, where a person can learn of his fatherhood via email? Well, good luck raising our nameless Junior without me. I'll always be grateful for your generosity in allowing me to escape relations with Him/Her. And you can continue believing parenting is the most important usage of time on our planet. I'll keep waving the flag for leisure. Because at age 30, I'm finally living a life without entanglements – and the ample joy of my daily affairs gives me abundant reason to keep living. I have a family who loves me and that is all I need in the way of love. Raising a child is nothing but difficult and – based on the life I've lived – I'd like to believe I'm done with difficult. You may think to yourself: what do you, a successful healthy man, know about difficult? But I have shared my life story with you, Sandy, and therefore you know: I've faced less hardship than many, but more than most. And I have prevailed – even if I'm the only one who fully comprehends the miracle of my own survival. And now it's my mission to spin the story of my survival: How I overcame hardships and drove my destiny toward a fatherless obscurity that — in the end — is the best solution for all parties. I can write it all down and that way I can feel better, knowing I've done right by my newborn child. I will not prostrate myself at the altar of your maternity. Marijuana and pornography and football are too important. And if you still don't understand how I can possibly type those words, well — then you're not too different from the rest of the world and, more importantly, you're not the woman for me.

I never sent this rambling response; I just printed it, intending to preserve my heated thoughts for a later date, or a later chapter, in *Why I Abandoned My Progeny*.

But I did delete Sandy's email; for I feared its presence in my inbox would tempt me to send my vicious reply. And I didn't want to tempt myself.

*   *   *

Four months later, Barbara Segal nee Pratt died in her sleep. The educated guess – later confirmed – was brain aneurysm. She wasn't breathing when Neil awoke that July morning, which was at about six. The ambulance came and the medics declared her dead. Neil phoned all of us from Long Island Jewish Hospital. That night in West Egg we dined on delivery pizza, discussing the life she'd led, the career she'd had, and the funeral logistics. The smells of warm dough and melted cheese filled the house.

With a strategic mixture of widening eyes and hand gesticulations and timely remarks, I tried displaying my oneness with the group's unalloyed grief. But in truth, my grief was adulterated, and my innermost thoughts veered from the japing and eulogizing of the larger conversation. I had plenty to eulogize regarding my mother, but my true feelings about her death were not something I could share with Neil and Nicole and Stephen – or with anyone. For amidst the group mourning, I was ecstatic about one thing: Barbara would never learn about her grandchild. And my grief, strong though it was, had been subordinated to this ecstasy. How was this possible? I pondered this and I realized: just as my mother had grown closer to Neil than she had to me, I had – in my own adult life – subordinated her to my lovers in the pecking order of my affections. There was nothing wrong with that, I supposed, except when it prevented me from bawling on the day of her death. How I longed to cry uncontrollably, if only to give Neil and Nicole and Stephen the impression that I was enslaved to a relentless spasm of melancholy! But no: I was conscientious to a tee. It was Neil who lost control every ten minutes or so. He went through a small plastic packet of pink tissues, discarding them into the warm open pizza box. They lay, snot-filled and crumpled, in a motley formation next to three uneaten pepperoni slices. At length Stephen, who remained standing for most of the evening, cleaned up around us, staying in the kitchen to boil water and set up a tea tray.

I wondered whether Neil was truly more bereaved than I was; or perhaps I was simply better equipped for tough times, all my lachrymal liquids dripped dry from my childhood of sobbing and brutality. And then I wondered if in some twisted way I had my father to thank for making me tougher.

When everyone else had gone to bed I crept downstairs and found my mother's weathered copy of *David Copperfield*, preserved from her undergraduate days at SUNY Buffalo. I turned to the passages where young Copperfield deals with his mother's death:

"If ever a child were stricken with sincere grief, I was. But I remember that this importance was a kind of satisfaction to me, when I walked in the playground that afternoon while the boys were in school. When I saw them glancing at me out of the windows, as they went up to their classes, I felt distinguished, and looked more melancholy, and walked slower. When school was over, and they came out and spoke to me, I felt it rather good in myself not to be proud to any of them, and to take exactly the same notice of them all, as before."

I read a few more pages before I went to bed. I took note of how Copperfield's stepfather, a character named Murdstone, was hardly bereaved at all; and for the first time in a long time I was thankful for Neil's presence in my life, for how he'd made my mother's last years among her happiest. There were worse stepfathers to be stuck with. And if his perception of me remained warped – if he had no idea I was capable of paternal dereliction, if he believed I was on the prim-

rose path to marriage and parenting – well, then perhaps another decade of knowing me would set him straight.

I began to grieve for my mother, now that the house had stilled. For I
was sleeping in the West Egg house but *she* wasn't in it. Tomorrow morning she wouldn't be at the breakfast table. Tomorrow night she wouldn't
be at dinner. Next time my family met up for a team homemaking project
she wouldn't be there. Next time I phoned West Egg she wouldn't pick
up. I'd receive no more surprise calls from her at my office; and I'd no
longer have a friend to discuss books and relationships with, to drive to
Gatsby's house with, and to smoke cigarettes with.

*   *   *

A few days later I began typing my story in earnest. After weeks I
shared my ambition with Nicole, as well as the idea that her child might
read it some day, in a quest to understand his or her solitary uncle. In an
email to Nicole, I typed:

"It's a fun, egotistical, cathartic process. My storyline may not be the
most precise – for this is a real life I'm describing, rather than a plotted
one; and my language may not be the clearest, since I'm just a football
writer, not a novelist or a poet; but if there's one cliché I've learned
from sports that applies to writing, it's that *will* can take you a lot further than *skill*."

Nicole became my sounding board. "It's mostly about football," I
told her on the phone one night. "And my mom. And masturbation.
I'm just a boy raised in the suburbs."

"By one parent," she said.

"Yeah, but where's the novelty factor in *that*?" I asked. "I'm nobody." Actors, alcoholics, anthropologists, athletes, cancer survivors,
coaches, comedians, drug users, executives, former first ladies, geishas,
immigrants, military personnel, minority leaders, news anchors, or-
phans, politicians, pornographers, rock stars, widows of newspaper
moguls – I had made a list, one day, in the book store, of the celebrities
who wrote autobiographies or memoirs. There were *thousands*. "It seems
like people care more about the teller than the story," I told Nicole,
after sharing my list. "People want celebrity stories, and I'm no celebrity. I'm not even an entrepreneur. I mean, who the heck am I? I'm 30,

and who have I become?"

"My stepbrother," she said.

* * *

So the first funeral I ever attended was my mother's, too.

I awoke at half-past-five to the heated arguing of Neil and Nicole, amidst the clacks and clangs of cups and silverware. I was in the basement. They were upstairs, in the kitchen. "Nic, go back to sleep," commanded Neil.

"I'm coming with you," said Nicole.

"You're young and you need to sleep. Come later, with Ari and Stephen."

"Dad, you're not going alone. We can leave a note telling the guys we left early and we'll see them there."

Minutes later I heard the front door slam and a car pull out of the driveway.

Stephen and I followed one hour later. He offered to drive my car and I let him, drifting into my own world of thought as soon as he merged with highway traffic. We were taking the Cross Island Parkway to a waterfront town called Beechhurst, where Neil's family were buried. I pressed my nose against the warm glass window and tried memorizing the view of the brown Long Island Sound beneath the bubblegum colored sky — hoping to forever freeze in my head the image of my mother's funeral dawn. The frosty clouds, smeared haphazardly across the pink sky, coupled with scattered streaks of glowing mandarin, had an instantaneous poignancy for me. But for all I knew, this was how morning always appeared, when driving West on the Cross Island. I blinked and leaned back in my seat. Air conditioning from a side vent tickled my chin.

* * *

A crowd of perhaps 50 surrounded the wooden box, including several West Egg high school students I didn't recognize: an anonymous, preppy bunch whom I'd mockingly scorned during my youth as Barbara's "other children." I held hands with Neil and Nicole as a rabbi read lines from a pocket-sized black book. Behind us were Barbara's coworkers from the English department. The women among them were mirthless. The men wiped their brows every few minutes as the heat of July pressed through their jackets and ties.

When the rabbi finished an electronic device lowered the casket. My mother was finally in the ground. A graveyard official handed shovels to Neil, Nicole, and me.

And now the real crying began.

It started with Nicole. She wiped her eyes on Neil's jacket sleeve, then mine, holding her shovel all the while. Neil had held tough throughout the ceremony, but now he grabbed me and Nicole and held us tight. His shovel fell to the grass. It felt like we were supporting his entire body weight. His sobs throbbed against us, his breaths wrenching and almost asthmatic.

I stood in the circle with Nicole and Neil, my shovel at my hip, my awareness too keen to forget that everyone was watching us. But in the absence of the sounds of shoveling, in the absence of the rabbi's words, in the absence of the mechanical hum of the lowering casket – now a solemn silence overtook the small crowd, and all I could hear were the cries of Nicole and Neil and the occasional airplane, departing from or arriving to nearby LaGuardia airport. Before I knew it my face was slick, and I was wiping my eyes on the black fabric shoulder of my stepsister's dress.

Neil was the first to start shoveling. Soon we joined him, and soon it was finished: earth had refilled the ground, and we turned away from the lumpy brown pile of dirt. It came to pass that the four of us lunched at a crowded Jewish deli-restaurant in Flushing. Its particular odor was a mixture of pickles and hot corned beef. There were cloud-white tablecloths and a full complement of Dr. Brown's flavored sodas. The necktie waiters hustled, all perspiring despite the air conditioning within, all carrying empty plates into the kitchen and trays of food back out to the tables.

When our food was served, almost 25 minutes after we ordered it, our harried waiter nearly dropped Stephen's Reuben with mashed potatoes. He was a pimply teenage boy, on the heavy side, and he apologized pro-fusely. But once he left us, with our dishes safely landed, we began an-other mourning discussion. Nicole spoke of shoe-shopping in Manhattan with Barbara on weekday afternoons. Neil shared a PG-rated version of his first date with Barbara. It was a version of events that propriety prevented me from correcting; and I wondered then if the older version of myself was content to be silent, to let the talking flow with a measure of self-censorship and an absence of abandon. It was a funeral meal, after all: why not permit a form of storytelling that brooked the artifice of adulthood, the ruse of revisionism, the hoax of hagiography?

I certainly wouldn't share *my* innermost thoughts – and I couldn't, as they entered and exited my brain at a rapid, relentless clip, like cars through a tollbooth, pausing and then zooming past the gate:

Maybe Barbara wouldn't have lamented a bastard grandchild.

Maybe she'd have embraced it, knowing what she did about my history, knowing that my presence in the child's life might have prevented another boy from growing up in a single-mom household.

Maybe she'd have become best friends with Sandy.

Well, it doesn't matter now. It's just like your beatings, or your slapping Shelagh, or your entire Boston existence. It's the past. The gate has fallen. Move on. Start a new history with Neil and Nicole. The old history can't help. It's a writing project, nothing more.

And nothing less.

Then I wondered when I'd next have a girlfriend, when I'd next be capable of trusting another person with the risks, physical and otherwise, of intimacy.

Time was, I'd have pondered suicide over a loss like this. No more. Suicide is a bailout for the young, a way to quit the season before you've sweated through the games. When you're 30, you've invested too much sweat to quit before the ending.

Still, the Hamlet question remains: what have I to live for, especially in the absence of lust as a goal? Who knows? Maybe this self-pity is endemic to my age. When you're five years old, you cry in pity for the zoo animals; when you're older you grow numb. So what's struck me is the sledgehammer of adulthood's numbing: inevitably it will smash me again; that's the price of living. So choosing to live is choosing to be grateful for those moments when the hammer's in the air, its energy potential rather than kinetic.

So my mom's elegy may also be my elegy for lost aims – aims as noble and quotidian as finding a girlfriend; that is, charming a woman with my life story, or its lilting recitation.

So what am I going to do now? What shall become my aim? I'm going to write this story of my life, how I ended up parentless by fate and childless by choice. And by then, maybe I'll figure out my goals for the next 30 years of my life. Maybe I'll find a yellow legal pad and write them all down. But first, I'm going to mourn my mom for the public, by being a little more present at this meal with my new family. That's what she'd have wanted. And that's what I want too. No shame in admitting I need Neil and Nicole and Stephen in my life – is there? Ah, you're not Zinsky the Obscure – you're Zinsky the Normal! You've gone from Zinsky's Quintessential to Zinsky's Quotidian! A person who needs people!

Returning my attention to the table, I couldn't but smile at my relatives, my mind giddily awash in its recent conclusions. So Neil and Nicole thought they had Barbara tales to share? Wait till they heard mine! One story, in particular, had congealed in my head over the past 48 hours. With little concern for coherence, knowing my audience could overlook a skipping record, a sputtering tire, I began to ramble:

"I remember driving around with her a lot, when I was five, six. She handed me the quarters for the meter and always said, 'Make sure you twist all the way.' One time, we took kind of a longish drive, out to this amusement park called Adventureland, which is all the way in Farmingdale. We got lost maybe four times on the way. Anyway, this trip was a big deal, because Mom and I were a lot like one of those poor older married couples who just stay home and watch TV. So, you know, every time we went out, period, it was an occasion, even if we were just going to Eddie's. So we finally reach Adventureland, and at the entrance the ticket guy straps my wrist with the bright orange pay-one-price band.

"We walked by this basketball booth where, if you made a shot, you won a stuffed panda bear. Mom asked if I wanted to try. I said, 'It's not worth your money, because I'm just going to miss.' She said, 'Come on, Ari, it's only a dollar.' And I said, 'Mom, I really suck.' So we kept walking and for the rest of the night we kept listing all these better ways you could spend a dollar. A comic book. Twenty five-cent gums. Four plays on a video game. A scorecard at the Mets game. Over an hour on a parking meter! A can of Tab – she drank tons of Tab, back when it was a popular drink. A pack of life savers. Postage stamps. Three songs on the Eddie's jukebox. We had so many examples.

"Anyway, we had the best time at Adventureland. I wore my orange wristband for the next six days. Mom kept telling me to take it off, but I just didn't. Finally one night at dinner, she says, 'Ari, for the 47th time, could you please grab the scissors and snip off that hideous bracelet?' And I started laughing, because she had this phlegmy way of stressing that first syllable in 'hideous,' as if she were a kindergarten teacher describing an ugly witch. But I was also laughing because whenever she repeatedly told me to do something, she always said, 'for the 47th time,' even if it was the second time, fifth time, or hundredth time. She asked why I was giggling and I said, 'When is it going to be the 48th time?' and we both sat there at that old oval table, laughing our asses off. Then she suddenly got silent. She said, 'Seriously, Ari. Cut it off.' So I did."

I chugged my black cherry cola can for a good five seconds. Neil straightaway signaled for the check and when it arrived – five minutes later, our heavy pimply waiter nearly tripping over a protruding chair to get it to us – Neil let it linger. The handwritten bill rested in its plastic black tray. I took out my wallet but Neil objected. "We've got time," he said.

"But the waiter doesn't," I replied. Neil nodded, and placed his credit card atop the check.

When we finally rose to depart, I went to the bathroom, so my family could exit ahead of me. When it was apparent they were all out on the sidewalk, I sought out our waiter, and handed him $20. "You don't have to do that, sir," he demurred, tucking the bill in his front pocket.

"And you don't have to do *this*," I said, gesturing broadly in the direction of our table, which had already been cleared. He nodded and backed away from me, eager to bring water to some incoming patrons. I strode toward the exit, eager to reach the sunny street where my family was still waiting.

The End

Fomite
Burlington, Vermont

Fomite is a literary press whose authors and artists explore the human condition—political, cultural, personal and historical—in poetry and prose.

A fomite is a medium capable of transmitting infectious organisms from one individual to another.

"The activity of art is based on the capacity of people to be infected by the feelings of others." Tolstoy, *What is Art?*

Flight and Other Stories - Jay Boyer
In *Flight and Other Stories*, we're with the fattest woman on earth as she draws her last breaths and her soul ascends toward its final reward. We meet a divorcee who can fly for no more effort than flapping her arms. We follow a middle-aged butler whose love affair with a young woman leads him first to the mysteries of bondage, and then to the pleasures of malice. Story by story, we set foot into worlds so strange as to seem all but surreal, yet everything feels familiar, each moment rings true. And that's when we recognize we're in the hands of one of America's truly original talents.

Loisaida - Dan Chodorokoff
Catherine, a young anarchist estranged from her parents and squatting in an abandoned building on New York's Lower East Side is fighting with her boyfriend and conflicted about her work on an underground newspaper. After learning of a developer's plans to demolish a community garden, Catherine builds an alliance with a group of Puerto Rican community activists. Together they confront the confluence of politics, money, and real estate that rule Manhattan. All the while she learns important lessons from her great-grandmother's life in the Yiddish anarchist movement that flourished on the Lower East Side at the turn of the century. In this coming of age story, family saga, and tale of urban politics, Dan Chodorkoff explores the "principle of hope", and examines how memory and imagination inform social change.

Improvisational Arguments - Anna Faktorovich
Improvisational Arguments is written in free verse to capture the essence of modern problems and triumphs. The poems clearly relate short, frequently humorous and occasionally tragic, stories about travels to exotic and unusual places, fantastic realms, abnormal jobs, artistic innovations, political objections, and misadventures with love.

Loosestrife - Greg Delanty
This book is a chronicle of complicity in our modern lives, a witnessing of war and the destruction of our planet. It is also an attempt to adjust the more destructive blueprint myths of our society. Often our cultural memory tells us to keep quiet about the aspects that are most challenging to our ethics, to forget the violations we feel and tremors that keep us distant and numb.

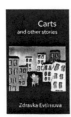

Carts and Other Stories - Zdravka Evtimova

Roots and wings are the key words that best describe the short story collection, *Carts and Other Stories*, by Zdravka Evtimova. The book is emotionally multilayered and memorable because of its internal power, vitality and ability to touch both the heart and your mind. Within its pages, the reader discovers new perspectives and true wealth, and learns to see the world with different eyes. The collection lives on the borders of different cultures. *Carts and Other Stories* will take the reader to wild and powerful Bulgarian mountains, to silver rains in Brussels, to German quiet winter streets and to wind bitten crags in Afghanistan. This book lives for those seeking to discover the beauty of the world around them, and will have them appreciating what they have—and perhaps what they have lost as well.

The Listener Aspires to the Condition of Music - Barry Goldensohn

"I know of no other selected poems that selects on one theme, but this one does, charting Goldensohn's career-long attraction to music's performance, consolations and its august, thrilling, scary and clownish charms. Does all art aspire to the condition of music as Pater claimed, exhaling in a swoon toward that one class act? Goldensohn is more aware than the late 19th century of the overtones of such breathing: his poems thoroughly round out those overtones in a poet's lifetime of listening."

John Peck, poet, editor, Fellow of the American Academy of Rome

The Co-Conspirator's Tale - Ron Jacobs

There's a place where love and mistrust are never at peace; where duplicity and deceit are the universal currency. *The Co-Conspirator's Tale* takes place within this nebulous firmament. There are crimes committed by the police in the name of the law. Excess in the name of revolution. The combination leaves death in its wake and the survivors struggling to find justice in a San Francisco Bay Area noir by the author of the underground classic *The Way the Wind Blew: A History of the Weather Underground* and the novel *Short Order Frame Up*.

Short Order Frame Up - Ron Jacobs

1975. America has lost its war in Vietnam and Cambodia. Racially-tinged riots are tearing the city of Boston apart. The politics and counterculture of the 1960s is disintegrating into nothing more than sex, drugs and rock and roll. The Boston Red Sox are on one of their improbable runs toward a postseason appearance. In a suburban town in Maryland, a young couple is murdered and another young man is accused. The couple are white and the accused is black. It is up to his friends and family to prove he is innocent. This is a story of suburban ennui, race, murder and injustice. Religion and politics, liberal lawyers and racist cops. In *Short Order Frame Up*, Ron Jacobs has written a piece of crime fiction that exposes the wound that is US racism. Two cultures existing side by side and across generations--a river very few dare to cross. His characters work and live with and next to each other, often unaware of the other's real life. When the murder occurs, however, those people that care about the man charged must cross that river and meet somewhere in between in order to free him from (what is to them) an obvious miscarriage of justice.

Fomite
Burlington, Vermont

All the Sinners Saints - Ron Jacobs

A young draftee named Victor Willard goes AWOL in Germany after an altercation with a commanding officer. Porgy is an African-American GI involved with the international Black Panthers and German radicals. Victor and a female radical named Ana fall in love. They move into Ana's room in a squatted building near the US base in Frankfurt. The international campaign to free Black revolutionary Angela Davis is coming to Frankfurt. Porgy and Ana are key organizers and Victor spends his days and nights selling and smoking hashish, while becoming addicted to heroin. Police and narcotics agents are keeping tabs on them all. Politics, love, and drugs. Truths, lies, and rock and roll. *All the Sinners, Saints* is a story of people seeking redemption in a world awash in sin.

When You Remember Deir Yassin - R.L. Green

When You Remember Deir Yassin is a collection of poems by R. L. Green, an American Jewish writer, on the subject of the occupation and destruction of Palestine. Green comments: "Outspoken Jewish critics of Israeli crimes against humanity have, strangely, been called 'anti-Semitic' as well as the hilariously illogical epithet 'self-hating Jews.' As a Jewish critic of the Israeli government, I have come to accept these accusations as a stamp of approval and a badge of honor, signifying my own fealty to a central element of Jewish identity and ethics: one must be a lover of truth and a friend to the oppressed, and stand with the victims of tyranny, not with the tyrants, despite tribal loyalty or self-advancement. These poems were written as expressions of outrage, and of grief, and to encourage my sisters and brothers of every cultural or national grouping to speak out against injustice, to try to save Palestine, and in so doing, to reclaim for myself my own place as part of the Jewish people." Poems in the original English are accompanied by Arabic and Hebrew translations.

Roadworthy Creature, Roadworthy Craft - Kate Magill

Words fail but the voice struggles on. The culmination of a decade's worth of performance poetry, *Roadworthy Creature, Roadworthy Craft* is Kate Magill's first full-length publication. In lines that are sinewy yet delicate, Magill's poems explore the terrain where idea and action meet, where bodies and words commingle to form a strange new flesh, a breathing text, an "I" that spirals outward from itself.

Zinsky the Obscure - Ilan Mochari

"If your childhood is brutal, your adulthood becomes a daily attempt to recover: a quest for ecstasy and stability in recompense for their early absence." So states the 30-year-old Ariel Zinsky, whose bachelor-like lifestyle belies the torturous youth he is still coming to grips with. As a boy, he struggles with the beatings themselves; as a grownup, he struggles with the world's indifference to them. *Zinsky the Obscure* is his life story, a humorous chronicle of his search for a redemptive ecstasy through sex, an entrepreneurial sports obsession, and finally, the cathartic exercise of writing it all down. Fervently recounting both the comic delights and the frightening horrors of a life in which he feels—always—that he is not like all the rest, Zinsky survives the worst and relishes the best with idiosyncratic style, as his heartbreak turns into self-awareness and his suicidal ideation into self-regard. A vivid evocation of the all-consuming nature of lust and ambition—and the forces that drive them.

Fomite
Burlington, Vermont

The Derivation of Cowboys & Indians - Joseph D. Reich

The Derivation of Cowboys & Indians represents a profound journey, a breakdown of The American Dream from a social, cultural, historical, and spiritual point of view. Reich examines in concise detail the loss of the collective unconscious, commenting on our contemporary postmodern culture with its self-interested excesses, on where and how things all go wrong, and how social/political practice rarely meets its original proclamations and promises. Reich's surreal and self-effacing satire brings this troubling message home. *The Derivations of Cowboys & Indians* is a desperate search and struggle for America's literal, symbolic, and spiritual home.

Kasper Planet: Comix and Tragix - Peter Schumann

The British call him Punch, the Italians, Pulchinella, the Russians, Petruchka, the Native Americans, Coyote. These are the figures we may know. But every culture that worships authority will breed a Punch-like, anti-authoritarian resister. Yin and yang—it has to happen. The Germans call him Kasper. Truth-telling and serious pranking are dangerous professions when going up against power. Bradley Manning sits naked in solitary; Julian Assange is pursued by Interpol, Obama's Department of Justice, and Amazon.com. But—in contrast to merely human faces— masks and theater can often slip through the bars. Consider our American Kaspers: Charlie Chaplin, Woody Guthrie, Abby Hoffman, the Yes Men—theater people all, utilizing various forms to seed critique. Their profiles and tactics have evolved along with those of their enemies. Who are the bad guys that call forth the Kaspers? Over the last half century, with his Bread & Puppet Theater, Peter Schumann has been tireless in naming them, excoriating them with Kasperdom....
from Marc Estrin's Foreword to Planet Kasper

Views Cost Extra - L.E. Smith

Views that inspire, that calm, or that terrify—all come at some cost to the viewer. In *Views Cost Extra* you will find a New Jersey high school preppy who wants to inhabit the "perfect" cowboy movie, a rural mailman disgusted with the residents of his town who wants to live with the penguins, an ailing screen writer who strikes a deal with Johnny Cash to reverse an old man's failures, an old man who ponders a young man's suicide attempt, a one-armed blind blues singer who wants to reunite with the car that took her arm on the assembly line— and more. These stories suggest that we must pay something to live even ordinary lives.

The Empty Notebook Interrogates Itself - Susan Thomas

The Empty Notebook began its life as a very literal metaphor for a few weeks of what the poet thought was writer's block, but was really the struggle of an eccentric persona to take over her working life. It won. And for the next three years everything she wrote came to her in the voice of the Empty Notebook, who, as the notebook began to fill itself, became rather opinionated, changed gender, alternately acted as bully and victim, had many bizarre adventures in exotic locales and developed a somewhat politically-incorrect attitude. It then began to steal the voices and forms of other poets and tried to immortalize itself in various poetry reviews. It is now thrilled to collect itself in one slim volume.

Fomite
Burlington, Vermont

My God, What Have We Done? - Susan Weiss

In a world afflicted with war, toxicity, and hunger, does what we do in our private lives really matter? Fifty years after the creation of the atomic bomb at Los Alamos, newlyweds Pauline and Clifford visit that once-secret city on their honeymoon, compelled by Pauline's fascination with Oppenheimer, the soulful scientist. The two stories emerging from this visit reverberate back and forth between the loneliness of a new mother at home in Boston and the isolation of an entire community dedicated to the development of the bomb. While Pauline struggles with unforeseen challenges of family life, Oppenheimer and his crew reckon with forces beyond all imagining.

Finally the years of frantic research on the bomb culminate in a stunning test explosion that echoes a rupture in the couple's marriage. Against the backdrop of a civilization that's out of control, Pauline begins to understand the complex, potentially explosive physics of personal relationships.

At once funny and dead serious, *My God, What Have We Done?* sifts through the ruins left by the bomb in search of a more worthy human achievement.

As It Is On Earth - Peter M. Wheelwright

Four centuries after the Reformation Pilgrims sailed up the down-flowing watersheds of New England, Taylor Thatcher, irreverent scion of a fallen family of Maine Puritans, is still caught in the turbulence.

In his errant attempts to escape from history, the young college professor is further unsettled by his growing attraction to Israeli student Miryam Bluehm as he is swept by Time through the "family thing"—from the tangled genetic and religious history of his New England parents to the redemptive birthday secret of Esther Fleur Noire Bishop, the Cajun-Passamaquoddy woman who raised him and his younger half-cousin/half-brother, Bingham.

The landscapes, rivers, and tidal estuaries of Old New England and the Mayan Yucatan are also casualties of history in Thatcher's story of Deep Time and re-discovery of family on Columbus Day at a high-stakes gambling casino, rising in resurrection over the starlit bones of a once-vanquished Pequot Indian Tribe.

Suite for Three Voices - Derek Furr

Suite for Three Voices is a dance of prose genres, teeming with intense human life in all its humor and sorrow. A son uncovers the horrors of his father's wartime experience, a hitchhiker in a muumuu guards a mysterious parcel, a young man foresees his brother's brush with death on September 11. A Victorian poetess encounters space aliens and digital archives, a runner hears the voice of a dead friend in the song of an indigo bunting, a teacher seeks wisdom from his students' errors and Neil Young. By frozen waterfalls and neglected graveyards, along highways at noon and rivers at dusk, in the sound of bluegrass, Beethoven, and Emily Dickinson, the essays and fiction in this collection offer moments of vision.

Fomite
Burlington, Vermont

Travers' Inferno - *L.E. Smith*

In the 1970's churches began to burn in Burlington, Vermont. If it were arson, no one or no reason could be found to blame. This book suggests arson, but makes no claim to historical realism. It claims, instead, to capture the dizzying 70's zeitgeist of aggressive utopian movements, distrust in authority, escapist alternative life styles, and a bewildered society of onlookers. In the tradition of John Gardner's Sunlight Dialogues, the characters of *Travers' Inferno* are colorful and damaged, sometimes comical, sometimes tragic, looking for meaning through desperate acts. Travers Jones, the protagonist, is grounded in the transcendent—philosophy, epilepsy, arson as purification—and mystified by the opposite sex, haunted by an absent father and directed by an uncle with a grudge. He is seduced by a professor's wife and chased by an endearing if ineffective sergeant of police. There are secessionist Quebecois involved in these church burns who are murdering as well as pilfering and burning. There are changing alliances, violent deaths, lovemaking, and a belligerent cat.

Still Time - Michael Cocchiarale

Still Time is a collection of twenty-five short and shorter stories exploring tensions that arise in a variety of contemporary relationships: a young boy must deal with the wrath of his out-of-work father; a woman runs into a man twenty years after an awkward sexual encounter; a wife, unable to conceive, imagines her own murder, as well as the reaction of her emotionally distant husband; a soon-to-be tenured English professor tries to come to terms with her husband's shocking return to the religion of his youth; an assembly line worker, married for thirty years, discovers the surprising secret life of his recently hospitalized wife. Whether a few hundred or a few thousand words, these and other stories in the collection depict characters at moments of deep crisis. Some feel powerless, overwhelmed—unable to do much to change the course of their lives. Others rise to the occasion and, for better or for worse, say or do the thing that might transform them for good. Even in stories with the most troubling of endings, there remains the possibility of redemption. For each of the characters, there is still time.

Signed Confessions - *Tom Walker*

Guilt and a desperate need to repent drive the antiheroes in Tom Walker's dark (and often darkly funny) stories:
• A gullible journalist falls for the 40-year-old stripper he profiles in a magazine.
• A faithless husband abandons his family and joins a support group for lost souls.
• A merciless prosecuting attorney grapples with the suicide of his gay son.
• An aging misanthrope must make amends to five former victims.
• An egoistic naval hero is haunted by apparitions of his dead wife and a mysterious little girl.
The seven tales in *Signed Confessions* measure how far guilty men will go to obtain a forgiveness no one can grant but themselves.

Fomite
Burlington, Vermont

The Good Muslim of Jackson Heights - Jaysinh Birjépatil

Jackson Heights in this book is a fictional locale with common features assembled from immigrant-friendly neighborhoods around the world where hardworking honest-to-goodness traders from the Indian subcontinent, rub shoulders with ruthless entrepreneurs, reclusive antique-dealers, homeless nobodies, merchant-princes, lawyers, doctors and IT specialists. But as Siraj and Shabnam, urbane newcomers fleeing religious persecution in their homeland discover there is no escape from the past. Weaving together the personal and the political *The Good Muslim of Jackson Heights* is an ambiguous elegy to a utopian ideal set free from all prejudice.

Meanwell - Janice Miller Potter

Meanwell is a twenty-four poem sequence in which a female servant searches for identity and meaning in the shadow of her mistress, poet Anne Bradstreet. Although Meanwell herself is a fiction, someone like her could easily have existed among Bradstreet's known but unnamed domestic servants. Through Meanwell's eyes, Bradstreet emerges as a human figure during The Great Migration of the 1600s, a period in which the Massachusetts Bay Colony was fraught with physical and political dangers. Through Meanwell, the feelings of women, silenced during the midwife Anne Hutchinson's fiery trial before the Puritan ministers, are finally acknowledged. In effect, the poems are about the making of an American rebel. Through her conflicted conscience, we witness Meanwell's transformation from a powerless English waif to a mythic American who ultimately chooses wilderness over the civilization she has experienced.

The Housing Market - Joseph D. Reich

In Joseph Reich's most recent social and cultural, contemporary satire of suburbia entitled, "The Housing market: a comfortable place to jump off the end of the world," the author addresses the absurd, postmodern elements of what it means, or for that matter not, to try and cope and function, and survive and thrive, or live and die in the repetitive and existential, futile and self-destructive, homogenized, monochromatic landscape of a brutal and bland, collective unconscious, which can spiritually result in a gradual wasting away and erosion of the senses or conflict and crisis of a desperate, disproportionate 'situational depression,' triggering and leading the narrator to feel constantly abandoned and stranded, more concretely or proverbially spoken, "the eternal stranger," where when caught between the fight or flight psychological phenomena, naturally repels him and causes him to flee and return without him even knowing it into the wild, while by sudden circumstance and coincidence discovers it surrounds the illusory-like circumference of these selfsame Monopoly board cul-de-sacs and dead ends. Most specifically, what can happen to a solitary, thoughtful, and independent thinker when being stagnated in the triangulation of a cookie-cutter, oppressive culture of a homeowner's association; A memoir all written in critical and didactic, poetic stanzas and passages, and out of desperation, when freedom and control get taken, what he is forced to do in the illusion of 'free will and volition,' something like the derivative art of a smart and ironic and social and cultural satire.

Fomite
Burlington, Vermont

Love's Labours - Jack Pulaski

In the four stories and two novellas that comprise Love's Labors the protagonists Ben and Laura, discover in their fervid romance and long marriage their interlocking fates, and the histories that preceded their births. They also learned something of the paradox between love and all the things it brings to its beneficiaries: bliss, disaster, duty, tragedy, comedy, the grotesque, and tenderness.

Ben and Laura's story is also the particularly American tale of immigration to a new world. Laura's story begins in Puerto Rico, and Ben's lineage is Russian-Jewish. They meet in City College of New York, a place at least analogous to a melting pot. Laura struggles to rescue her brother from gang life and heroin. She is mother to her younger sister; their mother Consuelo is the financial mainstay of the family and consumed by work. Despite filial obligations, Laura aspires to be a serious painter. Ben writes, cares for and is caught up in the misadventures and surreal stories of his younger schizophrenic brother. Laura is also a story teller as powerful and enchanting as Scheherazade. Ben struggles to survive such riches, and he and Laura endure.

Four-Way Stop - Sherry Olson

If *Thank You* were the only prayer, as Meister Eckhart has suggested, it would be enough, and Sherry Olson's poetry, in her second book, *Four-Way Stop*, would be one. Radical attention, deep love, and dedication to kindness illuminate these poems and the stories she tells us, which are drawn from her own life: with family, with friends, and wherever she travels, with strangers – who to Olson, never are strangers, but kin.

Even at the difficult intersections, as in the title poem, *Four-Way Stop*, Olson experiences – and offers – hope, showing us how, *completely unsupervised*, people take turns, with *kindness waving each other on*. Olson writes, knowing that (to quote Czeslaw Milosz)) *What surrounds us, here and now, is not guaranteed*. To this world, with her poems, Olson brings – and teaches – attention, generosity, compassion, and appreciative joy.
—Carol Henrikson

Raven or Crow - Joshua Amses

Marlowe has recently moved back home to Vermont after flunking his first term at a private college in the Midwest, when his sort of girlfriend, Eleanor, goes missing. The circumstances surrounding Eleanor's disappearance stand to reveal more about Marlowe than he is willing to allow. Rather than report her missing, he resolves to find Eleanor himself. *Raven or Crow* is the story of mistakes rooted in the ambivalence of being young and without direction.

Alfabestiario
AlphaBetaBestiario - Antonello Borra

Animals have always understood that mankind is not fully at home in the world. Bestiaries, hoping to teach, send out warnings. This one, of course, aims at doing the same.

Fomite
Burlington, Vermont

Visiting Hours - *Jennifer Anne Moses*
Visiting Hours, a novel-in-stories, explores the lives of people not normally met on the page—-AIDS patients and those who care for them. Set in Baton Rouge, Louisiana, and written with large and frequent dollops of humor, the book is a profound meditation on faith and love in the face of illness and poverty.

Entanglements - Tony Magistrale
A poet and a painter may employ different mediums to express the same snow-blown afternoon in January, but sometimes they find a way to capture the moment in such a way that their respective visions still manage to stir a reverberation, a connection. In part, that's what *Entanglements* seeks to do. Not so much for the poems and paintings to speak directly to one another, but for them to stir points of similarity.

Did you know that you can write a review on Amazon, Good Reads or Shelfari? Just go to the book page on the website and follow the links for posting a review. Books from independent presses depend on reader to reader communications.

CPSIA information can be obtained at www.ICGtesting.com
Printed in the USA
LVOW131933040713

341418LV00010B/1101/P